A NAME IN THE DARK

G. S. FORTIS

SOMETIMES THE MONSTER
WE FEAR MOST
IS THE ONE INSIDE US

A NAME IN THE DARK

G. S. FORTIS

BARDSDALE
— PRESS —

Copyright © 2020 by Gilmar Fortis II

First paperback edition April 2020

Book cover design by Natasha MacKenzie
Images © Shutterstock

ISBN: 978-1-7344909-0-9

www.gsfortis.com

For Taliesa

Acknowledgments

Writing this book was a long and difficult journey. Were it not for the support of my friends and family, I could not have completed it.

Thank you to those who read the first draft and provided their notes and encouragement, including Amy and Doug De La Piedra, Barbara and Frank Lin, Amy and Jeff Seastone, as well as Mischa Livingstone, Kara Rosella and Taliesa.

Special thanks to those who helped me take the book across the finish line. I'm especially grateful to Susan DeFreitas, the wonderful editor whose insight provided focus to the story, and to the team at Red Adept Editing—Sarah Carleton and Virge B.—who helped me refine my writing.

I am also very appreciative of Lorna Reid, who designed the book's wonderful interior, and Natasha MacKenzie, who created this beautiful cover.

Finally, I would love to express my gratitude to the city of Los Angeles. At times it's been a love-hate relationship, but you have provided a home for me, for Darcy, and for her band of misfits.

Chapter 1

Being a private investigator sucks. There was a time when I thought I would work from my own office, helping people with answers, and making enough money to cover rent.

Wrong. Wrong. Wrong. Some detective I am.

Angry muffled voices bleed through cinderblock walls—the fruits of my latest endeavor. To kill time until the argument is over, I sit on my bedroom floor, trimming my split ends with craft scissors. My caseload isn't steady enough to allow me to pay the bills or lease an office, especially with the high rents in Los Angeles. I guess a twenty-six-year-old doesn't exactly project the kind of experience people want when a marriage or lawsuit is on the line and they're shopping for a detective.

Granted, this latest job was personal and off the books. For the past two months, my roommate, Paige, has been dating a loser. She met Brock at a Vitamin Shoppe, and they bonded over their mutual passion for health supplements. He's a personal trainer—six foot four, two-hundred-plus pounds of muscle, and an absolute idiot. That's not my opinion. This guy literally believes the earth is flat.

It was no surprise that Paige fell for him. In most respects, she is an incredibly intelligent woman. However, when it comes to men, her romantic compass is about as reliable as an online horoscope.

It's fair to say I didn't like Brock from the moment I met him. It wasn't just because he put more effort into his looks than any woman I'd ever met or because his favorite—and only—conversation topic was *working out*. That alone would have neatly placed him in the same category as Paige's previous boyfriends, a parade of unworthy but ultimately harmless morons.

But Brock was different. He never invited Paige to his place. They could only go out on weeknights. He was invisible on social media. He was hiding something.

When I tried to talk to Paige about it, she didn't see it. That's Paige for you—blinded by love. Since work was "light"—nonexistent—I decided to snoop into Brock's past. My unsolicited and unwanted research led me to find out what he was hiding: a wife and infant daughter in Glendale.

I knew Paige was going to be devastated, but she was my best friend and needed to hear the truth. The news absolutely crushed her. I spent the afternoon pulling her out of her cocoon of grief and offering her a shoulder to cry on. Finally, she called Brock over to our loft. She was going to end it.

And here we are now, in hour two of "ending it."

The argument intensifies, and I peer at the sliding loft door that separates my room from the living room. As the yelling moves, my eyes drift over my travel posters of Los Angeles and the vintage metal lockers I use as a wardrobe.

Paige's voice rises as she rattles off a list of expletives describing how she feels about her soon-to-be ex-boyfriend. Part of me wants to be out there as moral support and backup. Then again, I've caused enough damage.

I put the scissors down and give my hair a break. They were just causing more damage anyway. I find a new way to distract myself with some leisure reading, *The Egyptian Book of the Dead*. A girl can never be too informed on ancient burial practices, and I need to do a bit of research anyway.

"Asshole!" Paige shouts from the next room. The text is too dense to read with all the screaming, so I close the hardcover volume and return it to a stack against my wall. There are piles of books all around my bedroom, like tiny skyscrapers forming a miniature metropolis.

The yelling escalates again. Paige roars, "Get out!"

Finally, we're coming to the end. I stare at the cold concrete that separates us. As footsteps resonate through the wall, I imagine Brock lumbering to the front door, his tail between his legs, saying goodbye forever.

"I'm not leaving!" Brock shouts.

I deflate.

Paige yells for him to leave. Again, he says no. A door slams. Something crashes. *A table?* Something breaks. *Glass?* Someone screams… *Paige.*

I'm instantly at the door, yanking it open. The heavy oak glides along its reinforced track and disappears into the wall. I barge into the living room, my hand sweeping the curtain of straight, black hair from my face.

Our entry table lies on the floor next to the front door. Next to it is our glass lamp, now shattered. Paige struggles to push Brock out, but he's too big. Her long blond hair obscures her normally beautiful face, which is puffy, red, and streaked with mascara.

This is a stark contrast to the girl I know. Paige is athletic and one of the strongest women I know. She works out every day and has the physique of an Olympian. But she's no match for the behemoth standing in her way. Brock's bulging biceps stretch the fabric of his sleeves as he grapples with her smaller frame. He pushes Paige back by her flailing arms, refusing to leave the apartment.

Paige turns to me, eyes wide as if suddenly remembering I've been in my room the whole time. "Oh shit, Darcy!" She rips herself away from Brock and runs to me. "I'm sorry!"

That fact that *she's* apologizing to *me* infuriates me more.

Brock's eyes follow Paige. "You!" he shouts, his face shaking with anger. "This is all your fault, isn't it?"

"Please, Darcy, don't," Paige implores, focusing only on me.

I ignore Paige and direct my comment to the guy behind her. "My fault? I'm not the one who cheated on his wife and lied!"

Paige places herself between Brock and me and gently pulls my face to look directly at her. "He's leaving," she assures me in a shaky voice. "Look at me. I'll get him out of here. Just... stay calm. It's fine." She whirls around to face Brock as he approaches. "You need to go."

This isn't a plea like earlier. This is a warning.

He charges toward us and easily pushes Paige aside. I stand my ground. My blood boils, and I clench my fists so I don't lash out.

His steroid-swollen head cranes down toward my five-foot, three-inch frame. "I always hated your yellow eyes." Yeah, that's the best insult he can muster right now. The first time he saw my eyes, he couldn't look away. He called them "freaky" at the time. My irises aren't just some faded-hazel hue but a deep, vivid, unnatural yellow.

An alert on my smartwatch goes off. Paige's eyes widen in alarm. This is the first warning and means my heart rate has hit one hundred sixty beats per minutes. I take a deep breath, remembering what Paige said. *Stay calm.*

My fists relax. "Leave."

He jams his finger into my chest, pushing me back. I stumble back from the forcefulness but keep my balance. "Don't tell me what to do, bitch."

Paige is at my side in an instant, an arm around my shoulders. "Darcy?" She grabs my wrist and looks at my smartwatch, trying to read the electrocardiogram on the display. My pulse is elevated but still in the safe range.

"I'm calm." Though I'm speaking to Paige, my attention remains on Brock. "Just go home to your wife, Brock." Then for good measure, I add, "Bitch."

Brock takes two quick steps forward and pushes me with all his might. I fly and crash into the wall behind me. My head slams against the concrete, and I slump to the ground. I rub the back of my head. My hand comes away red with sticky fresh blood.

And I am no longer calm. The secondary alarm on my watch chimes. My heart rate has now spiked to one hundred ninety BPM.

"Oh… shit," Paige mutters.

I rise, practically levitating from my seated position. Brock stands defiantly as I march toward him. My hand shoots up and grabs him by the throat. He tries desperately to knock my hand away, but he can't. Panic rapidly spreads across his face. He must realize there aren't enough metabolic steroids in his system to compete with my strength—my now-unnatural strength.

My mouth opens, but the voice that speaks isn't mine. It's a deep guttural inhuman sound from someplace dark and unholy. "I told you to go."

I have heard this voice many times, but Brock has not. I can tell by the look on his face that he's confused and very much afraid. He stares into my eyes—my glowing yellow eyes.

The room starts to shake and rumble. Poster frames clatter against the walls. Wind swirls.

Paige races past me and disappears into the bathroom, leaving me alone with Brock. The wind intensifies. Papers spin in a circle around the room. Objects slide off tables. My hand remains clenched around Brock's throat.

"What the hell?" he chokes.

Paige emerges from the bathroom, shaking a pharmacy vial and dumping the contents into her open palm. Bless her soul—she marches through the routine like we've practiced so many times before. She shoves three pills in my mouth then clamps down my jaw as if giving medicine to a dog. Her grip is strong, and she keeps my head still.

"Chew!" she orders.

I'm in enough control to bite the tablets and taste the bitter chalk as it starts to dissolve. I tuck the crumbs under my tongue. Then Paige releases my jaw and gets to work peeling my fingers off Brock's neck. The clock is ticking. My mouth tingles as my body slowly absorbs the medicine.

"Darcy!" Paige shouts. "You have to let go!"

I let go. Brock crumbles to the ground, gasping for air.

"Run!" she orders.

Brock remains still, unable to take his eyes off me—a deer in my headlights. Paige yanks Brock to his feet. This time, he doesn't resist as she pushes him across the room and to the door.

"What the hell is happening?" he rasps.

With a final push, Paige shoves Brock through the doorway and into the hall.

"What is she?" he asks as she slams the door in his face.

I watch all this unfold as I try my best to delay the inevitable. I hold my breath. My body stands frozen.

But my heart rate increases. It's only a matter of time at this point. Seconds.

Paige whirls to face me with a look of trepidation. "Shit." She sprints toward me, buries her shoulder into my midsection, and lifts me off my feet. Without slowing, she carries me across the living room.

Light as a feather, stiff as a board, I think.

Paige shot puts me through my bedroom door. I fly backward. The air pressure in my bedroom increases as I sail in slow motion. It's as if I'm suddenly caught in a vacuum. My ears plug, and sounds become muffled.

Paige grabs my loft door and slides it shut. The sound of the iron-hook slamming into place—locking me inside—echoes in my ears.

I land on the floor hard. I catch sight of my books and clothes rising around me and freezing in midair. Then I close my eyes and pass out.

Chapter 2

I guess I should explain how I came to be who I am. Or *what* I am.

I grew up in Malbrook, Pennsylvania. The town is a popular destination for tourists looking to spend time in Stone Lake, a giant reservoir in what used to be an old limestone quarry. It's a quaint little town with a rich history, family-owned shops, and good Christian people. It's also the most sinfully dull place you could possibly imagine.

My father, Benjamin Caine, owned a small mechanic shop in town. He was well-liked and had a reputation for knocking twenty percent off his advertised prices, which were for the tourists. He taught me everything I know about cars. His weekend hobby was fixing up barn finds and reselling them. Some days, I would help him clean an old engine block or rebuild carburetors. Other times, I might go with him on drives to hunt for obscure and authentic parts.

For better or worse, this was the only way we could communicate. It wasn't that he was cold or uncaring, but he did suffer from an overdeveloped masculinity. He was competitive with other men, only cared about things he considered "manly," and buried his insecurities in silence. Don't get me wrong—I loved my dad. He just didn't have the programming to engage with an adolescent girl, even his own daughter.

My mother, Alice Caine, née Gatlin, spent her whole life in Malbrook. She was popular in high school, the kind of girl whose pretty face won her beauty pageants, student elections, and the attention of everyone around her. After graduation, she continued to cultivate her popularity by volunteering with the local clubs, heading the boosters, and hosting monthly dinner parties.

My mother named me Darcy after her favorite character in her favorite book, *Pride and Prejudice*. At least, that was what she would tell people. I was never quite convinced she read the thing. She often said giving me a literary name would help guide me in school—as if that would work better than taking an active interest in my life.

Now, to be fair, both my parents loved me… in their own ways. They just didn't love me as much as they loved my big brother. Bennet was the pride and joy of the family. Two years older than me, he was the kind of kid you knew was destined for great things in life and not just because he inherited my father's masculinity and my mother's charisma. People recognized it the moment he walked onto a baseball diamond.

That kid could throw. When he would wind up, a hush would settle over the stands. His arm moved so fast you could hear it whipping through the air. By the time he was a freshman in high school, he was throwing eighty-five-mile-an-hour fastballs for the varsity team.

My parents attended every game, even the ones out of the county. My mother was an intimidating force on the high school booster club, and in her first year as president, she set a record for fundraising. My father had been managing Bennet's career since middle school, befriending and inviting scouts and recruiters to see the next Nolan Ryan.

So I did what most young teens do when overshadowed by an older sibling—I rebelled. It will be no surprise to anyone who knows me that I went through a pretty serious goth phase. I'm talking black lipstick, nose ring, and dark clothes. Okay, so that last part hasn't changed much. My best friend was a girl named Vivien Lemaire. Whereas I dipped my toe in goth culture, Vivien was all in. She wore leather corsets, was pierced from head to toe, and sported a purple pixie cut.

Vivien was also the Svengali who introduced me to the occult. Together we read tarot cards, used spirit boards, and studied astrology. She was a self-proclaimed Wiccan and taught me to how to chant. We would spend many hours in the deep Pennsylvania woods at a place called the Witching Well or Wishing Well, depending on who you asked. The well was a circle of granite stones no more than a foot high that surrounded a trickling hot spring. Local legend said the Shawnee tribe originally built it as a place to worship the Great Spirit. Because the Shawnee believed the Great Spirit was a goddess called Our Grandmother, this magical spot allegedly became a mecca for witches in Colonial America. They would come here to worship, practice, and pray. And that was what Vivien and I would do— practice our chants, pledge ourselves to the Triple Goddess, and pray for our deepest, darkest desires.

My foray into rebellion didn't elicit much attention from my parents. Aside from issuing the occasional grounding when I skipped school or forcing me to attend counseling sessions with our Baptist minister, my parents remained focused on their favorite child. And then, in Bennet's junior year, he suffered an elbow injury that threatened to derail his athletic career—the kind of injury no doctor wanted to risk with surgery.

That changed everything. Neither of my parents coped well with setbacks, especially ones like this. My father turned his attention to his work and his cars. My mother put even more effort into the community. They threw their energy into anything but staying home to confront my brother's pain and depression.

Actually, to say Bennet was depressed would be an understatement. He was destroyed. My brother and I weren't particularly close at that point, but it killed me to see him like that, not just because his dreams were ruined but also because of the cruel way my parents were behaving. They treated him like some dark secret they wouldn't acknowledge, like a burden, like a disappointment... like me.

So I started to take care of him. When he couldn't go to school, I brought him his homework. I cooked his meals and made sure he ate well. I even did his laundry—which, because he was a seventeen-year-old boy, required a firm constitution. We started spending so much time together that I found less and less time for Vivien, which she did not appreciate. She cut me out of her life and found some poor freshman girl to corrupt.

After much research, I found a physical therapist the next county over who was willing to treat Bennet. Three days a week after school, I would drive him back and forth. Those long drives in the car gave us some quality one-on-one time. Over the next few months, he and I would share our deepest secrets and our greatest hopes. We became as close as a brother and sister could be.

And by some miracle, Bennet got better. When he finally returned to the baseball field, I was his most enthusiastic and vocal cheerleader. Things started to return to normal for the

Caine family—they were better, even, than they'd been before the injury. Bennet's future was once again looking bright, and I was no longer the family's black sheep.

Until I ruined everything. It started slowly at first. I felt ill—fever, nausea, dry skin. My mother believed it was because I drank too much soda. When I started vomiting toads, my parents thought it would be a good idea to take me to the doctor.

The hospital didn't help. If anything, the situation grew worse. Levitation, speaking in tongues, physical contortion… the medical staff was baffled by what was happening. My father was horrified by the trauma my body was going through. My mother was convinced I was just trying to get attention. Bennet was worried sick.

One good Christian doctor at St. Samaritan Something-or-Other instructed my parents to take me home and contact the church. Even with all his medical and scientific knowledge, he correctly believed I was possessed by a demon—an honest-to-God denizen-of-hell demon.

There was nothing else the hospital could do. Under the cover of night, so as not to alert the neighbors about my disgraceful condition, my parents brought me home. My mother called the pastor of our church, but he could do little to help. When it came to demonic possession, it turned out there was only one group out there who knew their shit: the Catholics.

That was a bitter pill for my Baptist mother to swallow, as she couldn't stand Catholics almost as much as she couldn't stand Methodists. Rumors about my situation began to spread around town, and my mother became increasingly resistant to reaching out for help. She didn't want anyone to know what was happening in her home.

So Bennet made the phone calls. He was the one who sought recommendations and lobbied the archdiocese for evaluations from priests. With no help from my parents, he succeeded in getting two exorcists to come to our home.

They performed the Rite of Exorcism in an attempt to rid me of this demon. At that point, I was completely unaware of what was happening. The demon had control, and I was in an oblivious slumber. Later, I was told that it was unlike anything the priests had ever seen. The demon would not let go of my body.

Two days after they began the ritual, things went from bad to worse. I was never given *all* the details of exactly what happened. They'd bound me in my bed for the exorcism, but at some point during the rite, I was able to break free of my bonds. I attacked the priests then escaped the confines of my room. I rampaged through the house, obliterating everything in my path. My father and brother tried to restrain me, but I had grown too powerful. I turned my attention from destroying the house to attacking my assailants.

Eventually, they were able to restrain me again, and the priests resumed the rite. It took another two days before they were able to subdue the demon and I could regain consciousness. But the damage was done.

Bennet was dead. And I had killed him.

I was devastated. My brother with the bright future ahead of him... my brother who'd fought to help me... my brother whom I'd come to love more than anyone else in this world... had died by my hands. No matter how much the priests tried to convince me that it was the demon who had committed this act, I could not shake the guilt.

Then they gave me more bad news. The demon was not completely exorcised. I remained what the priest called a *demoniac*—a girl possessed.

Just as the demon had kept control of my body while my

mind and soul were subdued, I now had control of my body while the demon lay dormant within. They had done everything in their power to rid me of the evil spirit and had managed to suppress it, but it would return. The episodes would be shorter, only lasting a few hours, before I would resume command of my body. But during that time, there was no telling what kind of destruction and terror I would dispense.

Before he left, one of the priests gave my parents information he believed might help me purge the demon from my body. As part of an exorcism, priests would attempt to learn the name of a demon to drive it out of a victim's body. My particular demon never revealed its true name. If I could learn it, another Rite of Exorcism could be performed to successfully drive this evil spirit from my body. The priest also warned us that this entity had grafted itself to my soul. If I were to die before casting out this demon, it might very well carry my soul with it to the depths of hell, where I would burn for all of eternity.

After the exorcism, my eyes took on a vivid yellow color, a constant reminder to my family that there was still evil dwelling inside me—a demon that had murdered my brother. My mother, in particular, was unable to cope with my presence. She resented what I had done to Bennet, to the family, and to her. She claimed it was my fault for opening my soul to the powers of the devil during my goth phase. To this day, the knowledge that this might possibly be true sickens me.

While my mother wanted to hide me from the world, she also didn't want me in her home. Her conflicting desires developed into hostility. She hated me and every day made it a point to let me know. My father, despite all his machismo, did nothing.

So I left. I bounced around the country, visiting different

churches and priests in an attempt to research my demon's name. I eventually made my home in Los Angeles.

I promised myself that I would learn this demon's name and drive it out. I would rid my body of this evil. In the meantime, I decided to give it a temporary name, something I could call it whenever I looked in a mirror and stared into my yellow eyes.

So I named it Dudley.

Chapter 3

I wake on my hardwood floor. My head pounds from either a migraine or a small hamster playing trance music in my skull. Fortunately, I'm still in my bedroom.

There's a reason Paige and I moved into a loft converted from an old battery factory. Its high ceilings, oak flooring, and concrete walls are perfect for containing a demon. We installed a grid of iron bars in my windows, and the sliding bedroom door is secured from the outside with a T-shaped iron crossbar that locks into brackets.

I lift my wrist and cycle through the displays on my watch to check last night's maximum heart-rate reading. Two hundred three beats per minute. That's not good. If I have too many nights like last night, I'll die of a heart attack before I'm thirty.

I slowly rise to find my room a complete mess. The bed is askew, with blankets and pillows in piles on the floor. Books are everywhere. My bedside lamp lies shattered on the floor, which sucks because I don't have the cash flow for a Target run right now.

A broken photo frame of Bennet and me is at the foot of my

metal dresser. I crawl over, carefully pick away the glass fragments, and pull out the photo. It's the last photo I have of the both of us, from when I was sixteen and he was eighteen. His thick arms are wrapped around me as I struggle to get away. We are laughing. Even at that age, he looked like a man. But he would never become one.

Since this photo is the original print I took from home, I decide to put it away for safekeeping. I pull on the top drawer of my dresser, only to discover it's jammed because of a large dent on the side. I say *dresser*, but it's actually a filing cabinet. All my bedroom furniture is metal. I've broken too many pieces of cheap particleboard to keep buying that crap. Instead of an armoire, I have a series of lockers. My bedside table is steel. My bedframe is iron. Not exactly girly.

I retrieve the mallet I keep around for post-possession cleanup and use it to hammer the metal back into place, and I slip the photo into the drawer. Then the cleanup begins. Books are restacked according to genre. I shove the bed back against the wall. The broken glass gets swept up and dumped in an empty wastebasket.

I lift an old jean jacket from the floor to check if there is any more glass underneath. Instead, I find something else. A snake. A black viper, specifically.

It whirls its head in my direction, hissing, ready to strike. I throw the jacket back over the serpent and shuffle away. I've been in this situation before—too many times to count. It still grosses me out to think that thing came out of my mouth in the middle of the night.

I reach beside my dresser and grab a pair of snake tongs and a burlap bag I keep for just such occasions. I lift the jacket slowly and use the tongs to snatch the serpent. These guys can be venomous, so I'm careful, gentle, and quick. I deposit the offending creature in the bag, which I then cinch up.

Now I have to get rid of another stupid snake. I can feel myself getting anxious and realize the Xanax Paige fed me last night has worn off. It's early, and I have a long day at work ahead of me, so I rifle through my bottles of benzos. I opt for Klonopin to calm me down for the day.

I'm not an addict, by the way. I don't take these for recreation or to tranquilize myself against first-world problems. I do this to keep Dudley from getting the best of me. If I get too worked up or angry or generally lose control, I become more susceptible to one of my "Satan spells," as Paige likes to call them. So I have to remain calm and totally Zen.

Half a milligram of Klonopin twice a day usually does the trick. If I need faster relief, I take six milligrams of Xanax, crushed, under the tongue. The medication also helps shorten the spells and minimize the damage.

Last night's aftermath is way too much to deal with before my first cup of coffee. I knock on the wooden door that barricades me inside and wait for Paige to answer.

She calls through the door, "Darcy or Dudley?"

This is our routine after incidents like last night. She's never personally witnessed an entire episode, just the teaser. When my heart rate hits one hundred sixty beats per minute, we know we're moving into dangerous territory. At one hundred ninety BPM, I'm in full fight-or-flight mode. There's no going back, and she has seconds to either contain me or escape.

I've made her promise not to linger for the whole show. It's too dangerous. Her instructions are to keep the door locked until the next morning. She can't open it until she can confirm it's me and not Dudley.

"It's Darcy."

"Let's hear it."

I sigh. "Can we skip it just this once?"

"Hey, it's your rule."

I clear my throat. Then with absolutely no enthusiasm, I start singing.

"Cheer, cheer for old Notre Dame,

"Wake up the echoes, cheering her name,

"Please don't make me sing the whole thing in shame."

No self-respecting demon would ever utter those words, let alone sing them.

I can hear the iron hook scrape out of its latch. The pocket door slides on its track and disappears into the recess of the cinderblock wall. Paige Whitaker stands there in shorts and a gray Dodgers T-shirt. Her blond hair is tied in a ponytail and soaked with sweat. As with every morning, she has already burned a thousand calories before I've woken up. Meanwhile, I'm a disheveled mess and look like a public-service warning.

We stand there facing each other, and I'm reluctant to speak. I want to apologize for sticking my nose where it didn't belong. I want to apologize for leaving her alone last night when I should have been there. I want to apologize for losing control and putting her in a potentially dangerous situation.

"I'm sorry," she says, beating me to the punch. "I should have seen what a scumbag he was."

"I'm sorry. I didn't handle it right. And I never should have left you alone with him."

"No. I shouldn't have let him inside. That was my fault!"

"Men," I mutter.

"Boys," she corrects me and brings me in for a hug.

Paige is the closest thing I have to family now. I never want to see her hurt, and I never want to be the cause of her pain.

Which is why I don't say anything about how sweaty and smelly she is right now. "Did he ever come back last night?"

She shakes her head. "No. I don't think we'll ever see Brock again."

"Good."

"Darcy?"

"Yeah?"

"What's in the bag?"

I forgot about the bag in my hands and its contents. "Laundry?"

The bag squirms, flopping against her back. She wriggles away, her body contorting. "Gross!"

Paige twirls on her bare toes and heads to our dining table, reaching over her shoulders to brush away the lingering sensation from her back. I step into our long, narrow living room and walk toward the front wall. From the coat closet, I pull out a portable terrarium. Fortunately, nothing is inside this time, so it's fairly easy to dump in the new guest and quickly close the blue plastic top to seal it shut.

"I'm going to call him Sir Hiss," I call out across our loft.

"Don't do that! You'll get attached."

"Sorry," I say to our new houseguest in a quieter voice. "Paige doesn't like reptiles."

Well, not reptiles per se, just the hell spawn that emerges from my stomach.

I decide to take an extra-hot and extra-long shower. After, I wipe the fog from the mirror and take a moment to appraise myself. Despite whatever resentment I still hold for my mother, I count myself lucky that I inherited her high cheekbones and smooth skin. My long black hair helps me look youthful, but I wonder how much longer it will stay black before the wear and tear of demonic episodes turns it white.

Eventually, I find myself staring into my eyes. Only my irises are yellow, so people don't notice the color until they get up close. Once they do, they usually can't look away. Some people are unnerved by the color. Others are fascinated by it. I'm long past the charade of constantly wearing sunglasses, so when people ask about my eyes, I say I wear colored contacts as a fashion statement. I still haven't figured out what that statement is.

They say the eyes are the windows to the soul, and as I stare at my own reflection, I suspect the adage is true. However, in my case, I don't see my soul—I see Dudley. I see a stranger's eyes glaring back at me—a vile, malevolent demonic spirit that hates me with the burning fury of a thousand suns, a creature utterly pissed because he's subdued in the body of a twenty-six-year-old woman.

"Good morning, Dudley."

My stomach churns, so I know I've pissed him off. I do this from time to time to remind him who's winning this battle. Or maybe I do it to remind myself.

Being possessed feels a lot like being sick—or more accurately, like that day before you get sick. My throat is scratchy. I suffer from aches and chills. Ever since Dudley came along, I'm constantly cold. I guess compared to the thousand-degree heat of an eternally burning hell, eighty degrees might feel a bit nippy.

I choose my outfit for the day from the various lockers in my bedroom—jeans, boots, and my thick black field jacket. Even though it's going to be a warm spring day here in Los Angeles, I know I'll need to stay bundled. Plus, my jacket has plenty of pockets, so I never have to carry a purse.

When I emerge from my room, I can hear Paige taking her turn using the shower in our shared bathroom. On our dining table, I find a bowl of oatmeal with fruit and a hot cup of coffee waiting for me, courtesy of Paige. She's always looking out for me, which includes making sure I eat well.

I take a seat at our table—a repurposed barn door on wrought-iron legs. This was our first joint purchase at the Rose Bowl Flea Market after we signed our lease, and it now provides a place for us to eat and work. Paige's corner is adjacent to a large metal shelf unit that houses her various computers, gaming consoles, cameras, and other electronic equipment. To say she's a techie would be an understatement. Anything with a transistor and a circuit board is catnip for her. During the day, she works from home as a freelance web designer, building websites for small businesses and organizations. It's mostly just retooled WordPress templates, and she could easily charge eight hours of work for two hours of effort. But that's not Paige. She has too much integrity for that.

On my corner of the table sits a stack of books and a single laptop that I use for streaming and online shopping. I have a constant rotation from the library and can read up to four at a time—though not in the same genre. I usually have one fiction, one nonfiction, one reference, and a wild card.

My phone chirps with a text from Father Ramon: *I have a new client for you. Available?*

I don't have to bother checking my schedule. I quickly type back: *My calendar just opened up.*

Finally, a new gig. Maybe I will be able to afford a new lamp. I dig into my oatmeal before heading out to my day job.

Chapter 4

Los Angeles Central Library is a short fifteen-minute bike ride from home. It's chilly on this March morning, probably in the midfifties, so I'm thankful I have my jacket to shield me against the subarctic temperatures.

When I hit the homeless camps outside the series of rescue missions, I pedal as fast as I can until I reach the stretch of secondhand and knockoff stores that make up the first floor of old masonry skyscrapers built one hundred years ago. I twist and turn through bike lanes until I can see the purple rectangular bell tower rising above Pershing Square.

In ten city blocks, the population transforms from homeless people dressed in fatigues and living out of shopping carts to everyone wearing Hugo Boss and Donna Karen.

I lock up my bike at the rack outside the Central Library entrance. A wolf whistle sounds behind me, followed by, "What's a fine girl like you hanging around the library for?"

I smile and turn. Terrell Jenkins, one of the security guards, stands by the entrance with his arms folded. An African

American with wiry frame and years of experience in his face and eyes, Terrell is a notorious flirt. But at sixty, he's harmless and the only man I know who can still pull off that whistle and not offend anyone.

"Just trying to make an honest living and keep myself off the streets," I say, offering him a wink as I approach the door.

Terrell holds the door open as I walk in. Most guys come across as creepy when they flirt and catcall. Not Terrell. Maybe it's because of his age, or maybe he's refined his skill over the years, but whatever his secret is, it works.

"Oh, look, another beautiful angel coming to work!" I hear over my shoulder. Terrell holds the door for another librarian. Meg is in her late fifties and looks like a grandmother from any Norman Rockwell painting. Terrell is just as sincere and charismatic when he flirts with her as he is with me. She can't help smiling either.

So begins my day at the Los Angeles Central Library. Until my job as a private investigator can pay the bills, I'm stuck working here part-time. I started as a volunteer here so I could gain access to Los Angeles County special collections. My research into the occult and biblical references required access to rare and out-of-print books. If I were ever going to learn Dudley's true name, I had to study everything from the ancient Sumerians to modern Satanism. Eventually, the city hired me part-time to cultivate their Californiana collection, an archive of books, maps, photos, and art relating to the history of California—and especially Los Angeles—from the Spanish and Mexican periods to the present.

This morning, I cover a shift for a coworker, putting away books in the children's department. The room's 1920s design is virtually unchanged, with its wrought-iron grillwork that separates it from the main rotunda underneath the pyramid of illumination. The pyramid is decorated with Egyptian-inspired iconography—in particular, the sun symbol. Topping the pyramid is a golden arm holding a torch.

Some argue this is a symbol of enlightenment. Others argue it's a symbol for Luciferianism, a belief system that identifies Lucifer as a figure of enlightenment not unlike the Greek Titan Prometheus. Lucifer literally means "light bringer."

These are the thoughts that run through my scattered mind as I'm putting away copies of Dr. Seuss under the pyramid: symbolism in the library, my never-ending research into religion and evil, the socioeconomic differences I see on my bike ride to work... and the enormous Latino eyeballing me from the picture-books aisle.

He's been watching me for about ten minutes and absentmindedly holding a copy of *Where the Wild Things Are*. While I admit it's a great book, it shouldn't take him that long to get through it. This must be the potential new client.

I'm not about to ask him. I could be wrong. He could just be a huge fan of Maurice Sendak. I am. But in case he is a client, I push my book cart down a vacant aisle away from everyone else so we might have some privacy.

It doesn't take long for him to appear at the end of the row of books. He approaches slowly. I keep my eyes down—I don't want to spook him.

"Darcy Caine?" he asks in a thick Hispanic accent.

"You looking for a book recommendation?"

He doesn't seem to appreciate my sense of humor. Few people do. "I was told you could help us."

Us, he said. Curious. "Who sent you?"

"Father Ramon."

Bingo. "What can I do for you?"

"It's not me. It's my boss. Her daughter is missing."

"You call the police?" I ask.

"We can't call the cops."

This raises red flags. Even though he found me through Father Ramon, whom I trust implicitly, something is telling me that if this guy doesn't want the police involved, then I probably don't want to be involved either.

"Why not?"

"Let's go talk to her. She can tell you."

Another red flag. *Where is his boss, and why isn't she here? Where is this guy trying to lure me?* He isn't a typical errand boy. This guy is six feet tall, wears cowboy boots, and has rough hands. Even though I'm a woman, he positions his body square to mine with his hands ready at the hip. I can tell whether a man knows how to handle himself by the way he stands, and this guy has seen his fair share of fights.

I decide to push. I continue putting away books, looking anywhere but at him. "This isn't how this works. If she needs my help, she can come see me."

"Father Ramon said you could help her."

"God helps those who help themselves."

He's getting pissed now. I can tell he's not used to being denied. I'm not worried, though. *What's he going to do, punch a girl in the middle of a library?*

He slaps the books out of my hands and onto the floor. "Listen, bitch…"

Maybe.

He grabs my arm and pushes me against a wall. He's strong, with the beefy biceps a person gets from manual labor or beating people to a pulp. I glimpse the bottom part of a tattoo on his right shoulder peeking from under his short sleeve—a crudely drawn arrow pointed down.

"My boss wants your help. Father Ramon gave us your

name and where to find you. Are you going to help us, or am I wasting my time?"

I finally look up. My yellow eyes stare deep into his soul. He rips his hand away, not expecting this. I feint a move forward, and he rocks on his heels. I smile to see I intimidated him for just a moment. He sneers.

Someone whisper-screams, "You there!"

At the end of the aisle stands a mousy Hispanic woman. She's stern, with her hair tied in a tight ponytail and dark eyes piercing through horn-rimmed glasses. Her petite figure and porcelain skin make her appear much younger than her forty-five years would suggest. Some of our coworkers have even remarked that we look like sisters, which makes me question how old I must look.

"What's going on here?" she reprimands as she comes closer.

"Everything's fine, Lupe." I return my attention to the man, locking my eyes on his. "Tell your boss I'll think about it."

He straightens his shirt before turning away. Lupe presses herself flush against the book stacks as he trudges past her and disappears into the rotunda. We listen to the receding echo of his cowboy boots clacking on the hard marble floor.

Lupe hurries to me and looks me over. "Are you okay?"

"I'm fine."

"Was this another one of your customers?" She bends down to pick up the books from the floor. "I told you I don't want them coming around here."

Guadalupe Navarro is my supervisor at the library. She knows about my side gig as a private detective. Since I only work part-time for the library, she can't prohibit me from working elsewhere. That doesn't stop her from judging me for it, though.

"Sorry," I say.

She rises, carefully putting the books away, then turns to

look at me. In heels, she's roughly my height, but I always feel an inch or two shorter than she. With a gentle sweep, Lupe brushes the fallen hair away from my face. "Such a pretty girl. I don't know why you don't spend more time looking for a nice man to take care of you. Then you wouldn't have to bother with that terrible business."

I turn away, embarrassed by the compliment and overwhelmed by the kindness. Dating has always been a challenge with my condition. Whenever I find myself getting into a serious relationship, I end up sabotaging it. Most guys already think girls are crazy, so I dread having to explain that I have a literal demon inside me.

"Men aren't interested in girls like me." I try to make it sound tough, but I reveal more pain than I intended.

Lupe shakes her head. "Be careful. You'll be thirty sooner than you think, then men will wonder what is wrong with you."

Even though Lupe is trying to offer helpful advice, the words irk me more than I'd care to admit. I bite my tongue out of respect, but I can already anticipate this moment replaying itself in my mind over the next twenty-four hours as I think of the laundry list of things I should have said.

I return to putting away the rest of the books and change the subject. "Sorry about that." I nod in the direction of the recently departed trespasser. "It won't happen again."

Lupe takes the hint and turns to walk away. She hesitates then looks back at me. "You're not going to work for him, are you?" she says with tinge of concern.

"A girl's gotta make a living."

She scowls, finding no humor in my remark. "He seemed very dangerous," she says before disappearing around the bookshelf.

She's right. Before I take the case, I need to learn more. I decide to go to church after work.

✐

A bike ride to Pasadena is out of the question, so I pedal home to swap my mode of transportation. I lock my bike in our building's underground parking structure before settling into my trusted Mini Cooper.

A friend in the police department tipped me off two years ago to an upcoming police auction, so I was able to get the car for cheap. It's a black 1990 Mark V—mini even by Mini standards—with yellow racing stripes that stretch from bumper to bumper. As a British import, it has a manual transmission and the driver's side on the right. Parking next to high curbs is a constant battle in this city.

The engine is a work in progress that has been cobbled together using parts from a Honda Civic, a moped, and even a lawnmower. I credit my father for teaching me how to keep the engine running and make the most of duct tape. If I had the money, I could restore the heck out of it.

With a turn of a key, the engine sputters to life, and I embark on the half-hour journey through the Arroyo Seco watershed to Father Ramon. Five years ago, I read an article in *Vanity Fair* about a priest in Los Angeles, Father Ramon Castillo, who was making a name for himself as one of the most accomplished exorcists in America. Since his ordination, he'd conducted over twenty exorcisms throughout Southern California. The Vatican had even summoned him to lead a training session from around the world at a yearly conference for other exorcists. I like to pretend they call the event Ex-Con.

I was living in New Orleans at the time, searching for help from the priests and faith healers in the area. Since that had turned up nothing, and because I was still desperate for answers, I packed my things and moved to Los Angeles. I spent a few weeks stalking him outside the church until one day I caught him walking alone. I accosted him in the park, and I explained my situation. Since the article had been published, he'd received many inquiries from people who were convinced they were possessed, so he was naturally skeptical about my situation. I encouraged him to get in touch with the Vatican—they had a whole file on me. After confirming my story, and with permission from the Los Angeles bishop, he agreed to help me in any way he could. We've been friends ever since.

Our search to uncover Dudley's real name began in the libraries throughout Los Angeles and in every special collection resource we could find. We have spent countless hours digging through volumes of books. Father Ramon leveraged every connection he had to get us into museums and personal collections to study artifacts and materials not available to the general public. The Vatican had even sent him some rare and valuable texts as additional resources. For five years, we have been searching for the name of the demonic entity inside me.

Despite our best efforts, we're not any closer than we were on day one of our search. There are a lot of demon names. Sometimes I wonder if we'll ever figure it out.

Father Ramon was quick to notice I had a talent for research, an eye for detail, and an exceptional memory. I credit this to the years of research I had already conducted on my own. He used his connections to help me land work with a private investigation agency. We mostly handled workers' compensation claims for insurance companies, and I would perform sub-rosa investigations—secret surveillance of individuals, such as filming a forklift operator waterskiing a week after he'd filed a claim for a back injury.

I was good at my job. Damn good. In no time, I was the number-one surveillance investigator on the team.

When I considered starting my own business, it was Father Ramon who encouraged me. After completing my required field hours and acquiring the finest online bachelor's degree in criminology that money could buy, I became a certified, licensed private investigator and started my own business. Father Ramon connected me with my first client, and he continues to send work my way. He has a good relationship with his flock, and they have no reservations about going to him with their troubles, both in the confession booth and outside of it.

Once I've parked in Old Town Pasadena, I send Father Ramon a text letting him know I have arrived then stand across the street from the church. The sun sits low on the horizon, backlighting the old Romanesque church with its hundred-forty-foot campanile overlooking all of Pasadena. The redbrick structure is modeled after the bell tower at the Santa Maria Church in Trastevere and looks like something right out of medieval Italy. This tour of Los Angeles history is courtesy of my experience working in the Central Library.

Father Ramon emerges from the church. It's probably blasphemous to say, but Ramon is a good-looking man. He keeps fit, not just for the health benefits but also to keep himself ready for the next marathon exorcism. He's not yet forty, but his thick black hair is already showing signs of gray.

This evening, he's wearing his civvies—blue jeans and a gray polo shirt—and not his usual clerical shirt and collar. He crosses the street and smiles as he approaches. "Hello, Darcy. It's good to see you."

He knows better than to hug me or even to venture a handshake. That's another result of demonic possession—I can't have physical contact with religious leaders. Instead, he raises his hand in greeting, and I wave back.

"Hello, Father Ramon," I say.

I've met a lot of priests in my time, and there's no consistent convention for how they wish to be addressed. Ramon Castillo is probably the friendliest priest I've ever met. He likes people to call him Father Ramon.

We walk into Old Town and find our little coffee shop down a redbrick pedestrian alley. He's friendly with everyone in the neighborhood, saying hello to shop owners and locals by name. The café sits deep in the alley, with an external counter under a red-and-white awning. He orders in Spanish, pays for my coffee as well as his, and tips generously.

We find a small table and enjoy our coffee over some casual chitchat. He asks about my life and work at the library. I update him on Paige and her recent breakup.

Eventually, we talk about the strange visitor to the library. Father Ramon identifies him as Hugo Escalante, an employee of a woman named Carmen Viramontes. "I knew her husband very well. Marcos. He came to church every Sunday and was a generous supporter of the parish."

Generous supporter. That means he's a rich guy who donates bunches of money.

"Marcos passed away two years ago."

Don't I feel like an a-hole.

"He always spoke of his wife with great love and affection."

"You've never met her?" I ask.

"Marcos and his wife immigrated from Mexico years ago. Neither of them ever gained legal residency. Before he passed away, he confided in me that she suffered from a crippling fear that if she ever left the house, she would be caught and arrested."

"That would explain why she hasn't called the cops." It makes sense. A woman whose residency is in question would probably have a greater chance of being deported than having her missing child found.

Ramon continues. "Carmen's housekeeper, Leona, is her go-between to the outside world. Leona came to me after services on Sunday and asked to speak with me privately. She told me Elizabeth, Carmen's daughter, had gone missing. Vanished without a trace."

"A runaway?"

"They don't think so. Elizabeth is a freshman at USC and, by all accounts, an A student. Her mother called the school, and it seems she stopped attending classes with no notice."

"That doesn't mean she didn't run away," I say.

"Carmen may not be a legal resident, but she's a wealthy woman. Elizabeth has a bank account at her disposal. She hasn't touched it since she disappeared."

"How does Carmen make her money?"

Ramon answers my questions. They may seem random, but by now, he's used to my zigzagging thought processes. "Marcos ran a very successful chain of electronics stores. Super Tech."

As clear as day, the commercial I had seen a handful of times runs through my mind. A man in a plaid suit stands in an electronics store. He swings a long sword through giant price tags and yells, "Nobody slashes prices like Teddy!"

Teddy.

"I thought those stores were owned by someone named Teddy," I say. "The cheesy guy in the ads."

"That's an actor. When Marcos came to the States, he didn't have much money and spoke very poor English. When he opened his first store, he wanted to put a face behind the store that people would find likable. So he hired a white actor to pretend to be the owner."

"And neither he nor his wife ever became a citizen?"

He nods. "It's complicated. And at this point, she's been

here too long without a visa or green card to seek citizenship."

It's not uncommon for undocumented residents to operate small businesses. I don't know how they do it, but they do. The fact that Marcos was able to not only open one business but a whole chain is impressive. I make a note to myself to look into that and figure out why I haven't become more successful with my advantage of being a natural-born citizen.

It seems like a pretty obvious case of a runaway... except the money. I wonder why Elizabeth didn't clean out the account when she ran away. I would have.

I did.

I agree to visit Carmen tomorrow and get more information about the case. I haven't had a paying gig in two months, and I need the money—and a new lamp.

We chat for a bit longer before Ramon segues into the subject of my life. "Have you had any occurrences recently?"

I consider telling him about last night's episode but decide against it. There's no reason to worry him. I casually try to cover and tell him everything's perfectly all right now. "All fine here, thank you. How are you?"

He stares. I can read people pretty well, and I can tell he's reading me and not buying my story. Ramon knows me better than I give him credit for, so he also knows I'm done talking about myself.

"There's an upcoming exhibit at the Fowler Museum," he says. "Ancient Aztec Art. I thought a visit wouldn't hurt."

In our research to find the name of this demon inside me, we've decided to move beyond the typical Judeo-Christian demons and investigate other religions and mythologies. After all, God and the devil are older than Judaism and more pervasive than the usual Euro-Middle Eastern history, so we might find Dudley's real name mentioned in the texts or artwork of other civilizations.

I have to give Father Ramon credit—for a Catholic priest, he has an open mind about other religions. Sometimes.

"I'll check it out," I say.

"May I accompany you? Two sets of eyes are better than one."

We decide on a weekend and set a date.

I enter the front door of our apartment to find Paige behind a small fort of bankers' boxes. She pokes her head out from behind the cardboard fortress like a meerkat.

"Hi," she says in a guilty tone that matches her expression.

I know immediately what's happening. Without saying a word, I dump my keys on the table near Sir Hiss's terrarium and join her on the floor near our couch. "Where did we leave off?"

Paige hands me an accordion file filled with documents. "You're on *T*'s," she says. "I'm still on *C*'s."

I remove a handful of name-change forms for the County of Los Angeles.

"How was work?" Paige asks, making idle chitchat as she pores over the paper in her hand.

"I saw Father Ramon tonight."

"Tonight?" She whips her head to the window, as if only now realizing it's dark outside. "Does this mean you have a new case?"

I shrug, trying to be nonchalant. "I'm meeting someone tomorrow. We'll see."

Paige returns her attention to the files in her hand. "I ordered dinner. Chinese." She glances up at me. She knows Chinese is my favorite, so this must be her way of apologizing for the evening ahead.

"Sounds perfect," I say to let her know that I'm okay with tonight's plan.

She smiles, and we dig into the work for the evening.

Paige grew up in foster care as a ward of the court. Since she turned eighteen, she's been trying to track down her birth mother. The only evidence she has that her mom was ever a part of her life—other than her fading memories—is a photograph she keeps as a memento, a washed-out Polaroid taken at a beach. In it, a young blond woman wraps a towel around a toddler girl with shoulder-length blond hair. They're both facing the camera with the biggest smiles you can imagine. And yes, the young mother looks a lot like Paige.

When I say "fading memories," it's because Paige still remembers the day in the courthouse when her mother gave up custody. She was four. After that, Paige quickly got lost in the system. She was shuffled around to a number of foster parents who collected kids as meal tickets, cashing in on state benefits to earn a living. By Paige's account, the best of these foster parents were only verbally abusive. The worst… well, I don't need to paint the picture.

Paige believes her mother abandoned her as an act of protection. The vague memories of her mother involve living in small motel rooms, moving around a lot, and watching her mother cry—hardly a stable environment for bringing up a daughter. Her mother made a sacrifice twenty-one years ago, and Paige now believes she can take care of her.

With no help from government agencies, Paige has taken up the search on her own. She even hired a private detective at one point. Yes, she found the investigator through Father Ramon. Yes, that was how we met.

Three years later, I'm still helping her search through boxes of old files on the off chance we stumble on some nugget of information that we missed the last time we did this—some random document related to the birth or history of Paige Alexandra Whitaker. The two documents she does have are an application for a Social Security card and an order terminating guardianship, in which the names of the judges, attorneys, and her mother are redacted. Both these forms have the same date.

The fact that there are two documents with the same date for a Social Security number and a termination of guardianship suggested one thing—Paige Whitaker is not her real name, and her mother created a whole new identity on the day the child was legally abandoned.

Our online searches resulted in nothing. No forms seemed to exist for this name-change document... until we found a government warehouse where the hard copies were kept. Paige and I borrowed the documents a couple of months ago. Well, "borrowed," may be taking some artistic license. The process did involve Paige reconfiguring my City of Los Angeles employee access card for administrative access to every government building in the county, and I did have to pose as an internal auditor at the Hall of Records. But we fully intend to return every single box as soon as we're done.

Now that her relationship with Brock is over, Paige has pulled these boxes out of our downstairs storage locker. Clearly, his recent departure has reignited her obsession with finding her mother. We comb through the boxes, looking for evidence that a four-year-old girl changed her name to Paige Whitaker. The Chinese food arrives, and we continue to read one legal document after another. We're still reading when the Chinese food has been eaten and the leftovers have been put in the refrigerator.

It's one in the morning by the time my eyes are so watery I can't look at another piece of paper. I wish I could stay up later, but exhaustion sends me off to bed while Paige continues her search. There's no point in telling her she should to go sleep too. There's no stopping her. We've been here before. We'll be here again.

Chapter 5

I call Carmen's house and speak to Leona about setting up an appointment. The housekeeper's voice is sharp and direct and vibrates over the phone. Every syllable is overenunciated as if she's delivering a direct order to an inferior.

Leona requests that I come this morning and explains that Mrs. Viramontes is anxious to meet me. My schedule at the library is flexible enough that I can come and go as I need and no one bothers me, which is helpful for playing hooky. I ask Leona for directions, and she's further annoyed that I would bother her with such trivialities. After I hang up, I decide to make her my prime suspect out of spite.

I slide open my bedroom door. On normal nights, Paige doesn't bother to barricade me in. We've been living together for two years, and at first, we practiced the ritual of entombing me. Nothing ever happened. Then one morning, Paige left for an all-day seminar and forgot to unlock me.

By the time I woke and called her, she was too far to come back. I spent the day in my room. I should not have had all that

Gatorade the night before. Since then, unless I'm worked up or not feeling well before bed, we leave my door unlocked. Paige feels safe enough by now—though I think she locks her bedroom door.

There's no sign of her this morning, but our living room is a disaster. Boxes and papers litter the entire expanse of the floor. I can only presume she's out on a run. It's a little late for her to be doing that, but I'm not surprised since she was up until all hours last night.

I leave send her a quick *Good morning!* text and head off.

Carmen Viramontes's house is situated in a beautiful Pasadena suburb, lined and shaded by an endless column of elm trees. There are few cars parked on the street among these sprawling homes except for the trucks of gardeners and various utility vehicles at work. All the nice cars are parked in the driveways and behind the gates. The house sits behind a large wrought-iron gate surrounded by a ten-foot-high hedge.

I press the buzzer at the gate and announce myself. The iron bars slowly wheel open, and I hike up the driveway to an enormous Arts and Crafts home—sage green with cedar trim. The rich perfume from the rose gardens on either side of the driveway hits me like a punch to the face. The area around the house is clearly inspired by Japanese landscaping.

Leona is waiting for me on the porch and watches me trudge up the driveway. She's tall and composed and looks as austere as she sounded on the phone. Her perfectly coifed hair bun matches her perfectly tailored tan suit.

She furrows her brow as I approach. "Darcy Caine?"

I know what she sees—a little grungy girl with a heavy jacket and lesbian boots. I'm not the private detective she was expecting. She's also not what I was expecting. My impression over the phone was that she was a maid, but she's clearly more a majordomo… or majordoma… or whatever the female equivalent is.

However, there is one thing that strikes me about her—she's white. Carmen Viramontes, immigrant from Mexico and undocumented resident, has a white housekeeper. That is a fantastic reversal of fortune.

I extend my hand in greeting. "Yes. Leona? Nice to meet you."

Leona gives me a firm handshake. When most people first meet me, they do a double take when they see my eyes. Not Leona. She has too much social decorum for that.

She escorts me inside, and I'm equally impressed by the interior. A dual staircase in the foyer greets visitors, the two sides winding their way up to a vast upper floor in perfect symmetry. Dark wainscoting is juxtaposed with clean white walls. Everything is meticulously placed and meant to amaze.

I'm guided through the drawing room—yeah, this place has a drawing room—past the dining room, and to the kitchen. The moment I step inside, I'm hit by the fragrance of smoke and spices. The kitchen is busy with prep work. One servant is cutting vegetables on large board while another is hand-mixing some sauce in a wood bowl. In the middle is a woman stirring a steaming skillet. She wears an apron over her white blouse, and from behind, I can't help but notice her voluptuous figure.

"¡Váyanse!" Leona commands. The two other servants stop what they're doing and quickly leave. Only Leona and the woman remain.

Leona offers me the beverage of my choice. I ask for English breakfast tea—"if it's not too much trouble"—with milk. I try to gauge Leona's reaction, and though she hides it, I suspect she's mildly impressed with my choice.

As Leona prepares my tea, the woman at the stove turns to

look at me. She's beautiful. Though she must be in her late forties at least, her piercing eyes and long black hair make her appear much younger. Her hair reminds me of my own and gives me hope for keeping it long when I'm her age.

"Thank you for coming." The woman walks toward me. This has to be Carmen. I extend my hand for a shake, but she greets me with a hug instead. "I'm so glad you could come. Please, sit."

She has a thick Hispanic accent. English is clearly her second language, but she's comfortable speaking it.

Carmen guides me to sit at a stool at the kitchen counter. "Are you hungry? I have so much food here. Do you like paella?"

Before I can answer, she's pulled out a plate. She scoops up a generous serving of rice, shrimp, and sausage from the simmering pan. "It's my personal recipe. Do you like spicy food? It's not too spicy."

As Carmen and Leona meet at the stove, there is a silent exchange between them. Carmen nods then returns to me with the plate. "I'm sorry. Cooking usually helps relax me, but ever since Elizabeth..." She trails off. "Please, I hope you enjoy."

Leona returns with my tea then takes a seat at a stool in the corner. She's not going to leave us alone. Carmen stands silently waiting. I take a bite.

"How is it?" she asks.

"Delicious," I say. And I'm not lying. It's been too long since I've had a home-cooked meal. Neither Paige nor I can cook. Though my mother was never one to cook anything more exotic than spaghetti with jarred sauce, having something hot off the stove reminds me of home. "This is amazing! Where did you learn to cook like this?"

"My mother," Carmen says proudly. "She taught me everything I know."

Still standing, Carmen asks me if I found the place all right. I tell her yes and compliment her on her home. It's minor chitchat, but I can tell Carmen is comfortable and accustomed to playing the hostess. Her responses feel scripted as she describes the recent restoration of the house and the great effort that went into upgrading the design while remaining true to the original architect's intentions.

She keeps staring at my eyes. She doesn't mention them, and I'm sure Father Ramon told her to prepare herself. Still, to most people, they can be disconcerting.

While we talk and I eat, I observe Carmen's body language. She remains standing, her hands folded neatly before her. Aside from her frantic cooking when I walked in, she's a poised and warm hostess. Two minutes into conversation, she still hasn't mentioned her daughter's disappearance. Though this might make some people seem suspicious, it reminds me of my mother. She would always put on a front with people, never letting anyone know the real inner turmoil going on inside. I remember after the exorcism, when she would keep me locked inside during the day. She would tell people I was recovering from chicken pox. Or on a school trip. Or visiting family in Idaho. Anything but the unseemly truth.

I don't find this front suspicious. I find it familiar. Meanwhile, Leona sits quietly. She offers nothing and waits patiently for the next directive from Carmen.

I'm the one who brings up Elizabeth. "How long has she been gone?" With one hand on my fork, I use the other to pull out my trusty composition book and start taking notes. As much as I want to be respectful of the situation at hand, I can't stop eating.

"Since last week. She attends school at USC and lives here. She's a freshman, but I let her have her freedom. If she's gone overnight, she'll send a text just to let me know she's safe."

"When was the last time you saw or heard from her?"

"Wednesday morning before she left for school."

I ask about Elizabeth's phone, thinking we could track its location. Carmen has already tried, but it's been turned off. I ask about Elizabeth's car. Carmen says they found it in a school parking lot. We run through all the *For Dummies* ways to track down a person, and it sounds like Carmen's done everything she can to find her daughter—except call the police.

"Tell me about her friends and boyfriends."

Carmen exchanges a glance with Leona. "She had a boyfriend, but I don't even know his name. He never came to the house. I didn't think it was serious, but a week before she disappeared, I overheard her talking with him on the phone. She was telling him it was over. It sounded like an argument. I asked her about it later that night, but she didn't want to talk to me about it. When it comes to sex, you know how mothers and daughters can be."

"Yes. Yes I do." *No. No I do not.*

"Since that argument and since she disappeared, I worry that…"

She stops herself—the first break in her composure. I don't press, hoping for more genuine emotions to break through. Instead, Carmen collects herself. "I worry that he might have something to do with this."

I'm disappointed by the lack of an outburst. "Do you know where he is or how I can find him?"

Carmen shakes her head.

Turning to Leona, I ask, "Did you ever meet him? Do you know anything about him?"

She is momentarily caught off guard. "No. I'm sorry."

Back to Carmen, I ask, "Is he a student?"

"I think. But I don't know if he goes to USC."

I ask about Elizabeth's friends, and Carmen is forthcoming about everyone she knows. I get a list of friends' names and numbers, though she claims to have called most of them and says they are all worried and no one has information.

We keep talking, and I ask another round of questions that seem to go nowhere. Carmen is starting to open up, and her answers finally feel off script. I ask, "Can I see her room?"

Leona rises and leads the way, and I walk beside Carmen up the stairs to the second floor. The fact that there are no personal decorations downstairs doesn't register until we make it to the top. I realize I saw no family photos, souvenirs from vacations, clothes, or bags lying around. Downstairs is only for show.

Upstairs is a different matter. Family portraits line the wall—images of Elizabeth growing up and professional photographs of Carmen, including some that suggest she used to be a model or an actress. There are portraits of a man I can only assume is—was—her husband.

There are no candid shots. These are posed portraits, assembled to show a family. Curiously, they don't show the entire family together. Everyone is there, just in different pictures. Even my dysfunctional family posed for a group photo once in a while.

One picture strikes me—a man standing in front of a store called Super Tech. It's not Teddy. "Is this your husband?"

Carmen nods. "Marcos. The day he opened the first store." I can tell by Carmen's tone that we're back on script.

I toss some underhanded softballs to see if any useful information can be culled from casual conversation. "Still open?"

"No. This was taken in 1993. We had to expand years later and closed down the first store."

I point at the photo. "That must have been a proud day."

"Yes. When Marcos arrived in America, he had only a hundred dollars. He worked and saved up many years to open that store. He was a hardworking man, and it was important to him to prove he could live the American dream."

Carmen wipes a tear from her cheek and waits for me to finish admiring the photo. Instead, I think about her delivery. I've only taken one acting class, but I can tell she's totally indicating.

At this moment, I can't figure out what bothers me about the whole thing. *Unhappy marriage? Business in debt? Loan sharks? My only suspect, Leona?*

I shake it off, and we continue on to Elizabeth's room. I immediately see her mother's influence in the decor, though this is the most brightly colored room in the house. Shades of blue and red adorn most every inch of the room. There are fewer pictures of Elizabeth here than in the hall but plenty of pictures of friends. The ones of Elizabeth are from the past few years, as suggested by the red sweater with USC on the chest.

My phone comes out, and I take photos while Carmen and Leona watch patiently. I capture snapshots of the occasional knickknack that catches my attention. Mostly, I take pictures of pictures.

Near the bed are two items of note, a crucifix on the wall and a statue of the Virgin Mary on the bedside table. I'm careful not to get too close to them.

I can't help but notice how much Elizabeth's room reminds me of my room when I was younger. A collage of photos above her vanity shows her with friends, just like the one I had. A crucifix hangs above her bed. I had the same thing. Instead of USC cardinal-and-gold pennants, I had blue-and-white pennants. My mother wanted me to be a Nittany Lion, and I was supposed to go to Penn State after high school… before the whole demon thing happened.

I find what I'm looking for when I locate Elizabeth's laptop sitting on her bed. It strikes me as curious that a freshman at USC would leave for school in the morning and not bring her laptop. I don't mention it.

"She might have a great deal of information on her laptop. I would like to borrow it to see what I can find."

At this, Leona says, "I don't think we can let you do that."

I look at Leona then at Carmen. My impression now is that Leona is there to protect Carmen. Possibly from me.

I wait for an answer but don't press. Carmen then speaks up. "I'm sure Father Castillo told you about my situation—why I cannot go to the police. I don't know what my daughter has in her computer, but I simply cannot risk letting it out of my home. If you would like, you may look through it now. While I am here."

I can't say I blame her. If my home and residency were in jeopardy, I might be wary about letting a computer with potentially damaging evidence leave my house. In an effort to assure her, I explain what I'll be looking for on the computer. Emails. Search history. Social-media profiles. A diary. I open the screen and talk her through my search. As expected, the computer is password protected.

"Now what?" Carmen asks.

I restart the computer in safe mode and remove a flash drive from my pocket. Paige created an application for me to use for just such an occasion. I talk Carmen through the task at hand— an attempt at a brute-force attack to crack the password and access the computer. She stares back at me with a confused expression then keeps a worried eye on me while I work. I can only imagine that my explanation reinforces her fears about my taking the computer. But it's not like I could use Elizabeth's laptop to access all their personal banking files, steal their private fortune, and collect enough evidence to have them deported.

Paige could, but I don't tell Carmen that.

In about five minutes, I finally have access to Elizabeth's desktop. I open her emails, and we scan them, looking for communications between her and her friends. As I expected, there's very little. Most people Elizabeth's age communicate almost exclusively from their cell phones. Email is too formal.

I look through her files to see if she keeps a journal. Nope. There are plenty of folders for homework and college classes. Elizabeth seems like a good student.

Then we hit the browser. I go straight to Facebook and give her timeline a cursory glance. There's been no activity in the past week. I check her About page. USC student. No relationship status. I scroll her more than three thousand friends—just a bunch of happy teens and young adults in college, too many to research right now.

When I search through the security settings in her browser, I'm able to reveal many of the passwords she has saved. Without drawing too much attention to my actions, I quickly export the passwords from the browser and onto the USB drive. I search for other accounts and social media but find nothing on her laptop. Like other teens, she accesses most of her accounts through apps on her phone, so the laptop doesn't offer much. I scour her search history. There's nothing atypical—no weekend getaways, remote locations, or How to Disappear without a Trace—so I close the laptop and retrieve the USB stick.

This anonymous boyfriend makes one suspect—two if I still count Leona. I agree to help Carmen take the case. She's appreciative and offers a hug as thanks. I propose a fee—more than my usual—and Carmen accepts without a hassle. Leona produces a signed check that Carmen fills out.

Before I leave, Carmen insists I take some more paella. I don't want to be rude, so I accept two large containers. I'm beginning to like Carmen.

Leona walks me to the gate, and who should I pass while I'm leaving but Hugo—Mr. Library himself. He emerges from the cab of a delivery van for Super Tech and glares at me when we catch each other's eye. I smile and nod. He counters with a sneer and marches into the house.

Leona watches our silent exchange. "What was that about?"

"We're in a book club together."

My Spidey senses tell me not to trust Hugo. I'm also not sure of his role in this whole thing. The fact that he was driving a Super Tech van suggests he works directly for the electronics chain—the business—and not Carmen personally. But his appearance at the library and then Carmen's home tells me he's more closely involved with Carmen than just on a professional level. When I combine that with the tough-guy attitude, I decide to add him to my list of suspects.

I wonder if that was what bothered me about the Super Tech photo and Carmen's Razzie performance in the hall. *What's the personal connection? Is he her boyfriend?*

It's weird for me to think about a grown woman having a boyfriend. The term sounds so juvenile. Then I remind myself that I'm an adult, and I don't have a boyfriend. Now I feel like a loser.

Chapter 6

When I get home, our living room is spotless. There is no sign of the boxes, and the papers that had once littered the floor are gone. Paige looks up from her spot at our dining room table as she slurps up leftover noodles.

"What happened to—"

"Don't ask," she says. That pretty much tells me all I need to know. After yet another attempt to glean new information from the mountain of documents, she has achieved nothing. She changes the subject. "How did your meeting go?"

I can tell Paige is looking for an opportunity to take her mind off her search, and I'm happy to oblige. After putting away the paella for later, I take a seat at the table across from Paige, grab some chopsticks, and dig into a box of dumplings. "Can you run some background research on a Carmen Viramontes?"

"Who's Carmen Viramontes?" Paige asks, setting her noodles on the table next to me.

"Widow in Pasadena who owns a chain of electronics stores.

Husband was Marcos Viramontes. Her daughter, Elizabeth, is missing."

"Runaway?"

"TBD. The mom is undocumented, so I don't know how much you'll be able to find online with a cursory search. You might have to be creative."

Paige smiles. *Creative* is my way of saying she may have to bend the laws just a bit. Paige loves being creative. Whenever I get a job, I bring Paige in for some black-hat help and give her a cut. Not that it matters. We share so many costs at this point that we should just open a joint bank account and become common-law partners.

As we eat, Paige shows me what she is able to uncover—a lot of reviews about the Super Tech chain, which has seven locations in all. Some online reviews mention Teddy, the proxy for the franchise. No one mentions Carmen or Marcos. The Viramontes have done a pretty good job of staying out of the public eye.

Using the passwords I captured on the USB stick, we log into Elizabeth's Facebook account. We each scroll through Elizabeth's profile and begin the task of researching the timeline, friends, and photos of Elizabeth Viramontes. In reverse chronological order, we begin detailing the days, weeks, and months before her disappearance—attending a football game with friends, checking into bars in downtown LA, sharing posts from celebrities and news sites.

After about an hour, I recognize one face that keeps popping up. It's a young man in his early twenties with angular features and a pointed goatee that makes his whole head look like a triangle. In some posts, he's tagged as Sebastian Gallo. We open his profile and begin scanning his page. Scrolling down, we find more pictures of him and Elizabeth—posing at a concert, hugging on the beach, holding hands at the mall, kissing at the park.

"I think we found the boyfriend," I say.

The amount of information at this stage is limited. There's no evidence that he's a student at USC or any other college. There's no indication of his job. What is clear, however, is that he likes to "party."

Judging by the requests on his wall, he's also the source of the party. There are numerous posts of people asking, "Can you hook me up?" Others are looking for "T," and some are flat-out placing volume orders for cocaine. Sebastian Gallo is a drug dealer.

"This guy is a real winner," Paige remarks. "Why would she date him?"

I shoot her a look. *Pot. Kettle. Black.*

"Shut up," she says, glaring at me out of the corner of her eye. "How do you want to proceed?"

"Let's use Tiffany."

Tiffany Maddox is a catfish profile we created on another case. She's a young woman who works at Hooters to put herself through school at a fashion college. Tiffany has a Facebook profile, a Twitter account, several dating accounts, and a blog dedicated to fashion. Most of the content was my handiwork. The images are all of Paige. It took some convincing, but I needed someone superhot, and Paige's body has often been described as "redonculous." After we launched the various online profiles, Tiffany soon gathered thousands of friends and followers of people she'd never met in real life. Paige and I both later admitted to being jealous of Tiffany's online popularity.

Paige logs into Tiffany's Facebook account and sends a friend request to Sebastian. Five minutes later, we get the alert that Sebastian has accepted our request. Of course he has. *Thank you, Tiffany Maddox.*

Now that we're connected, we can view even more of his photos, check-ins, and likes. It's like getting an engraved invitation to invade someone's privacy. All it takes is an attractive profile picture and a man's desperate need for sexual validation.

We scroll through his albums and find more photos of Elizabeth and him. He has many pictures of them at dinner, at clubs, and at the beach. I also notice pictures of them with a group of mostly guys, none of whom I recognize from my glance at Elizabeth's friend list or the photos on her walls. A lot of these guys are heavily tattooed. I presume they are friends of his.

"Look at this," Paige says, pointing at the screen. It's a check-in to La Lucha, a bar in Lincoln Heights, eight days ago. Paige brings up Elizabeth's Facebook page on another tab. She scrolls down and points to a check-in to La Lucha from the same day.

"Curiouser and curiouser," I say. *Good catch, Paige.*

While we continue to search, we get a message from Sebastian: *S'up?*

Paige groans. "Here we go. A well-orchestrated attempt to sound cool and casual."

I take over the keyboard and write: *Oh nothing. S'up with you?*

He responds: *Just chillin like a villain.*

I accelerate the process: *I'm looking for a party. You look like someone I need to know.*

Sebastian responds: *You no it girl.*

The typo kills me, but I keep going: *What's fun?*

He answers: *Rave tomorow.*

When I meet this guy, I promise myself I will buy him a dictionary. I accept the invitation, and he sends me the address.

"Raves are never a good idea," Paige says. "Maybe we shouldn't go."

I review the invitation. *Underground party on the outskirts of town at the invitation of my prime suspect? Oh yeah, this is going to end well.*

Chapter 7

My Mini Cooper speeds along the 210 freeway late in the evening. Paige rides shotgun, navigating from her phone while I drive. To our left is the entire San Fernando Valley—a blanket of warm lights spread out in a grid that goes on forever.

I exit the freeway and proceed up a canyon highway. Within five minutes, we've left Los Angeles and are winding our way up a forgotten rural road. As we make our way up the hill, the ranch houses are spread farther and farther apart until they eventually disappear. There's not a single car or street lamp in sight. The cityscape has long since disappeared from my rearview mirror. My headlights, the only source of light, illuminate a cracked and patched stretch of asphalt with a curtain of darkness on either side.

"Keep going for another mile," Paige says.

I think about Paige's search. I know the impasse is causing more pain than she cares to admit, so I can't stop thinking about how to help her. The wheels in my mind keep turning. "You know the weird thing about all your documents?"

"What?"

"Everything such a secret. Not just your information but even the judge's information."

Paige considers this. "'Judges', like, multiple judges? Or 'judge's,' like one judge?"

I shoot her a smile. "Good question. Seems strange, though, that they keep omitting that name, don't you think? I wonder if it's the same judge on all those forms." My stomach gurgles.

Paige turns to me. "That was loud. Did you eat something you shouldn't have?"

I didn't eat anything unusual, but I'm feeling suddenly ill. I'm queasy, and I can feel myself warming up more than usual.

"You don't look so good," she says.

We're too close to turn back now. "I'm fine," I lie. Deep down inside, I hope someone at this rave had the presence of mind to order portable toilets.

"Okay," she says, not sounding convinced. "Make the next left."

I'm feeling more nauseous the farther we drive, so I accelerate to get there faster. I make the left turn. Then I slam on the brakes. My tires screech as they skid across the road.

Paige lurches forward, her phone flying out of her hands and her hair shrouding her face. "What the hell?" she cries, wiping the hair from her face.

"Do you see that?" I yell.

She looks through the windshield. "What?"

Just as I feared. I whip the Mini into reverse and peel out backward. My rear tires run off the road and rise up an embankment. The car stops, and a cloud of dust rises around us.

"What are you doing?" Paige says.

"Cemetery."

"Oh."

Once the dust settles, I get a better look at what lies before us. Three figures stand in the road, staring at our car. One is an older woman, probably in her sixties, dressed in a floral print dress, her brunette hair puffed up in a bouffant.

Beside her are two children, a boy and a girl. They are roughly the same age, nine or ten. The girl is wearing a gingham dress, and the boy is dressed in a blazer and shorts, with an old schoolboy cap.

"What do you see?" Paige asks. She can't see them. The reason she can't see them is because they're ghosts.

It suddenly becomes clear why I've been feeling so uneasy. We've been driving alongside a cemetery. The moment I turned and saw those three figures, I knew what they were. They're not transparent like the ghosts from stories or reality shows about ghost hunters. They appear as tangible as any other person—at least to me. To Paige and most everyone else, they are invisible.

The ability to see the undead roaming the earth is one of those perks of being possessed by a demon. The first time it happened, it scared the bejesus out of me. After I was shunned in Malbrook, I got a room in an old hotel in Philadelphia. The first night there, I was trying to get some sleep when I discovered that the sliding glass door to the balcony was open. I got up to close the door and noticed movement outside. I slowly stepped out, and on the adjacent balcony, I saw a woman trying to push her child over the railing three floors up.

I screamed. The woman and her child froze and whipped their faces in my direction. Then she pushed the child over. I quickly looked to see what would happen to the body, but it disappeared in midair, and the woman was gone. Or so I thought. When I turned around, she was on my balcony, right in front of me.

Then she tried to push me off the balcony. I thought I felt

her cold spirit hands press through me. What I actually felt was her energy, though. It wasn't tactile. There was no physical impact, just the sensation of a frigid wind passing through me.

After that, I ran down to the lobby and learned that years earlier, a woman had killed her three children by pushing them off the balcony. One of her kids even went willingly. Then the woman killed herself.

That was my first ghost. Now I see them often enough that it unnerves me—like when I find a spider in the bathroom—but doesn't send me running in a panic... like when I find a spider in the bathroom.

Over the years, I've discovered there are two kinds of hauntings. The first is a residual haunting. These ghosts are less like spirits and more like the energy of victims playing like a looping video. A ghost will appear and disappear, replaying moments from its former life. Residual hauntings usually occur in a place where a traumatic event, like a death or horrible accident, occurred. Other hauntings of this nature can occur in places of some spiritual significance, such as the location of a secret.

The other kind of haunting—the kind I'm looking at right now—is an intelligent haunting. The spirit knows that it is dead, and it's on a mission. Some spirits are trying to right a wrong. Others are trying to reach out to someone they love. A few have unfinished business. There are many reasons why someone's soul might not move on to the next plane.

The three ghosts stare at me, walking from side to side but never toward me. Their feet meet the boundary of the cemetery grounds but never cross it. They can't. Their mouths move in an attempt to speak, but ghosts make no sound. I'm sure they're asking for help, but I can't go near them. Cemeteries are hallowed grounds. There is nothing I can do for them tonight.

"Do I want to know what you're looking at?" Paige asks.

She doesn't, because—unfortunately for Paige—I need her to go through there.

"It's nothing," I lie.

A pair of headlights approaches from the direction we came from. I turn off my headlights, and we're shrouded in darkness.

Music blares from a Volkswagen Beetle as it turns into the cemetery. Its lights illuminate the three ghosts, and it drives right into them without hesitation. For a moment, the spirits disappear. Once the car passes through, its rear lights bathe them in a red glow. As it continues onward, the light diminishes until the specters disappear into the shadows.

Paige's phone vibrates, and she checks the screen. "He says he's inside already."

As she talks, I stare at the cemetery gates. "Is there another way, around the cemetery?" I ask. Paige unbuckles her seat belt. "What are you doing?"

"It's only a mile from here."

"You can't go alone."

She opens the car door. "I'll be fine," she says with absolutely no confidence. She slowly steps out.

"Paige, get back in here! It's too dangerous!" It was never my intention to let Paige go in there alone. I was supposed to be by her side the whole time.

She ignores me and walks toward the cemetery. I get out on my side and only take a few steps before stopping. I sense a force field around the cemetery, repelling me. The ghosts watch me, waiting.

"Be careful," I call. She stops, suddenly looking afraid.

"At the rave," I clarify. "Be careful at the rave."

She nods. "I've got my Taser. I'll be fine." Paige stands at the gate, not crossing the threshold. She turns back to me and takes a deep breath. Like a sprinter at the starting gun, she bolts into the cemetery and past the ghosts. I can still hear the echo of her heels long after she disappears into the darkness.

The dull bass of electronic music thumps in the distance. Above the trees, a soft glow warms from the event the sky just over the horizon. The rave must be closer than I thought.

After an hour, I start to get hungry. Luckily, I always keep snacks in my car. It's an important life lesson I learned from several all-night stakeouts and the time I got stuck in a SigAlert on I-5 that shut down traffic for two hours.

I open the rear hatch and find some crackers. As I'm sitting on the hood of my car, enjoying my saltine snack and a bottle of water, I notice more headlights coming up the road. I'm curious about who the latecomers are, so I pay close attention. Then I notice red and blue sweeping lights. Police cars. A lot of them.

This can't be good. I reach into my pocket, pull out my wallet—no reason to wait until the last minute—and use a hands-free earbud to start calling Paige.

One by one, police cruisers and SUVs stream past me and into the cemetery. Near the end of the line, a cruiser pulls up to me and shines its directional light in my face. I hold up my private investigator license before I'm even asked.

"Private investigator! I'm the one that called it in!" I shout, trusting that my confident lie will buy me a free pass. Without a word, the cruiser turns away and follows the convoy into the cemetery.

Paige's phone goes to voicemail—not surprising, since she's at a rave. I try texting her: *Cops on the way! Run!*

Sirens blare from inside, and I can see the glow of police lights swirling from past the cemetery. I try to ignore the ghosts who follow me as I walk down the road to find a better angle to look. The dull bass from the music stops. Too many moments pass, and I consider running inside.

Now, I know I said I cannot enter hallowed grounds… but that's not entirely true. I can, but the experience is excruciating. I once made the mistake of riding in a car that drove onto a cemetery a few years ago. I felt like I'd entered an activated microwave oven. My skin started to burn, and it was like I was being cooked from the inside out.

That was the last time. My concern for Paige is overwhelming, and I think about making the attempt again. Or I could drive through. That might be faster. Hopefully, I wouldn't lose control of my car and crash into a tree.

Headlights appear from deep within the cemetery. Moments later, dozens of cars race through the cemetery, not just on roads but across the grass and over the flush markers on the ground as well. Car engines rev, and then footsteps thunder as hundreds of silhouettes stampede out of the cemetery and onto the country road.

Reaching through my driver's-side window, I turn the lights on. The three ghosts are still there. Trying to ignore them, I look past among the fleeing partygoers. There's no sign of Paige among the masses.

"Paige!" I call into the cemetery. "Paige!"

"Darcy!"

Turning, I see Paige emerging from the shadows deep inside the cemetery. She runs, pointing farther in, where I spot a figure in a black hoodie dashing down another knoll. He narrowly misses getting hit by a car that skids on the grass.

I waffle. *Run or drive? Run or drive?* With every second I debate, he's getting farther away. I decide to run.

My feet pound on the asphalt, and I sprint down the street. Cars speed past me now, trying to get away. I round the corner and head around the bottom edge of the cemetery. The hooded figure emerges from the grounds. He races across the street and into a field on the other side. I close the gap fast.

Then I biff it on a ditch and slide face-first into the ground. I hear footsteps behind me, and Paige zooms past me. Her strides are long and quick, and I mutter an insult because she's running effortlessly in heels.

I push myself up and follow her onto the nearby field. The dirt is uneven, so I keep stumbling. My effort is unnecessary, though. With Paige's speed and stamina, the subject is no match her, and she delivers a flying leap and tackles him to the ground.

When I reach them, Paige has our suspect in a full nelson. Arms up, he sits cradled in her lap. Both of them are covered in dirt.

"Get off of me!" he shouts from under his hoodie. I jog over slowly then take a moment to catch my breath. I pace back and forth, hands on my hips, straining for air.

"Seriously?" Paige asks incredulously as I pant.

I hold up my finger, asking for a minute. My sides cramp with stiches, and I grimace in pain.

"What the hell are you doing?" the hooded figure shouts again. When my wheezing stops, I reach over and pull away the hood to reveal…

"Sebastian Gallo."

He stops struggling. "So what?"

Red flashing lights alert us of an oncoming vehicle. We duck down low, and Sebastian momentarily stops struggling until the police cruiser passes.

"You're not cops?" he asks.

I get nice and close so he can see my eyes. Even in the dark, their bright color is clear. He pulls away.

"I want to talk about Elizabeth Viramontes."

He strains within Paige's CrossFit hold, but she keeps him

still. "Who are you with?" he spits out, still struggling.

I reach into my pocket and pull out my private investigator license. I shove it in his face. "Elizabeth's mother hired me to find her."

He stops struggling, a quizzical look on his face.

"Are you going to cooperate?"

He nods.

Paige loosens her grip. Sebastian immediately shoves her off and makes a run for it. I quickly reach out, grab him by the hood, and yank him to the ground. With a crunch he lands flat on his back. He gasps, the air knocked out of him.

"Damn it, Sebastian," I say.

He struggles to breathe while Paige wraps him up again. I take this moment to make some things clear. "Listen, this place is crawling with cops right now. I have no problem calling some attention our way to let them know I've caught one of the dealers they were looking for tonight. I'm going to assume you've got shit on you right now—enough for a felony?"

It takes a moment for Sebastian to catch his breath. I hope he is beginning to realize he's in a no-win situation. "What do you mean, 'find her'?" he asks.

If he's pretending not to know about the fact that she's missing, then I have to play along to get him to talk. "She disappeared about a week ago. When was the last time you saw her?"

"I don't know."

"Guess."

"Two weeks? A month?"

"Try eight days ago," I retort. "Right before she disappeared."

Paige chimes in. "La Lucha. Sound familiar?"

Sebastian gulps. "Elizabeth and I had gone out for drinks."

"You were broken up. Why get together? Did she need something you were selling?"

He snickers. "She was scared, all right?"

"Of what?" I ask.

"You don't know what you're getting into," he says dismissively.

"What was she scared of?"

Sebastian leans toward me. "Santa Muerte." He spits on the ground.

I don't know much about Santa Muerte, but I know this is cause for concern. It's an offshoot of Catholicism, a cult that worships a female deity known as the Saint of Death—a deity that looks like a skeletal Virgin Mary. The cult is infamous for their sacrifices, both animal and human, throughout all of Mexico.

I continue questioning. "Elizabeth was involved in Santa Muerte?"

He nods. "When we started dating, she introduced me to it. She bought into the whole thing. I thought it was a joke... at first. But they're into some crazy shit. No chick is worth that, so I broke it off with her."

"If she was into it, then why was she scared? Why reach out to you?"

"It was getting too much even for her."

"Why? What happened?"

Sebastian looks away, shaking his head. I cross my arms. I've got all night.

He sighs. "It all started when this crazy old woman showed up to the temple—the one down in East LA. They used to sacrifice chickens when I was there. When the old woman showed up, it got worse. They were killing cats. Dogs. Elizabeth said she was a witch. A lechur... or something, I don't know.

Elizabeth wanted to get out because…"

Paige and I exchange a look. I wonder if he's really trying to sell me on the story of some witch.

"Because…?" I say, prodding him to continue.

"Because she was afraid they were going to kill her. You want to find out who took her, go down to the temple on Whittier."

Sebastian is not to be trusted, but no one would be stupid enough to offer this as a reasonable story behind Elizabeth's disappearance. When people lie, they try to come up with a story that's believable. When people tell you an absurd story, there's usually some truth behind it.

Red lights flash again, and we all duck down. Another police car passes, shining its spotlight around the field and over our heads. As it passes, I reach into Sebastian's pockets and start pulling out vials and bags and tossing them to the ground.

He protests. "Hey!"

"Shhh…"

Paige keeps him cinched up. I reach into his back pocket and pull out his wallet. Once the cruiser passes, I take a picture of his ID with my cell phone. "Just in case I need to find you again."

With no other reason to keep him, I give Paige the go-ahead to let him go. Again, he pushes her away. He rips his wallet out of my hands, collects his drugs from the dirt, then scrambles into the shadows of some nearby trees and disappears.

We wait, careful to avoid any remaining police cars. Then we trudge back to the car. As I huff and puff, Paige chastises me. "You need to start jogging."

"I know."

⟋⟍

Santa Muerte means "Saint of Death." I know that already, but when I start my online research the minute I get home, everything I read underscores that notion. By whatever power this entity—spirit, deity, or demon—is granted, its sole mission is to bring death.

Most stories of death center on a being whose purpose is to lead souls from this world to the next. The grim reaper, with his giant scythe, is reaping the dead to bring them to afterlife. Charon ferries a boat across the River Styx to the underworld. There's actually a word for a being with this mission—psychopomp. A psychopomp guides the deceased to their final destinations.

That term does not apply to Santa Muerte. For her, death itself is the objective. The term Santa Muerte refers both to the cult and to the being the cultists worship. She goes by many names, including the more formal Nuestra Señora de la Santa Muerte. The Saint of Death resembles a cross between the grim reaper and the Virgin Mary. She has a bare skull for a head and is draped in the blue-and-red robes of the Holy Mother.

I grab my phone and scroll through the photos I took in Elizabeth's room. There it is before me, a red-and-blue color scheme that suggests some tenuous connection. Could Sebastian be telling the truth? I keep reading.

The cult itself is an offshoot of Catholicism. Its true origins are unknown, but its popularity throughout Mexico has exploded in recent years, so much so that the Catholic Church had to officially condemn its practice. That did nothing to quell its supporters.

I read my discoveries aloud to Paige throughout the night. By two in the morning, she's had enough and decides to go to bed. She mumbles something on her way out.

I mumble back, "Okay."

"Did you hear me?" she asks.

"Yes?"

"I said, 'Promise me you're not going to stay up all night reading.'"

"Just five more minutes."

As she disappears through her doorway, I can tell by her expression that she doesn't believe me. Honestly, I don't believe me, either, because once I get started, I can't stop, the same way Paige can't stop exercising once she gets going, I can't stop reading. Time slows down. The pages go by in a blur. I can't remember how many times I've stumbled on a curious book at the library, and once my shift ended, I spent the rest of the evening in some nook, unable to leave until I got to the last page. The same is true of research. Once I get invested in a topic, I'm like Alice stumbling down the click hole—I keep going.

I find information on Santa Muerte's prevalence in Mexico and its migration into the United States. In recent years, the popularity of Santa Muerte has been attributed to the growing power of Mexican drug cartels. The practice of worshiping the Saint of Death is connected to both those who work for the cartels—who summon her power to destroy their enemies— and those seeking protection from them. A common practice for followers is the ritualistic sacrifice of animals to appeal to her. Then there are the news articles. Every week, there's another ritualistic decapitation of men, women, and children in her honor. There's plenty of conflicting information from various websites, and I can't tell which is legit and which consists of the ramblings of some mommy blogger looking for hits.

I try to find information on this temple Sebastian mentioned in East Los Angeles, but apparently, no one bothered to create an entry for Dangerous Death Cult on Yelp. This might take some good old-fashioned detective work.

"What are you doing?"

I look up to find Paige standing at her door with a disapproving scowl on her face. She's not wearing the same outfit she wore moments ago. Now she's dressed in her morning-workout gear.

"What?" I ask.

"You stayed up all night!"

That can't be right—it's still dark. I look out the picture window. Through the buildings and skyscrapers looking east, I get a glimpse of a warm glow rising in the horizon. The time on my laptop reads 5:02 a.m.

My eyes rise to meet hers. "Oops."

She shakes her head and walks across the room to take a seat across from me at the table. "What did you find out?"

I close my laptop and stretch. "Well, if Elizabeth was involved with Santa Muerte... she's in real trouble."

"If she is involved, and if she is in trouble, what's the next step?"

I cast a glance at the terrarium. Inside, the snake slithers across the transparent container wall, looking for a way out. "I think I need to pay a visit to Fiona."

Chapter 8

I make sure the lid on the terrarium is secure. The last thing I want is this denizen of the underworld to escape in the back seat of my car then attack me while I'm doing sixty-five on the 10 freeway.

"Thank God," Paige mutters when she sees me packing him up. She stays seated at our table about as far away from me as she can without going into another room.

My stomach churns. Anytime someone utters a phrase or idiom that references God or heaven, I can feel Dudley writhing inside me. Allergy season is the worst. When I start sneezing and find myself on the receiving end of a barrage of "Bless yous," I get physically nauseous.

"Yes," I say to Paige. "Say goodbye to Sir Hiss."

"I hope Fiona puts it in a meat pie."

"Shhh. He can hear you!" I yell as I sweep out the door.

It's a short drive to the studio where I'm set to meet Fiona after her taping. For those of you who don't know, I should mention that the Fiona I'm meeting is *the* Fiona Flanagan—Irish celebrity chef, media proprietor, and owner of the Flanagan Foods brand, the same Fiona Flanagan who has a cooking show at eleven o'clock in the morning on local networks, enthusiastically introducing audiences to long-forgotten recipes with her musically thick County Cork accent.

When she demonstrated how to cook eighteenth-century dessert recipes on YouTube a few years ago, Fiona became the latest chef to reach stardom. Her grandmotherly appeal won the hearts of millions online, and she leveraged that popularity to launch a media and commercial-food empire. You can't walk into the baking aisle of a grocery store anymore without seeing her silver hair and smiling face plastered on boxes and ads.

So why am I driving onto a movie studio lot at 3:35 p.m. to meet some celebrity chef, and what could this possibly have to do with my case? Because Fiona Flanagan is an honest-to-goodness witch. I show my ID to the guard at the entrance and follow his directions to guest parking. Once I park my crappy Mini between a Tesla and a Mercedes SUV, the walk to Fiona's office isn't far. I enjoy the carnival show of costumed actors dressed as accident victims, a set crew pushing a mangled car though the giant doors of the massive stage, and tourists piled into a stretch golf cart, getting a glimpse of daily life on set.

I'm tempted to remove my sunglasses. If there's any place I might fit in, it's here. But I don't. I need to keep a low profile when meeting with Fiona.

Stage 9 sits in the center of the lot and for all intents and purposes looks exactly like the others—an enormous beige fifty-foot-high block with no windows. I approach a side door where two red flashing lights warn that a recording is in progress. Two studio guards are waiting.

I flash my pass, and one of the guards opens the door for me. I step into an unlit anteroom. When the door closes behind me, I'm shrouded in darkness.

Another door opens, admitting me to a long hall. Thunderous applause breaks out as I move down a familiar passage. As the cheers and clapping die down, Fiona's amplified voice fills the building. Her rolling *R*'s and lilting consonants fill the stage like a concert.

"There are two keys to a true and fine sambocade. One, dried elderflowers. You'll be finding them at your local natural food store or coop. And I cannot stress this enough—accept no substitutes. And two, rosewater!"

I've been here enough time to know my way around the base of the bleachers where two hundred captive audience members watch their host. The stage is constructed to look like the inside of an old European cottage. Stone and wood surround all sides, and a wooden kitchen island sits center stage. A plump, energetic woman waddles around the island. Her green apron is covered in flour, as are her hair, hands, and face.

She's a whirling dervish of energy as she grabs premeasured ingredients and tosses them into the bowl from the top of the key. "Sugar!" Toss. "Egg whites!" Toss. "Vanilla!" Toss.

As much as I'd like to linger and watch the spectacle—one that keeps 3.5 million viewers tuned in every day—I keep moving down the labyrinth of halls until I reach the green room. Its walls are literally green. The room has plush leather seats and a television where I can watch the rest of her show. I help myself to a bottle of water and wait for the show to finish.

My phone chirps with an email alert. Lupe is reminding me that we have an exhibit opening tomorrow in collaboration with the Getty Museum. The curator is currently at the library, making some last-minute changes. Once the finishing touches are completed, someone needs to catalog everything going on display. Apparently, I just volunteered for the graveyard shift for cataloging tonight. I send her an email confirming that I'll be there.

"Thank you, my darlings. I'll see you tomorrow!" Fiona waves and sends kisses to her audience before disappearing through a back door.

Cue credit roll. Cut to logo. Fade out...

Fiona bursts through the door and explodes into the green room. She doesn't even hesitate as she charges toward me with open arms. "Ah, Darcy, my dear! You're looking absolutely wonderful!" She envelops me in a hug, which lasts a good five seconds and ends with a big squeeze.

She releases then reaches for my sunglasses and lifts them to see my eyes. "And a good afternoon to you, too, Dudley." My stomach grumbles a response. "I was ever so pleased to hear from you. What brings you to the lot today?"

I reach down, grab the tub, and show it to her. "I brought a present."

She claps her hands in delight. "Marvelous! Let's take it to my office."

Fiona leads me through the halls and out the rear of the sound stage, where her private golf cart waits. She hops in, and I hurry to get in before she peels away. We zip through the narrow streets of the studio lot, maneuvering past construction vehicles, lighting equipment, and large backdrops.

"How have you been?" she says nonchalantly as she steers through a troop of World War II soldiers.

My right hand grabs hold of the roof rail, and my other holds onto the terrarium. "Fine. Still working at the library."

"Aye, that's grand. Keeping out of trouble, right?"

I close my eyes when she narrowly avoids a collision with a tour cart. "Yeah. No trouble."

In less than a minute, we arrive at her Spanish bungalow.

Fiona once told me it used to be Paul Newman's office. She screeches into her private parking spot and jumps out before the cart has settled. I manage to keep up with her while I lug the snake container. Inside is a small waiting room supervised by a receptionist. In a production office, you usually find some pretty young thing, five days out of college, at the front desk. This office is no exception.

"Hiya! You have three messages!" shouts the young graduate. From her Southern accent, I recognize her as Eva Jean, whom I spoke with earlier today.

Fiona burns through assistants faster than I go through toothbrushes. Eva Jean is cute and perky. My prediction is she'll fail miserably in the next two months then move back to Enid, Oklahoma, and tell everyone how people in LA are fake and that was why she left.

"Not right now, my dear!" Fiona says without slowing down.

I wave politely to the new girl as I keep up with Fiona, who leads me down the hall. Her *office* is a large and sterile kitchen. A granite-top island with a stainless-steel range top sits at the center, four pots simmering. A steel hood hovers over the burners as smoke rises out of the kitchen. The walls are lined with glass shelves that hold every imaginable ingredient a person could need—and some that any average mortal would never need. Four industrial glass-door refrigerators stand guard, displaying a colorful variety of produce, meats, and frozen goods.

In stark contrast to the set where she produces her show, this kitchen is modern and sleek. Fiona's on-screen persona evokes a sense of the old world—earthy, green, and venerable. In her private life, Fiona prefers a clean, contemporary style.

She finally slows down and settles onto a kitchen stool by the island. "Okay, love. Let's see this beauty."

I rest the carrier in front of her then take a few steps back for protection. Fiona calmly reaches inside and pulls out the snake. It coils itself around her arm. It's blacker than I remember, like an inky rope with two glassy eyes. She raises it to look straight into those eyes.

The timbre of her voice lowers as she admires it. "Aye, look at you. Creature of darkness. You're not from this plane. What have your eyes seen?"

I get chills thinking about it. No, this snake isn't your typical egg-born reptile. It was created in some other place—a place I'd rather never visit, thank you. And it found its way inside me. *Thanks, Dudley.*

"I named him Sir Hiss."

Fiona ignores me and caresses this deadly creature with loving charm. She shows no fear despite the fact that its venom could kill with a single bite. Couple that with whatever hellish powers it might possess, and this serpent could do all kinds of damage.

Fiona probably knows all about that. She's so charismatic and affable that it's easy to forget she's a witch—and not some crazy old Wiccan who practices a few chants and prays to the blood moon. No, this woman is over four hundred years old and survives by the grace of a dark magic that I will never fully comprehend.

I had only been living in Los Angeles a few months when Fiona showed up at my door, unannounced. At that time, I was living in a pay-by-the-week motel in Boyle Heights, so imagine my surprise when a celebrity just showed up one day. She came inside and, with no preface, announced that she knew about my possession and about the demon inside me. I was dumbstruck. *How could she know?*

She extended her hand, and a candle levitated off my bed

stand. I watched as it floated in midair before me like a dandelion seed on a gentle breeze. Fiona spoke as the candle made its way to her, and she explained she was a witch. She said she could sense my arrival and had spent the last month tracking me down. The candle landed gently in her outstretched hand. Then she blew on it, and it exploded into dust, the particles spreading out and disappearing in the air.

Sitting in my dingy hotel room was this strange woman who I recognized from television and magazines. She had searched to find *me*, wielding powers I hadn't even realized existed. This woman wanted to help me. At that time, I wasn't sure if I could trust her.

Five years later, we've become close. I come to her when I need guidance or advice. When I vomit up some creature from the underworld, I happily give it to her. I still don't know if I can completely trust her, but she's the only person besides Father Ramon who understands the evil inside me—who understands, firsthand, the dark and mysterious world I only imagined during my ill-advised goth phase.

Fiona rises and carries the snake to a wall of steel drawers. She carefully selects one of them and presses on its face. It slides out smoothly. Without saying a word, she holds her hand several inches away. As if instructed, the snake extends its long body from her hand and slithers into the drawer. When it finally uncoils the remainder of its body and its tail disappears inside, Fiona pushes on the soft-close door and returns to her kitchen island.

"Thank you, my dear, for another fine gift."

I have no idea what she does with these things. Frankly, I don't want to know. Fiona is not one to stand still for long, and before I realize it, she's whisking some new ingredient into a steel bowl.

"I've got a new case," I announce.

"Is that so? Another referral from Father Ramon?" She's trying to remain polite, but I can sense the animosity when she says his name. It's no secret that witches and the church have a long and bitter history. I suspect that Fiona's personal history may include some particularly harsh encounters.

"Missing girl," I answer. "Mother's looking for her."

"Runaway?"

"I don't think so."

"What are you thinking?"

I hesitate. "I'm not sure. How much do you know about Santa Muerte?"

Fiona stops whisking. I watch her carefully. She doesn't look up at first. She places the bowl on the counter and takes a deep breath. "You're joking me."

I lean over one of the pots and inhale deeply, taking in scents of simmering meats and vegetables. It smells amazing. "It sounds like this girl was mixed up with the wrong crowd."

When I look up at Fiona, she has a serious expression on her face. "Wrong crowd? That's a very different thing than cults."

"I don't know. Her boyfriend is pretty convinced. He claims the girl was trying to get out. Some old woman was scaring her off. A lesh… lech…"

"*Lechuza*," Fiona finishes.

"That's a witch, right?"

Fiona nods. "Aye. From Mexico. Mighty powerful," she says grimly. "They're known for their ability to shape-shift."

Looks like I came to the right person. "Is Santa Muerte real?"

Fiona crosses to her wall of cabinet drawers and appraises each one. "There has always been a great fascination with death." She selects one and opens the drawer. Her hand disappears inside then emerges holding a frog. She strolls to the kitchen island.

"Every culture, across every age, has tried to understand death. What happens when we die? What happens after?"

She pulls out a paring knife, and I know I'm not going to enjoy what I'm about to witness. She presses the frog on its back against the granite. It squirms to escape. Her grasp is steady.

"There is a great power in death. Not life or the afterlife but that singular moment of death."

Without hesitation, Fiona stabs the frog. It convulses as she digs the knife into its chest. Then with a quick flick, she lifts the blade so I can see. Sitting delicately on the steel is a tiny yet still-beating heart.

She grabs the heart in her other hand and squeezes it in her fist. She mutters in an Irish-Spanish accent, *"Muerte Santisima."*

Her hand opens, and green flame explodes from her palm. It remains lit as she continues to speak. "Death has always been part of the Mesoamerican culture. Hundreds of years ago, they worshiped gods of death and sacrificed each other as payments of devotion. When the Spaniards colonized Mexico with their Christianity, they brought with them the holy saints, the Grim Reaper, and more death. Over time, those who practiced the old ways found a way to combine the old gods and their new one. From those practices, new religions formed that held the power of both. None was more popular than the cult of Santa Muerte."

She closes her hand, and the fire is extinguished. Smoke seeps from her fist. "You're asking me if Santa Muerte is real. It's very real. And you don't want to go messing about with them, Darcy."

I shake my head. "I have a job to do. There's a girl out there in trouble. She needs my help. And I'm asking for your help. If she's involved in this, then I have to get involved in this."

Fiona takes several deliberate steps toward me. I instinctively back up, not sure what she's going to do next. "That is a profoundly foolish idea," she says in a menacing tone. "Very dangerous people pray to that unholy saint. God only knows what lengths they would go through to harness your power should they discover what lies inside you."

Chapter 9

Fiona's warning is sincere—that much I know. There is a lot of magic in this dark world that I may never understand. Deep down inside, I know I should listen to her, but all I can think about is Elizabeth.

"What did Fiona have to say about your case?" Paige asks when I walk inside the door.

"To stay away."

Paige pulls her laptop back and scans the screen. She clicks on her mouse and types, resuming her work. "Does she not realize telling you not to do something only encourages you?" she asks, eyes still on her screen.

"That's not true," I say defensively.

"Are you going to drop the case?"

"No, but it has nothing to do with Fiona or her warnings of Mexican cults or gods of death."

Paige looks up. "What's that, now?"

I look at the time on my phone. "I told Lupe I'd make up some extra hours."

"Tonight?" she asks, confused.

"There's an exhibit opening tomorrow. They're probably still setting up. While I'm there, I'm going to do some more research on Santa Muerte—see if I can find anything in the archives."

⌒

By the time my car pulls up in front of the Central Library, night has completely settled on the city. Winds have brought in a thick fog, obscuring the tops of the surrounding skyscrapers within low-lying clouds. It's not dark, though. Fog diffuses the city lights throughout all of downtown. It's cold, especially for me.

I leave my car on the empty street and hurry around to the side entrance. From my cell, I call the security desk for admittance—standard practice for after-hours access. However, no one answers. By chance, I check the door and find it unlocked. This is not an uncommon practice when the guards know people will be coming in and out for a project. I hurry inside to escape the frigid air.

When I walk through the doors, I'm reminded of why I love the library at night. During business hours, it's bustling with activity. Visitors and tourists crowd the lobby, chatting loudly and ignoring library etiquette. But this late, there's not a single soul around. The only sound is that of my boots on the marble tile as I step toward the main lobby.

Normally, there are at least two guards on duty at the security desk. When I find it empty, I presume they are upstairs with Lupe as she reviews the finishing touches on the exhibit. For the next month, the library is offering a free exhibit of Los Angeles street photography from 1900 to the present. The exhibit hall is upstairs, adjacent to the rotunda.

I proceed down the narrow hall that leads me to a powered-off escalator then stop. Perched on the rubber handrail is an owl.

Two black eyes, set against a white heart-shaped face, stare intently at me. I recognize it as a species of barn owl, but it's unlike any I've ever seen before. It's massive, with gray—almost silver—feathers wrapped across its body. The library has its share of birds wandering inside. One might spy a crow or pigeon or the occasional small wren. But this is the first time I have ever seen an owl.

The raptor cocks its head, appraising me. Then it spreads its broad wings and launches, flying up the escalator path to the next floor. I step onto the first step of the escalator and peer up. The owl disappears around a corner.

Something is not right. Slowly, I climb the static escalator steps to the second floor. No sign of the owl.

I stand in the original part of the building with a pyramid on its roof, symbolic statues of enlightenment standing guard within, and cryptic messages in ancient languages carved into its stone walls. In 1986, two mysterious fires decimated the structure, which led to a major renovation that included the expansion of a modern structure—a cavernous atrium that doubled the footprint of the building.

I turn, walk toward the newer structure, and emerge from a hall to the overlook that provides a bird's-eye view of the atrium. From my vantage point, I can see the six stories below. Each floor is staggered before me like a giant step, descending to four floors beneath street level. Directly across from me are a series of colorful art installations hanging from the red-orange girders that frame the atrium's ceiling.

With the lights off, the only illumination comes through the glass ceiling from the soft glow of the skyscrapers that loom above the library. I turn away from the atrium and proceed down the hall. It's dark, with only the light from the atrium behind me and the rotunda before me. My boots continue to echo on the marble flooring as I approach my destination.

I am horrified and heartbroken by what I see. Lupe lies in the middle of the room. Her body is splayed across the marble floor, her lifeless eyes staring in my direction. And blood is everywhere.

Despite my initial caution, I instinctively hurry to her side and slide to my knees down beside her. Tears well up in my eyes, and I brush them away with my sleeve. Lupe Navarro, whose spirit made her seem larger than life, now looks so small and cold. I restrain myself from touching her—from checking if, by some miracle, she's alive. I have enough sense to know not to disturb a crime scene.

The gaping wound in her chest suggests how she died. At first, I think it's a gunshot wound. Then I realize it's far, far worse. Her sternum is broken through, and where her heart should be is an empty bloody hole.

My head whips around the room, searching for a perpetrator or someone who means me harm. When I hear the flapping of wings over my head, I look up. The owl circles above, looping around the enormous chandelier that hangs above the rotunda. A circle of forty-eight glass bulbs surround an interior ring of zodiac symbols cast in bronze. In the center is a blue glass sculpture of planet Earth that glows from within.

I stand up, keeping my eyes on the owl. It seems like it guided me here on purpose. I wonder if it's trying to warn me or show me something—some clue on the faded mosaic of the ceiling tile. Or…

The hairs on the back of my neck rise. The sound of fabric dragging across the floor behind warns me of the incoming attack. The owl was a distraction. I jump forward, roll, and come to my feet to meet my assailant.

Before me stands a haunting specter. A woman's pale face

stares back at me. Except it's not just a pale face. Black shadows sit where eyes should be, and it's skeletal, as if the flesh and blood have been drained, making it look like a mask shrink-wrapped over a skull. Ornate black tattoos dot the skin in a design that is all too familiar. She wears the dark-blue-and-red robes of her spirit.

This is Santa Muerte.

Her clawlike hand reaches for my chest. Instinctively, I reach out and grab her arm. The moment we make contact, a flash of heat erupts between us. The pain forces us both to recoil. I stumble backward and inspect my hands. My palms are red from where I touched her skin.

She looks at me, confused. I am not what she was expecting. Slowly, she floats clockwise around me, the hem of her robes trailing on the ground. Sharp nails extend from her hands. Lupe's blood drips from the same hand she used to attack me.

I back away, not sure how to handle her—or how to handle *it*. What is this thing? I've lived with demons, and I've seen ghosts, but I have never seen anything like this before. Never have I been faced with something so… monstrous.

She continues to circle me. The hem of her robes drags across the floor as if she has no feet. Her mere presence gives me chills, like the ghosts I've seen.

This thing is no ghost, though. She's a corporeal entity, real and tactile. I made contact with her—with it. And it hurt. *Why?* I've felt this burning before, when the bare hands of a religious figure were laid on me, which means the pain exists because I have a demon inside me and she is a saint.

An evil saint. And judging by the angry expression on her face, she intends to do to me what she did to Lupe. Santa Muerte stops then floats counterclockwise. I keep my distance, thinking that if she keeps this up, I can escape down a hall. Hopefully, I can run faster than she can float.

She springs forward with impossible speed, and I realize there's no escaping her. Again, her clawed hands shoot for my chest. I grab hold with both hands. The pain is excruciating, but I don't let go.

I fall backward, and Santa Muerte is on top of me. My hands burn as they grip her arms, and I can tell by the anguish on her face that she feels the same agony. She pushes her weight on top of me. She's impossibly strong. Supernaturally strong.

Then I push back with a strength that's not my own. Dudley is coming.

The black sockets where her eyes should be widen in recognition of the power emanating from me. Her skull-like grin lunges toward me. The gravity of her weight pushes hard against me with a strength I can barely resist.

Her sharp bloody claw continues reaching forward— toward my beating heart. I cry out to push her away. Her grimacing teeth inch closer. Her eyes stare straight into mine as her face nears.

I fear she's going to bite into my face at any moment. Her mouth opens slightly. She looks like she's smiling. Then a hollow voice whispers four little words:

"I know your name."

A chill sweeps through my body. Those words weren't for me. They were for Dudley.

The owl swoops down just above us, delivering a screech cry. It flaps its wings and disappears down the hall. Santa Muerte jerks suddenly.

"No!" she cries.

I'm confused, but when her body tugs again, I realize what is happening. She slips off me as if pulled by an invisible force. Her hands scrape on the marble tile, trying to get back to me.

She snarls, trying desperately to claw at me. Then, with a final jerk, she's pulled into the hall and dragged headfirst.

Instinctively, I lunge for her. She knows my demon's name, and I'm not letting go of her that easily. My hand grasps at the hem of her robe, and as she moves, I go with her. I use both hands to hold her robe as we slide through hallway. She tries to swipe me away with her claws, but in her straightened position, she can't reach.

The atrium looms up ahead. The only thing between us and a seven-story fall is a sheet of tempered glass with a steel top rail. *Shit.*

I contort my body and dig the heels of my boots into the ground. I try to gain traction, but it's not working. As we near the glass, Santa Muerte rises off the ground to clear the rail. The owl flaps its wings as it maneuvers past the hanging art installation. The bird is pulling her—guiding her.

Santa Muerte flies over the rail. My boots slam into the glass, and I literally pray it doesn't shatter. My body crumples against the divider, and a spiderweb of fractures spreads across the pane, but it holds. The inertia of her flying body rips her from my grasp.

"No!" I yell.

I watch as Santa Muerte sails across the open expanse of the atrium. She doesn't fall—she glides along an invisible horizontal trajectory. The owl circles back toward me, but Santa Muerte keeps sailing to the far wall. She crashes through a window and disappears into the night. Broken glass rains to the ground eighty feet below.

The owl continues its dive toward me, and just when I think it's going to attack, it swerves. With a final screech, it flies back across the expanse of the library and escapes through the broken window. Only now do I notice red-and-blue flashing lights bleeding through the glass and into the atrium. The police. If they're not already inside, they will be in moments.

That's why Santa Muerte was pulled away. I dig into my pocket and pull out a pill box—Xanax. *Shit.* Lupe's blood is on my hands. I chomp down on a handful of pills—maybe too many, but with the police just moments away, I can't risk Dudley rampaging through the library.

"Cheer, cheer for old Notre Dame,
"Wake up the echoes, cheering her name."

I'm hoping my singing will keep Dudley at bay. I pull out my phone and send a quick text to Paige: *SOS. Library. Now!*

I keep singing.

"Send a volley cheer on high,
"Shake down the thunder from the sky!"

So far so good—no Dudley.

Voices shout from downstairs. I can hear them sweeping the area. I close my eyes and do my best to remain calm. Sometimes I can keep my cool and suppress the demon. I hope this is one of those times.

Footsteps charge up the escalators. Flashlight beams sweep across the ceiling as they get closer. I look at my smartwatch. My heart rate is at one hundred eighty beats per minute.

One eighty-six. One eighty-seven…

I stay still and take deep breaths. I think happy thoughts and go to my happy place. I think of kittens and ice cream sundaes and a warm fireplace and…

One eighty-eight. One eighty-nine…

The voices are near the top of the escalator. My body goes

limp. The Xanax is already slipping into my bloodstream. My mouth feels numb. There's nothing else I can do. I glance down at my watch.

One eighty-nine BPM, hanging steady.

One eighty-eight.

One eighty-five…

Bright lights blind me as barrage of boot steps approach. "Freeze!" a voice shouts from behind the flashlights. "Hands in the air."

My hands slowly rise. I'm serene. I'm tranquil. I'm tranquilized. Dudley isn't coming.

Chapter 10

It's raining. A Los Angeles Police Department base camp is set up on Fifth Street, with pop-up canopies clustered together to shield the officers and stations from the weather. There's even a tent over my Mini, where technicians in white Tyvek coveralls scramble to recover any possible evidence.

Handcuffed, I sit on the rear bumper of an ambulance while a paramedic checks me for injuries. When he's done, a forensics technician collects samples from my fingers, nails, skin, hair, and clothes. Those samples include Lupe's blood. I am officially suspect number one.

Down the street, a barricade blocks satellite news vans from getting near the library as they prepare for the eleven-o'clock news cycle. Paige arrives, drenched from the rain, and is allowed to wait with me at the ambulance while two uniformed officers hover above us. I'm not sure how Paige made it past the barricade—whether it was through her good looks, sheer persistence, or a criminal lie—but I'm glad she's here.

She stays by my side even once the technician is done, but

we don't dare discuss what has transpired tonight. Not with the officers around. In the silence, my mind races with all the new information.

Santa Muerte is real.

Santa Muerte murdered Lupe.

Santa Muerte knows my demon's name.

This changes everything. My search for Elizabeth has led me down a path I didn't expect—a path that may finally rid me of this demon. I need to figure out why Elizabeth was taken so I can find her. If I find her, I find Santa Muerte. Then I need to force Santa Muerte to give up the name. I have no idea how I'm going to do any of those things.

An older uniformed police officer hurries from the library and comes toward me, ducking under the canopy. "Ms. Caine? I'm Sergeant Ortiz. The detectives would like to speak to you now."

It's time. I stand, and Paige rises with me. The officer holds up his hand to Paige. "Just Ms. Caine."

I give Paige a reassuring nod. "It's okay."

Still handcuffed, I follow Sergeant Ortiz into the rain. I shrug and keep my head down as we jog into the library. The cold rain pelts me.

The moment the officer and I step inside, we come across a flurry of activity at the security desk. A forensics photographer is taking photos of the ground behind it. I never checked behind the desk when I walked in earlier that evening. That was a foolish move on my part. I knew it was strange that there was no security there. I should have investigated.

I stop and turn to Sergeant Ortiz. Rainwater drips from my damp hair onto my face. "Was it Terrell?"

He exchanges a look with another officer standing by the crime scene, who shakes his head. I'm hit with two feelings back-to-back. The first is relief that it wasn't Terrell. The second is guilt because of my relief. As awful as the feeling might be, I'm glad the body isn't my friend's.

"Miss?"

I look up to see Sergeant Ortiz waiting. I'm not sure how long I have been staring at the scene near the security desk. "There may be another one." The words come suddenly from my mouth as if spoken by their own volition. When I realize everyone is staring, I shake myself out of my trance. "There are usually two guards working at night. Someone else must be around somewhere."

One plainclothes detective starts barking orders to spread out and search. Officers rush out, talking into radios and heading in different directions. Sergeant Ortiz gestures for me to keep moving.

It takes considerable effort to pull myself away and follow him to the escalator. This is where I first saw the owl. *What was its role? Was it Santa Muerte's pet or some familiar spirit? It must have been down here, keeping watch, while Santa Muerte...*

Sergeant Ortiz and I climb to the second floor. The cuffs make it difficult to hold the handrail, so I move slowly up the steps. The rotunda is filled with technicians, uniformed officers, and plainclothes detectives. Work lights are set up, shining on the body of Lupe, which, fortunately, is now covered by a sheet.

Ortiz stands by my side and waves for someone's attention. "Detective! She's here."

From the group of investigators emerges the detective. He's younger than most everyone here but passes through the scrum with the confidence of someone with authority. His brown suit has lost its form as if it's the only one in his wardrobe and has been worn too much. He lets it hang on his lean frame in the same casual way that one wears pajamas. An ugly blue tie dangles from his unbuttoned collar.

Once he reaches us, he proceeds to ignore me, looking around the room. His fingers run through his tousled hair, doing little to improve his disheveled look. When he finally turns to me, he eyes the cuffs on my wrists.

"Take those off," he orders.

Ortiz removes the cuffs without questioning.

"I've got it from here," the detective says.

Ortiz collects the handcuffs and walks away. The detective looks around the room. At the moment, no one is close by and within earshot.

Finally, he turns to me. He's tall, so I have to tilt my chin up to meet his face. It's a good face, rough and handsome. He doesn't even flinch when he looks at my yellow eyes. With my wrists free, I wrap my arms over my chest. I'm shivering from the cold and the situation.

The detective asks, "Do you need a blanket?"

I shake my head. More water drips down my face, and I self-consciously wipe it away.

"Are you okay?" he asks, checking me over. His voice is deep, with the remnants of a New York accent.

"Yes."

"You're not hurt?"

"No."

"Cops treated you okay?" He sounds genuinely concerned.

"Yes."

"Good. You know I have to yell at you now, right?"

"I'm ready."

In an instant, his tone changes from concerned to severe. "What the hell happened here, Darcy?"

Detective David Resnick and I have known each other a long time. Being a private investigator, I have crossed paths with him more than a couple of times. Some of my cases had to do with crimes committed in his bureau. He used to work in Gangs and Narcotics in Hollywood, and one of my first cases had to do with a drug dealer named Rollo who was selling cocaine to child actors on a studio lot. Luckily for me, I'm immature enough to pass for a sixteen-year-old and was able to help David nab him in a sting. That bust made him a high-profile star in the LAPD and provided him the path to move up to Robbery-Homicide. Since then, he's been my go-to for inside police information.

A few months ago, he moved to the Central Bureau, which puts the library in his jurisdiction and makes him the detective on scene tonight. At the moment, I'm not sure if that's a good thing or a bad thing for me.

"Didn't you get my statement from the first officers on the scene?" I ask.

"I want to hear it from you."

No, he wants to catch me in a lie. He stares down at me, and there isn't a hint of friendliness in his eyes. Tonight, he means business.

"I came in late to set up for an exhibit tomorrow," I say. "No one was at security. I came up here and found Lupe. Then the police arrived." The fewer details I offer, the better.

"That's all you're gonna give me? You're a better storyteller than that."

"You want a story or the truth?"

David glares at me, but I don't let him intimidate me. It's a tough world, and I've spent the better part of it dealing with dangerous criminals, aggressive cops, and literal demons. When you're my size, you have to learn how to punch, curse, and spit with the boys if you don't want to get pushed around. Unfortunately, when a woman asserts herself like that, she soon earns the reputation of being a bitch.

David knows this about me. He even once admitted it's what he likes about me. Tonight, however, he's the detective and I'm a person of interest. I don't blame him for wanting the truth, but I can't afford to provide that. I wouldn't even know where to begin.

"Was there anyone else here when you arrived?" he asks.

"No."

"Why is there blood on your hands?"

"I'm sorry," I say, looking down at my recently washed hands. They're still pink with the stain of blood. I nod in the direction of where Lupe still lies. "I wasn't thinking when I checked to see if she was okay."

"You know better than to touch a body at a crime scene."

"That *body*," I say angrily, "was my friend." I realize he has a job to do, but I'm getting tired of him treating me like one of his usual suspects. We go back a long way, and he should know me better.

David pulls away, and I can sense his regret for pushing too far. Despite his tough-guy attitude, I know he cares about me. He scans the room again. "Sorry. And I'm sorry about Lupe, but you and I both know you're not telling me everything."

"Can I be perfectly honest with you?"

His demeanor softens. For a moment, the old David I know is standing before me. "Of course."

It kills me to keep him at bay, but I have to. "I've given you my full and complete statement. And that's all I'm going to say tonight."

David has lived in Los Angeles for the past twelve years, but he's a true New Yorker. He grew up in Brooklyn—Vinegar Hill, to be exact. Life wasn't easy for him when he was young. He was in constant trouble because of his big mouth and quick fists. Having spent his life fending for himself on Flushing Avenue, he didn't exactly develop the temper and patience of a Tibetan monk. So I expect David to rip me a new one, but he doesn't. He just scratches his perpetual day-old beard and shakes his head.

"I don't know what happened," I add after an uncomfortable silence. "I don't know who did it. I came here tonight and found her. Found this."

Another detective approaches us. He walks with a swagger as if to bring attention to his masculine stride. The horseshoe moustache is another component of his macho facade. He wears a more expensive suit than David but is stiff and uncomfortable in it despite his lean build. Judging by the can of Coke in his hand, I'm guessing he's not much of a coffee drinker. His hair is thickly unnatural with a too-perfect hairline—probably courtesy of some hair plugs that have since healed. I can't decide if he looks great for sixty or terrible for forty.

David stiffens and mutters, "Try not to be a smartass for two minutes."

That remark stings. I mean, it's true, but still…

"How's it going?" the detective asks us.

"Ed, this is Darcy Caine. Darcy, this is my new partner. Well, I'm his new partner. Detective Ed Snyder."

I nod a hello.

Snyder barely offers a grunt my way before turning to David. "What's her story?"

"She's all right, Ed."

"She's a suspect."

"She's a witness," David counters.

It's a relief to hear that I'm actually not suspect number one. At least, not in David's eyes. He shifts slightly, placing himself indirectly between Snyder and me. This subconscious gesture doesn't go unnoticed by me. He knows I can handle myself, but that doesn't stop him from protecting me. It's one of the things I love about David.

Sorry, not "love." It's one of the things I *like* about David. That's what I meant. Like.

Instead of giving Detective Snyder a piece of my mind, I bite my tongue out of consideration for David. He's the junior detective, and the only reason he's questioning me is because of our history. Otherwise, Snyder would be trying to sweat me.

Snyder shoots me a look. "Then let's hear it, witness. What time did you get here?"

"Nine o'clock." I glance at David. *See? No smartass remark.*

"Why didn't you call the police?"

"By the time I found Lupe, you guys were already outside."

"What were you doing all the way down the hall, sitting against the railing with blood on your hands?"

"I was being emotionally distraught," I say.

"That supposed to be funny?"

"My friend was murdered tonight, so no. I'm sorry if I don't remember all the details. I'm still in shock."

Snyder glares at me then turns to David. "The captain is going to want a full report first thing in the morning. We'd better make sense out of all this crap. If we don't get an arrest soon—"

His threat is interrupted by commotion from an antechamber next to the rotunda. I can hear voices calling out. Officers start moving toward a doorway.

"We found the guard!" someone shouts.

A group of officers emerge from the hallway that leads to the gallery. A black security guard limps forward, resting his weight on two uniformed cops who walk on either side. He holds a white bloodstained cloth to his head, but he is very much alive and conscious. It's Terrell.

Snyder hurries toward the group. I instinctively move to

follow, desperately wanting to hug Terrell and see if he's okay. A hand grabs me by the elbow gently but firmly. David reels me in and leans into my ear. "Just wait."

Despite my normal tendency to ignore sound advice, I do as he instructs and stand by his side. Snyder exchanges a few words with Terrell, who is dazed but nods and shakes his head in response. I can barely make out what he says from across the room.

"No. Someone attacked me from behind... hit me on the head... I was able to make it to the rear hall and lock the employee door behind me. I called 911. At least, I think I did. I don't know what happened next. Then I woke up, and you guys were here."

He suddenly seems to notice the covered body in the center of the rotunda. Terrell's voice echoes in the chamber. "Is that Darcy?"

"Terrell!" I shout, wanting to put his fears at ease.

He looks up and sees me, and the relief spreads across his face. His legs give out beneath him, but another police officer keeps him on his feet. His aged body suddenly looks much older. I break free from David and hurry to Terrell. The police officers let me by, and I grab him in my arms.

"You're okay!" he says, holding me tight. He sobs against me. "I thought..." He trails off. "Who's that?"

David is behind me and asking the question I'm thinking. "Why did you think that was Darcy?"

I release Terrell and watch him wipe the tears from his eyes. "I was on rounds when Roger radioed from the front desk. Oh God. Roger?"

Roger Watkins. His must have been the body the police found behind the security desk. I didn't know him well. Roger was a security guard who usually worked the night shift. What I did know about him led me to believe he was a good guy. He was a grandfather from New Orleans, a veteran of the Vietnam War, and two years away from retirement.

Terrell looks at me, his face pleading to know if Roger is okay. I look back, silently telling him all he needs to know. He struggles to pull himself together. I grab his hand and wait patiently for him to process the news. Fortunately, so do the officers around me.

Terrell finally continues, "Roger—Roger said someone was here to see Darcy. I-I told him you were working in the gallery." Terrell turns to me. "I thought that was you here tonight."

My stomach sinks as I turn back to the body beneath the sheet. That was supposed to be me. Someone came to the front desk, looking for me. That person killed the front desk security guard, Roger Watkins. Then Santa Muerte came up here and found a small brunette working where I should have been. She killed Lupe, thinking it was me.

My mind continues to race through the situation. *Who asked Roger where I was?* He wasn't going to calmly radio for my location because the spirit of Santa Muerte drifted to his station. She and that owl were with someone else tonight. *Who?*

"Lupe?" Terrell asks. His question jerks me back to the present. "Is that Lupe?"

I turn to him and nod. Terrell covers his face with his hands, and I hold on to him as his legs begin to buckle again. Two people died, and it's clearly too much for him to bear.

"Did you see who attacked you?" Snyder asks Terrell. Then he points at me with his stubby finger. "Was it her?"

Terrell looks at him in disbelief. "Is this a joke? Someone was trying to kill *her!*" he says, holding me tighter. His eyes burn into Snyder's.

"Okay," David says, stepping between them. He turns to

Terrell and addresses him respectfully. "Sir, why don't we take you outside? We'll get you something to drink and have someone look at your head." He gestures to a uniformed officer, who tries to grab Terrell, but he shakes him off.

"I'm okay," Terrell says as he struggles to walk on his own. He looks at me and reaches out to squeeze my hand. "I'm glad you're okay, Darcy."

Snyder watches Terrell walk out then turns to face me. Neither of us says a word, but I know that in his mind, I've just been removed as a suspect, and that pisses him off. He turns and stomps away.

"Darcy?" David nods in the direction of the atrium.

Silently, I follow him to the hall and away from the eyes of the Los Angeles Police Department. The hallway floor is littered with yellow flags indicating every single drop of blood that spilled as Santa Muerte and I went sliding along the marble hall.

"I still need to make sense of what happened here tonight," he says, looking at all the evidence markers as we pass. He's talking not only to me but also to himself. "Why someone was murdered, why her heart was torn out, and what you were doing here."

"I know," I say.

"You working another case?"

"I'm working a lot of cases." It's a half-truth. In my defense, one case is a lot for me these days.

We stop at the railing that overlooks the atrium. The crack where I slammed into the tempered glass is marked with another flag of evidence. Another investigative team is checking the glass on the floor several stories below where Santa Muerte and the owl flew out the window.

David points. "Did you see that happen?"

I shake my head.

"We found blood in the shards inside and out on the street. It looks like someone did a Superman out of an eight-story window."

He waits for me to respond. I say nothing.

"Jesus, Darcy, you have to give me something. Are you protecting someone? Hiding from someone? There's no way you would have touched Lupe. You know how important a crime scene is." I can see him working the evening's events in his mind. I keep my expression blank. "You didn't touch her—you grabbed someone else. That's how you got blood on your hands. Maybe you struggled with this person. Maybe this person was the assailant. I don't know yet."

I still don't say anything. My attention stays focused on the crew cleaning the glass on the bottom floor.

"How many secrets are you keeping?"

David, if you only knew...

I finally turn to him. I'm reminded of how much I lie to people every day—about who I am, what I am, and what I'm doing. Some days it comes naturally, and I hate how easily I can deceive people. As much as I would love to let it all out, I can't reveal who I truly am.

David continues. "The best-case scenario is that we do figure out what happened here tonight—that I find out you're lying and hiding something from me and impeding a police investigation and we charge you for obstructing justice. That's the best-case scenario."

I can sense his reluctance to finish his thought.

"The worst-case scenario is that we put this all on you." He turns and walks away.

Chapter 11

The rain has passed. I'm not allowed to leave for another two hours. That's how long it takes forensics to wipe down and analyze my car for evidence, from the tires outside to under the seats inside. When Paige and I settle into the car, it still reeks of isopropyl alcohol and the metallic powder residue.

Before I pull away, Sergeant Ortiz leans in through the passenger window and comes face-to-face with Paige. My car is so small he has to take a knee to look inside. I can see his surprise when he realizes the steering wheel is on the wrong side.

He shifts his attention to me. "Detective Resnick wanted me to remind you that you are not to leave the county without letting us know."

I'm aware of the drill and thank the officer for his help this evening. He points down the street to the edge of the cordoned-off area. "The officers will open a path for you to leave. Drive slowly, because there are a lot of journalists and paparazzi out there tonight."

"Paparazzi?" Paige asks.

"Yeah," he says, resigned. "Some idiot called in a fake report that a reality TV star was here tonight. Now we have to deal with this shit, too. Be safe."

With that, he taps the roof of my car, and I'm good to go. As instructed, I drive slowly toward the police line, where a horde of people with video and still cameras shine lights in my direction. The police open a narrow path, and I cautiously make my way through it.

I have never had such a hard time seeing in my life. The lights are oppressively bright and sear into my retinas. Flashes pop off in rapid succession, creating a strobe effect. Video lights follow my progress as my car inches forward. Paige looks away, but I have to be careful not to hit any one of the dozens of pedestrians who press into my car. Once I'm finally past the last of them, I speed up. It's still night outside, and the stark contrast from blinding lights to darkness takes getting used to.

My Mini cruises through downtown for a few blocks before Paige finally asks, "What happened tonight?"

I tell her about everything—the owl, Lupe's dead body, Santa Muerte, the fact that Santa Muerte knows the demon's name.

"Holy shit. Holy shit! This could be it!" She's excited now. "If you get the name, you can exorcise it. You need to tell Father Ramon!"

I don't say anything. I just park and turn off the engine.

"Darcy?" she asks, but I don't respond. I start crying. My eyes are closed. Paige's arms wrap around me, trying to comfort me... trying to console me... trying to understand why I'm suddenly distraught.

I am at a complete loss of control as my crying intensifies. The sobs come out like barks, and my body convulses. My mind races through thoughts of regret, sadness, and torment. And guilt.

When the guilt hits, the tears come harder and faster. As much as I feel saddened by the deaths of Lupe and Roger, I'm not crying for any of them. I'm crying because of Bennet.

⌇

"What time is it?" I ask Paige once the tears have stopped and I'm finally breathing normally again.

"Four a.m.," she says, looking at her phone.

I've been crying for a solid half hour. The windows of my car have fogged up completely, diffusing the city lights. I wipe the last of my tears and lean back in my seat. I would have thought that after all of that, I'd be exhausted. But I'm past that point of being tired, and I still have four cups of midnight coffee coursing through my veins.

Paige sits there quietly. I know she wants to understand what's going on in my mind but is willing to give me space and time to talk about it. But there's really no good way to ever bring this up.

"Did I ever tell you how Bennet died?"

Paige is taken aback. "You never told me exactly how. You told me it happened when Dudley had control."

In the three years we've been friends, Paige has never probed for the gruesome details, which I appreciate, because the truth is much more complicated than I ever revealed. "That's not... entirely true."

Paige does her best to maintain her poker face. I take a deep breath and shudder from the cold and the anguish. "When I was possessed and they had brought me home, Bennet wouldn't leave my room. Nearly that entire time, he stayed with me. God only knows what he heard and saw, but he never left."

My stomach turns.

"That last exorcism, the priests told him he couldn't be in my room. So he stood outside my door. I can picture him standing guard outside my bedroom on the upper landing of our house. We had a beautiful house. It was one of those old post-war colonial houses with the old wrought-iron fence all the way around—a two-story house, three if you counted the attic.

"Bennet and I used to love sneaking out of the windows at night to climb on the roof and look up at the stars. There was practically no light pollution in Malbrook, so the sky was filled with stars. I haven't seen so many since I left home."

I think back, remembering how one time we snuck out with soda and snacks so we could watch the Perseid meteor shower. We stayed up all night and were so tired the next day that we both ditched school so we could sleep.

"Darcy?"

Paige is looking at me, and I realize I zoned out for a while. "Sorry."

"Why are you telling me about the roof of your house?"

"Because that's where I killed him."

Paige covers her mouth with her hand.

It scares me to tell her this. Despite everything we've been through, I still have secrets I'm not ready to share—secrets I'm afraid might be the straw that breaks the back of our friendship. "During the exorcism, I escaped. Or Dudley did. Since I was possessed, I don't remember any of this except what happened next."

"What happened next?" she asks.

"I woke up, and Bennet and I were on the roof. During my possession, I'd dragged him out up there. I was holding on to our chimney with one hand, and the other was wrapped around Bennet's neck. I was holding him over the edge—thirty feet in the air. We were both so confused in that split second—he at seeing me regain control, I at seeing him like that. I didn't know what was happening. It was like I'd just woken up from a dream. But when I woke, I lost the demon's power. I lost the strength to hold him up. And I let go."

Paige lets out a gasp.

"Bennet reached out for me. I tried to reach out for him, but it was too late. He was already falling." I rub my arm across my eyes, those stupid tears returning. "And he fell right on that stupid ugly wrought-iron fence."

I remember his face like it was yesterday—the horror when he was falling and looking at me. That was the last time I saw my brother alive. If only I could have held on. If only I never let go.

"So the demon receded into me on purpose, just for a moment, so I could see my brother die."

Paige takes a moment to digest this new information about me. I wait, not sure how she's going to react. Honestly, I'm not sure if she'll judge me or fear me.

"I'm so sorry," she says with sincerity.

"I let him go, Paige. He slipped right through my hands."

The servers at Canter's are rude, and the food is usually stale, which perfectly epitomizes the Los Angeles experience and explains why the restaurant has been around for ninety years. It's basically a home for all of Los Angeles's orphans—for people like Paige and me. It's also the perfect place to decompress after a shit night like tonight and one of the few places open at four in the morning.

The waitress pours us each some coffee without our asking. I order a spinach scramble, no sides. Paige orders a Denver omelet with a side of bacon, challah French toast, and half a grapefruit. Paige doesn't say anything after the waitress leaves.

Instead, she waits for me to indicate that I'm ready to speak.

"David is investigating the murder," I say.

"Oh?" Her voice rises an octave and stretches the one word into two syllables.

I can already tell what she's thinking, but I'm eager to move past it. "It puts an added spotlight on me, so I have to be careful."

"What are we going to do next?"

We. I enlisted Paige's help in this case for the tech side. When I needed bait to lure Sebastian out, I pulled her in deeper. But after what I saw tonight, and after what happened to Lupe, I'm reluctant to keep her involved.

"I don't want you to be any part of this," I tell her. "It's too dangerous."

"All the more reason why you need someone by your side."

"This isn't a normal missing-girl case anymore. I saw things last night that I have never seen before. Santa Muerte is real. And she's trying to kill me."

"You need protection," Paige says.

"You can't protect me from her."

"Well, we're going to find out."

I know there's no stopping Paige when she decides she's going to do something. And I'm acutely aware of how stubborn I can be. When the food arrives, we eat in silence—an immovable object and an unstoppable force having a nice quiet breakfast at five in the morning.

My phone rings, and it's a number I don't recognize. Curious who would be calling me at five in the morning, I answer. "Hello?"

"Hello," an automated voice responds. "This is City Librarian Charles Lynton. Due to the tragic events last night, the Los Angeles Central Library will be closed until further notice. There is no need to report to your normal shift until otherwise contacted by your supervisor…"

I hang up, not interested in hearing the rest of the call. Paige looks at me, waiting. "Robocall" I say. "I don't have to go to work today."

She nods then digs back into her grapefruit. We continue to eat in silence until Paige says, "Here's what I think. If Santa Muerte came to kill you tonight, then Santa Muerte is trying to stop you from finding Elizabeth."

I've already reached that conclusion, but I play along. "Why?"

She shrugs. "I mean, if you find her, then you'll discover who kidnapped her. Right?"

"Only in one particular scenario."

Paige sighs. I can see the wheels turning in her head.

"Because," I say, now using Paige as a sounding board, "Elizabeth must still be alive. Some person—or persons—kidnapped Elizabeth. And the only reason the person doesn't want me even close to finding Elizabeth is because she's alive. If she were dead, they could dump the body—who cares if I find her? But if she's alive, they need her alive for some reason." My mind shifts back to everything I know so far. "Sebastian said an old woman was involved. Fiona thinks it could be a *lechuza*—"

I stop cold.

Paige examines my face. "What is it?"

"The owl," I say. "Fiona said the *lechuza*…" I trail off and pull out my phone. I quickly dig through the bookmarks I made when I did my research on the Santa Muerte cult and spirit.

"What?" Paige asks more anxiously. I find what I was looking for and hand my phone to Paige. She grabs my phone and starts reading out loud. "According to Mexican folklore, the *lechuza* is an old witch—or bruja—who sold her soul to the devil in exchange for magical powers. Among her powers is the ability to shape-shift…" She looks up at me.

"Keep reading," I tell her.

"As a result, she can turn herself into a large bird, especially her namesake. *Lechuza* is the Spanish word for owl."

"The *lechuza* was there tonight," I say. "She was the owl."

Chapter 12

B y the time we leave Canter's, the rising sun sits low in the east. Morning commuter traffic has already started to build up as everyone on the west side heads east, and everyone on the east side heads west.

"When are you going to tell Father Ramon?" Paige asks.

"I can't. Not yet."

"Why not? Maybe he can help."

I shake my head. "Last night, I encountered a witch and an evil spirit of death who tried to murder me. If Father Ramon found out what happened, he would try to stop me from investigating further."

"But why? This could be the key. This… spirit, entity, whatever… knows your demon's name!"

Father Ramon may be my guide in this search, but he's also a man who's developed a healthy fear of evil. I know him, and I know he'd only get in my way. "He'd stop me to protect me."

Paige settles into the passenger seat and looks out the window. "What about Fiona?"

"Maybe."

Fiona has already warned me to stay away. She most likely knew Santa Muerte was real. The other question is whether Santa Muerte would have told the *lechuza* what she knows. *If they came to kill me last night, and now they know about Dudley, what might they try next? What could they use against me?* Before getting us home, I decide to swing by the library to see how things have settled down. Fifth Street is open again—the LAPD base camp is completely gone. There are still a few black-and-whites parked on the street, along with a long line of news vans. Reporters are stationed at the entrance, providing updated coverage for the morning news.

My Mini Cooper eases into commuter traffic. It's only seven in the morning, but gridlock has already set in. When a jackass in a BMW cuts me off in an intersection, I'm thankful I had a dose of Klonopin before leaving Canter's. I do my best to remain calm and Zen as I maneuver my car through a red light to avoid blocking traffic.

My attention shifts to my review mirror, and I see a truck behind me speed through the intersection. It's a Ford Super Duty that cut through the same light I did and is now stuck with its tail in the crosswalk. The vehicle looks familiar, I recall seeing it parked outside Carmen Viramontes's driveway. A car like that stands out for two reasons. One, nobody in Los Angeles drives a pickup unless it's for work. Two, a red vehicle stands out among the monochromatic cars in this city—most people here drive black, silver, or white cars. The windows are tinted, but the driver looks like Hugo Escalante—Carmen's personal errand boy.

"Paige?"

"Yeah?"

"We're being followed," I say. Paige starts to turn around, but I grab her shoulder. "Don't look!"

"Geez! Maybe start with 'Don't look' before telling me

what not to look at. Who's behind us?"

"Bright-red truck. I think that's Carmen's guy."

"How long has he been following us?"

"Not sure." My attention was so focused on the jackass in the BMW that I didn't notice who was behind me. My guess is that he was probably parked at the library and followed me as I drove past.

"Now what?" Paige asks.

With traffic at a standstill, there isn't much either of us can do. As the cars slowly begin to move, I decide there's only one course of action at my disposal. "Hold on," I tell Paige.

The next chance I get, I merge into the right-turn lane. On cue, he follows suit. I start heading east, deeper into downtown. Everywhere we turn, there's construction, adding to the congestion. Then I make an ill-advised left turn across two lanes of traffic and cut into an alley. I floor it, zipping past delivery trucks and dumpsters on this bumpy and dirty road.

In my rearview mirror, I can see the red pickup cut off several cars and follow us. Paige's head is turned around, and she's watching. "Shit," she says, "he's still following."

"I got it."

She turns to face forward again. At the end of the alley is the next major street and another traffic jam. "Darcy!" she yells, her voice panicked. "What are you doing?"

"Hold on."

Paige braces herself as I finally hit the brake and make a sharp right turn. Instead of merging into the street, I pull into the dedicated bicycle lane. Taking advantage of my car's compact dimensions, I zip along the narrow divide between parked cars and traffic. I nearly clip a few mirrors along the way.

Paige squeals as I continue to accelerate along the tiny path. With the intersection in reach, I push down on the gas and speed past all the other stuck motorists. I glance in my rearview mirror and see Hugo trying to follow, but he can't. There's not enough room for him to merge into traffic.

So long, sucker. The bike lane is my friend, and I keep traveling as far it will let me.

Paige is visibly excited. "That was amazing! You were aiming for that bike the lane the whole time?"

Yeah. Sure. Let's go with that. I keep driving east and then start to head north.

"Wait," Paige says, finally noticing we're not headed toward home. "Where are you going?"

"We're going to visit Carmen Viramontes."

The traffic is murder heading north, and there aren't enough bike lanes in the city to make this commute to Pasadena any easier. When Paige and I arrive at the quiet residential street, we see no sign of Hugo's truck. My guess is we have about twenty minutes before he gets here.

I don't usually arrive unannounced on any occasion—some of the lessons my mother taught me did stick. But I need to get some answers if I'm going to find Elizabeth, Santa Muerte, and my demon's name. And I don't want to give Carmen and Leona time to prepare like they did last time.

Paige looks around at the neighborhood, with its extravagant wealth, that sits isolated from the rest of the city. We approach the front gate and the ten-foot-tall hedge that surrounds the property, protecting it from the outside world. I buzz at the gate.

Leona answers and sounds surprised. "Do you have some news?"

"Not news. More questions."

"One moment." Minutes go by, and I'm surprised at the

time I have to wait.

"Does it usually take this long?" Paige asks.

"No." I shake my head in frustration. "They're hiding something."

With each passing second, I grow more and more concerned. When people ask you to wait, it's so they can prepare. When people prepare, it's for a show. When there's a show, it means someone's lying.

Five minutes later, I hear, "Come in." The iron gates open for us.

Paige and I walk up the driveway and find the Super Tech delivery van parked out front. Paige takes in the property, from the massive house to the manicured landscape. "Maybe we should get into the electronics business," she says.

"Yeah. Let's get on that."

Leona is waiting on the porch, and I can tell she's surprised to see Paige. "And who is this?" Leona asks with a hint of annoyance.

"My business partner," I say, "Paige Whitaker."

Paige extends her hand to Leona, but before she can even climb a single step on the porch, Leona whirls around and disappears into the house.

"I think she likes you," I tell Paige as we follow Leona inside.

She guides us into the drawing room—which is too bad. I was hoping for another free meal in the kitchen.

"Please have a seat. Mrs. Viramontes will be down shortly." With that, Leona leaves Paige and me alone.

"What's the plan?" Paige asks.

"Plan?" I say, shooting her a sardonic look.

"Right. Look who I'm talking to."

A few minutes later, Leona returns with Carmen. With the amount of time I've had to wait, I was expecting to see my hostess dressed up to receive me. Instead, Carmen is wearing only a housecoat. I wonder if I've interrupted her bath time.

Carmen immediately casts a cold stare on Paige. "I didn't realize you were working with anyone. I was hoping this job would remain private." No greeting. No questions about finding her daughter. Just concern that someone is working with me.

"You can trust her."

Carmen turns her glare on me. "My daughter has been kidnapped, and any day, I could be arrested and deported. I can't afford to trust anyone."

"Someone tried to kill me last night," I say with no attempt to ease into the topic. "Don't lecture me on not being able to trust anyone."

Both Carmen's and Leona's faces register shock. "What happened?" Leona asks.

"Did you hear about the murder at the library?" I ask.

"The story on the news this morning," Carmen answers.

"Someone thought that was me. They killed someone else instead."

Carmen sits down, stunned.

"You're in danger, now," Leona says. It's not a question but an observation.

"She is," Paige agrees.

It's too soon for me to mention Hugo and this morning's brief chase through downtown. I also know he's probably on his way here, so I need to get some answers before we get to him.

"Someone doesn't want me to find Elizabeth, which means she must still be alive. And," I add, "it also suggests I'm getting close to finding her."

"Did you find something out?" Carmen asks anxiously.

I exchange a glance with Paige—a look that says, *Follow my lead.*

"The boyfriend, Sebastian," I say to Carmen.

"Sebastian?" Leona exclaims. She and Carmen exchange a look, and I try to read their expressions. They are both surprised by the news, but I can't tell if there's concern there above the recognition.

"You know him?" I ask.

Carmen answers, "He worked for our main office for a while. We had to let him go."

"Because he was a drug dealer?" I ask bluntly. I do it to elicit a response. Again, Carmen and Leona exchange a look that tells me everything I need to know. They are very aware of his history. I offer a follow-up question. "Was Elizabeth doing drugs?"

Carmen shakes her head. "Absolutely not."

I shrug. "In my experience, when a young girl starts dating someone who deals drugs, it's usually not in spite of his dealing—it's because of it."

Leona takes over. "Did he kidnap her? Was he involved in her disappearance?" Leona is clearly concerned. I've known domestic staff to develop an emotional attachment to the children of their employers. I suspect Leona has more done her fair share to raise Elizabeth.

I shake my head. "He says he wasn't."

Carmen speaks up. "How can you trust what he says, especially if he is, as you say, a drug dealer?" She's on the attack now—questioning me. Doubting me. The genteel facade she put on in our first meeting is long gone.

"I never said I believed him." I do believe Sebastian, but I'm not going to reveal his story about a witch or my experience last night. "But he certainly has information that could lead me to her."

Carmen sits back, but Leona leans forward anxiously and asks, "Like what?"

Time to show a card. "Was Elizabeth involved in Santa Muerte?"

Carmen's eyes widen. This is where I was going with the conversation all along. I study her. She is shocked. *Is it because she didn't know or because I found out?*

Leona stands in front of Carmen, protecting her from my line of sight. "How dare you ask her that? Leave!"

This is clearly a sensitive subject. Judging by Carmen's expression and Leona's reaction, I've committed a grievous sin in even mentioning Santa Muerte. I've offended them. Or someone is hiding something.

I ignore Leona and keep my attention on Carmen. "Did you know Elizabeth was spending time with an old woman who was involved in the cult? Any idea who this woman is?"

I'm hoping someone will mention something about a witch, but I doubt it. Carmen looks down, recoiling deeper into her sofa. I can't tell if this is an expression of guilt or fear. Out of the corner of my eye, I can sense Paige tense up, preparing to move.

"I said leave," Leona repeats.

I turn my attention to her. "No." I peer around Leona at Carmen. "If you want me to find Elizabeth, you're going to need to tell me everything. And I mean everything."

"She's done answering your questions today," Leona says.

Carmen speaks up. "I don't know any old woman. And I cannot believe my daughter would ever associate herself with that disgusting religion." Now that Carmen has indicated her willingness to speak with me, Leona steps aside.

"Why did you send Hugo to follow me?" I ask.

"He's following you?" Carmen asks as Leona retakes her seat next to her employer.

"He was at the library this morning, looking for me. Why is he following me?"

"I don't know. I didn't know he was."

"What does Hugo do for you?"

"He worked for my husband for many years. He manages the stores—"

"Then why did you send him to contact me?" I ask. I know she's hiding something. "Why him specifically?"

Carmen looks from me to Leona.

"Carmen?" I prod. I don't want to give her time to formulate a response with Leona.

"I trust him," Carmen says.

"How can you trust someone you didn't know was following me?"

Carmen buries her face in her hands. She's on the ropes.

I keep hitting. "What was his relationship with Elizabeth?"

"Please stop."

Leona finally interjects, "That's enough." Her tone is stern and commanding, and this time, it gives me pause. "Hugo is a trusted member of this family. These questions are insulting to Mrs. Viramontes."

I don't care if Carmen is insulted. I need answers. "What is *your* relationship with Hugo?"

"I do not have a relationship with Hugo," Carmen snaps. "He is someone my husband trusted, so he is someone I trust. When Elizabeth first disappeared, I asked Hugo to find her. I could not trust anyone else. Especially the police."

"Are you involved in anything else illegal I should know about?"

"No. Absolutely not."

Oh yes, she absolutely is. "Hugo doesn't manage the stores, does he?"

"He worked for my husband!" Carmen shouts. She's defensive now. Emotional.

There's a lot Carmen's not telling me, and she won't tell me, especially with Leona protecting her. Maybe Leona is more than a maid. Maybe Carmen is more than an immigrant. Maybe their electronics empire is more than that.

My eyes dance around the room, and I take into consideration this enormous house in an affluent neighborhood. *Why does someone have a thug running personal errands, like tailing private investigators? How did Elizabeth Viramontes get mixed up in a Mexican cult known for its drug affiliation? Why would someone kidnap her? Who is Carmen Viramontes?*

It's an obvious and inevitable conclusion, and I'm embarrassed I didn't think of it earlier. Or maybe I did and just didn't want to admit it. I say, "It's not the stores he manages, is it?"

"He does," she pleads.

"It's another part of your business."

"No."

"Tell me!"

Leona finally shouts, "I sent him after you!"

I freeze. Carmen looks up, shocked. Paige leans forward beside me.

"Why?" I ask, unable to hide my frustration.

"I was worried about your investigation. Finding Elizabeth is…" She trails off, her voice cracking. "We must find Elizabeth. I told Hugo I wanted any updates. I didn't care how. Even if he had to follow you."

Part of me wants to walk away, but I'm in too deep now. Carmen and Leona are going to continue to hide information from me, so I can no longer rely on them for my search. Carmen is no longer my client—Elizabeth is. And when I find Elizabeth, I'll find Santa Muerte.

"If you want me to find her," I say to them, "if you want

her safe, then I don't want Hugo following me anymore. His presence puts her in jeopardy. Put a leash on him if you want me to find your daughter."

Leona stiffens. "You do not have to worry about Hugo anymore."

As if on cue, the front door opens. The sound of hard boot soles clacking on wood floors echoes through the house. Hugo enters the room. Everyone stops talking.

He's clearly surprised to see me. No one is surprised to see him. I raise my hand and offer a little wave.

"Will you excuse us?" Carmen asks.

With Paige in tow, I take my time as I stroll past Hugo and head outside. We climb down the steps of the porch to stand in the driveway, allowing a respectful distance for Carmen to handle Hugo and Leona.

Paige keeps her focus on the house as she whispers, "So, um, Carmen... she's a drug dealer, right?"

"Pretty much."

"That's comforting."

Carmen's angry voice blasts from the house. The sudden sharp yelling startles Paige and me. Hugo's voice counters but is immediately cut off. Leona shouts in English, and soon all three are speaking over one another.

Then silence. Paige and I exchange a look that says, *Should we run?*

The door opens, and Leona emerges. She's composed as she walks down the steps toward us, her head slightly bowed. She stands before me for a moment before speaking. "Mrs. Viramontes apologizes. Neither Hugo nor I will interfere with your investigation again."

Chapter 13

———◆———

"Elizabeth!" I shout, waking up.

I'm on the couch, where I landed a few hours ago. Or maybe it was longer than that. The last thing I remember is coming home with Paige, telling her I was going to close my eyes for a quick afternoon nap, and... now it's night outside. The only light comes from the kitchen—which does little to brighten the loft—and from a computer screen in Paige's corner of the dining table.

Her disembodied face looks up from behind the laptop. "Bad dream?"

"Dark magic. Missing girls. Bennet's death. Demons. The usual." The words come out through a raspy and halting voice. I rub my head, realizing that I slept in a funny position and haven't had enough water.

"I fixed you dinner," Paige says, nodding toward our coffee table. A cold glass of water sits there, condensation dripping down to the coaster. Next to it is a plate with a ham-and-cheese baguette sandwich and two aspirin.

I reach for the aspirin and water first. As I start chowing down on the sandwich, Paige turns on the kitchen light. It's dim enough not to shock my eyes with its brightness.

"I was thinking…" I say as she walks back to her computer.

Paige rolls her eyes. "Uh-oh."

"Shut up," I say defensively. "I was thinking… can you go on Facebook and track down all the locations Elizabeth had checked in? Then cross-reference it with all the places Sebastian checked in?"

"You were thinking this… when?"

"While I was sleeping," I say, my mouth full of bread.

"I thought you were having nightmares."

"It was a very busy nap. Can you do it?"

Paige's fingers are already clacking along her keyboard. That's all the answer I need. I take another bite of the sandwich and place a phone call.

"Fiona Flanagan's phone! How can I help you?"

I immediately recognize the Oklahoma twang. "Hi, Eva Jean. It's Darcy."

"Well, hiya, Darcy! How're you doing?"

Not wanting to get sucked into small talk, I get straight to business. "Is Fiona there?"

"I'm afraid not," she says, drawing out the last word. "She's in a meeting with her publisher to go over her upcoming book."

Publisher? "Where are you guys?"

"Why, we're in New York. Can you believe it? Fiona gets a call from her agent yesterday saying they've got cover art, and instead of—"

"Eva Jean?"

"Yes?"

"Just let her know I called." I hang up just as Paige plops down beside me with her laptop. "That was fast."

Paige mirrors her screen to our TV. "What's the deal with Fiona?"

"She's in New York. We're on our own for a while."

Paige pulls up an online map of Los Angeles. "I looked at all the check-ins for both, plus any posts in Instagram, Twitter, and anywhere else I could track down their digital footprints. Elizabeth, obviously, had more. This is what I found."

On the map appears a collage of bubbles in three different colors—red, blue, and purple. In some bubbles are the photos they posted at the location. There it is, the history of all their photos, mapped out across the city.

"Blue bubbles," Paige says, "are Elizabeth. Red bubbles are Sebastian."

"Why isn't blue the guy and red the girl?"

She sighs. "I'm making maps, not planning a baby shower. Can I continue?"

"Fine."

The maps show a higher concentration of the red and blue bubbles across the Los Angeles area. Elizabeth's bubbles are concentrated in the Pasadena, USC, and downtown areas. Sebastian is all over the map. I guess he's a drug dealer on the go. The fewest bubbles are purple.

"Purple bubbles," Paige says, "are where Elizabeth and Sebastian overlap." She punches a key, and the red and blue bubbles disappear. The purple bubbles are concentrated in Central and South LA. "These are where they overlap. And this"—she punches another key—"is where they check in at the same time."

Four purple bubbles remain. One is the La Lucha bar we first identified they'd checked in at, one is at USC, one is at the Cinerama Dome in Hollywood, and...

"Now," she continues, "remember when Sebastian said that

temple was in Whittier in East LA?"

The display zooms in to Whittier Boulevard with a single photo—the last purple bubble. A photo of an altar pops up. It's blurry, but there are clearly several figures standing in front of the altar, lit only by candles. Their faces are obscured by digital noise.

"I bet you anything that's your temple."

She clicks back on the map and provides a street view. It's a poor neighborhood with dilapidated buildings and vacant industrial lots. The building at the center of the image is a nondescript pale stucco commercial structure on Whittier Boulevard between a liquor mart and a discount clothing store. Two levels. On the bottom floor is a florist shop. Next to it is a grated door that does little to hide the steps leading up.

Paige points upstairs. "That's your temple."

Chapter 14

———— ◆ ————

P aige and I stand before a two-story building on Whittier Boulevard. A tattered sign on the first floor indicates that a florist used to occupy the street level. A rolling steel door is pulled down and locked, and faded graffiti marks the metal. There are plenty of storefronts here in Boyle Heights, but along this impoverished stretch, most of them have been closed for some time.

Beside the shop is an iron grate that blocks the entrance to an upstairs business. When I pull, it opens with a creak. The stairway is dark, but jarred candles provide some light. I scan Whittier Boulevard. Aside from the few cars that drive along the street, I don't see anyone.

"What do you think we'll actually find up there?" Paige asks.

I shrug. "I guess it would be too much to ask that Santa Muerte is actually up there, just hanging out."

Hesitantly, I walk up the steps. Paige follows. At the landing is an open door on the left. Carved on the door is a strange and unusual symbol.

"Stop," I say.

My arm holds Paige back as I inspect the symbol. It's burned onto the wood, probably with a soldering iron. Though roughly etched, it holds a roughly geometric quality. In the center is an oval dissected by two perpendicular lines that extend out of it. The vertical line has two slashes at the bottom to form an arrowhead and nine slashes at the top to form the fletching—essentially, aiming the arrow downward. In the four quadrants of the oval are different symbols: a four-pointed asterisk, a cross, a heart, and a triangle. The horizontal line has two more lines at each end to form crosses. And to the right of the oval, crossing through the horizontal line, sits a single backward *S* with spiraling loops at each end.

"What is it?" Paige asks.

I pull out my phone and snap a picture. "A veve."

"And what is that?"

"I've only ever seen this in voodoo. A veve is a religious sigil meant to act as a beacon for spirits. A way of summoning them or inviting their protection."

"I can guess which spirit this is for," Paige says.

I touch the wood, feeling the carving beneath my fingers. To my amazement, it's warm, as though someone had recently touched iron to wood. I know that's impossible. Then again, I've seen a lot of impossible things lately.

I touch the bottom of the symbol—the arrowhead. "I've seen this before," I whisper.

"Where?" Paige asks.

"Hugo has this tattoo on his right shoulder. I remember seeing it the first time I met him, at the library."

"Well, that would mean he's involved in Santa Muerte," Paige says.

"Yes. Yes, it would." If Hugo were involved, that could

explain how Elizabeth was introduced to the cult. It would explain a lot about Hugo.

With a gentle twist of the loose knob, I open the door. Inside, we find a makeshift church with folding chairs in place of pews. Instead of depictions of the Stations of the Cross, faded photos of people are pinned on the wall—family members, friends, and lovers. The offerings are so numerous they nearly coat the entirety of both walls with clutter. Strewn across nearly every inch of the temple floor are dried and crumpled flowers, scattered feathers, and clumps of melted wax. As a result, the concrete below is barely visible. From all this rises a sweet and putrid smell that burns the nasal passages.

I bend down and pick up a gray feather, mentally comparing it to the plumage of the owl I saw in the library. Those feathers were almost metallic in color—silver.

"Owl feathers?" Paige asks.

I drop the feather and shrug, not sure. We continue on. At the altar, in place of any depiction of Jesus, stands a six-foot Virgin Mary draped in fabric robes of blue and red and adorned in more flowers. Flaming candles and floral wreaths surround her. In place of a halo over her head is the shining blade of the scythe she holds. In her other arm, she cradles a globe. Instead of a peaceful woman's face, a skeletal visage gazes down at the floor as if lost in thought.

A heavy-set man rises from a chair and approaches us. He wears work pants and a black polo shirt with a white clerical collar. His bushy brow furrows as he gets near, looking us up and down.

"*¿Que quieres?*" he asks.

Paige and I exchange a look. I shrug as if to say, *Let's play along.* "We've come to pray," I tell him.

The padre sneers at us then spits. His phlegm lands with a

splat on the floor. "Come in," he commands.

Paige follows and turns to me. I close my eyes and prepare for the pain then take a step inside. A rush of adrenaline flows through me. My eyes pop open as warm blood courses through my veins—a sensation I haven't felt in a long time. I am light-headed. Dizzy.

"Are you okay?" Paige asks.

I nod. It was the opposite of what I was expecting. There's no pain and no adverse reaction to the holy ground, which can only mean one thing—this place is evil.

"*¡Apúrense!*"

Paige and I hurry forward to the altar. The padre shoves a basket in front of us. It takes a moment for me to register why.

"How much?"

"*Cinco.* Five."

My wallet comes out of my coat pocket, and I put a clean five-dollar bill in the collection plate. He grabs the bill and shoves it into his pocket.

"Each."

I put another five in the basket. He puts it in his pocket too. "What you want?" he demands.

Paige looks at me then at him. "To pray?"

He sighs impatiently. "*Si, si.* Pray. For what?"

Clearly, when people come to him—or to Santa Muerte—it's to ask for something. We hadn't planned on this, so I improvise. "I'm trying to get my boyf—"

"I need to find my mother."

I turn to Paige. Her eyes stay on Padre.

"Your mother. She lost?"

"My birth mother," Paige clarifies.

He nods then turns to me. "You?"

I shake my head. "I'm good."

He gets a good look at my eyes and peers close. "What about those?" he asks, pointing his fingers at them.

"Next time."

He shakes his head in disgust then turns to Paige. "Do you have a photo? A picture?"

Paige reaches into her pocket and pulls out the slim leather wallet case that holds her phone. She digs into one of its pockets and pulls out a photo. It's the same one I've seen many times, a faded picture of young four-year-old Paige with a beautiful blond woman. They're at the beach. Smiling. Holding each other as close as can be.

He takes the photo and disappears behind the altar. For a second, I can see her gesture as if to reach out and stop him.

I tap on Paige's shoulder. "Are you sure you want to—"

"Yes."

End of conversation.

Padre returns with a bucket overflowing with various items. He yanks on Paige's arm and positions her right before the altar then directs me to sit on a folding chair.

He pulls a repurposed dish-soap bottle and pours liquid in a circle around Paige. She looks at me, worried. I fake the most reassuring expression I have to offer and shoot her a thumbs-up.

He lights a match and drops it on the dish soap. Blue flames spread along the liquid, surrounding Paige. A yellow spray bottle comes out, and he starts squirting Paige with what I hope is a nonflammable oil.

He does all of this nonchalantly, without saying a word. He shuffles in a circle around Paige, stepping on the fire with no regard. He lifts Paige's arms to form a T and instructs her to hold that position.

The flames around her are slowly extinguished. It finally occurs to me that this may actually summon Santa Muerte. *What if she shows up? I'm not ready for her yet. Not now.*

"So does this bring Santa Muerte—"

"Shhh!" Padre shouts, silencing me with a finger to his lip. I shrink back in my chair. *I guess we're going to find out.*

Another item comes out of the bucket—a red candle. He lights it then begins rubbing the stem of the candle up and down the sides of Paige's body. In his other hand, he raises the photo high in the air.

Finally, he starts speaking.

"¡Gloriosa Dama de la Santa Muerte!
"Señora de la Noche
"Niña Blanca."

Like an earthquake, a single jolt shakes the room. Padre stops and looks around. He was not expecting this. I rise from my chair and look around, worried Santa Muerte may actually appear at any moment.

Padre gulps then continues.

"Gracias por todo lo que haces
"Gracias por escucharnos hoy.
"Venimos a ti con un deseo
"Por favor, escúchanos a los mortales en tu gracia.
"Pedimos que aquello que esté perdido, se encuentre
"Pedimos que lo que esté roto, se arregle
"Pedimos que los seres queridos que se fueron, regresen
"Pedimos que aquello que esté incompleto, se complete."

Winds begin to rise and swirl through the room. The photos on the wall flutter rapidly. Flower petals and feathers sweep across the floor. The flames on the candles flicker.

Paige turns her head to me. "Is that you?" she shouts above the howling air.

"No!" I respond, shaking my head.

But I'm not sure. My heart begins to race. My hand jitters in excitement. My cheeks feel flushed. I haven't felt this warm in years. I check my watch for my pulse: one hundred five beats per minute. I'm safe.

I may not be doing this, but I'm connecting to it. My eyes lock onto the statue. Maybe this thing will morph into the actual entity.

"Keep going!" I shout to Padre above the wind. I ready myself for a fight.

He takes a deep breath and shouts the next part of the prayer.

"¡A cambio de escucharnos!
"Ofrecemos nuestros regalos, son tuyos para siempre
"Remedia nuestro dolor!"

The winds intensify, ripping the photos and flowers from the wall. Debris whips around the room in a counterclockwise motion.

"Darcy!" Paige shouts.

As the chaos around me intensifies, my body temperature increases. It's as if I'm wrapped in a dozen flannel blankets. I haven't felt this warm since the first time I upped my Klonopin dosage.

Padre has a look of fear as he continues to shout.

"¡Alivia nuestras almas
"Oh, Patrona Santa de la Muerte, concédenos vida!"

The circle around Paige reignites. Bright-red flames explode ten feet into the air. Padre stumbles back, trips, and falls. Paige shields her face as the flames grow around her. Instinctively, I dive into the circle of flames, tackling Paige. We roll to the floor, and I pat her down to make sure she's not on fire.

The inferno becomes a violent vortex of orange and red, rising into the middle of the room. Padre's had enough and bolts for the door. Paige and I scramble away from the flames. The fiery tornado grows higher and higher, reaching to the ceiling. I climb to my feet, ready for Santa Muerte.

Then suddenly, the vortex collapses. The winds stop. The debris spills to the ground. And I'm cold again.

Paige dives forward toward the circle. I react too late and can't stop her. She shuffles to her feet, clutching the photo of her mother. Without turning to me, she asks, "Do you think it worked?"

I don't know what to say. Whatever happened here was enough to scare the padre. I think it's safe to assume we're breaking new ground.

Or are we? Something happened to scare Elizabeth. Maybe she witnessed something similar. Or maybe she was part of something worse.

We wait in silence. Nothing more happens. Then I say, "We should go."

I get up and escort Paige to the exit. As we walk, I notice the bare walls on either side. Then I stop.

One single picture remains on the wall. Crossing past the chairs, I make a beeline for the wall and get a closer look at the photo. It's a young man embracing a girl, facing the camera. They're happy. She's a pretty young Latina. He's a rough-looking rebel. It's Elizabeth and Sebastian.

I pluck the photo from the wall and turn it over. On the

back is a message: *I'm sorry*. It's dated yesterday.

Paige's hand rests on my shoulder as she looks at the photo I'm holding. "Holy crap, he was just here." I look back at the statue. Leaves and feather are still falling, giving the impression that it's snowing inside. "It worked."

Paige's hand slides away. Without looking, I can sense her disappointment—it didn't work for her. "Yeah. I guess."

"Let's go."

As Paige and I make our way out, I take one last look at the altar at the end of the room. Despite the violence and chaos that just happened, the flowers are undisturbed, and the candles are still lit. Then I do a double take. Maybe it's in my mind, but I swear the statue of Santa Muerte has moved. And now it's staring right at me.

Chapter 15

A fter the incident at the temple, I need a drink. Well, we both do. I drive us to our favorite bar in time for happy hour.

It's the type of bar that's hidden from the general public, and to find it, you have to navigate through the dining area of a popular French brasserie called Orléans. Most people pronounce it "Orleans," as in the infamous Louisiana city, but I've found if I pronounce the correct way, I get better service. It's a bright and airy space with tables crammed close together to accommodate the crowds hankering for unpretentious home-style French cooking. With so many people, the din of conversation is nearly deafening.

Paige and I bypass the restaurant and make our way along the back wall to a door marked Employees Only. We pass through it and descend a narrow wooden staircase that creaks with every step. At the bottom is an ever-present doorman in a black suit. From experience, I know he won't let us by without a password—or a suitable bribe. The password changes nightly, a policy the owners instituted to keep out unwanted patrons. Tonight, it's *Cassis*.

He opens an unmarked red door for us.

The bar doesn't have a name, which helps keep it off the maps and online reviews. Those of us in the know call it the Cellar. It's intimate and designed to feel like an upscale speakeasy from the 1920s. Exposed brick walls and red leather chairs absorb the dim lighting from the tiffany lamps. A piano player is tucked away in the corner, banging out a jazzy cover of a classic '80s song on an old upright.

I'm drawn to a beacon at the back of the room. Hundreds of bottled spirits, backlit by an amber glow, sit on shelves that rise to the ceiling. We take a seat on the barstools, and the bearded bartender emerges from the shadows and slides two cocktail napkins before us. He's wearing a button-down shirt and a formfitting waistcoat that hugs his lean torso.

"Old-fashioned, Darcy?" he asks.

"Thanks, Chester." *Is it bad when you're on a first-name basis with your bartender?*

He turns to Paige. "Dirty martini?"

She nods.

Chester is a bartender who takes his time with each drink. He prechills each glass with ice then gets to work mixing. In no time I have my old-fashioned with a single ice cube and an inky-black maraschino cherry, and Paige has her perfect martini with a swirl of cloudy brine and two olives. We take our drinks to a quiet booth in the corner while the piano player moves on to a new song.

"Question," Paige says as we slip in.

"Shoot."

"What if Elizabeth isn't entirely innocent in all this?" She pops the first olive in her mouth.

It's a question I've considered. Somehow, this young college girl got mixed up in Santa Muerte. That doesn't happen accidentally. Either she sought out this cult, or someone introduced her.

"Okay," I say. "How did she find her way to that temple?"

"You said you recognized the symbol from Hugo's tattoo."

"Hugo introduced her to Santa Muerte?"

"Either that, or it's a crazy coincidence."

The pieces do add up. Sebastian was the first person to confirm Elizabeth's involvement in Santa Muerte. By his account, *she* introduced *him* to the cult. And now I can tie Hugo into it as well. Which leaves me with just one question.

"Who is the *lechuza*?" I ask.

Paige shakes her head. "I don't know, but you think she was there at the library?"

"If what Fiona said was true, she could have transformed into the owl..." My attention shifts from Paige to a large bald man in a suit, approaching her from behind. He's mean looking, like he was asked to leave prison for being a bad influence on the other inmates.

I don't notice the second guy sliding into the booth beside me until he's already seated. He's just as rough looking as the first man and similarly bald but more stylish in his attire. He wears a finely tailored suit—charcoal pinstripes—with tan shoes and a belt to match. The wrinkles on his face are not from age but from a hard life of constant scowling and sneering. His decision to wear a V-neck T-shirt under his suit jacket seems a curious fashion choice.

What catch my eye are his tattoos, which rise from beneath his white shirt. I can barely make out the tops of Russian cathedrals. Around his neck is a serpent coiled like a noose.

"May we join you?" His voice is deep and rough with a thick Russian accent. I see more tattoos, epaulets on his shoulders. He's not trying to impress. He's trying to intimidate.

I'm about to decline when Paige answers. "Actually, we're in the middle of a private conversation, so if you wouldn't mind...?" She waits for them to leave. They don't. "Seriously," she continues, undeterred, "we don't feel like getting hit on right now."

Poor sweet Paige. Most times, she's the smartest girl I know. And honestly, I can't blame her for assuming these guys are here to pick us up—most strange guys who talk to her are after one thing.

"Paige," I say, disappointed, "these guys aren't hitting on us. These gentlemen are drug dealers."

At first, she clearly thinks I'm joking. I admit, my comment was made to both put them off their game and defuse the situation. To get through this conversation, I'm going to have to put on my tough-girl face and let these guys know I won't be pushed around. But... I don't want them to shoot me. I'm going to have to walk a fine line.

Paige scoots away from her guy. "Seriously?"

I jab a thumb at the guy beside me. "I think this one is." I point my index finger at the one beside her. "I think he's the muscle."

She looks her companion up and down. Even sitting, the Muscle towers over her.

"I take it we don't have to introduce ourselves, do we?" I ask.

The Russian next to me takes my hand and kisses it gently. "It is pleasure to make your acquaintance, Darcy." He turns to Paige and reaches out for her hand. She recoils. "And you, too, Paige. Or should I say, Tiffany Maddox? My name is Yury. Yury Vilonov."

It's one thing that he knows our names. That he knows the catfish name suggests he might be connected to Sebastian.

"Okay, Yury Yury Vilonov," I say. "And where is our

mutual friend, Sebastian?"

Yury Yury exchanges a look with his partner. "Sebastian is missing."

Missing? The wheels in my mind start spinning. *Where could he have gone? Did he find Elizabeth?*

"Are you here to ask me to find him?" I ask.

Yury Yury stifles a laugh. "Fuck him. He runs from city. I don't care."

Chester arrives and sets two chilled glasses of vodka before Yury Yury and the Muscle. He looks at me. "Everything okay?"

"We're okay," I say, nodding.

Paige pipes up. Her voice trembles as she says, "Can I order an angel shot?"

This is a nervous mistake on her part, because now the clock is ticking for me to figure how the who, what, and why of this situation. In many bars you will find a poster in the women's restroom with a notification to the female patrons—if any men at the bar are harassing you, if your date is making you uncomfortable, or if you need assistance for any reason, order a fake drink from the bartender or wait staff, and they will enlist security's assistance. That fake drink is called an angel shot.

Chester registers this and casts a worried look at the two guys. "Sure thing."

He walks back to the bar, so now I only have a minute or two before the bouncer comes. My attention returns to Yury Yury. He smirks, downs his drink, then tries to act nonchalant as he continues. "I understand you are looking for Elizabeth Viramontes... I'm looking for her, too."

"Aren't you a good Samaritan."

He doesn't care about Sebastian but wants Elizabeth—which, I guess, means they're probably not together.

"I hope you are able to find her," he says. "In fact, I'm willing to help in any way I can. Perhaps with your expenses. Borz?"

The Muscle reaches into his coat pocket. Paige lets out a tiny yelp. Everyone freezes. I shoot her a look, urging her to pull it together. She's visibly shaking now. I can even see a tiny bit of sweat forming on her brow.

The Muscle proceeds to pull an envelope out of his pocket and drops it on the table with an emphatic thud. His hand rests for a moment on the package, and I stare at the tattoos that wrap around every finger. My eyes follow as the Muscle's hand pushes the envelope across the table and leaves it right in front of me. It swells enough for me to see the thick wad of cash through the opening. Yury Yury says nothing. He just keeps smiling.

"In exchange for…?"

He shrugs. "Perhaps when you find Elizabeth, I could persuade you to bring her to me."

Yury Yury's tattoos suggest he's a high-level Russian mobster. I've seen tattoos like that recently—in photos of Sebastian's friends on Facebook. Which probably means Yury Yury is Sebastian's boss. Which means he wants Elizabeth for less-than-altruistic reasons.

"You want her as leverage? A bargaining chip?"

He smirks. "As you say, I'm a good Samaritan."

"I'm afraid to ask what you would say if I decline."

His smile drops. "Then don't."

I shake my head. "Your offer is tempting, but the fact of the matter is, I have no idea where Elizabeth is." I place my hand on the envelope and slide it back to the Muscle.

In a flash, the Muscle's hand lands on mine. He presses down hard, using his weight to hold down my wrist.

Yury Yury leans in to me. "I said, don't."

I turn to face Yury Yury. "And I said, you can have it back." I jerk my hand out from under the Muscle's.

Yury Yury reaches for his coat. My hand slams on Yury Yury's hand, keeping his arm in his pocket.

"Darcy!" Paige yells. "Calm!"

Everyone freezes and looks at Paige. She stares at me with nervous, pleading eyes. It suddenly occurs to me why she's been so nervous. She isn't afraid of Yury Yury. She isn't afraid of the Muscle. She's afraid of me.

"Stay calm," she says again in a soothing, quiet voice.

Yury Yury turns to me with a curious expression. He looks me up and down, trying to understand why Paige would tell *me* to stay calm in this situation. I can feel his hand relax under his coat as he releases the hard pistol buried under the fabric.

"Is everything all right?" Chester appears beside our table, this time with the doorman and a second, larger bouncer on either side of him. Both guys have arms that stretch the limits of their black cotton T-shirts.

I turn to Yury Yury and pull my hand off his. "Is it?"

With no response from anyone, Chester continues. "Gentlemen, I'm going to have to ask you to leave."

Yury Yury keeps his eyes on me, ignoring Chester and his guys. The Muscle stands to face them.

"*Stoy!*" Yury Yury commands. The Muscle freezes but doesn't back down.

Yury Yury slides the envelope off the table and slips it into his coat. He pulls out a single hundred-dollar bill and places it under a saltshaker. "For your drinks and your troubles."

Yury Yury waits for me to respond. I say nothing. The conversation is over as far as I'm concerned.

"You are full of surprises, Darcy Caine. You will probably find out later who I am. And you will probably learn why you should fear me." Yury Yury pulls out a business card and places it next to the money. "If you find Elizabeth, you will call me and name your price."

He turns to eyeball Chester but doesn't say anything. He merely opens his arms as a display of compliance. Chester and his guys open a path for them to leave.

Before he walks away, Yury Yury says, "If you do find Elizabeth and do not call me…" He shakes his head. "It would be very unfortunate for you. And you, Paige," he says, casting a glance at my trembling friend. "And maybe even that priest in Pasadena. Good luck." He walks out of the bar, followed by his Muscle and the two guards.

"Jesus, Darcy," Chester says after they disappear through the front door. "Who was that?"

My stomach growls, and I cover it with my hand as if that will do anything. "Just another happy customer." I try to act casual, but the truth is, I'm a bit rattled by this recent interaction. These guys mean business, and the fact that they know about everything, from Paige to Tiffany to Father Ramon, means they've done their homework. It means they know how to get to me and the people I care about. "What the hell happened to your password policy, Chester?"

"I'll talk to the guys," he says, contrite.

"Yeah. Wouldn't want anyone dangerous getting in here."

"I got it."

"Like a terrorist."

"I got it!" he shoots back.

"Chester," Paige intervenes, "how about another round?"

He turns without answering.

When he's far enough away, Paige asks me, "Are you okay?"

"Yeah, I'm fine."

She shakes her head. "I mean, are you calm?"

I inhale deeply. I check my watch. My heart rate is high but within the normal range and slowing down. My body is relaxing with each breath. I don't feel Dudley coming on. "I'm okay."

"Then can I freak out right now?"

"Yeah. You go."

"What the hell, Darcy?" she says in a voice a few decibels too loud. She looks around the bar then quiets herself. "Now we have the Russian mob involved?" She grabs the rest of her martini and downs it in one gulp.

"Yeah, I totally didn't see that coming," I say in a calm, collected voice.

"How did they get involved?"

I offer my best guess at this time. "I think Sebastian works for him. Or he did until he skipped town."

"Do you really think he skipped town?"

"I'm trying to be optimistic."

"What's the pessimistic answer?"

I stay silent, which gives Paige the answer she didn't want.

"Shit." She grabs my drink and downs it.

"What this means is that Sebastian is—was—some low-level dealer who switched from Carmen to Yury Yury. That's how Yury Yury knew about Tiffany and about us."

Chester returns with our drinks—on the house. Paige downs her second martini. I grab my old-fashioned and start nursing it before she has a chance to claim it.

Paige takes a bite of her olive. "And he wants Elizabeth as a pawn in his drug war with Carmen?"

"Yeah. As if we didn't have enough to deal with," I answer, biting down on a cherry.

"Jesus," she says. My stomach growls. "Now we're caught in the middle of some drug war?"

"If we are, it's still probably the least of our worries."

Paige shoots me a look. "That's comforting."

Chapter 16

It's morning. I lie in bed, thinking about last night's altercation. It's not clear whether Yury Yury works for himself or for some larger organization. Either way, I start counting everyone I need to watch out for—drug dealers, Santa Muerte, the LAPD, and now the Russian mob.

I pull myself out of bed and head out to the living room. With no cause for alarm, I'm able to slide my door open without having to sing the Notre Dame song. Paige is in the loft, waiting for me. I'm not sure how long she had been standing there, but knowing her patience and resolve, I'm aware that it could have been all morning.

What strikes me is how she's dressed—a black T-shirt, black pants, and black shoes. She looks like she's going to a casual funeral. Then I notice she's holding the same outfit on a hanger, presumably for me.

"What's up?" I ask.

She pushes the hanger forward. "I need you to change."

"What's going on?"

"I found him, Darcy."

I struggle to catch up. "Found who?"

"The judge."

It takes me a moment, but I get there. Paige has figured out the redacted name of the judge on all the legal documents hiding her past.

"You were right," she continues. "It's not me I should have been searching for—it's the judge! I thought about how you said it might be one judge on all those same documents. And I thought, 'That's weird—how many judges approve all those different kind of forms? There are all different courts—different judges.' So I did another query. I wanted to know which judge did all three—name change, Social Security, and termination of guardianship."

"And you found one."

"And I found one. Get this—his name is Judge William Whitaker."

I cock my head. "Whitaker?"

She nods vigorously. "I was four years old, and the court had to assign me a new name. He gave me his."

I'm impressed. If I could convince Paige to abandon her high-salary, low-effort career, she could become one hell of a struggling private detective.

"Now," she says, holding the outfit out for me, "I need you to change. And please don't ask why."

Paige and I have an understanding. "Please don't ask" is the cue for unconditional friendship. It's our way of saying, "The shit is about to go down, and I need someone by my side when it does."

I grab the outfit and change in my room. Of course, I keep my jacket on. A plain T-shirt isn't going to keep me warm. When I emerge, she grimaces at the jacket but says nothing.

"Can you at least tell me where we're going?" I ask as we walk out the door.

"Bellagio Country Club."

⟍⟋

The Bellagio Country Club is a private club tucked away in the foothills of the Santa Monica Mountains. Located off the meandering roads of Bel-Air, the property is a collection of Spanish-style clubhouses and includes private pools, tennis courts, and an eighteen-hole golf course. It's the type of establishment where the elite have come to play since the Golden Age of Hollywood.

Normally, it would be impossible to gain entrance to this club unless you were willing to pay the two-hundred-fifty-thousand-dollar initiation fee plus yearly dues. Or unless your best friend convinced you to pose as a member of the event staff for a private reception. So here I am, wearing a white apron over my black outfit—sans warm and cozy jacket—holding a silver tray of canapés for the wealthy and powerful citizens of Los Angeles. It's a private luncheon on the deck of the main clubhouse, which overlooks the city from its rich and insulated perch. The day is clear and sunny, providing a view from downtown to the ocean beaches. Banners and signs mark the occasion—a fundraiser for some local politician running for reelection at the end of the year.

I move through the crowd, putting on my best smile and trying to pretend I actually care about my job. The appetizers clatter on the metal tray as I shiver from the unobstructed wind that sweeps through the hills. I'm on the lookout for one person—Judge William Whitaker. Not only did Paige find his name, but she also cyberstalked him and discovered he'd be at today's reception. How she found that out she refuses to tell me, for my own legal protection.

"See him yet?"

I flinch and turn to find Paige behind me, holding an empty tray. She scans the crowd, looking at everyone but me.

"Don't sneak up on me!" I reprimand her.

"Find me as soon as you see him."

"Yeah, I know the..." Before I even finish my sentence, she's gone.

Earlier, she sent me a text—a photo of the judge at another one of these events. He's a good-looking man in his sixties with thick wavy silver hair on a face with sharp, chiseled features. He has a warm, genuine smile, even in the posed photo Paige found.

I keep looking out for this silver fox as I navigate the elite of Los Angeles and hope I don't drop these canapés. After an hour of serving appetizers to the city's preeminent stakeholders, I'm about ready to call it—no Judge Whitaker in sight.

An event assistant wearing a headset stands in the corner on the deck. He's clean-cut, Ivy League, and very nervous. I ditch my tray and pull out a blank sheet of paper. With great determination, I march up to the young man.

My eyes lock on his, and I quickly issue an order. "I need eyes on Judge Whitaker."

"Wh-What?"

I grit my teeth impatiently and wave the sheet of paper too fast for him to read. "Whitaker! Who has eyes on Whitaker?"

"Why do—"

"What's your name?"

"Preston?"

Of course it is. "Okay, *Preston*?" I say, emphasizing his question. "Someone smashed the headlight of Judge Whitaker's car, *Preston*? And I need to know where he is. Now!"

Preston? clicks on his headset. "Anyone have eyes on Judge Whitaker?" I shoot him an impatient glare, and he adds,

"Please?"

The funny thing about people is if you act like you hold a position of authority, they will respect it. Take Preston? here. I can tell by his Cole Haan shoes and hundred-dollar haircut that he has more money in his bank account than I do, and unlike me, he actually belongs here. But if I act like he's supposed to answer to me, well, he'll answer to me.

Preston? nods as he listens to his earpiece. "N-Napa Lounge," he stammers.

I'm off before he can finish. Paige is still meandering around with an empty tray. When she sees me charging forward, she falls in pace with me. I grab her empty tray from her. Another cute hostess is offering a selection of finger sandwiches to trophy wives. Without a word, I swap it out with Paige's empty tray and leave behind a group with befuddled expressions.

"Where?" Paige asks.

"Napa Lounge."

We hurry down the long hall, our feet pattering on the Spanish tile. And there, off the main hall, is a placard marked Napa Lounge. We charge inside. The lounge is sparse and white—oppressively white. The only color in the room comes from the wood beams across the ceiling, which match the brown carpet. Even the four men standing in the center of the room are white. They turn to look at us when we barge in with only a single tray of offerings between us.

"Oh, good," one of them says. "I was wondering if we'd get any food in here. Come in, come in." He waves us over, and we approach. My hand extends to offer the tray of new appetizers. Paige is empty-handed.

In the center of the group is a tall man with thick silver hair and wire-framed glasses. He smiles at us and allows his companions first dibs. This is Judge William Whitaker. As the men pluck food from my tray, Paige lasers in on the judge. Her stare doesn't waver, even as he appears to become uncomfortable.

"Can we order some drinks, too?" asks another man. He turns to the others. "Should we get a bottle of scotch?" Then he addresses us again. "Can you get us a bottle of scotch?"

I glance at Paige. She says and does nothing. Not wanting there to be an uncomfortable dead silence, I start stalling. "Sure thing, gentleman. Any particular bottle? We have Glenlivet, Glenfiddich, Glengarry, Glen…"

"I'm Paige Whitaker!"

Everyone is quiet and turns to face Paige. She continues to stare at Judge Whitaker. He takes her in, trying to process her sudden unprovoked announcement.

"Ross," I finish, and an even more awkward silence falls.

Whitaker turns to his friends. "Would you mind excusing us?"

The other men slowly step away, leaving only the three of us in the lounge.

Whitaker turns to me. "And you are…?"

"Oh. Darcy Caine." Not sure how to greet a judge, I wave. "Hi."

He smiles. "I'm going to assume you're going to be part of this conversation, but if you wouldn't mind, could you close the door for us?" He points at the door to the hall. As I move to close it, he turns to my friend. "Paige, why don't we have a seat?" He gestures to the corner, where several armchairs sit in a semicircle.

I shut the door, deposit my food tray on the nearest table, and join Paige and Whitaker. He studies Paige thoughtfully. He's still smiling, though now he seems mildly amused.

Finally, he speaks. "You found me. After all this time, you finally found me. It's been—what? Twenty years?"

Paige nods.

"I've always wondered about you. How you turned out. If you were okay. I hoped that one day you would find me. That's why I gave you my name—the only clue I had to offer. And look at you. Here you are, this beautiful young lady. And since you've found me, I have to imagine you're very bright. It looks like things turned out okay for you."

This time, Paige doesn't nod. As he reviews the expression on her face, his smile fades just a little. "Did you ever get adopted?"

Paige shakes her head. I'm suddenly struck by how quiet she is. Paige only has two speeds—Stop and Go. *Go* is how she escaped the foster system. It was how she taught herself everything about computers. It was how she'd found her way to this man after all these years of searching for answers. But Paige has the same insecurities and vulnerabilities as everyone else, and when you hit that chink in her armor, she slams on the breaks and *stops.*

"She didn't," I answer, knowing that the fact she was never adopted is a particularly painful subject for her. I take her hand and offer a reassuring squeeze. If Paige can't speak, then I'll speak for her. My attention returns to Whitaker. "She left the last foster home the moment she turned eighteen. Got a job, found her own place to live, and put herself through two years of junior college. She's a web developer now. Very successful. And the best person I've ever known."

Whitaker's smile returns. "I'm happy to hear that. So, then, what brings you here? To me?"

I wait then answer for Paige. "She's looking for her birth mom."

This time, Whitaker's smile not only fades but disappears completely. "Why?"

"Because," Paige says, breaking her silence, "I want to know what happened. I want to know why she left me. If she's okay. If…" She trails off then redirects her queries. "Do you know her?"

Whitaker shakes his head. "I know you've been better off without her, Paige. I'm sorry you didn't have an easier life growing up. You deserved better. But I see you now, here before me, and it looks like you turned out to be the best possible version of yourself. I don't think that would have been possible with her."

"Why not?" Paige shifts to Go. She's eager for information and willing to fight for it. "What was wrong with her? Was she in trouble? Was it drugs? Was it…?" Paige trails off. "Did she need help? I can help her now."

Whitaker leans forward to meet Paige and takes her hand in his. It's not a forward advance. It's not romantic, just caring. "You cannot help her."

Paige's shoulders sag in defeat.

"Cannot help her?" I repeat. "Paige can't help her now? That means you know where she is."

Paige perks up.

The doors swing open, and a Bellagio manager steps into the room with a security guard. Behind him stands Preston? with his headset still on. The manager points at us. "Those two. They're not part of the staff. Escort them off the grounds."

The security guard approaches us. We turn to Whitaker, hoping he'll speak on our behalf.

Instead, he pats Paige's hand. "Things turned out for the best for you. And that is all the information I am willing to offer." He lets her hand fall and leans back in his chair.

"Let's go." The security guard grabs Paige and me by the arms and tries to lift us. He fails. Neither one of us is willing to move yet, and despite our relatively small size, it's going to take a lot more than one overweight guard to move Paige's earned strength or my raw power.

He tries again, but we don't budge. Whitaker is looking away now, ignoring our presence.

"I said, let's go!" the guard orders.

"Judge?" I ask.

He glances at us. "I'm sorry."

The guard is about to grab us one more time when Paige and I simultaneously stand.

"That's more like it," the guard says smugly. "Let's go." He motions to grab Paige, but my arm snatches him in mid-reach.

"You touch her one more time," I say, my yellow eyes boring into his, "and I will break your arm." I squeeze, applying enough pressure to let him know mean it.

I push him aside then wrap my arm around Paige's. We walk out of the Bellagio Country Club. Preston? hides behind the manager as we pass.

✴

The entire drive home from the Bellagio Club, Paige is quiet. When we final get home, she goes straight to bed. She doesn't deal well with defeat, and she's back to Stop.

I put a kettle on the stove and boil some water. Once it has heated to a rolling boil, I pour the hot water into her favorite cup, a small ceramic mug she bought at Disneyland, featuring the character Chip from *Beauty and the Beast*. I suspect, on some level, she identifies with a partially broken character. Once the tea has steeped for three minutes, I quietly knock on her door and let myself in.

The blinds are closed, shrouding the room in darkness. Despite this, it's a cheery space—much cheerier than my utilitarian room, with bright-colored rustic furniture and posters of art exhibits from local museums. With the exception of a speaker system, there's little tech in here. This is where she goes to unplug each night.

I set the tea down on her bedside table and have a seat on her bed.

Under a bundle of blankets and pillows, Paige stirs. "Chamomile?"

"Chamomile," I answer.

She emerges from her cocoon and sits up. Her eyes are red and puffy—she already had a good cry while I was in the kitchen. She drops a single tissue on her bed and takes the cup in her hands. The steam rises from the beverage, and she inhales its aroma but doesn't drink. We sit in silence for a while.

Paige finally speaks up. "You know, I don't care if I'm better off without her. I want to know what happened."

"I know."

"I can't stop asking, *Why?*"

"I know."

"What if I'm going to make the same mistakes?" she asks.

"You won't."

"I already am."

She's talking about her relationships with men. Paige has no memory of her father and no indication that he was ever in the picture. This is why she's never even considered looking for him. It's always been about the search for her mom. By learning why there was no father and why her mom left, she also hopes to understand why she keeps going after the wrong men.

"You're not your mother. You're not your foster parents. You are not your name or that judge's name. Paige Alexandra Whitaker is all you and only you, a beautiful, intelligent, amazing woman. You made her—no one else gets credit for that."

"I'm a mess," she says.

"Well, that too."

She kicks me through the blankets but also smiles a bit. "I guess that's why we get along so well, since you're a disaster."

"We're quite the duo."

Chapter 17

I watch as Paige falls asleep wrapped in a cocoon of blankets. She still clutches a single tissue. With empty teacup in hand, I sneak out the door. For better or worse, Paige's early night has afforded me the opportunity to pursue the next step in my search for Elizabeth—alone.

Paige hasn't let me out of her sight since Lupe's death. She was with me when Hugo pursued us, she was there when I confronted Carmen, she experienced the Santa Muerte temple with me, and she was on the receiving end of Yury Yury's threat. Things are getting more and more dangerous, and I don't want her getting hurt as I continue my investigation.

Tonight, I'm going to find Sebastian. Despite Yury Yury's claim that he's skipped town, I still need to confirm that for myself. Seeing as how Sebastian was recently at the temple, I believe he still loves Elizabeth and is looking for her. I grab my jacket, car keys, and the photo Sebastian left at the temple, with the words *I'm sorry* on it.

"What are you sorry for?" I ask myself. I also make sure to

grab my trusty Taser this time. Aside from a missed dose of Klonopin and Dudley on the bench, that's going to be my only defense for tonight.

Using the photo I took of Sebastian's ID, I enter his address into my phone's map and drive out to Harvard Park in South Los Angeles. Despite its name, Harvard Park is neither prestigious nor parklike. My little car nearly loses its muffle as I drive over one pothole after another. Each house I pass on this dark street is small and in disrepair, and every single one has bars on the windows and doors.

I picked a bad time of day to drive here. I don't like guns, and I never have. My father used to take me shooting when I was young and ingrained in me the long and proud history of gun ownership. It didn't take. Despite my profession, I don't own or carry a gun. But at times like this, I think I should. There's no telling what I'll find in here.

My navigation app brings me to a block where the homes are either abandoned or unkempt—it's hard to tell which. After I park, I walk slowly to my destination. The house is dirty, with drab olive paint peeling off the walls and an overgrown brown lawn. I step up the stone steps onto the bungalow porch then look around the empty neighborhood. There are no streetlights on this street, only the glowing windows from a few houses. At least some people are home.

It's important that I talk to Sebastian and I find out why he was at the temple. If Sebastian was willing to go back to there after everything he told me, he must be convinced that Elizabeth is in real and immediate danger. And if he's sorry, as the photo says, he must have done something.

I consider my options. *Call the police?* No. *Call Paige?* No. I have to knock on the door and man up.

My fist slams on the door. Or really, I pound with authority on the iron gate that blocks the door. It rattles under my fist. No one comes.

I pound on the door again. The door cracks open. A man stares at me through the metal screen. He keeps himself in the shadows of the dark room, so I can't make out too many details of his face.

"Is Sebastian here?" When the guy doesn't answer, I continue. "He told me to come by."

"Who's Sebastian?" His voice is deep, with a guttural toughness and a distinct Latino accent.

"Don't screw around. Is he here or not?"

Sure, it's a little suspicious that someone like me would pound on a door like this in the middle of the evening. I can tell he's trying to shake off the fog of whatever narcotic he's recently taken. He keeps looking at my eyes, probably trying to figure out if he's imagining their yellow hue.

He sniffs and wipes his nose. "Are you a cop?"

"Do I look like a cop?"

"If you're a cop, you have to tell me."

That's not true. I can tell this guy gets his legal advice from movies. "I'm not a cop. Where can I find Sebastian? He's not answering my messages."

"Why are you looking for Sebastian?"

I sigh as though this is a terrible inconvenience. "He didn't tell you I was coming by? Maybe he didn't want you to know. Ugh!" I feign anger, and I can tell this guy is unsure how to deal with me. "I'm so pissed at him right now. This, and blowing me off at the concert… you know what? Screw him!" I pull out my phone and start to walk away.

"Wait," he says.

I stop and try not to smile, knowing I've gained some trust. I turn around. He pulls opens the door as wide as it will go and leans his face against the iron gate. I can see him clearly now. The two sides of his face are different. The left side is scarred from a deep and violent burn, the healed wounds giving the appearance that his skin is melting. His left lower eyelid droops slightly and glistens with constant tearing.

"What's your name?" Two-Face asks then takes another deep sniff.

"Tiffany."

"Tiffany." He unlocks the metal gate and steps onto the porch. A rough skinny hand reaches out to me. "It's nice to meet you."

I don't even realize there's someone behind me until an arm wraps around my neck and a damp, pungent cloth covers my mouth. I struggle, but the sweet-smelling fumes fill my lungs with each desperate breath I take. The more I fight back, the more quickly I get drowsy. I know it's a losing battle. I know when I wake up, I'm a dead woman.

My eyes flutter open, and it takes me a few moments to remember my last waking moments. I try to sit up but can't. My arms and legs are pulled to the far corners of a metal table by some rope I can't see. I'm gagged and can still taste the remnants of sweet chloroform in the rag in my mouth.

"She said her name was Tiffany, but her driver's license says Darcy. Darcy Caine."

I tilt my head up and can see Two-Face and three other guys surrounding me. My cell phone is in his hands. He rifles through the credit cards and IDs tucked inside its case. The rest of his group hovers over me, blocking my view of the room, which is no matter, because my vision is blurry. I see only the four Latino males of various heights and builds in wifebeaters and Dickies jeans.

Am I in the house? Have I been moved somewhere else? All my clothes still appear to be on, so I silently thank God for that small miracle.

"She was looking for Sebastian—that's why I called you!" Two-Face is pretty agitated and talking on the phone. He keeps wiping his nose with his arm, which can only mean he's tweaking right now. A nervous, violent meth head—this is not going to end well.

He looks at me. "Black hair. Twenties."

With all eyes on me, there's not much I can do. I struggle against my binds—I'm trapped.

Two-Face paces around the room and continues to go through my wallet. "Are you coming down here or not?" Then he freezes as he stares at the last card from my wallet. "Shit, man. She's a private detective?" He flashes my ID in my face as if that's information I didn't already know. He is not happy with the response from the other line. "You know what? Fine. We'll handle this."

He hangs up and throws my phone and cards on the floor. The others follow him as he moves away, and my line of sight is opened to the rest of the room. It looks like a shop of some kind, with a low ceiling and metal shelves all around. Glass tubes and plastic jugs litter each tabletop. Beakers. Pipes. Hoses. I'm in a meth lab.

As my vision clears, I can see a giant crucifix hanging on the far wall. I strain to look, and the image comes into focus. Not a crucifix. A person.

Sebastian. Long copper pipes pierce his arms, legs, and body and impale him on the wall. Blood drips from his mouth onto his bare chest. A slice carved along the base of his stomach allows his entrails to dangle from his drying wound.

Panic sets in as I register what I'm looking at. I try to scream out, but the gag muffles my voice. My wrists chafe as I struggle against the rope.

One of the cohorts pipes up. "What do we do with her?"

Two-Face stares at me. I can guess what he's debating. He approaches me and gently touches my leg. I kick and struggle, trying to recoil from his touch.

"Get my knife," he finally says.

I try to use all my strength to break the binds, but I can't.

"Open her shirt," orders Two-Face.

One of them rips open my shirt, and buttons go flying. I feel exposed, violated, and for the first time in a long time, powerless. My arms continue to push and pull against the ropes holding me down.

The alarm on my watch goes off, but no one pays attention. Two-Face stands over me. I stop struggling and brace myself for their next move. The goons start praying in unison. Some chant in Spanish I don't understand.

What the actual hell are they doing? Again, I struggle against the restraints, trying to escape—trying to warn them through my gag that things are going to end badly… for them.

Two-Face raises the knife above my chest. My heart races, and sweat beads down my face. My body is heating up. Adrenaline is pumping.

"*Muerte Santisima…*" he says.

Not this shit again. The secondary alarm goes off. I'm in fight-or-flight mode now.

The room starts to shake. Two-Face wavers, looking at what is happening around us. It's like an earthquake in here. Bottles and lamps crash to the floor. A shelf tips over and spills glass jars everywhere. A wind blows through the house.

The praying stops as the air pressure increases. My ears pop. Two-Face turns his attention down to me. I look him dead in the eyes. The last thing I remember is the horrified expression on his face when my binds snap apart like Silly String.

It's sticky. That's the first thing I realize when I wake up. I open my eyes but see nothing. *Am I blindfolded?* No, it's still night out, and there are no lights on inside. I struggle to stand and realize I'm no longer bound. My hands and arms are covered in some weird viscous glaze.

I feel my way to the door and find a switch. Reluctantly, I turn the light on.

There's so much blood. It's everywhere—on the floor, splattered across the walls, covering me. Most of my clothes are torn, and I'm not sure by whom. I walk around the space, careful not to step on the many shards of glass, and examine what I did. Or rather, what Dudley did.

I find the first body. He lies on the floor, his chest ripped open. It looks like someone tore him open like a bag of potato chips.

The next body is nearly decapitated, except his lower jaw remains attached to his neck. I find the rest of his skull slammed against the wall and lying on the floor.

The third body I find is impaled against the floor with chair legs. It looks like he's been stabbed many times. He never stood a chance.

I finally locate Two-Face. He got the worst of it. As best as I can tell, he was trying to run away, perhaps trying to hide in the bathroom. His body has been folded in half backwards. The back of his head lies on his ass. This contortion resulted in breaking open his abdominal lining, spilling his guts onto the floor.

Unable to control myself, I vomit where I stand. Not that it makes much of a difference in this mess. I know I should hurry up and leave, and I know I need to hide my tracks. I can't. I collapse to the floor and cry.

I knew Dudley would come out again someday. Part of me always felt safe because he was inside me, ready to take over as a survival mechanism. But I didn't anticipate this. I feel a regret I haven't felt since Bennet died.

Now four more people are dead because of me. For the past ten years, I've been able to control this darkness in me. I've been able to keep this demon from hurting anyone. And now a terrible mistake has been made that can never be undone. It can never be fixed. The pain I feel isn't just emotional—it's deep in my gut. And I sob.

Eventually, I pick myself up, knowing what I have to do. I begin the process of self-preservation. I find all my personal effects—my Taser, my ID, my credit cards.

My phone rings. I struggle to silence it in case someone is outside. The caller ID shows it's Paige trying to call me. *Shit.* Now I'm really in trouble.

I find every scrap of my clothes and put it in a bag. Realizing I can't walk out the door looking like Carrie drenched in blood, I decide to take a quick shower. I put a plastic bag over my scalp, to prevent my hair from falling into the tub, and rinse as much blood off as I can.

Through a window, I peer outside to get a sense of where I am. I haven't gone anywhere. This is the house I arrived at hours ago, on the same shitty block in Harvard Park.

My phone vibrates with a text from Paige: *Where are you?*

Unfortunately, I don't have time to respond. I put on some sweatpants and a hoodie I find lying around and proceed to wipe my fingerprints from anyplace I can remember touching. It's still not good enough. I find a jug of isopropyl alcohol and pour it over everything. Before I walk out the door with all my belongings, I light a match.

With the hood over my head and my eyes down, I walk out the door. The night sky shrouds me in darkness, and I'm happy for the nearly vacant street. Head down, I charge in the direction of my car.

The only other soul around is a man walking a pit bull. As I approach to pass, the dog starts barking at me. Animals hate me. And just my luck, this stupid mutt is bringing some unwanted attention my way.

"Easy, Bruno." The guy pulls on the choke chain as I try to pass. "Sorry, he's usually not this aggressive."

I nod my thanks as I try to walk by. By pure stupid luck, I glance up as a car drives by, and its headlights illuminate my face. I quickly turn away and hurry to my car.

Behind me I can hear the dog owner yelling, "Fire! Fire!" as I slide into the driver's seat.

Safely inside, I jam the key in the ignition and twist. The engine turns. I peel out and speed away as fast as I can.

〜

On my way home, I steer my Mini onto San Julian Street in Skid Row. The sidewalk is one long tent city, with homeless people gathered together over burning trash cans to keep warm. My car barely slows to five miles an hour as I roll down my window. The pungent smell of body odor and urine punches me in the face.

At this moment, I appreciate having a right-side steering wheel as I toss my clothes into a burning trash can. I'm bummed that my jacket was in that bag. I really liked that jacket.

My Mini continues its slow crawl, and my eyes connect with a particularly homely woman. She's slim and, like so many others here, haggard. The flames from the trash can illuminate her features. Once upon a time, she may have been beautiful, with smooth skin and long blond hair. Now her skin is dark and wrinkled like weathered leather. Her hair is matted with a layer of filth and dirt. But her eyes reveal an intense madness, like she's about to snap.

I think about what Judge Whitaker said about Paige's mom. *You cannot help her.* I drive away.

✺

I arrive home and rush to get inside the loft. Paige is pacing in the living room. She freezes when I walk through the door.

"Where the hell have you been?" she yells. "I've been freaking out all night! Why didn't you answer my texts?"

I charge past her toward our bathroom. Paige rushes to intercept me. She blocks my path with a stiff arm across the doorway.

"Darcy!"

I look up at her, the cowl of the hoodie still covering my head.

She reads the expression on my face and registers that I'm wearing different clothes. Her arm falls. "Oh shit. Dudley?"

Without answering, I move past her and hurry into the bathroom. I take a Silkwood shower in scalding-hot water and make sure to clean myself completely. Only when my skin turns pink from the scrubbing do I finally shut off the water.

Paige is standing outside the door when I emerge with only a towel wrapped around me. "What happened?" she asks. She sounds worried and confused.

The only thing I say is, "You and I were together all day."

My damp feet slap against the kitchen tile as I grab a bottle of water and a granola bar. She doesn't say anything to me, but she looks afraid. "Where were you?"

I don't answer her. After what I just went through, I don't know how.

"Darcy?" she asks, her voice trembling with fear.

"Lock me in." I pull my sliding door shut and wait.

Only when I hear the metal arm bar barricading me in do I allow myself to relax. I make a cocktail of Xanax, Klonopin, and Excedrin PM and go to sleep.

Chapter 18

It takes me a moment to discern the pounding on the door from the pounding in my head. I pull myself out of bed and drag my sorry ass to the door. "What?"

Paige says from the other side, "You have a visitor." Her voice is oddly casual, especially considering how I left her last night.

"I'm not entertaining today. Tell them to go away."

"It's David," she says in a singsong voice.

Shit. Shit, shit, shit.

I change out of my clothes and into something nice—too nice. Then I change out of that outfit into something more relaxed but still flattering. Despite telling myself I don't care what other people think, there are times I do care and people I want to impress. Right now is one of those times, and Detective David Resnick is one of those people.

I jerk on the door. It doesn't budge. "Paige? It's still locked."

"I need to hear it," she replies.

Oh God, no.

"Is he out there?"

"Uh-huh."

"Please don't make me."

"Sorry," she says.

I sing as fast as I can.

"Cheer, cheer for old Notre Dame,
"Wake up the echoes, cheering her name."

Before I'm even finished, the hook scrapes out of its lock, and the door slides open. Paige offers an apologetic look. I ignore her and walk briskly past to find the young police detective sitting on the couch. The first thing I notice is David is wearing a new suit—a taupe two-button and a significant upgrade from his Kohl's collection. His thick hair is still unkempt, and his perpetual four-day-old beard could still use a shave, but he looks much more refined.

"What was that about?" he asks.

"Oh, it's an ongoing bet I lost." *Along with my dignity.*

As I move farther into the room, I notice another person near the kitchen—his partner, Detective Snyder. In his left hand, he holds a can of Coke, apparently his go-to source for caffeine. I offer him a nod. He offers back a grunt in greeting and grooms his moustache.

David rises from the couch and approaches me. I'm never sure how to greet him. *Should we shake hands? Should we hug? Should I jump into his arms and ask him to whisk me away?*

We shake hands.

"We were in the neighborhood and thought we could drop by." He looks me up and down, in the way guys do when they think they're being subtle but aren't. I feel both vindicated by my choice in outfits and self-conscious that I didn't have more time to get ready.

"This is some door," growls a voice behind me. Snyder plays with the pocket door, sliding it in and out of the brick wall that separates my room from the living room. The heavy oak makes a dull roar as it moves along its track.

"Yeah," I say, "a girl can never be too safe in this neighborhood."

He studies the iron latch that securely, and formidably, locks it into place. "The lock's on the outside." The hook clamps into place, offering a deep metallic clank.

"Well…" I start, exchanging a look with Paige as I struggle for a reasonable excuse.

Paige finishes. "Sometimes I need a little peace and quiet when she's acting up…?"

"And why would you be acting up?" Snyder asks.

"PMS," I reply.

And with that, Snyder concludes his questions. If there's one thing that stops men—even detectives—from asking questions, it's a woman's bodily functions. Satisfied, I take a seat on the couch, and Paige joins me.

"Sorry. I'm a little out of it this morning," I say while trying to tousle my hair.

"Rough night?" Snyder asks. There's no mistaking the stern tone.

This isn't going to be a friendly visit, and I'm now on the defensive. "I'm not a morning person," I say matter-of-factly.

"It's eleven in the morning, Darcy," David says, standing over me. "Hot date last night?" He smiles as if he's teasing me.

This is no tease. He's searching for answers to different questions and talking around the subject he's investigating—

which, chances are, has everything to do with what transpired last night in Harvard Park. I know this what he's trying to do because it's what I do.

Now I need to counter and to learn what he knows without giving anything away. I also need to know what Paige might have already told him. Everything counts on our keeping our stories straight. The last thing I want is to get caught in a lie and taken to police holding. Nothing good would come of locking me in a jail cell with a hundred other women with anger-management issues.

I don't answer his question. I ask my own. "What brings you here?"

"Can't I come by and say hello?"

"You're on the clock. Didn't think you'd have time while you're working."

"I was in the neighborhood."

I do my best to remain calm despite panicking on the inside. I decide to redirect the conversation. "Have you found any information about Lupe's killer?"

"Killer?" Snyder asks. He closes in on us—on me—and leans in. "Was there only one killer?"

"Was there more than one?" I ask.

"Do you know something?"

"Less than you, I'm sure, Detective."

Snyder steps away, clearly annoyed by my response.

"No updates," David says, shooting Snyder a glance. He turns back to me. "Sorry. We're still looking."

"Thanks. I appreciate your checking in." I hope that is the end of the conversation. I lean forward and get ready to stand, but David continues speaking.

"You hear about the house fire last night? Happened in Harvard Park 'bout eleven thirty." He's given me something, expecting I'll give something in return. I don't.

I sink back into the couch. We're going to be here a while. "Are you with the fire department now?"

"Were you out last night?"

"Are you suspecting me of arson?" I ask.

"Should I?"

"Do you have a reason to?"

Detective Snyder sighs in the corner, causing David to flinch. It's becoming clear that Snyder has, once again, extended David the courtesy of leading this interrogation—I mean, interview. As of now, Snyder is less than impressed, and his patience is waning.

"I might," David says, shifting gears again.

Shit. He has something.

My mind races, but I don't let him see. I run through the checklist from last night. *Did I remove all the evidence of my being there? Did I leave anything behind?* I can't keep up the act much longer. I need to cut to the chase.

"Why are you here, David?"

"Where were you last night?" The playful tone in his voice dissipates. He wants an answer.

Paige pipes in. "I told you, we were both here last night. Drinking wine and binge-watching *X-Files*."

It's sloppy but effective. I go with it. "I was here last night. Drinking wine and binge-watching *X-Files*."

"So I've heard," he responds, shooting Paige a warning look.

Snyder mutters something. I don't catch it, but it makes David uncomfortable.

I repeat my earlier question. "What brings you here?"

David pulls out his notepad. It's cute when he tries to act like a grownup around me. "I've got a witness who claims he saw someone last night who fits your description."

Shit. Stupid dog walker.

"My description? Beautiful, demure young woman with impeccable fashion sense?" I'm trying to keep up the breezy atmosphere. Even as the words escape my mouth, I can hear the desperation. This is not going well.

"Girl with yellow eyes."

I need to start wearing sunglasses more often. I smile for David. "Can't be too many of us in LA."

"No. Not too many."

"If you want to know if I'm going around setting house fires, the answer is no."

I know why he's here. He needs to say it.

"Not just fire. There were five bodies in the house. Fire department thinks it was intentional. That makes it a homicide."

Paige stiffens behind me. I don't look, but I hope she doesn't give anything away with her expression.

"I was here last night," I repeat, "drinking wine and binge-watching—"

"Jesus Christ," Snyder says.

My stomach growls loud enough for everyone to hear.

Snyder approaches and hovers over Paige and me. When he finally speaks, it's to me. "Five bodies! In a house that happened to be a meth lab." He extends the index finger of the hand holding the Coke right at me. "And a person matching your description leaving the scene."

David puts his notepad away and takes position behind Snyder. As the senior detective, Snyder has now taken over. David has to defer to the ranking officer.

"Now," Snyder continues, "if you want to answer our questions honestly and completely, we're happy to do that here. Keep dicking us around, and we'll do this at the station—maybe even put you in a lineup and see if someone can ID you at the scene."

I share a glance with Paige. If they put me in a lineup, this dog lover might have a pretty good chance of IDing me. David might also have evidence I don't even know about.

Paige repeats herself adamantly. "Like I said, we were here last night. Watching TV."

David paces behind Snyder, running his fingers through his hair in that way he does when he's debating.

"Fine," Snyder mutters. "Why don't we go to the station? Get your things."

I pipe up. "Not until I can arrange for my attorney to be present."

Snyder stops. David finally steps in and whispers into his ear. I can make out, "Can you give us a minute?"

He and Snyder have a silent exchange. The senior detective is clearly not happy about being asked to leave. Finally, he shakes his head and walks away. He slams the door closed behind him and disappears into the hall. David turns back to me and nods toward Paige.

"Okay, Darcy, can we talk privately?"

More than a little worried, I look at Paige.

"Actually," she says, "I'd prefer to stay."

David shoots me a look of dismay. "What the hell? I got my guy to leave."

"Fine," I relent. "Paige?"

"No."

"I tried."

Paige doesn't budge. We sit there looking at David, challenging his next move. His shoulders sag in defeat. He knows this isn't a fight he's going to win.

"Four of these guys we haven't ID'd, yet," David says. "We

know the place was a meth lab, so they probably weren't there to spread the good word. We did ID a Russian-mob kid. Sebastian Gallo, street dealer, arrested a handful of times going back to juvie. No one on the force is going to miss them. And no one on the force is going to work overtime to find out who did this one. But the bodies..." He hesitates. "They were in pretty bad condition. Aside from being burnt"—he looks at me—"they were mangled. Someone or something tore them up pretty bad."

He pauses and watches me. I can see him trying to make sense of what he saw and how I fit in. I can also feel Paige tightening up, putting two and two together about what happened last night.

"I know you were there last night. What the hell happened?" His voice betrays how desperate he is, not because he wants to know why but because he wants to know how.

I finally give him an honest answer. "I don't know what happened to them."

David shakes his head. "Fine, but I don't think they kidnapped Elizabeth Viramontes."

I have a pretty good poker face, but when David announces Elizabeth's name, my jaw drops.

"We know you're working for Carmen. We know you're looking for her daughter."

I have to give David credit. He's been slowly playing me the whole time with a pretty solid hand. With as much as he knows about the Viramontes case, I have no idea how much evidence he has on me regarding the arson.

And murder. Murders. I am so screwed.

"It's a missing-girl case. That's all," I offer.

"This one's not just a missing-girl case. How much do you know about the woman you work for? Who do you think this

Carmen Viramontes is?"

I hesitate. "Widow. Undocumented. Inherited the electronics chain from her husband, which is probably a front for her drug dealing."

I feel pretty confident at the moment. The fact that I've figured out she's a drug dealer gives me a free prize on my first spin. *Spin again to solve the puzzle.*

"You think she's just a drug dealer?" he says incredulously. *Lose a turn.*

"Her family runs one of the largest drug cartels in Mexico, the Galeana Cartel. They're worth nearly a billion dollars. And Carmen? Her husband used to be the chief distributor of cocaine, marijuana, and heroin in LA. And that electronics chain? That was her doing, her invention. They own a factory in Juarez, Mexico, and place the drugs in the electronics boxes they ship here directly. Once they receive the shipments, they remove the drugs for distribution and launder the hundreds of millions of dollars they take in each year through the chain. She's not just a drug dealer, Darcy. She's a drug lord."

Bankrupt.

The weight of all this sits in my stomach like a brick. She doesn't keep herself trapped in the house to avoid getting deported—it's probably because there's a bounty on her head from any number of rival cartels. And Hugo must be some sort of capo.

And Leona? Could she be the consigliere? Underboss? Bagman?

Paige sinks into the couch behind me, and David sits down near me. "She's dangerous, Darcy," he says. "A ruthless, manipulative, evil, and incredibly smart woman who won't let anything stand in her way. She's known as the Vibora Negra— the Black Viper. The LAPD is in a joint task force with the FBI and the DEA. No one in law enforcement has even set eyes on her—she stays in that compound twenty-four seven. We know who she is, we know what she's been doing, and we are putting together enough evidence to put her away for a long time. Just walk away before someone gets hurt—before someone *else* gets hurt."

I look up and meet his eyes. He seems sincerely worried about me. "How long have you been working on her case?" I ask.

"I'm not. Not anymore. When I was with GND, we busted up a small ring. Tried to connect her husband to it but failed. You know why? Carmen. She covered his tracks like you wouldn't believe."

And now he's with Homicide. I repeat this in my mind before I respond. "You're with Homicide now. How'd you know I was on the Viramontes case?"

"Word got back to me. Girl with the yellow eyes hanging out in Pasadena. Shows up again last night in Harvard Park. Not too many girls like that." He tries to play it off as casual. I admit, it gives me a warm, fuzzy feeling inside knowing someone is looking out for me.

"I don't need anyone looking out for me," I grumble. I don't know why I say it.

"Tough shit, Darcy. That's what I'm doing."

Swoon. "What about Elizabeth? She's still missing. Someone has to find her."

"It doesn't matter."

This pisses me off. "How you can say that? A girl is missing out there."

David retreats. "I'm not saying her life doesn't matter, but you've probably figured out by now she was taken by a rival cartel. She's being used. The most dangerous thing you could do is find her. Then you'll be in real trouble."

I think about Yury Yury and his threat. David has a point.

If I find Elizabeth, and people learn that I have her, then I'm in real trouble. Rival cartels are going to be hunting for me. "Do you know who has her?"

He shakes his head.

"Do you know how she's being used?" I can read the reaction in his face. He's hiding something. "What do you know?"

"It's out of your league, Darcy."

Out of my league? He doesn't even know about the death cult and the witches.

"That was a dumb move, going to that house alone," he adds after a moment of silence. I can tell he's getting frustrated because his New York accent reemerges and gets thicker. "I don't know what the hell happened there or how you got out of it, but this ends now. Drop the case. Back away."

He doesn't ask me to agree. We've known each other long enough for him to know how stubborn I am. Most men would attack me for my resolve. David respects me for it.

Before he reaches the door, I ask, "Am I under investigation by the LAPD for last night?"

David pauses then turns to me. "Five drug dealers from two different gangs were killed last night. That means two rival gangs have bounties out for the murderer. If the LAPD implicates you in their deaths, the last thing you need to worry about is getting arrested."

This is both an assurance and a warning. The LAPD is going to leave me alone for my own safety. Any gang looking for revenge is going to come after me if they find out the police believe I'm a suspect.

"There's only so much I can do," he adds. "There's already a lot of heat on you. The murder at the library. Last night's fire. The missing girl." He shakes his head. "I'm worried you may already be in more trouble than you even realize."

This, coming from a guy who doesn't know I have a literal demon hibernating inside me. I'm in a no-win situation.

David opens the door and joins his partner in the hallway. Snyder shoots him a look so intense that I can only imagine the admonishment he'll receive later. I know David is protecting me against his senior partner and possibly the rest of the force. Snyder turns to leave, and David trails behind him.

When I close the door, I can feel Paige's penetrating gaze behind me. I turn around to face my own chiding.

"What... happened?" she demands.

I spend half an hour explaining what transpired and the hour after that listening to Paige lecture me about my reckless and dangerous decisions—about how stupid I was to go out there alone... about putting myself in a situation where I lost control of Dudley... about not telling her what happened when I got home. She builds up so much momentum that she even yells at me about forgetting to pick her up from the airport last year.

As Paige's voice starts to get hoarse, she finally slows down and looks at me. Over the past sixty minutes I've slowly curled myself into a ball on the couch. I stare straight ahead, absorbing the slings and arrows with nary a snarky response.

"What?" she says.

I look up. With shame and fear, I utter the one thought I haven't been able to shake since last night. "I murdered someone, Paige."

The words taste like bile as I speak them—the final ugly admission of what I did. I committed an act that can never be forgiven and can never be undone. Ten years ago, I took my brother's life. Since then, I've managed to keep the demon inside me at bay. I've found ways to contain this evil—by confinement, by sedation, or by isolation. Until last night.

Paige sits next to me and takes my hand. "You're not a murderer."

"I killed them!"

"The demon killed them, not you. It's not your fault."

I shake my head. David and Paige were right—I shouldn't have gone to the hideout alone. This time, my reckless behavior had deadly consequences.

"It's my fault." The realization and nausea set in. "I took their lives."

"They would have taken yours," she says. "Darcy, these were not innocent people. You heard what David said about them. They were drug dealers. They were ready to kill you, probably because they've killed before. Maybe they planned to again. Dudley or no Dudley, you did the right thing protecting yourself."

I nod. Part of me feels relief hearing Paige say this. Her words echo the thoughts I wouldn't allow myself to believe. Self-defense is the only possible justification for what I did. I squeeze Paige's hand in thanks.

But even if my actions were justified this time, I am reminded about the deadly power I have in me. This is a power that once stole the life of someone who was innocent and whom I cared about very deeply. Now more than ever, I need to find Santa Muerte. I need to find my demon's name.

My head rests on Paige's shoulder, and I pull her hand to my chest, not wanting to let go. I need to get rid of this demon before I hurt someone I care about again.

Chapter 19

Today is the day I meet Ramon for our visit to the Fowler Museum for the Aztec exhibit. I need to talk to him about what happened in Harvard Park, and I have a favor to ask of him. The museum sits on the UCLA campus, tucked away among the grassy knolls that rise around it. Its tall redbrick walls and Italian arches lead up to the terra-cotta roof, a style that blends in seamlessly with the Romanesque architecture featured in the university's other structures.

Inside, Paige and I follow Father Ramon through the exhibit for Aztec artifacts. Since I no longer have my field jacket, I wear a long, thick overcoat. It's a little too formal for a trip to the museum. Paige says it's the nicest piece of clothing I own. She's not wrong.

For Father Ramon, this visit to the museum is an opportunity to search for more demon names. I'm here because I'm hoping to learn something more about Santa Muerte. From my meeting with Fiona and my wiki research, there's a lot suggesting her origins go back to the Aztec Empire.

The gallery is dimly lit, with spotlights directing visitors from room to room. Gold and silver jewelry dangles from wood carvings. Small statues hide under glass cases. Clay pots and other cookware show hints of everyday life in ancient Mesoamerica.

I find it difficult to fathom time—real time, like ages and epochs. History has become a hobby of mine as I've conducted my research into demonology. I've learned so much about the history of religions, the different cultures, and the people of all eras.

I must confess, in everything I've studied about religion, God, and this demon inside me, I've only grown more confused about the truth of heaven and hell, unsure which religion, if any, is right. Nearly every known religion recognizes the existence of demons. The Ancient Greeks, Sumerians, Egyptians, Buddhists, Hindus, and those who practice Abrahamic religions have not only confirmed the existence of demons but have identified many by name as well. They may not all agree on the definition of good and who God is, but they all believe in and fear the same evil.

Then there's Quetzalcoatl. In front of me is a large statue of the serpent god worshipped by the Aztecs. It's a simple dark-gray stone carving that resembles a coiled snake with a masked man emerging from its mouth. The story of Quetzalcoatl carries a lot of similarities to the Christ story. The bringer of bread sacrificed his life for mankind. He was resurrected, destined to return to his people after death.

"Darcy," Paige calls, bringing my wandering thoughts back to Earth. "Check this out." As I approach, she points at a glass case in which a giant headdress sits on a mannequin's featureless head. From the gold crown explode hundreds of colorful feathers—blue, purple, red, and green. Paige reads the museum description. "When the conquistadors arrived, they discovered the Aztecs possessed an excess of gold and silver. Though it was often used for jewelry and decoration, what the Aztecs truly prized were colorful feathers. This was more valuable than their gold and silver, which they willingly gifted to the Spanish visitors."

"Gifted?" I say suspiciously. If there's anything I remember from my world history class in the tenth grade, it's that the Spanish took what they wanted from the Aztecs.

I look at another stone carving nearby. This one is clearly of a woman wearing a crown of skulls. Her face is also depicted to look like a skull.

I grab Paige and drag her close. "Look," I say, pointing. If I didn't know better, I would say this is Our Lady of the Holy Death—Santa Muerte herself.

Father Ramon joins us and reads the museum label out loud. "Mictecacihuatl," he says, perfectly pronouncing a name that looks like someone took a nap on a keyboard.

I give it a shot. "Mic-tika-waka."

"Meek-tay-kah-see-wah-tl," he repeats.

"Meek-tay-kah…"

"See-wah…"

"See-wah…"

"Tl. Meek-tay-kah-see-wah-tl."

"Meek-tay-kah-see-wah-tl." I finally get it right.

"Lady of Death," Father Ramon reads from the label. "In Aztec mythology, Mictecacihuatl was the ruler of the underworld. Her role is to watch over the bones of the dead. She still presides over some festivals celebrating Dia de los Muertos—the Day of the Dead." He shakes his head and walks away.

"I don't think he's a fan," Paige says.

The Santa Muerte cult represents itself as a Christian

church, despite being officially condemned by the Vatican. It's no wonder Father Ramon is quick to dismiss anything related to Santa Muerte. This one is personal.

"What do you think?" Paige asks, looking back at the display.

I follow her gaze. My curiosity is piqued. "There could be something to this."

I'm talking not just about Santa Muerte but about my own personal situation as well. Maybe Dudley's identity has roots in Aztec culture. Maybe that's how and why Santa Muerte recognized the demon in me. Maybe this case is leading me down a path for a reason.

I shudder at the thought of having to endure yet another unsuccessful exorcism. I cannot describe how painful an exorcism attempt is. It's a searing, tearing agony that courses through every inch of my body, like I'm peeling all my skin off then taking a bath in isopropyl alcohol… that's been lit on fire.

As we continue our stroll through the museum, I learn more and more about the Aztecs. They did not believe their many gods were evil. They were strict and demanding gods, yes, but not evil. After the conquest by Spain, however, many priests would characterize some of those earlier gods as actual demons.

The final relic we encounter is a replica of the Aztec sun stone, carved into a circular rock face. It's twelve feet wide, with ornate symbols in concentric rings. In the center is an angry god holding a human heart in each of his hands. Human sacrifice was part of their culture, but the act of removing the human heart reminds me of Santa Muerte—and of Lupe. *Poor Lupe.*

Ramon walks Paige and me out and offers to drive us to my car. I'm quiet, hoping he'll pick up on the fact that there's something I want to discuss. As we approach his white Prius, I ask Paige to give us a moment. She knows what I'm about to ask, so she goes for a short walk to give us space.

I take a seat in the passenger side of his car. We're alone in the concrete parking structure south of Sunset Boulevard. I can hear the din of traffic racing past in spurts.

"What is it?" he asks.

It's difficult to spit out. Finally I say, "I need reconciliation."

Ramon is taken aback. "You want to confess? You've never wanted to confess before. What happened?"

I take a deep breath, then I start talking. I tell him about the case, about Carmen and her drug empire, about Lupe's murder, and about Santa Muerte.

♒

Ramon sinks into the driver's seat, trying to absorb everything I've just told him. He blesses himself, and I struggle to contain my internal revulsion at this act. Dudley tends to cause some minor discomfort whenever I'm near Father Ramon, which I've learned to endure. But when he says or does things—whether out of instinct or habit—that are innately religious, Dudley can cause serious pain.

"I never should have involved you in this case," he says. "I didn't realize where it would lead. So much darkness and evil."

"Well," I begin, reluctant to mention why I'm sharing this with him. "I haven't gotten to the worst part yet."

His face falls. "What's worse than that?"

Then I tell him about the meth lab. About how I found Sebastian. What they tried to do to me. And what I did to them.

I can tell Ramon is struggling to find the words to talk with me. He's usually forthright, but this time he is deliberate. "You have sinned, Darcy."

"It wasn't me," I say, shaking my head. "It was the demon."

Ramon shakes his head. "I'm not so sure."

I'm taken aback. "You think I wanted to kill them?"

"This entity inside you doesn't merely emerge and cause destruction then retreat. This demon wants you dead so it can bring you back to hell with it. Why would it emerge to save you from getting killed?"

I'll be honest—I've asked myself this question before. I've never come up with an answer I liked. Maybe I'm about to find out why.

Ramon continues. "The demon does not have power over your body whenever it wants. It only appears at times when you lose control of your inhibitions—when you *let* your emotions get the best of you."

He takes a deep breath. "This demon didn't use your body to kill those people. You willingly harnessed the demon's power."

I struggle with this notion. I don't want to admit I committed a murder. *Then again, why else would I feel such guilt?*

"How do I control this demon?" I ask.

"You can't. The question is, how do you control yourself?"

I am the first person to admit I'm my own worst enemy. Self-discipline is not exactly one of my shining attributes. I think about the consequences of what I've done. Dudley has given me the power to commit a sin, one that could damn me to hell. Even if I exorcise him from my body, I'm now guilty of a mortal sin— murder. *And the punishment for that is damnation... right?*

For now, there's only one thing I can do. I look at Ramon. "I need to make my confession."

His eyes widen in shock. "Are you sure? You're asking me to bless you. You remember what this feels like."

I nod. He's done it once before. Dudley does not like to be blessed, and he lets me know in the most excruciating way possible.

He starts his car, and we drive out to the entrance to pick up Paige. I direct Father Ramon to an old fire road in the hills where we'll have some isolation. We make our way as far as you can get from civilization and still be within the Greater Los Angeles Area. Once we park, I can tell Paige is worried. She came all this way to protect me, and here I am, putting myself through another ordeal.

I turn from the front seat and look at her in the back. "I need you to go for a walk."

She shakes her head, confused but resolved. "No. I'm staying." There's a reason why she wanted to come. After everything that's happened in the past few days, she doesn't want to leave me alone.

Father Ramon opens his driver's-side door then addresses Paige. "Paige, may I speak with you?"

Reluctantly, she exits the car. In the passenger's-side mirror, I can see them talking at the rear of the car. I can't hear what they're saying, but from the shaking of her head, I know she's reluctant to leave.

It's hard to say no to Ramon. He has a calm, reassuring voice—a voice of certainty and reason that's difficult to contest. It's what makes him a good priest and an excellent exorcist. Father Ramon has attempted five exorcisms on me and conducted three confessions, and not once has he let Dudley take control of me. Though we have been unsuccessful in expelling the demon from my body, Ramon is the only priest who's been able to keep it in check. I trust Paige with my life, but I trust Father Ramon with my soul.

Whatever he says makes its way through to her. She turns and starts hiking up the dirt road. The rear hatch opens, and Ramon starts digging around. We're actually going to do this.

I wrap the lap belt around both my wrists then pull until

the safety lock engages. My heart is racing, anticipating what's going to come next. I hope it stays under one hundred ninety beats per minute.

The rear hatch slams shut. Ramon's footsteps crunch on the dirt road as he makes his way to the passenger side. I take deep, measured breaths to stay calm—a little trick I learned watching Lamaze videos on YouTube.

The door opens. Ramon has a bible in his hand and his purple stole wrapped around his shoulders.

"Oh shit," I mutter, unable to control myself. My body tenses from anxiety, trying to steel itself for the experience.

Ramon grabs my seat and pulls it forward, further tightening the belt. "Ready?"

"Yes." I shake my head. *Nope.*

He crosses himself, and my stomach twists like the worst cramps I've ever had.

"In nomine Patris et Filii et Spiritus Sancti…"

He's doing it in Latin. *Shit.*

I scream. It's so loud my throat strains and cracks. My body writhes in the confines of the seat belt, twisting and turning. I close my eyes, trying to block out the pain.

Father Ramon presses his hand firmly on my chest. It burns as if it's searing my flesh. The overwhelming pressure keeps me trapped in my seat. The pain courses through me, but I'm unable to move from beneath his grasp.

The alarm on my watch goes off. My heart rate is now over one hundred sixty BPM. This is par for the course, and I know Father Ramon will be able to keep Dudley at bay. He always has.

"Deus meus, ex toto corde pænitet

"Me omnium meorum peccatorum
"Eaque detestor, quia peccando."

An inhuman wail escapes my lips. It's agonizing, and I scream the whole time. The taste of blood pools on my tongue.

"Non solum pœnas a te
"Juste statutas promeritus sum."

I keep screaming. How Father Ramon manages to keep performing the prayer is a mystery, because I scream for a solid five minutes, and I don't stop until he says his final "Amen." Then I pass out.

⌢

It's dark when I wake up. I look at my alarm clock to see it's 3:33 a.m. *Perfect.*

I don't remember what happened after the confession. I don't remember how I got home or how I got into bed. Knowing Paige, she probably drove me home, threw me over her shoulder like a lumberjack, carried me upstairs, and tossed me into bed.

My muscles ache, and my throat is sore, probably from all the screaming. On a lark, I sit up and look at my nightstand. Sitting there are a full glass of water and two aspirin.

Thank you, Paige. I take the aspirin, drink the water, and go back to sleep.

Chapter 20

Lupe's funeral is at the Westwood Memorial Cemetery. It's a strange little burial ground, small and unassuming, just a patch of green grass surrounded by skyscrapers amid the Wilshire Corridor. That suits me just fine. I stand on the roof of a nearby parking structure with a bird's-eye view of the ceremony. I want to be here, but since I'm unable to stand on cemetery grounds, this is the closest I can get. Out of respect, I wear my best outfit—a black pantsuit with my thick wool overcoat and pumps.

It's an intimate ceremony with maybe thirty people in attendance. I recognize a few coworkers as well as Paige, who's wearing a modest black flare dress. Lupe's son stands at the head of the casket, saying a few words that I can't hear.

I scan the rest of the cemetery. David Resnick and Ed Snyder stand a respectful distance away. Once again, Snyder is clutching his daily can of sugar and caffeine. For a change, both are wearing black suits. I can't help but notice this is yet another new suit for David. Maybe Ed finally convinced him to update his wardrobe.

They stand near David's blue Dodge Charger, his police-issued cruiser. That means they're here on official business. It could also mean they're looking for me.

The services conclude, and the attendees slowly make their way past Lupe's son to offer final condolences. As the people head back to their cars, David intercepts Paige. They exchange a few words, marked mostly by Paige shaking her head.

Finally, she moves past him. When no one else is around, it looks like Snyder starts reprimanding David, who takes it on the chin, nodding and listening. Snyder ducks into the passenger side of the car and disappears. David does a quick check of the area—no one is around, so I'm the only one who sees him flip off Snyder before he slips into the driver's side.

I head down the stairwell to my car on level three. The last of the other guests' cars are pulling away when I hear the click of Paige's heels echoing in the stairwell. She rises from up the steps and approaches my car.

"What did David want?" I ask.

"He wanted to make sure we weren't still looking for Elizabeth."

"What did you tell him?"

"I pleaded the fifth."

I laugh and open the driver's-side door. "And what did he say to that?"

She opens her door. "That I've been spending too much time with you."

In that lighthearted moment, when I feel calm and safe for just a second, everything changes. An arm comes out of nowhere and wraps around Paige's throat. A gun is pointed at her head.

"Paige!" I cry out instinctively.

She screams and struggles, but her assailant presses the muzzle of his gun harder against her temple to quiet her. Yury Vilonov issues his order. "Quiet."

Paige complies and stops struggling.

Yury is a very different man from the last time I saw him. He's panic-stricken and nervous, and his clothes are disheveled and dirty. New scars and bruises mark his face. It looks like he hasn't slept in days.

He points his gun at me, and my hands go up. "You, come here!" he says.

I follow his orders and step around the car. "Whatever you say, Yury," I say in the best soothing voice I can muster. "You're in control."

He looks around the parking structure to make sure we're alone. The gun swings from pointing at me to pointing at Paige to pointing at the air. There's no one here.

"Yury?" I ask, bringing him to the present. "You want to tell me what's going on?"

He points the gun back at me, which is not what I wanted. "They're dead."

"Dead?" I ask. "Who's dead?"

"Everyone. All of them. Even Borz."

"Borz?"

He shakes his gun at me. "You know Borz. You met Borz. Borz!"

"Right!" I say, realizing Muscle's name was probably Borz. "Borz. Great guy, Borz. Right, Paige?"

Paige nods as best she can under Yury's grip. "Yeah. Borz."

"Dead!" he repeats.

"What happened?" I ask.

A car drives by in the distance, its radio blaring. The booming bass must freak Yury out, because he swings his gun wildly.

"Yury! It was just a car." I move into his line of vision. "Come back to me," I say, trying to get him to focus on me and only me. "Tell me what happened."

Even though he's looking right at me, it takes him a minute to focus. "It was *d'yavol*," he says. "A devil."

Okay. I move a step back, and he keeps the gun aimed at me. Paige's eyes widen in fear.

"I saw it," he says. "I saw it kill them all." I keep moving, but the gun stays pointed at me. "We shot it, but it did nothing. It tore my men to pieces like a wild animal. I escaped."

Dread fills my entire body.

"I ran away, like child," he continues. "Last night was worst night of my life."

"Last night?" I ask.

He nods. "*Da*. Last night."

I relax just a bit. It wasn't me.

As I let a breath out, Yury cocks his gun. "You don't believe!"

"No!" I shout, recoiling. "I believe! I believe!"

Paige panics. "She believes! She believes!"

Convinced he's not going to shoot me at that moment, I ask, "What did it look like?"

"It was horrible. It had robes like… like death. A skull for a face. Claws for hands. It… it ripped their hearts right out."

I nod. "It was a woman, wasn't it? A demon dressed in the robes of a woman?"

An expression of relief washes over Yury's face. Someone believes him. He's not going crazy. "You see her? You know too?" He lowers his gun.

He releases Paige. She runs over to me, and we maneuver ourselves behind my Mini. Suddenly, I wish I had a car larger than a lunch box—something we could hide behind.

Yury points the pistol in the direction of the cemetery. "Your friend? Her heart was torn out?"

I nod. "Yes. It was terrible."

"Did you see it? The creature?"

"Yes. I've seen the creature."

Tears well up in his eyes. He rubs the gun against his face, wiping the tears away. "I knew you would know. I knew. This is Sebastian's fault, right? You know Sebastian. He was in cult."

He charges toward us. Paige and I jockey for position, each one trying to shield the other for what comes next. As he nears, we cringe in anticipation of a bullet. Instead, he pulls a wad of cash from his jacket pocket.

"Here. Here is money. Find me Sebastian." He shoves the money into my hands. "Sebastian was in cult, and this is his fault. Find him and bring him to me."

I look at the cash in my hand. It's no small sum. The amount that would make life just a little bit easier.

I press the money back into his hands. "Sebastian's dead."

Yury looks at me then at the money. He shoves the cash into his coat pocket then turns and walks away. Paige and I stay behind the car, ready to run and hide.

Yury stops and turns back to us. "It's over, then. You cannot stop the evil once it decides it wants you." He walks down the ramp and disappears around a corner.

Chapter 21

Paige and I stand quietly as the elevator from the underground parking structure slowly rises to our fifth-floor loft. My pumps were killing me, so I took them off, and now Paige towers above me. She already has a couple of inches on me, but since she still has her heels on I feel especially diminutive. We've barely said a word since our interaction with Yury Yury.

The elevator doors open. Paige and I emerge into our empty hallway. The concrete is cold against my bare feet, but it's only a few yards until we get to our unit.

"So Santa Muerte is out there, killing other people?" Paige asks.

"She took out Yury's gang. Who knows if there's been anyone else."

"He didn't mention the old woman."

"No."

As we approach our unit, I notice light streaming out of our living room into the hall. The front door is open. *Did we forget to close it this morning?* A moment later, a lean figure emerges wearing a gray trench coat and a fedora.

My initial suspicion is that this is some assailant ready to kill us. When the figure spins and pulls a pistol, my first reaction isn't to run. My first reaction is to say to myself, *I was right?*

Paige pulls me into an adjacent hall as two shots ring out. One bullet clips the corner near my head. Paige shoots me a look of alarm and frustration. "Run!" she shouts.

I drop my shoes, and we sprint down the hall. The hard sound of Paige's heels as she runs is echoed by a similar clacking made by our attacker. My back is turned, so I pray we can make it around the corner before the next gunshot.

We whip around the corner as two more shots ring out. My focus shifts to Paige, and in that moment, my only concern is that she is okay. Judging by the speed and determination of her running, she seems fine. *Thank God*, I think, despite the discomfort that causes. I don't care—I need to make sure she makes it out of here okay. I stay on her six as we sprint down the hall, keeping myself positioned between her and our assailant.

Through my panting breaths, I yell the only plan I can think of. "Fire escape!"

We turn another corner and come to the frosted-glass window, which, of course, is closed. Paige slows down, and I overtake her. In a full-bore sprint, I jump, tuck my knees under my chin, and cannonball my way through the glass.

The shards claw at my wool overcoat and my skin as a hundred tiny fragments explode around me. I ribcage it against the iron railing, which stops me from falling the remaining five floors to the ground. My bare feet plant on the grating of the fire escape, painfully digging into the sharp metal.

I struggle to stand as Paige jumps through the now-open window. When she lands, her high heels immediately get caught in the metal grid. She kicks off her shoes and grabs me by the arm to drag me toward the ladder as another gunshot pierces the unbroken glass in the window. He's getting closer.

We're in the alley behind our building, with no cars or people in sight. Paige leads as I follow her down the series of zigzagging steps, and we make our way down as fast as we can. We slide, run, and climb—barefoot—as fast as we can down the fire escape. I ignore the pain as the metal tread from every step cuts into the soles of my feet. I wonder how Paige can move with such speed and grace with no shoes and a calf-length dress. Then I realize she's hiked up her skirt enough to stretch her stride, and I also remember how calloused her runner's feet are. When you run the equivalent of a marathon every three days, your feet can take a beating.

We make it two flights before our attacker appears above and takes aim. I risk looking up to see if I can get a glimpse of his face through the iron grate that separates us. I don't see the face, but—

A muzzle flash distracts me. I duck on instinct as if that that would do any good. The bullet bounces off the iron grating. A loud, sharp ding reverberates as the bullet ricochets in another direction.

My attention shifts to Paige. *Is she okay?*

She doesn't slow down. I see no impact wound. The momentary relief dissipates as I realize we're nowhere near safety.

We keep going down as fast as we can without stopping. The farther down we go, the more iron separates us from the shooter.

Two more shots. Bullets zing in every other direction but ours. Paige is still okay.

He stops shooting. I glance up and see our assailant climbing down after us. *One more flight to go.*

Instead of taking the ladder the remainder of the way, Paige launches herself over the rail and free-falls the last ten feet. Her feet plant on the ground, and she rolls onto her shoulder to absorb the impact.

Then she stands there, waiting for me to catch up. She's a clear target, so I do what she did to catch up, but I totally biff the landing, pain shooting through my bare feet and my shins. I stumble forward into the street.

"Come on!" Paige shouts, still standing on the sidewalk.

I sprint for her, pushing her toward safety. I position myself behind her as we run as fast as we can across the street. Another gunshot explodes. My eyes are on Paige to make sure she's okay.

Bam! A searing pain punctures my shoulder. It knocks me off balance and onto all fours. Blood splatters onto the pavement before me—my blood.

For a moment, I'm frozen in shock. A fiery agony burns in my shoulder followed by a dull ache. *Holy shit. I've just been shot.*

Paige drags me to my feet and pulls me to a doorway across the alley. "Run!"

Another gunshot. This one misses us both. We fling ourselves through the open back door of a local business. I land on hard linoleum, and Paige smacks her head against a wall trying to catch me. We find ourselves on the floor in the kitchen of a local bar. A busboy yells at us, but Paige pulls me up and pushes me past him.

The pain intensifies. Adrenaline pumps through my blood. The electrocardiogram on my watch goes off—heart rate is rising. My brain is activating every chemical in my system to nullify the pain and keep me moving.

Everything whirls around me. I'm starting to lose my perception of what is happening and, with that, my control. On top of the panic of being chased and shot and keeping Paige from getting hurt, I'm now worrying about Dudley.

We barge through the kitchen and emerge in the lounge. It's dark and noisy—probably happy hour. There are way too many innocent bystanders for my comfort. Paige doesn't miss a beat and drags me to the bathroom as I keep my head down. I can hear her utter some expletives at what I assume is a line of women waiting to get in.

We burst through the door, and I stumble across the cold floor. The next thing I know, I'm sitting on a toilet in a stall with Paige standing in front of me. She checks my watch to read my heart rate.

"Oh... fuck!"

That's not good.

She tosses my wrist aside then digs through the pockets of my overcoat. She pulls out the Xanax and shoves a handful of pills in my mouth, which feels cottony. I chomp down. The tablets dissolve under my tongue.

"Breathe. Swallow. Breathe," she says in soothing tones. It's good advice, but I'm distracted by the pills. They taste funny. Different. And it takes me a moment to realize that Paige's hands are covered in blood.

"Are you okay?" I grab her hands, inspecting them.

"I'm fine! You're the one who's shot."

Thank God.

It hurts all over. I lower my head again and finally notice my feet. Bloody footprints lead from outside the bathroom right up to me. As I sit, a small pool of blood is forming under me. From my feet. From my shoulder.

My head is spinning. My heart is racing. This could be very, very bad.

I try holding my head as if that could stop the dizzying effect. My right arm dangles limply at my side, and when I try to lift it, nothing happens. *Why won't my arm move?*

"Do you want me to call 911?" a woman's voice asks.

"No!" Paige calls then calmly adds, "We're fine." She turns back to me, reconsidering. "Do you want me to call 911?"

I shake my head, still trying to breathe and calm myself down. If Dudley emerges at a hospital, it could be worse. I don't want to do anything but focus on calming myself down.

I pull out my phone and say two words. "Father Ramon."

Paige searches through my phone. "Okay, I'll call him. Stay calm." She opens my coat with her free hand. "Jesus, Darcy. You're bleeding a lot."

"Yeah. And my arm doesn't work anymore."

Paige looks down at my limp arm. "Shit!"

She backs away and disappears from my view while I stay in the stall. "Father Ramon? It's Paige." My eyes start to close, and I listen to the conversation. "She's been shot, and I need— yes. Where? You sure? We can be there in fifteen minutes."

Bam! A loud bang rings out in the bathroom. My eyes open wide. I'm worried it's a gunshot. I hear it two more times—a sound like someone is hitting a metal object. With one more bang, a metal plate clatters on the floor and slides to where I can see it, along with a dozen other small white objects.

Paige crawls into view and picks up a fistful of pads. She pulls open my coat, opens my blouse, and applies pressure to my shoulder. I howl in pain. My good arm swings, and I slap the stall divider. The metal crumples under my palm, collapsing into a misshapen dent. A woman screams from the other side, and a toilet flushes.

Paige jumps back, a look of panic on her face. I know what she thinks this means. She thinks Dudley's coming.

"I'm fine," I mutter, trying to take deep breaths. This doesn't feel like a normal episode. Something is different.

She looks at me, not quite satisfied.

"Cheer, cheer for old Notre Dame," I mutter through gritted teeth.

"I'm getting us a car," she says. "Just try to stay calm. Go to your happy place." She taps on her phone, opening a rideshare app.

I start thinking about what Ramon said. It's not Dudley—it's me. I try to find something to focus on to stay calm. To stay in control. Kittens. Blue skies. Long walks on the beach. Ben & Jerry's. Four milligrams of Xanax with an old-fashioned chaser. David.

David?

I have no idea why his name pops in my head, but I go with it. David sitting on my couch. David with his buttoned shirt tucked into his stupid jeans and his half-tied tie. David and I walking on the beach. Under blue skies. With Ben & Jerry's. And kittens.

"Darcy…?" Paige's voice is a muffled whisper in the distance.

I sit on the toilet while a gaggle of aspiring trophy wives stare at me, and I bleed from a gunshot wound into a wad of tampons, chewing on a fistful of benzodiazepines, dreaming about David, hoping a demon doesn't emerge to kill everyone in sight.

I realize there's now a hole in the collar of my coat. And it's got blood all over it. I poke my finger in it and wonder which brand of stain fighter might help and whether I should sew or patch up the hole. On top of being shot, I'm now mad about the one outfit I own that Paige actually likes. If only my high school guidance counselor could see me now.

"Darcy?"

"Hello?" My head wobbles. I feel drunk.

"Darcy!" shouts Paige. I focus for only a second before my head droops. "Jesus you've lost a lot of blood. Darcy!" I snap out of it and look at her. "Car's here."

She hoists me up and wraps my good arm around her. We stumble out of the stall. I'm woozy, but I can make out the faint shapes that stare at us as we make our way to the dining room. *This is so embarrassing.*

When we get outside, I'm surprised at how dark it is. I've lost all sense of time. *How long were we in there?*

She opens the rear door and dumps me into a silver Prius. *Why does everyone have a Prius?*

I can't keep my eyes open, but I hear the driver ask, "Holy shit, is she all right?"

"Just drive!" Paige tells him.

My cheek rests against the cool glass as the driver zips through the streets of Downtown Los Angeles. I look up and stare at the concrete towers with their tiny rectangles of illuminated windows converging into points in the sky. I close my eyes.

I'll just rest for a minute.

Chapter 22

I have no idea where I am. The pungent odor of menthol burns my sinuses. When my vision comes into focus, I find myself in a small beige room. A few small windows near the ceiling indicate that it's night outside.

My head rolls to the side. I'm lying on an uncomfortable narrow bed with metal rails boxing me in on both sides. My left arm is connected to an IV line, which is connected to a clear saline bag hanging from a stand.

In a chair beside my bed sits an elderly woman crocheting black fabric. She must be in her eighties. Her gray hair is tied back in a ponytail. She's wearing sweatpants and an exercise hoodie.

"Paige?"

The old woman looks up and smiles. "How are you feeling, sweetie?"

"I'm so confused."

She holds up her project—a black mesh vest. "What do you think? It's for my grandson." She leans in to whisper. "He lives in West Hollywood, if you get my meaning."

"Okay... where am I?"

With great effort, the woman rises from her chair and collects her materials. "I'll get the doctor for you." She shuffles to the door and covers the ten feet in just a few short minutes. Her arthritic hands open the door, and she steps in a hallway. "She's awake!" she screams then shuffles away.

Paige rushes into the room, sliding to a halt just inches from my bed. She's dressed in light-blue nurse scrubs with white rubber clogs.

"You're a nurse?" I ask, still a bit loopy and trying to get a handle on things.

Paige looks at me, relief overtaking her. Her eyes well up. Then she smacks me. "God damn it, Darcy! You scared the shit out of me!"

"Geez, sorry."

I try to lean up and feel a dull pain in my shoulder. My arm sits in a sling, with a bandage that wraps around my chest. A red stain blossoms through the gauze that covers my gunshot wound. Instead of my pantsuit, I'm wearing teal nurse scrubs. My feet are bandaged, and I can only imagine how torn up my soles are from running down the fire escape.

"Okay, where am I?"

"Hollydale Homes," the doctor says as he walks in.

He's African American, probably in his sixties, with a thick white beard that frames his cheerful smile. He peers at me through square-framed spectacles that perch on his nose. Father Ramon trails behind him and stands at the door.

"Hollydale Homes?" I repeat. The name is familiar. It's a nursing home in Silver Lake and was in the news recently for... something I can't quite remember. My memory is usually reliable, so this is going to bug me.

"That's right," the doctor says, pulling up a stool and taking a seat at my bedside. It's not uncommon for nursing homes to have a medical staff on premises full-time.

"Darcy, this is Dr. Savell," Father Ramon says. "He's the only doctor I could trust and who I knew would be available at this hour."

That's smart thinking on Father Ramon's part. Bringing me here was a lot safer than taking me to a crowded hospital.

Dr. Savell maneuvers my injured arm, rotating it through the normal movements. "You're lucky. There are a lot of joints and bones in this region."

"It's doesn't hurt that bad," I say, proud of my toughness.

"That's probably the morphine," he says, peering over his glasses.

When he tweaks my arm a bit too far, I flinch, pulling it back. He ignores my discomfort and grabs my hand. "That's odd," he says as he continues to articulate the entirety of my arm, hand, and fingers.

"What's odd?"

Not answering, he removes the IV from my arm. With practiced care and experience, he bandages the puncture. Then he pulls out a blood-pressure gauge and stethoscope. The cuff inflates around my arm and takes the reading. I glance at Paige, who watches with a worried expression. Dr. Savell removes the stethoscope and leans back with a discouraged look.

"What's wrong?"

His eyes stay low as if he's pondering his own diagnosis. "Nothing," he says, sounding mildly shocked. "And that's what's so peculiar. You were shot in the shoulder, and when you came in, I was sure you had suffered nerve damage. But now it seems you didn't. You lost a lot of blood, so your pressure should be low. But it's normal." Finally, he looks up at me. "Is this because of the demon?"

I look at Father Ramon. "We can trust him," he says.

Dr. Savell smiles. "I've been helping Father Ramon for—what? Five years now? I've treated many of the people he's cured." He looks me over. "But I've never seen anyone like you before." From his coat pocket, he pulls out an ophthalmoscope. "May I?"

I nod, and he proceeds to examine my eyes. "Very, very interesting." His process is analytical. Direct. Fearless. "So it's still in there?"

"Yes."

"Have you always been able to heal this quickly?"

I exchange a look with Paige. She sits next to me and takes hold of my hand. She squeezes mine gently as if to reassure me.

I finally answer. "I think I noticed it the first time about a year ago. I was biking to work when my foot slipped off my pedal and smashed into my leg. It tore a gash right into my shin. By the time I got to work, I had blood dripping all the way down into my boot. It was deep. I thought for sure it was going to scar. It didn't."

"How long did it take to heal?" Dr. Savell asks.

"It was gone the next day. No scar."

"It's been ten years, Dr. Savell," Paige says, taking over. "Ten years, and she's not any closer to getting rid of this… demon… than she was when it first possessed her. Over the years, little by little, it's taking more and more control of her body. She's getting colder even on warmer days. The attacks happen more frequently." As Paige speaks, I cast a guilty look at Father Ramon. "Twice in the past month. And now it's healing her body."

Dr. Savell turns to me. Despite my best efforts to remain impassive and indifferent, there's no stopping the tears welling up in my eyes. My stupid ugly yellow eyes.

"She's afraid of what this means," Paige continues then turns to Father Ramon. "I know you've been trying to help her—we all have. But she's afraid this means it's here to stay."

And there it is—the bitter, cold truth. The dread I've only revealed to my best friend. The thing I'm afraid to speak of for fear of making it real.

"That's why we need to find..." She glances cautiously at Dr. Savell. "This name, no matter what. No matter where."

Father Ramon steps forward. "I'm sorry, Darcy. I didn't realize."

I try to offer a reassuring smile. "I have to find Santa Muerte."

Father Ramon shakes his head. "It's too dangerous. You don't know what this might do to you. There are other ways to find the name."

I place my hand over my chest. Where my heart is. Where Dudley lives. "I don't know what *this* will do to me if I can't get rid of it soon."

Dr. Savell rises, breaking the tension in the room. He pulls a bottle of pills off a shelf. "Pain killers," he says, handing it to me.

"Codeine? Oxycodone?" I wipe my eyes, trying to rein in the emotional moment with humor.

"Tylenol."

I pocket the pills and mutter, "Thanks."

"You said you've had two recent episodes? How are you managing them?"

"Um, Xanax and Klonopin."

"Uh-huh," he mutters. "Prescription?"

I shrug guiltily. "I know a guy."

He grimaces and pulls out a pen and prescription pad. "Dosage?"

"Half a mill of the Klonopin twice a day. Six for the Xanax to mitigate the episode."

He scribbles on the pad then tears off two sheets for me. "Congratulations. You're now my patient."

When I stand, the pain in my feet reminds me that I'm not entirely healed. Since I dumped my footwear during this evening's earlier chase, Dr. Savell provides me with a pair of the ugliest shoes I have ever seen—Crocs, men's size ten to accommodate the bandages wrapped around my feet. With our prior outfits either covered in blood or full of bullet holes, Paige and I are stuck wearing the nurse scrubs. And since I'm freezing, Dr. Savell digs up an old hoodie with the logo of a men's erectile-dysfunction medication printed on the breast—a gift from a pharmaceutical rep.

Now I remember why I've heard of Hollydale Homes. The local news featured this facility as it was covering a report on the surge of STDs in nursing homes. This city is so weird.

Dr. Savell escorts us through the halls of Hollydale. The building is Spanish Colonial, with various apartments and activity rooms throughout. When we walk outside, I get a sense of its large scale. The complex is perched on the side of the main hill that rises above Silver Lake.

"Now that you're my patient," Dr. Savell says before we leave, "if you need anything, please call me." He pulls out a business card and hands it to me. When I try to take it, he holds fast. "I mean it. I don't care if it's medical, paranormal, both, or neither. You call me."

I take the card, feeling admonished but also relieved to have someone else in my corner. When Dr. Savell leaves, Father Ramon turns to us and takes a moment to look at my wounded arm in its sling.

"I'm so sorry," he says, shaking his head. "Why didn't you

tell me about the demon?"

"You've already done so much for me," I say. "I didn't want you to worry about me."

"I'm worried about you even more now." He chuckles in mild exasperation. "I don't want you working on this case for Carmen anymore or chasing after Santa Muerte. I want you to promise me."

I don't say anything.

"Promise me, Darcy. Promise me this, and I promise you that we will find this demon's name." He locks me in his gaze, and I can't look away.

I roll my eyes. "Fine."

"You promise?"

"Yes," I say impatiently. "I promise."

"Okay. Now, remember, I'm a priest. A promise to me is a promise to God."

"I know."

Father Ramon seems satisfied. He offers us a ride home, but we decline. Paige pulls out her phone and calls for a rideshare. We say goodbye to Father Ramon, and I make another promise to visit him soon so we can resume the search for Dudley's true name.

As we watch him drive away, Paige asks me, "Did you just lie to a priest?"

"Yep."

"You are so going to hell," she says then winces in regret. "Sorry. I didn't mean that literally."

On any other occasion, I might actually take that personally, but not tonight. I have other things on my mind. As our rideshare pulls up in a Ford Escape, I know we've already wasted too much time tonight. The person who kidnapped Elizabeth and is working with Santa Muerte is the same person who tried to kill me tonight. With my good arm, I drag Paige inside the car.

"Hey!" she says. "What's the hurry?"

We slide into the back seat, and I tell our driver we have a destination change.

"Where to?" our driver, Ted, asks.

"Pasadena." I turn to Paige. "We're going to see Carmen."

Chapter 23

Ted drives us through the late-night streets of LA. The fog has rolled in, so the city lights are diffused in a soft glow as we drive along Los Feliz Boulevard.

"Why are we going to see Carmen?" Paige asks, confused. "And why in the middle of the night?"

Struggling against the pain of my shoulder, I pull out my phone then dial and place a call.

"You remember what David said," Paige says. "She's dangerous. The last thing we need to do is go back there."

The phone rings then ultimately goes to voicemail. "She's not answering," I say, hanging up. "Shit."

"Darcy! What's going on?"

"I know who kidnapped Elizabeth."

Ted finally looks in his rearview mirror.

"What? Who?" Paige asks.

"The same person who tried to kill us tonight. Leona."

Ted casts another glance our way.

"That was Leona?" Paige exclaims.

"At first, I thought it was Hugo," I continue. "He always wears cowboy boots. And the person chasing us was definitely not wearing cowboy boots."

Paige squints at me like I'm insane. "Most people don't wear cowboy boots!"

"Yes, but when they were chasing us, didn't you hear the sound of their hard-sole shoes on the floor?"

Ted finally pipes up. "Okay, is this some immersive theater thing? Are you two actresses? Because I'm not paying for the show."

Paige ignores him. "No. I was too busy running for my life to notice their shoes."

"Leona wears hard-sole shoes. High heels or saddle shoes. I noticed that when I met her. And I heard that same sound when we were being chased."

"Okay, someone with hard-soled shoes was chasing us."

"Not just someone—a woman. The person chasing us had a woman's figure—a woman's stance. And I looked up when she was shooting at us from the fire escape."

Ted interjects, "This isn't very convincing. You guys need to work on your bit."

"And you saw Leona?" Paige asks.

"Well, no." I recall what I saw moments before the muzzle flash forced me to look away. "I couldn't make out the face, but... I saw long black hair hanging down from under the hat. It had to be Leona."

Paige shakes her head, and I have to admit it's pretty thin evidence. "But why, then?" she asks.

"She's the one executing the power move. Leona wants the most valuable thing Carmen has—her empire. It wasn't the Russians. It wasn't some rival cartel. It was the person right next to her. Leona. She's the one who kidnapped Elizabeth."

Paige considers. "That's a gutsy move."

"Leona knows Carmen can't go to the police."

Ted cranes his neck to address us. "Why can't Carmen go to the police?"

I indulge him. "Carmen is the head of a major drug cartel here in Los Angeles. Calling the police would jeopardize her entire operation. She'd be arrested before anyone bothered to look for Elizabeth." I turn back to Paige. "And Leona knows that."

"Damn," Ted says.

"And we're just going to walk right into Carmen's house, knowing that Leona tried to kill us and could very well be there right now?"

"I have to warn her."

Paige squirms in her seat. "Maybe we should call the police. Maybe we should call David."

I shake my head. "We won't have to. If I'm right, the cops are already there."

⌇

Ted slows down just enough so Paige and I can exit the vehicle. Then he peels out and disappears around a corner. The street is quiet, but since the recent shooting incident and my conversation with David, I'm now looking for anything remotely suspicious. I'm not surprised when I see a panel van parked a few yards away.

"Follow me," I tell Paige and do my best to march gingerly on wounded feet in the oversized Crocs.

I knock on the passenger door. The van rocks slightly as someone inside makes his way to the door. Moments later, the window rolls down. A man inside is dressed as an electrician, but I know he's a cop.

"Do you know what time it is?" I ask.

He sneers at me through his bushy goatee then looks at his

watch. "What do you want?"

"David told you to keep an eye out for me, yes?"

He looks me up and down, no doubt taking in my Crocs, scrubs, and bloody arm in a sling. "You must be Darcy," he says nonchalantly.

I nod, not sure if he figured this out because of my spunky reputation or because of the disastrous spectacle before him. "I wanted to let you guys know I'm going in to talk to Carmen."

Goatee looks around. "You do understand the concept of being undercover, right?"

"I'm not attracting any more attention than you are with this unmarked kidnapping van. Seriously, do you guys think you're being inconspicuous?"

He rolls his eyes. "God damn it, what do you want?"

"I thought I'd offer to wear a wire if you guys want."

"Snyder was right. You're a smart-ass," he says, rolling the window back up and ending our conversation.

"Well, I guess it's comforting to know the police are here," Paige remarks.

"Yeah. Gives me the warm and fuzzies."

We walk toward Carmen's house. "How many cops did you see in there?" Paige asks.

"Two more."

We come up to Carmen's gate, and I'm about to buzz when I notice that it is unlatched. I open the door. "This isn't good."

Paige nods at the van. "Should we ask for backup?"

I'm already limping through the gate. "I'm sure they'll come if we need help."

We approach the porch and see that most of the lights are on in the house. There's no movement from inside. It's still and peaceful and altogether disconcerting—too quiet even for a Los Angeles suburb this far away from any major thoroughfares.

We walk up the wood steps to the front door. As I continue to scan the area for danger, Paige grabs my hand. "Look."

The front door is ajar. Drawn on the door in crude red paint is the all-too-familiar sigil of Santa Muerte. The same symbol from the temple. The same symbol from Hugo's tattoo.

"Shit," I say. "This can't be good."

I try the handle, and the door opens. Paige reaches into her coat pocket and pulls out a handgun—a black semiautomatic subcompact. I'm momentarily stunned. "What are you doing with a gun?" I say in a decibel level somewhere between a loud whisper and a quiet shout.

"I bought it."

"When?"

"It doesn't matter." Paige takes a step toward the door.

I stop her with my arm. "When?"

She sighs. "Two years ago."

We moved in together two years ago. Apparently, Paige bought a gun when we decided to be roommates. She bought it in case she would ever need to use it… on me.

I let go of her arm. I can't blame her really. I just wish she had told me.

"You know how to use that thing, right?" I ask.

"Yeah. I watched a video on YouTube."

"That's comforting."

Paige smirks. "Yeah. Now you know how it feels."

I step through the doorway with Paige at my heels. It's eerily quiet in here, too. Nothing is out of place. Everything is as it always is. Except no one's here. I begin to worry we're just breaking and entering.

Then I smell smoke. Following the scent, we walk through the living room and into the kitchen. On the stove is a smoking pot on a burning flame. I hurry over to the range and turn off the burner. The inside of the pot is completely dry, like someone was trying to boil water hours ago and it evaporated.

With my good hand, I move the pot off the hot burner. On the kitchen counter is a selection of raw chicken and vegetables. Some are half-cut. I touch the chicken.

"Gross," Paige mutters.

"It's warm," I whisper. "It's been out for hours."

The back door opens, and Leona walks in holding an arrangement of cut flowers. She's unarmed, so I feel confident we have the drop on her.

"Leona!" I call out.

She looks up at us. I'm starting to walk toward her when it all goes suddenly wrong. Leona's expression turns to one of horror. The flowers explode against her chest. Blood sprays out, and she falls backward out of the door.

Instinct takes over, and I duck and cover. "Paige!" I yell.

Paige ducks with me. "What?" She's clearly panicked but not registering the spectacle. She's reacting to me.

It dawns on me that I never heard a sound. No gunshot. No impact from the shot. No scream from Leona. I stand up and look at the back door.

Paige is freaking out now. "Darcy! What's going on?"

I point to the door. Paige shakes her head. "What about it?"

It opens, and Leona walks in holding an arrangement of flowers.

Paige repeats her question. "What am I looking at?"

Leona looks up in horror. Or more accurately, Leona's ghost looks up in horror. The flowers explode against her chest. Blood flies everywhere. Leona staggers back and out the door. Again.

This time, I notice something different. It wasn't a gunshot that ripped into her. Something punched a hole in her chest.

The figure returns through the door again. This time, Paige raises her gun and aims.

It isn't Leona walking through the doorway. It's a young woman in her early twenties with long black hair. She shuffles in, eyes cast down. Her face is pale and drawn like she hasn't had a decent meal or good night's sleep in weeks.

"Elizabeth?" I whisper.

Elizabeth Viramontes looks up. She's confused when she sees me—actually, she seems generally confused about everything. Her eyes are bloodshot from crying.

I gently place my hand on Paige's pistol and lower it. "Are you okay?"

The young girl's lips quiver. "What did I do?"

I take a few steps forward then stop.

Elizabeth raises her hands. They're stained with a coat of dried crimson flakes that resemble old gloves. "What did I do?" she asks again.

What did she *do?* It's only then that I register the spectacle before me—Elizabeth Viramontes, her hands coated in blood, wearing a familiar blue-and-red gown.

Her body suddenly jerks and spasms with impossible movements. Elizabeth cries out in pain as she falls to her knees.

Paige pulls me away, suddenly alarmed. "Darcy! Run!"

But I don't. I stand, watching something I've never seen from the outside. Leona's apparition passes through Elizabeth's body, blocking my view. The ghost looks up as the same spectacle plays out just like before. A look of horror. The blood. She falls back and disappears through the doorway.

Where Leona once stood, Santa Muerte rises from her knees. Her skeletal face stares at me, and her cracked lips spread in a gruesome grin. This time, however, I see her in a new light. I see a kindred spirit, a girl consumed by fire. I see Elizabeth, possessed by Santa Muerte.

She strikes with incredible speed. Her claw-like hand reaches for my chest, and I know in an instant what is coming. As fast as I can, I reach out and grab her arm. Grimacing through the pain in my shoulder, I resist her strength.

Just like before, the contact creates an excruciating shock. I resist letting go and power through the pain. Two unnatural and diametrically opposed forces are colliding in a physical plane where they do not belong—polar opposites fighting against each other and against the energy that possesses us.

Her bony arms feel like sticks under sheaths of skin. Grasping them, my hands are seared with hot pain. I twist her arm to wrestle her away. She launches herself with full force against me, and we fly across the kitchen against a kitchen cabinet.

We spin and crash onto the floor, with me on my back and the spirit above me. Her wide skull-like grin lunges toward me. Her weight pushes me down with a strength I can barely resist. Her fingers continue reaching toward my chest—toward my beating heart. I cry out to push her away. The grimacing teeth inch closer. Her eyes stare straight into mine as her face nears.

As she gets closer, I fear she's going to bite into my face at any moment. The black voids where her eyes should be bore into mine. I call out, "Elizabeth!"

For a moment, the specter hesitates. The figure above me flickers like a glitching ghost. The skeletal face disappears, and in its place, I see Elizabeth. Two frightened eyes look back at me.

I remember that moment when Dudley released me and let me see Bennet die. In the same way, Elizabeth has regained control of her body. Santa Muerte is gone.

"Elizabeth!" I shout again.

Panic washes over her face. She stops struggling with me.

"What's happening?"

"Stay with me!" I shout. "Don't—"

Too late. The Lady of Death resumes control of Elizabeth's corporeal body. Her skull-like mask returns. Once again, her hand pushes for my heart. Sharp nails dig into my skin.

Bam! A gunshot rings out. The impact strikes the entity above me, forcing her off. Instinctively, I cry out, "No!"

The spirit rolls into the air and lands on her feet a few yards away. I look up to see Paige aiming the gun again, ready to pull the trigger again.

"Don't!" I cry out again. I leap up and push the pistol away as another gunshot rings out. I can't let Paige hurt Elizabeth. She knows my demon's name. She can save me.

Santa Muerte crouches on all four and hisses at us, readying for another attack. Just as she's about to lunge, she stops. Her heads whips toward the front of the house as if she is listening.

Something screeches from outside. A sound I've heard before. An owl.

Santa Muerte face turns to me, fury washing over her face. Just like at the library, a mysterious force pulls her and sucks her out of the open doorway. I run out the back door and watch as she disappears into the night sky.

My eyes are drawn to the ground outside and the steps at my feet. Several feet away in the grass, lying on her back, is Leona. Blood has pooled around her body and has soaked into the ground.

Shouts of the police announcing their presence echo behind me. I slowly raise my arms, my wounded shoulder limiting how high I can lift that arm. I step backward, and I sense an energy pass through me.

Leona's ghost emerges through my body and materializes before me. I watch as she replays the moment of her death. Her face twists in pain and shock. She stumbles back, and her spirit crumbles before me then settles into the body lying on the grass.

It's like I said—there are two types of ghosts. A residual ghost is like an energy force playing in an infinite loop. Residual ghosts do not interact with the real world any more than a projected movie would. Like Leona's ghost.

Then there are intelligent ghosts, the kind trapped on this plane of existence who know they are trapped. These ghosts interact with the living—or in some cases, possess them. Elizabeth is possessed, just like me.

I take a knee and feel a police officer grab my arm and jerk it behind my back. My bad shoulder burns as the muscle tears in his grip. I don't care. Elizabeth is still alive, possessed by the spirit who knows my demon's name.

Chapter 24

It doesn't look good for Paige and me at first glance. That night, we entered the premises of a known drug dealer without permission. Police stationed at the scene report hearing gunshots. Then they arrived to find Paige holding a gun and me standing over the body of a dead woman.

That was why I didn't resist when they arrived and why I didn't complain when they wrenched my injured shoulder to handcuff me. I didn't offer any resistance when they escorted me to the driveway and shoved me into the back of a squad car. It's also why I didn't say a single word when they started asking us questions. I didn't even ask for a lawyer.

The red and blue lights move across the front yard as a helicopter spotlight sweeps the grounds. I look out the back seat through the window to Paige, who sits in the back of another squad car. Through an open door, a plainclothes detective listens to her as she talks. I have no choice but to trust that Paige isn't saying anything relevant. There's a good chance I won't talk to her until after the police have both our statements, and the worst thing we could do is offer contradictory information.

Strike that. The worst thing we could do is tell the truth.

Through the rear window, I can make out a soft glow over the manicured bushes—certainly emanating from the television crews filming this breaking news story. My cuffed hands sit in my lap. At least the LAPD was kind enough to front cuff me on account of my shoulder. I rotate my arm, trying to find a comfortable position.

Paige finishes her interview. The detective closes the door on her and turns away, a look of disgust on his face. *Good girl, Paige.*

At this point, the police know I'm not saying anything to them. I'm not talking until someone I can trust arrives. When David opens the door and slides into the back seat with me, I breathe a sigh of relief. He's the only one I know will have my back in this.

"I'm swear to God, Darcy, you'd better have a damn good explanation for this, or I'm letting you rot in jail."

My knight in shining armor. "Is the medical examiner here?"

David shakes his head, already growing impatient. "Yeah, he's here. Why?"

"Here's the deal. First, you're going to talk to the cop on surveillance tonight. He's going to tell you Paige and I arrived at ten fifteen. This is going to be corroborated by a rideshare receipt you'll find on my phone. Second, the medical examiner is going to determine that the time of death was well before that time frame. And for the trifecta, Leona wasn't killed by a gunshot."

"The police on duty report hearing two gunshots."

"Yes, Paige fired her gun—"

"What the hell is Paige doing with a gun?"

"I know! It's ridiculous. And believe me, I'm going to have a talk with her about it later."

"This isn't a joke, Darcy."

"Leona's heart was ripped out, David."

He stops. I can see the thoughts racing through his mind. This information is good and bad at the same time.

"Just like Lupe?" he asks.

"Just like Lupe."

"That puts you at two crime scenes with the same MO."

"I know, but it also means she wasn't shot. I don't know when she died, but it was well before we got here."

"This is a colossal mess," he says, pinching the bridge of his nose in frustration. "You wanna explain why there was a report of shooting outside your apartment this afternoon?"

Oh, right. "You heard about that?"

"Yeah. When a dozen people call 911, it gets around the department. Was that Paige, too?"

"No, no, no. Someone else shot me." I nod toward my injured shoulder.

He looks at me and does a double take, seeming to notice my bandage for the first time. "You were shot?"

"A little bit."

David grabs my shoulder and inspects the wrapping. The remnants of dried blood are still caked on my clothes. "You okay? Do we need to get you to a hospital?"

I shrug him off. "It's fine. I'm fine."

"You've seen a doctor? He said you were okay?"

"Yes, that's why I'm dressed like a nurse tonight. And hey, it's the twenty-first century. We have women doctors now."

"So you saw a woman doctor?"

"That's... neither here nor there. Big picture, David!"

He rubs his temples. "You're exhausting. Let's get back to tonight. Why did you come here?"

"Because I thought Leona shot me, and I came here to warn

Carmen Viramontes about her."

"Leona?"

"Yeah."

"The dead woman?"

I sigh. "I'm willing to admit I was wrong about that one."

David stares at me for a moment before saying, "You honestly think anyone's gonna buy that story?"

"Look, once the ME confirms the time of death and the fact that she was not shot, and the police on scene confirm the time frame, you'll see it confirms my statement."

"You haven't provided a statement."

"I just did."

"I am not the detective on scene, you..." David punches and kicks the seat in front of him over and over and over. The entire car shakes as he violently releases all the frustration I'm causing him. Then he stops.

"Better?" I ask.

David opens the door and exits the car. He slams the door shut with more enthusiasm than is necessary. I watch as he marches toward Ed Snyder. *Good old fun-filled Ed.* They have a brief and heated exchange then disappear into the house together. I look out the window at Paige, who is also watching the scene. She shakes her head.

A few minutes later, David comes marching out of the house alone. He stomps his way to my car, opens the back door, and slides in beside me. He doesn't immediately say anything.

I finally ask, "Well?"

"You were right—it wasn't a gunshot. And her heart's missing. I don't have an exact time of death, but it's roughly two hours ago."

"See? It couldn't have been me."

"Where were you two hours ago?"

"Hollydale Homes. Seeing my new doctor."

He shakes his head. "I wish you'd listened to me and stayed home."

"That's where I was shot, remember?"

He sighs. "Right."

"David," I say, keeping my tone serious, "they know where I live."

He nods his understanding. The body count is piling up, and someone means to add me to the list. "Do you know where Carmen is?"

I shake my head. "I haven't heard from her. I came here to warn her. If she's smart, she's hiding."

"Why did Paige fire her gun?"

If I give David a reason, and Paige gives a different one, we're screwed. "I don't know."

This is the safest answer I can provide. I can't speculate, so whatever motivation Paige conjures up, I can't contradict. If Paige says she saw an assailant, that's her reason. If she says she saw an ethereal spirit from another dimension attacking me, my answer still works.

"You're in more trouble than you're worth."

That hurts me more than I care to admit. The last thing in the world I want is for David to feel that. It would be nice if he could be the type of guy who, for once, thought I was... worth the trouble. David exits the vehicle and closes the door behind him.

"You're not the first person to tell me that," I say to no one.

He walks over to the detective who was questioning Paige earlier, who is now with Snyder. They talk, and I can tell that David is working to convince him of something. The other detective continually shakes his head then finally lifts his hands in defeat. He yells something unintelligible as he points at Paige, then me, before finally walking away.

David tries to walk away, too, and Snyder grabs him. I can only assume Snyder is trying to talk some sense into David. Hopefully, David will make an irrational decision for my benefit.

I spend the next fifteen minutes watching David talk to several different people—presumably other detectives and the commander on the scene. Eventually, David signs off on some document before he walks over to the police car that's holding Paige. He opens the door and helps her out then uncuffs her. When he heads over to me, she follows him.

He opens my door and sweetly says, "Get out of the car." I shimmy my way to the door, and before I'm even standing, David is walking away. "Let's go."

I hurry after Paige, who's following David. My feet are still sore, so I quickly fall behind them. "What about my cuffs?"

David ignores me, so Paige turns to me. "I think he's mad at you."

"What did I do?"

"And he took my gun," she adds.

"David! Why did you take her gun?"

He doesn't even slow down. "One, she's not supposed to be carrying a gun around. It's illegal."

"Then write her a ticket. I'm sure she'd be happy to pay."

"Hey!" Paige objects.

"And two," David continues, "it's evidence in a murder investigation!"

"She didn't shoot Leona!"

"Doesn't matter."

We continue following him to his police-issued blue Dodge Charger parked in the driveway. He opens the front door for Paige, and she slides inside. I wait at the rear door, but he ignores me and climbs into the driver's seat. I struggle to open the door with my cuffed hands then tumble inside and fall into the back seat.

"No help?" I say to Paige.

"That's for the ticket comment."

David starts the engine and pulls forward. The movement of the car shuts the door for me. The Charger pulls out through gates, and as I deduced, the residential street is lined with news vans, reporters, and cameras. Uniformed officers open a lane as David slowly navigates his way through the crowd. Flashbulbs go off. The car finally emerges from the crowd.

David sighs. "I'm going to take you home so you can pack your things. You can't stay there if this person who took a shot at you knows where you live. Do you have somewhere you can stay? With someone you trust?"

Yeah, I have someone in mind.

Chapter 25

David's car winds its way through the Santa Monica Mountains along Mulholland Drive. We made the stop by our loft. While David stood guard, we quickly packed our necessities and left before anyone tried to murder us. Again.

I stare out the back window as his car takes the serpentine route along the crest of the mountain. At times, I'm staring at the vast sea of lights to the north in the San Fernando Valley or the endless lights of the Westside to the south. It's peaceful up here, the kind of place I need to be for now.

"Who do you think killed Leona?" David finally asks.

I'm not sure what to tell David. I know *what* killed her. My list of suspects is also shortening down to the semifinalists.

"I'd look into Hugo," I say.

"The enforcer?" he asks. Clearly, he's familiar with Hugo's work.

"Yeah. Hugo Escalante. Enforcer and children's-literature enthusiast."

The Dodge turns into a private driveway and stops at a large iron gate. I reach out through the window and enter in the code that was given to me.

"Who the hell do you know who lives up here?" David asks.

"A very old friend."

The gate slides open, and David pulls into a circular driveway that loops around a metallic fountain that resembles a Cubist sculpture of a tree. We park at the front door of the house—a modern geometric structure of glass, steel, and cement. From this angle, it looks like it's only one story, but I know from prior visits that there are two more floors below, wedged into the side of the Santa Monica Mountains.

David follows as Paige and I wheel our luggage up the well-lit path to the front door. Before we ring the bell, the door swings open to reveal Fiona, dressed in casual but luxurious loungewear. She hurries forward.

"Hello, my darling!" She embraces me tightly. It's automatic for her, and it's not until I wince that she looks at my sling. "What happened to you?"

"Got shot," I say casually.

"Did you deserve it?" she asks with the same casual air.

I grimace.

She turns to Paige. "Look at you. So beautiful!" She engulfs Paige in a hug.

Fiona's eyes turn to meet David. "Aye, and look at this one."

David is dumbfounded, his jaw nearly on the ground. Admittedly, part of the reason I didn't tell him I was staying with Fiona was so I could see that look when he first saw my celebrity friend. It was totally worth it.

"You must be David," she says.

"That's right. It's, uh, nice to meet you." He reaches out his hand, but she slaps it away and embraces him.

"Please, I feel like I already know you. Darcy is always on about you."

My smile slips away, and my stomach sinks. "No. No I don't."

Fiona ignores me. "You were recently promoted to Homicide, right? Congratulations."

I sometimes think there is no hell worse than the damnation of embarrassment.

David casts a sideways glance at me. "Yes, that's right. Thanks."

Fiona is beside herself. "Look at him, dear. Such a handsome fella. I bet you're an excellent detective."

David shrugs. "I... try."

"He took my gun away," Paige chimes in.

"What?" Fiona exclaims, dismayed. "You cannot go about this awful city without a gun. You can borrow one of mine."

David shakes his head. "Wait... what? No. Don't give her a gun!"

Fiona smiles. "Look at him." She turns to me. "He *is* cute when he gets angry," she says, agreeing with something I never actually said—not even once.

David shoots me a look.

"Well," I say, "This has been fun, but I think we've imposed on Detective Resnick enough." I drag my luggage forward and corral Paige and Fiona into the house. "Thank you for the ride and—you know—the whole keeping-us-from-getting-thrown-in-jail thing. Drive safely. Bye!"

I shut the door on David's face. "What the hell, Fiona?"

She only smiles. "I like him. He's cute."

"Yeah, I know!"

David calls through the door with crystal-clear clarity. "So, uh, will the gate open automatically on the way out?"

I die inside.

Fiona approaches the door and speaks through the solid oak. "Yes, dear. Thanks again for bringing the girls."

David calls again, "Okay." Silence. "Bye."

Fiona locks the door. She mutters something against the door and gestures with her hands. I know she's casting a protection spell, so when Paige casts a concerned look my way, I nod to assure her everything is fine. When I spoke with Fiona on the phone earlier in the evening, I asked if Paige and I could crash at her place because we were no longer safe in our apartment. Fiona agreed, no questions asked. If she can extend that courtesy and trust to someone who could potentially bring a shitload of trouble into her home, I need to trust she intends to keep us safe.

"We're safe now." Fiona turns and struts past us, moving deeper into the house. "It's late. You'll be wanting to see where you'll sleep."

The weight of my mortification keeps me in place until Paige pushes me forward. We follow Fiona downstairs to the bedrooms. The stories of her home are inverted from the way they would be in a normal house. The top floor is for socializing—it's where the kitchen, dining room, and living room are located. Downstairs are the private quarters and study.

She guides us to a guest bedroom larger than our living room, with two beds and its own bathroom. Opposite the beds is a view overlooking the entire Los Angeles Westside, from downtown to the ocean.

Fiona glances at her Breguet watch. "I'll let you sleep in." She turns to me. "I know you'll have a lot to tell me, but I'm thinking it can wait until the morning." She excuses herself and closes the door.

I pull off the Crocs and dump them in the nearest trash can then examine the bandages around my feet. The blood has soaked through, so I retreat to the bathroom. After washing and rewrapping the wounds and pulling on some thick wool socks, I emerge to find Paige standing on the balcony. I join her to admire the view of Los Angeles at night. An endless sea of city lights stretches out before us.

"Are we going to be safe here?" Paige asks.

"This is the safest place for us."

Paige turns to the room we'll be sharing. "Am *I* going to be safe in *here*?"

We have never shared a room. She's become accustomed to sleeping two locked-and-barricaded doors away from me every night. And now I know she kept a gun with her, too.

With little more to discuss, Paige collects a pillow and blanket and leaves to sleep on the living room sofa. I close the door and lock it, for whatever good that might do. As an added precaution, I reach into my suitcase, pull out two Klonopin, and swallow them. I don't bother changing clothes. I pass out in my nurse scrubs.

I wake up to the smell of bacon, eggs, and other delights wafting from the upstairs kitchen. I groggily open my eyes and discover a fresh mug of coffee at the bedside table. With great reluctance, I sit up and grab the beverage. The porcelain is still hot, and the first sip is a mélange of floral and earthy flavors. *Perfection.*

Before heading upstairs to the kitchen, I take a moment to change out of the scrubs and into something normal. I remove my sling and take off my top. With a wet washcloth, I wipe away the dried blood around my shoulder. The bullet hole is sealed shut, but the wound and stitches remain.

It's hard to imagine that I was shot less than twenty-four

hours ago. I rotate my shoulder, testing its strength. When I stretch too far, the pain hampers my movement, but remarkably, I feel like I'm nearly at full strength.

I unravel the bandages on my feet. Likewise, any hint of injury is gone. Perhaps the reason my feet healed faster was because of the superficial nature of the wounds, unlike the muscle-and-nerve damage to my shoulder. There are no abrasions or cuts on the soles from the metal tread of the fire escape—though I could use a pedicure.

I grab my coffee and head upstairs. Paige sits on a stool at the granite kitchen counter. She's dressed in her normal running outfit, but on this particular morning, she's not a matted mess of sweat. By this hour, she has usually finished her first ten miles. On the kitchen island and on the counter before Paige is a feast of bacon, country-fried potatoes, waffles, fruit, and more coffee.

Taking a seat next to Paige, I can see she's transfixed by Fiona, who's holding an egg. "Okay," Paige says, "sunny-side up."

Fiona holds an egg in her fist. She smiles then rubs her other hand over the closed fist. With a flick of her wrist, she smacks the egg with one hand against the counter then opens the shell over Paige's plate. Out plops a perfect sunny-side-up egg. Steam rises from the round yolk.

Fiona turns to me and smiles warmly. "Good morning." She slides a plate stacked with food in front of me.

Paige is still staring at her plate. "This is insane." She turns to me. "Did you know she could do this?" Then she asks Fiona, "What if I wanted green eggs? Could you do that?"

"How long has she been doing this?" I ask Fiona.

"All morning, dear," Fiona says with a patient smile. She cracks another egg on the counter and deposits one green poached egg on Paige's plate.

"This is insane," Paige says again.

Fiona turns to me. "How are you wanting your eggs?"

"Scrambled, please."

"No!" Paige shouts. "That's boring." She turns to Fiona, "Can you add other ingredients? Can you do an omelet?"

"Let's not ask our hostess to perform for us," I suggest.

She watches as Fiona shakes two eggs in her hand then cracks them open. Warm, moist scrambled eggs collapse onto my plate. "That's insane," Paige repeats.

I've been lucky enough to see Fiona cast some serious spells, so I know these minor tricks are nothing for her. Still, it feels like witnessing tiny little miracles. For Paige, this is something else. She's always been one to try to understand how things work. She'll disassemble something just so she can see how all the parts create a whole. That's how she got into computers—locked away in her room, she tried to understand how a CPU, RAM, a motherboard, and a hard drive could transform ones and zeroes into something presentable. Paige's mind won't rest until she understands.

"Okay," Paige proceeds meekly. "Like, how do you do… this?"

"You mean magic?" Fiona asks.

"Is that what this is? I mean, I know you're a…" Paige hesitates.

"Witch?" I finish for her.

"Is that okay to say?" Paige asks. "That's not a derogatory term?"

"Not at all, dear," Fiona says.

"I'm sorry. I don't know the difference between magic and witchcraft. Or if it's okay to say *witches* or *wizards* or *sorcerers*."

I drop my fork. "Paige!"

Paige freezes. She turns to Fiona, who smiles. "I'm afraid

your friend is winding you up," Fiona assures her.

Paige punches my arm—the injured one. I flinch, expecting intense pain. Surprisingly, the wound doesn't split open. Still, Paige is strong, and it hurts.

"Okay," Paige continues. "So, with magic, how do you do it? Can you just conjure up anything you want?"

"No, it doesn't quite work that way. Think of magic as a way of transmitting, transforming energy or matter." Fiona lifts an egg. "I can heat this egg, and I can mess about with them to cook them any way I want. But I cannot make an omelet because I cannot change the egg into onions or ham or cheese."

"But you made it green. There's no green inside. How did you do that?"

"I know how to manipulate what's inside this shell. Inside are other elements—sulfur in the whites and iron in the yolks. You combine those, you get green."

Paige is clearly fascinated by all this. Truth be told, I never asked Fiona for the details of her magic. Maybe I was embarrassed or afraid I was being nosy. So I let Paige continue while I stuff my face with scrambled eggs. Which are delicious, by the way.

"You don't need a wand or a staff or a broom?"

Fiona bursts out laughing. "Only if I'm wanting to sweep. Wands and staves have their place, and truth be told, some prefer to use them, and some spells require them. Some spells require an incantation. Some spells are so powerful that two or more witches are needed to harness the energy. A coven, if you will."

Paige leans forward, enthralled. "You mean, combining your power?"

"Not necessarily," Fiona answers with a smile, happy to oblige her eager audience. "Some spells can be incredibly complicated, with multiple parts. You may have one witch use a conjuration spell to summon power, while another uses an enchantment to harness and hold the power."

Paige nods. "A team."

"Aye. As for myself, I learned that I only need to use a handful of spells on a daily basis. These are conducted with simple chants or by the use of everyday items I carry with me at all times"—she reaches into her pockets and pulls out three gold coins, a vial of salt, and a crystal—"much like you carry your keys, wallet, or cell phone." She waves her open palm over the items, and one by one, they disappear.

"How did you learn to do all this?" Paige asks.

"My mother. She was a very powerful witch herself, and she taught me everything she knew. Over time, I developed my own style and discovered a few things myself. But my passion for the arts—and that's what they are—was all because of her influence."

I stop eating as Fiona mentions her mother. Casually, I try to register Paige's expression. It's blank.

Paige stands and reaches for her headphones. She takes a deep breath to compose herself. "I'm sorry for pestering you with my questions."

"Paige…" I start.

"I need to get my run in. Breakfast was delicious," she says to Fiona. "Thank you." She disappears out the door for what I can only imagine will be a marathon.

When she's gone, Fiona turns to me. "Did I bollocks it up?"

"It wasn't anything you did." I go back to eating my breakfast.

⌁

After breakfast, I help Fiona with the dishes. It's the least I can do for the feast she provided. As I'm drying the last of the bowls and putting them away, I sense Fiona staring at me.

"Yes?" I ask.

"Are you wanting to tell me what happened last night?"

I guess it's time. "I just need to get a refill on my coffee," I say, picking up my empty mug. Fiona waves her hand over the top of my cup. It fills from within. *So much for stalling.*

We take a seat on her sofa, which overlooks the Westside of Los Angeles. "I first saw Santa Muerte at the library," I begin.

I proceed to tell her about Lupe's murder and seeing the spirit for the first time. I tell her about the owl too. Then I talk about Carmen and the cartel, what Paige and I witnessed in the temple, Sebastian's death, getting shot, and what happened last night. I give her every detail I can think of—anything that might help her help me. She's surprised by none of it.

"You know what I've been going through, don't you?" I ask.

"There isn't much magic that happens in this city that I don't know about," Fiona says. "That's how I found you so many years ago."

I lean forward. "Do you know who she is?"

"I wasn't sure then. I'm sure now."

"Who?"

"Her name is Melchora. She is a bruja, which is a kind of witch. The *lechuza* you've been looking for."

I have limited experience with the supernatural. Ghosts, Fiona, and my demon were everything I knew until I encountered Santa Muerte. Now Fiona is telling me about a bruja being "a kind of witch." *How many kinds are there? What else is out there?*

"I have tried to keep you from this world," Fiona continues. "But this seems to have been a long time coming. Somehow, you quelled a demon inside you. A demon that has mighty power. There are others out there who will wish you harm and some who will want to use you. And now this one knows your name."

This gives me chills. "Melchora. How do you know her?"

Fiona rises from the sofa and offers a remorseful smile. "I think you should follow me."

"Uh-oh. This doesn't sound good." I'm rising to follow Fiona when Paige enters through the front door. She's drenched in sweat from her short but evidently intense run. She grabs a water from the refrigerator before realizing Fiona and I are watching her.

"Better?" I ask.

Paige shrugs and takes a big gulp then takes another look at us and hesitates. "What's going on?"

"Fiona wants to show me something, and I think it's bad. Wanna come?" I smile, pleading for a friend.

Paige and I follow Fiona slowly down a staircase that leads to the bottom floor. Fiona guides us to a locked door, which she opens by muttering a chant I can't understand. We step inside a large room with a dark tinted window and yet another view of the city. On the back side is an entire wall of stainless steel, apothecary drawers, and cabinets. A long, glass table sits in the middle of the room, a decorative bowl with stainless-steel balls in the exact center of it. Fiona walks to the wall and selects a drawer halfway down. She opens it and removes a snake—the same one I gave her when I last saw her.

Paige squirms. "Oh geez."

Fiona walks toward us with the snake. "I have a confession. I haven't been completely honest with you about what I do with these specimens. It's important to tell you that these creatures possess a tremendous amount of magic."

"What kind of magic?" Paige asks.

"The kind of magic that can only be created in another world," Fiona answers in an ominous tone.

"Hell," I add. "She means the kind of magic that can only

be created in hell."

Fiona nods. "Aye. They are very powerful. A rare commodity."

She lets go of the snake and steps toward us. Paige and I step back. The snake winds itself around Fiona's arm then slithers its way up to her neck.

"A month ago," she says, "you brought me a particular specimen, a snake with bands of red and black. Its Latin name is *Micrurus diastema*. A coral snake normally found in Mexico and Central America. Extremely venomous. And by way of you, an incredible gift. A powerful gift." Fiona stops and rests her hand on the corner of the table, and the snake slithers its way down her arm and coils itself into a ball on the glass. "A valuable gift."

It suddenly occurs to me where Fiona is going with this. "Did you sell it? Have you been selling"—I gesture to the wall of stainless steel drawers—"all of them? This whole time?"

"These items are highly sought among those like me. It would be selfish to keep them to myself."

"You're selling them for profit!" I shout.

Fiona shrugs. "These items are not common, everyday items. You will not find them in a shopping mall or online—well, maybe on the dark web. No matter," she adds, trying to stay on course. "We sell, trade, and barter when we need to. I myself buy from others all the time. It's what we've always done."

Paige shakes her head. "We? Who's *we*?"

"And"—I bury my head in my hands—"you sold one to her, didn't you? Melchora?"

"The coral snake," she admits.

"When?"

"Oh, three weeks ago."

And there it is. "Right before Elizabeth was kidnapped," I say.

It's no coincidence that Fiona knew so much about Santa Muerte and the *lechuza*. That's why she warned me to stay away. She had met the *lechuza*.

On instinct, Paige approaches Fiona to confront her. Then she stops when she realizes the snake is still coiled on the table. "Wait a second. Are you saying this snake that Darcy… vomited…was used to possess Elizabeth with this demon?"

"Oh, it's not a demon," Fiona corrects. "She's a powerful spirit, yes, but not a demon."

"But," Paige counters, "Elizabeth is possessed. Like Darcy."

"Possession is not exclusive to demons, my dear."

I'm not concerned with the semantics but with the notion that this whole thing—Elizabeth's kidnapping, her subsequent possession, Leona's death—was put into motion by me.

As if reading my thoughts, Fiona comes close and rests a hand on my shoulder. "Aye, my dear. It's not your fault."

"More like yours," Paige says.

I wave my hand at Paige. I love that she defends me, but now's not the time. Fortunately, Fiona doesn't take it personally and ignores Paige's comment.

"Frankly, I'm surprised Melchora is able to wield such magic," Fiona says. "I didn't think she was that powerful a witch."

"Another thing you were wrong about," Paige mutters.

"Paige!" I say. "That's enough."

She crosses her arms.

"Oh dear," Fiona says, turning away. She collects the snake off the glass table and returns to her wall of drawers. When she extends her hand to the empty drawer, the serpent obediently slithers back into its container. She slowly closes the drawer.

Paige and I exchange a look, trying to read each other's thoughts.

Fiona finally turns to face us. "What do you intend to do?"

"I'm going to find this thing," I say, "and I'm going to make it reveal the name."

"Are you sure you want to do that?"

I'm a bit taken aback by this comment. In light of recent events and the revelation that she's profiting from me, it's becoming clear that my possession is a benefit to Fiona.

"Yes," I say. "I'm sure."

"Because," Fiona continues, "someday, perhaps sooner than you think, you might be able to harness even more power than you think you have. Imagine what you might be able to do with it."

"She can't control—" Paige starts.

I point my finger at Paige—a final warning. I hate having to be the big sister right now, but I need to hear what Fiona has to say, and I can't have Paige pissing her off. It doesn't matter whether or not Fiona is giving me good advice—she's giving me information.

My attention returns to Fiona. "Go on."

Fiona focuses her attention on Paige and calmly continues. "All I'm saying is that perhaps Darcy has not considered what a blessing this might be for her."

"How…" Paige chokes on her words. Then she resumes. "How could this possibly be a blessing?"

Fiona approaches me. With a finger, she pulls down the collar of my sweater to reveal my healed wound. Even Paige is surprised by its improved condition.

"This is how," Fiona says.

She pinches her thumb and index finger together in midair and pulls. Slowly, the suture begins to unravel itself until the last of the threads is pulled out. It hovers for a moment in the air. She snaps her fingers, and a flash of fire consumes the string. A wisp of smoke is all that remains.

Her lips widen, and she puts on a smile. I've seen this smile before—it's the expression she shows on TV every day—a warm, loving mask meant to endear and captivate an audience. "As with any good talent, all you have to do is learn to control the power."

I don't look at Paige. Even out of the corner of my eye, I can tell what kind of judgmental stare she's casting in my direction.

But I have one question for Fiona. "How?"

Don't ask me how I convinced Paige to leave Fiona and me alone for fifteen minutes. I have no idea how, but I'm fairly certain it wasn't particularly diplomatic. Fiona stands at the far end of her glass table while I stand at the other end.

"Magic is all about control, Darcy," Fiona says. "But you cannot control the elements until you can control yourself. The same goes with your demon. This entity inside you has great power. You have that power, too. I know you can feel it. What you're needing to believe is that you can control it whenever you want."

I make the mistake of rolling my eyes. "Fiona. I hardly think—"

"*Eiteogach!*"

Before I can even finish the thought, a steel ball from the decorative bowl is hurled toward my face. It slams against my cheek and bounces into the wall behind me.

"What the shit, Fiona?" I yell, rubbing my now-bruised cheek.

"Now you try."

My face scrunches up, and I feign trying to Force push a ball at her. It doesn't work. "See? I can't do it."

"*Eiteogach!*"

Another ball launches from the bowl. This time I'm ready,

and I duck—or more accurately, fall to the floor. Staying under the table, I yell at her through the glass that separates us. "Knock it off! Seriously, someone could lose an eye!"

Fiona stands and backs away from the table. Then that stupid witch does it again. "*Eiteogach!*"

This time, the ball rises from the bowl then slams down through the glass table. Shards rain down around me, and the metal orb slams into my chest. My body flies backward and slams against the wall. She's actually trying to hurt me.

Fiona walks toward me. "You know you can stop this. All you have to do is take control."

I'm getting angry. My blood warms, and the electrocardiogram on my watch starts to beep. "He's coming out!" I warn her.

"No!" she shouts. "Harness the demon's power!"

Harness the demon's power. Those are the same words Father Ramon used to describe what I had done. He believed I was permitting the demon to take control. Fiona believes I can wield its power.

Neither of them have any idea what I'm dealing with. They don't understand the pain like I do. They don't live with it every day. They don't know what it's like to have an evil, destructive force inside that threatens to destroy you and everyone you love. They don't get it. The more I think about that, the angrier I get.

Fiona raises her arms. "*Foluaineach.*" The bits of glass rise slowly from the floor in front of me. My heart beats faster as I watch them point their jagged edges at me. My hand shakes. Then a breeze wafts through the air, and my hair flutters across my face. He's coming.

Fiona yells, "*Eiteogach!*"

"No!" I cry. A hurricane wind explodes from my chest, pushing the broken glass away and toward Fiona.

With catlike reflexes, Fiona slams her forearms together. "*Armas!*" she yells.

The shards bounce away as if deflected by some invisible shield. The air continues blowing around the room. The shattered glass on the floor skittles in a circle. The sound grows louder.

Fiona's lips curl in a wicked grin. "You did it!" she cries above the noise. "You're doing it!"

I can sense Dudley emerging. I shut my eyes. I don't want to see what happens.

"Nooo!" I roar above the howling wind that swirls around me.

In the blackness, Fiona calls out, "*Bhí an saol ina chalm.*"

A soft, cool breeze breaks through the vortex. For a moment, it's as if I'm at the beach. The fragrance of water and salt fills the air, and I can almost hear the waves lapping on sand. The warmth inside me subsides. My breaths are calm. The wind dies down and dissipates.

Fiona's dulcet voice breaks through. "*Bhí an saol ina chalm.*"

My eyes are still closed, but I sense a calm in the room. Dudley's not coming. Somehow, by some magical means, she's tranquilized him. I open my eyes.

I'm still on the floor, with my back against the wall. The glass table is now intact as if nothing ever happened. Fiona stands at the far end, smiling at me through its transparent surface. Even the steel balls are back in their bowl, perfectly situated in the center.

I feel my face where the steel ball hit me. It's not tender. It's as if this never happened. *Did this happen?*

"There now, dear," Fiona says. "Was that so hard?"

✺

Fiona opens the door to Paige, who's standing there, freshly showered and dressed. "What happened?" Paige demands.

Fiona turns to me. "She controlled it."

"Hardly," I say, still rubbing my cheek despite it not being sore.

Fiona steps past Paige, and we follow her. "You protected yourself. You conjured the wind. You moved the broken glass."

"But I was only able to stop him from taking over because you were there."

"This time," she argues. "Just to show you that you can do it. All you must do is open yourself a wee bit. Find that boundary that gives you both the power and control."

Fiona leads us to another room. It's a small study with bookshelves and an ebony wood desk. A floor-to-ceiling safe sits in one corner.

"Now, something for Paige." Fiona spins the safe handle and yanks open the door to reveal a trove of pistols, rifles, and shotguns.

My jaw drops. "Why in the world do you need guns?"

"I don't need them. But even I enjoy the power of a good high-caliber firearm. Now…" She turns to Paige. "Let's see, dear. What should we give you? Ah!" She pulls out a small handgun. "One of my favorites, the Glock 36." With expert dexterity, she pops out the magazine and displays the gun to Paige. "Forty-five caliber. Standard magazine load of six. Easy rack." She pulls back on the slide and inspects the chamber. "Empty." She pops the magazine back in. "Slim, so you can tuck it your jeans with no one the wiser," she says, handing the gun and a shoulder holster to Paige.

"Thanks!" Paige says, inspecting her new gift.

Fiona turns to me. "Would you like protection?"

"No. I have Paige."

She closes the safe and turns to inspect us. "Well!" she says, clapping her hands and turning to Paige. "Now that you are once again properly armed and you"—she looks at me—"have… Paige, I'm thinking it's time for a field trip."

"Where?" I ask suspiciously.

"Oh," she says with a smile, "you'll be liking this place."

Chapter 26

F iona's Land Rover screeches to a valet stand near the corner of Hollywood and Vine. Paige and I quickly step out of the vehicle, thankful to have arrived safely. This is an area where old Hollywood meets new Hollywood. Brand-new twenty-first-century buildings mingle others nearly one hundred years old, many of which are in various states of disrepair. Their facades are a neoclassical style, built of old redbrick with intricately carved entablatures etched into the masonry. I often wonder who is occupying the upper floors, where many windows are frosted with dirt or blocked with stacks of old paper piled against the glass.

A cool morning breeze whips through the street. I flip up the collar of the double-breasted jacket Fiona loaned me. The golden-brown Harris Tweed isn't my normal fashion choice, but she insisted I "dress for the occasion" and not like some "dosser in mourning."

Fiona accepts a ticket from a valet and joins us on the sidewalk. We follow her to a front door of one of the older buildings, a gothic structure ten stories tall. She punches a code into the security box, and a loud buzz-and-click sound informs us the door is now open.

Fiona turns to Paige. "I'm sorry, dear. This is as far as you go."

Paige looks at me. We discussed this on the car ride over. The place was "not for the uninitiated," Fiona said—which to me meant *not for Muggles*. Despite Paige's initial protestations, she ultimately understood that this was a world where she was not permitted.

"Text me when you're done. I'll be at the coffee shop next door." Paige gestures to her laptop bag, letting me know she'll be able to keep herself busy for a while. Then she disappears around the corner, and I follow Fiona inside.

"You're right," Fiona says. "She's protective of you."

"She would take a bullet for me."

Fiona glances at my shoulder. "Maybe to return the favor."

We enter a lobby to find one uniformed guard standing by two old elevators and another sitting at a reception station. Fiona approaches the reception guard.

He smiles as she arrives at his desk. "Good afternoon, Ms. Flanagan. It's good to see you again."

"Thank you, Charles." Fiona scribbles information in a logbook.

Charles smiles at me. "Good morning, miss. I hope you're having an excellent day."

I nod a thank-you.

Charles turns back to Fiona. "New member?"

"Not yet. She's a guest."

Charles continues to smile. "He won't allow guests." This is stated as a fact, not a challenge or confrontation. His tone is cheery, like a kind stranger commenting on a sunny day.

Fiona finishes her entry in the logbook. "He'll allow this

one." She leads me to the elevators. The other guard nods to us. Fiona pulls out a black plastic card and waves it at a sensor panel at the elevator. A light flashes green, and the elevator door opens.

We step inside. The elevator door closes. We stand there, not moving.

"What floor?" I ask.

"Just wait."

Moments later, the intercom system crackles to life. "No guests, Ms. Flanagan," says a disembodied voice with an English accent.

"I'm aware of the rules. He'll make an exception," Fiona answers.

"He never makes exceptions," says the voice.

"Just tell him this—tell him I bring two guests."

There's a pause before the speaker crackles again. "I only see one other with you."

"Tell him."

Silence follows. After a couple of minutes, the elevator jostles with no forewarning. We rise, and I watch the light panel and read the floors as they go by. *1, 2, 3, 4, 5...*

Then the panel goes black, but we keep moving. Finally, the doors open. Fiona steps out, and I follow her into a large two-level penthouse. Every wall is covered in dark oak panels framed by ornate molding. While some panels display framed photos and paintings, many others are carved with symbols, sigils, and veves.

My eyes rise to the mezzanine level, where two rows of tables overlook the space. There are people seated and chatting noisily, most of them either drinking some cocktail or smoking. Directly above is an enormous skylight that stretches the length of the floor.

Fiona leads us to a reception stand, where a tall, thin man

towers over us. He wears a pinstriped suit. That outfit, coupled with his bald head, makes him look like Jack Skellington.

"Did he make an exception?" Fiona asks with a wry smile.

"This way, please," Jack says. I recognize the voice I heard on the elevator.

We follow Jack up the stairs that lead to the mezzanine. As we climb, I notice more and more faces turning in our direction. And when I say *our direction*, I mean *my direction*. By the time we're at the top of the stairs the entire place is completely quiet, and all eyes are on me.

By all accounts, everyone looks normal—well, normal for Los Angeles. There are people of all ages, from teens to the elderly, and all ethnicities. Some are dressed in suits, some in eclectic casual garb. One woman is even dressed in yoga pants and a hoodie. Still, there's something off about all of them. As we hurry through, I don't have the time to observe them and put my finger on it.

Jack leads us past a large island bar where I spy a selection of top-shelf-only spirits. We move down a hallway, past various clubrooms and antechambers. Still, there are carvings of symbols on the walls—symbols I recognize from years of researching religions, magic, and the occult. We pass one after another. There are some with Christian origins. Egyptian. Celtic. Hindu...

We walk through the main dining area. Three living trees burst from the floor, their gnarled trunks twisting over the tables while their large limbs sprout a canopy of leaves. Black-and-white photos of members are hung on the walls, memorializing past events at the venue.

And every time we approach a new group of patrons, they stop and stare. No one speaks, not even in hushed tones, as I pass. It's as if they collectively understand the same secret.

Whatever that secret is, it seems to be about me.

We finally arrive at an oak door at the end of a long hall. Jack Skellington knocks. "They're here."

The large wooden door creaks open. Jack nods to us and retreats down the hall.

Fiona waltzes inside, and I follow. I'm not sure what to make of this room. My first impression is that it's an office. It has a standard desk, some chairs, and shelves. But there are various vials and strange items lined up along those shelves. An old apothecary cabinet lines one wall while wood filing cabinets line another.

The old wood desk in the center is cluttered with stacks of books, papers, and gold bars. Stacks and stacks of gold bars. Behind the clutter sits a man I presume is of Middle Eastern descent. He's dressed in a finely tailored tan linen suit, a white button-down shirt, and no tie. His thick salt-and-pepper hair is perfectly cut and blends into a well-groomed beard that does nothing to hide his strong jaw.

As Fiona steps in, he rises quickly from behind his desk. "Fiona," he says in a deep voice with a thick accent that confirms his Middle Eastern heritage. "It is so good to see you again." They exchange a hug and a two-cheek kiss.

His eyes turn to me. "This must be her." He extends a hand to me. "My name is Ammon."

I reach out to take his hand. "Hi. I'm Dar—ow!" I pull my hand away and recoil. I look down at my palm and can see it's red where my skin touched his.

Ammon peers into my yellow eyes. "Fiona was right. You've bested a demon."

My stomach growls as Dudley responds, like a dog suspicious of a stranger. "I hardly think I've bested him. I'm stuck with him, is more accurate." I continue to clutch my hand.

It feels like I just grabbed a hot iron. The skin on my palm starts to bubble with blisters.

"I apologize for the little test," Ammon says. "I had to make sure the story Fiona told me was true."

"Ammon, I'm offended," Fiona says with a bit of melodrama. "Would I lie?"

The pain worsens, and I start to get a little pissed. Here I am with third-degree burns, and these two are making chitchat.

Ammon pulls a handkerchief from his inside jacket pocket and uses it to lift an amber stone from the desk. It's roughly the size of an egg, and it's translucent, which makes it seem to radiate light. He extends the stone to me. "Hold this with your hand."

I don't move.

"It will help. I promise."

I look at Fiona, but she offers no guidance. Gingerly, I reach out with my good hand and tap the stone gently. It feels cool to the touch. I take it with my hurt hand. As soon as my fingers wrap around the stone, the pain begins to subside.

"Thanks."

He raises an eyebrow.

"I don't mean it to sound sarcastic," I say. "It's just the way I talk. You'll get used to it."

"You won't," Fiona adds.

Ammon gestures for us to sit then returns to his chair behind the desk. "I can presume you wish to nominate young Darcy for membership to the Mancery? While I must admit she is an impressive individual, I'm not certain she qualifies. And if she did, you know this isn't how it's done."

"I'm not here to discuss her membership—at least not today."

The Mancery? Membership? What is this place?

"Then why are you here? More to the point," he says,

looking at me, "why is she here?"

"Because another member is trying to kill her," Fiona answers.

I feel like a kid watching Mommy and Daddy talk about me and my future as if I'm not in the room. I mostly have no idea what they are talking about. However, when Fiona mentions "another member," I realize she's talking about Melchora.

Ammon shrugs. "I don't think I need to describe to you the width and breadth of members we have in our association." He turns to me. "No offense, young lady, but you're hardly the only person threatened by one of our members."

"That's comforting," I mutter.

Fiona shoots me a look, reminding me not to be myself. "Darcy, why don't you tell Ammon what happened last night?"

I look at Ammon. He stares at me impassively, perhaps thinking there is nothing I can tell him that would affect him in any way. Judging by his office and the magical rock in my hand, he's clearly a powerful individual—but I don't think he's a witch. He's something else. And someone this powerful has probably seen, well, some crazy shit.

But for some reason, Fiona thinks what I have to say may compel him to help us. Despite some initial stuttering, I talk. I tell Ammon about the events that transpired at the library. Santa Muerte. My getting shot. Leona's ghost. Elizabeth's possession. The police.

When I mention the police, Fiona interrupts. "Melchora has summoned the spirit of Santa Muerte and used it to possess the child. But she's being careless and is attracting a lot of attention. Attention we don't want."

Ammon laughs. "Truly, Fiona? You're now concerned about bringing attention to us?"

Clearly, this is a shot at Fiona's fame. I once asked her why she pursued such a high-profile career. I wanted to know why someone so concerned with keeping her powers a secret would choose a path in the public eye. Her answer was the same one she offers Ammon tonight.

"Go away with ya if you think I'm going to spend another four hundred years hiding from the rest of the world. I've a right to make a living, just like anyone else. And nothing I do threatens you or anyone else at the Mancery. But Melchora..."

She lets the name settle on Ammon. As he considers the weight of this, I pick up where Fiona left off. "I don't think Melchora's done," I say. Ammon looks up at me. "There is some plan in motion, and it has to do with Carmen Viramontes's empire."

"Who is Carmen Viramontes, and what is her empire?" he asks.

"She's the leader of a drug cartel. It was her daughter who was kidnapped and possessed by the spirit of Santa Muerte. Whatever Melchora is trying to do, this is just the beginning."

"Drugs are a dirty business," Ammon mutters.

"A business with which we do not want to associate," Fiona says. "Now that the police are sniffing about, they're going to follow her tracks right back to us. You and I have fought hard to make sure the Mancery has maintained its secrecy."

"Fair enough," he says. "I will look into Melchora. She has not visited our establishment for a while. If what you're suggesting is true, her membership is the least of her concerns." He turns to me. "That doesn't explain why you're both here today."

Fiona leans forward. Not sure what to do, I lean in too. "I want the dowsing pendulum," she says.

I look at Ammon. He leans back, perturbed. He must know

what she's talking about. I certainly don't.

"So you can find her?"

"So Darcy can."

"I've told you many times, Fiona. It's not for sale."

"Would you consider a temporary exchange? A loan, if you will."

Ammon shakes his head dismissively. "An exchange? What could I possibly wish to exchange for lending out the pendulum?"

"The blood of a demon?"

My heart skips a beat the moment those words come out of her mouth. I slowly turn to face her with a look that could kill. "Seriously?" *First, the animals I've vomited up and now this?* "I'm not your personal goddamn vending machine, Fiona!"

I consider her a friend and an ally, but every now and then, I'm reminded of how very Hollywood she can be. One minute, she's my best friend and ally, then suddenly, she's making promises on my behalf and expecting me to provide her whatever she wants.

"We need the pendulum," she shoots back. "You need the pendulum."

"Why? Can't we find Melchora on our own?"

"That's not the question. The question is, can we find her before she strikes again?"

Damn it, that's a good point. There's no telling when Santa Muerte may strike again—and when she does strike, whose life might be lost.

I turn to Ammon. "This pendulum... what is it?"

Ammon smiles. Clearly, Fiona's proposition has whetted his appetite. He rises from his desk and steps through a door into an adjacent room. Moments later, he returns with a small wooden box. It's unstained, with a pale color and glassy grain that appears petrified. A tree is carved on the lid, its branches and roots wrapping into a perfect and circle around the tree.

He opens the box and lifts a silver chain. From it dangles a large clear crystal.

I shrug. "Neat. What does it do?"

"*Finna Fiona*," Ammon says.

Slowly, the pendulum begins to swing. At first, it's a normal rocking, back and forth. Then it stops. It levitates at a ninety-degree angle, pointing at Fiona.

"I crafted this from a piece of Iceland Spar I recovered from a shipwreck off the coast of Norway," Ammon says. "I suspect it belonged to a shaman who guided boats at sea. Speak the words, and it will guide you where you want to go."

I admire the pendulum. It's transparent, like glass. As light hits it, it doesn't refract the light like normal crystal. I have never seen anything like it. It's beautiful.

My attention shifts to Ammon, who watches me carefully. I can see him stifling the faint hint of a smile.

Leaning back in my chair, I shrug. "Why do you want my blood?"

"*Stöðva*," Ammon says. The crystal drops, its weight returning to normal. He returns the jewel and chain to the box and closes the lid. "That is none of your concern. Do we have a deal, or not?"

"Aye," Fiona says.

"No," I say.

Ammon turns to Fiona. "She can be quite rude."

I shake my head, not willing to let them shame me into compliance. "Look, Ammon, it is my concern. The last time I opted into this whole donation program, this one"—I jab a thumb at Fiona—"eBayed it to a witch, who later tried to have me killed. So pardon me for being a little gun-shy this time around."

Fiona rests a hand on my arm to calm me. "Darcy, please…"

I pull my arm away. "Look, if you harvest me for more parts, you need to make a deal with me. Not Fiona. Me. I'm willing to discuss this exchange. But I need to know this blood isn't going to come back and bite me in the ass." My heart races. I take a deep breath, trying to relax before the alarm on my watch goes off.

Ammon doesn't bother looking at Fiona. His eyes stay focused on me. "I spent my entire life studying magic—a lifetime that dwarfs yours by comparison. In that time, I have focused my attention on components and ingredients. Some are common. Some are not. And I have the unique training and ability to imbue the properties of these items, permanently, into other objects. Like that stone you are holding."

I had all but forgotten the stone. I look down and open my fist. The stone rests lightly in the palm of my hand. No pain, no blisters—as if nothing ever happened. Actually, better—my skin isn't even dry anymore.

I look up at Ammon. He's holding his handkerchief again and opening it to me. Gently, I lay the stone in the fabric, careful not to make contact with him. He wraps the fabric around the stone and places it back on his desk.

"A demon's blood is not something easily procured. I have never had the chance to work with it. I don't know anyone who has. I can't say for sure what use it will be. We are talking about the life force of an eternal and powerful entity—a thing that can cross the very planes of existence. I need to study it. To learn from it. Then if I can harness its power and use it in some… object… I cannot promise that someone somewhere down the line won't use it against you."

With my luck, I'm sure someone someday will.

"Then I think you'll need to up the ante if you want this sweet A positive," I say, tapping my forearm.

With a deep, resigned sigh, like so many other people make when dealing with me, Ammon asks, "What would you like?"

Now we're getting somewhere. "This Santa Muerte spirit knows my name. Its name."

Ammon's eyes widen. "Indeed?"

"Indeed. I need to know how I can control Santa Muerte and force her to reveal the name. Do you have any magical thingamajigs that can do that?"

Fiona finally chimes in. "Are you sure you want—"

"I'm sure," I interrupt. *There she goes again, trying to get her way.*

Her shoulders sag. "Very well, dear."

Ammon considers my request. He quietly rises and disappears through the back door. Moments later, he returns with another box. This one is made of wood blacked with resin. Gold hieroglyphs—character texts and images— cover each side and the top. He turns the box to me and opens the lid, revealing the contents.

Inside is a folded piece of ivory cloth. Ammon gestures for me to take it. I hesitantly reach into the box and lift the fabric. Despite its gossamer texture, it's curiously heavy. I unfurl it to reveal a long and delicate veil made of a silky mesh. The material is so fine it's translucent.

"Whosoever dons this veil is compelled to tell the truth," Ammon says. "Place this on the head of the spirit, and you can ask for the name."

Great. So I just need to get close enough to Santa Muerte to drape this over her head. Then I interrogate her for Dudley's name. I return the veil to its box, and he closes the lid. He places this box next to the one containing the pendulum. There sit the two keys to solving my case and my life. One key will help me find Elizabeth. One key will help me learn my demon's name.

"Do we have a deal?" Ammon asks.

Truth be told, I'm a bit naive when it comes to the details of donating blood on the black market. "Do you need a drop right now? Do I go to the local Red Cross and have them draw ten milliliters?"

Ammon and Fiona exchange a brief chuckle.

"Dear," Fiona finally says. "He doesn't want *your* blood."

I wrinkle my brow. "He just said he wanted..."

Oh no.

It occurs to me what is so funny—and not so funny. They don't mean to draw my blood while I'm me. They want to draw it from me while I'm Dudley.

The words struggle to come out: "Well... what do... how... are we going to do that? When are we going to do that?"

Ammon smiles and raises his hands. "Why not now? Why not here?"

My stomach sinks. This is not like the exercise Fiona and I did in her house. This isn't finding that fine line. What we're talking about is unleashing the deadly and dark force inside me. This will be a full demonic episode.

After sitting in silence for too long, Ammon finally asks again, "Do we have a deal?"

Paige is going to kill me.

Chapter 27

A mmon and Fiona lead me through the club. Once again, all eyes are on me as we navigate our way through the place. Ammon leads us down a long hallway to a locked door. He presses a smart card against a reader then enters a six-digit pin into the keypad. The light turns from red to green.

"High-tech?" I ask.

Ammon smiles as he opens the door. "Everyone here knows magic. One of our members is nearly one thousand years old, knows the secrets of life and death, and once resurrected a woman who had been dead for a month. He still doesn't understand email. Sometimes, technology is better."

We pass through the door and down another hall. We arrive at a large circular room. Huge blocks of limestone form the rounded walls, with each block etched in more symbols. At one end is an old wooden cabinet, and in the middle is a stone altar roughly the size of a cot.

Fiona closes the door behind us after we enter. It scrapes shut with a thunderous boom, shutting us inside. I give her a questioning look, but she merely returns a smile.

Drawn on the floor is a perfect circle about thirty feet in diameter. There are no symbols inside it—just a blank canvas. Ammon opens the cabinet and collects four candles. He lays them at four opposite points of the circle.

Fiona takes my hand and leads me to the altar. As I near, I notice it's completely covered in the carvings of various runes and symbols. There are so many, overlapping each other, that they look like graffiti. I surmise that the reason it has so many symbols is because a lot of ceremonies have been conducted on it over the years. I also notice there are manacles connected to the stone. *They look comfy.*

"We can always back out if you want." She guides me onto the altar.

"Shut up, Fiona. Let's get this over with."

I'm sure she's trying to be reassuring, but after the way she's been acting lately, I suspect she has some ulterior motive I haven't figured out yet. I know enough not to trust Fiona or Ammon, but I'm also realizing that I can be as valuable to them as they can be to me. I may provide them some long-term benefits, so I don't think they intend to do me harm... today.

Fiona gestures at the tweed coat I'm wearing. "You'll be needing to remove this." I take off the garment and hand it to her. Dressed only in my T-shirt and jeans, I'm suddenly freezing. At least, for now. "Shoes, too, dear," Fiona says. "It's all part of the... process."

Ritual, she almost said. As in *ritual evocation* or *ritual sacrifice.* Begrudgingly, I remove my boots. She gestures to my socks, and I peel them off and stuff them in the boots. I'm suddenly conscious of fuzz between my toes.

I lie down on the cold stone, and Fiona shackles me to the altar. It is just as uncomfortable as I imagined. She jerks down on the chains to remove the slack from my arms and legs then uses a metal lock to keep them in place. When I pull on the chains, there is no give.

Ammon walks into my line of vision, and I see he has lit the four candles. He walks inside the circle, waving a burning censer that dangles from a gold chain. The perfume fills the air, a combination of floral and sage that is quite calming. As the smoke settles on the floor, it solidifies into a drawing—a five-pointed star, along with a variety of hieroglyphs.

Fiona stands beside me and ties a leather strap around my arm then cleans a spot on my forearm with alcohol. A butterfly needle with a long tube connected to the end appears in her hand. She glances at me. I nod.

She plunges the needle into my vein. I watch as blood drips out of my arm, through the hose, and into a golden chalice on the floor. It's a lot more blood than I was expecting. She finishes the job by taping the needle into place.

Ammon appears above my head, holding a small wooden stick wrapped in leather.

"What's that for?" I ask.

"So you don't bite your tongue off."

Well, that's a considerate touch for someone who's about to lure a demon out of my body. This is the second time this week I've been shackled to a table. I'm beginning to suspect I may be partially to blame for this coincidence.

Ammon looks down at me. "Are you ready?"

"Are you?" I ask.

"I assure you, I'm well prepared."

"Then sure. Why the hell not?"

He places the leather bit inside my mouth then steps backward until he is outside the circle. He steadies himself then begins to chant.

"O Daemon, audi me
"Prodi et detege se."

With a jolt, pain suddenly courses through my body. I close my eyes as I writhe and pull at the chains, which keep me steady.

"Imprecor Aerem
"Imprecor Aquam
"Imprecor Terram
"Imprecor Ignem."

A fiery burn permeates my entire body. I scream through the bit as the pain continues to explode from deep inside.

"O Daemon, audi me
"Te complectimur in cameram."

Ammon's voice projects throughout the chamber as he switches languages. "I, Ammon of Egypt, do invite you, oh magnificent and formidable one, to our humble chamber!"

I open my eyes. I can see the flames of the four candles explode upward into the room like fireworks. In my mind, I can hear Father Ramon's voice. The pain is exhausting. I can't focus. Something is crawling out from within my stomach. It claws at my throat. Trying to get out.

Again, I can hear Father Ramon telling me to stay in control. I can't. It hurts too much. My jam slams shut, and the wooden bit bursts between my teeth.

Slowly my senses start coming back to me. My eyes remain shut as my consciousness returns, and I try to make sense of where I am. I'm cold. The floor is hard. I'm on my side. Something shuffles close to my head. It makes a *click, click, click* sound.

I open my eyes. My shirt is gone, and I'm only wearing my bra and jeans. The rough, cold floor sticks to my skin. I'm curled in a fetal position inside the edge of the circle. I can see its painted border right at my face.

Click, click, click, click, click…

When I roll over, I'm met by a horrifying sight. A sea of insects crawl over each other right in front my face. Thousands of centipedes, spiders, beetles, and other nasty bugs form a thick blanket two inches deep.

I scramble away and to my feet, swatting at anything that might be on me. The insects quickly fill the void left by my absence in the ring but do not cross its border. A perfect circle of bugs forms in the center of the room. They continue to crawl over each other, unable to penetrate the magical barrier and escape the ring. Their spindly legs and bony pincers continue to *click, click, click.*

It occurs to me where all these bugs came from. I spit, just in case I have any lingering bugs in my mouth. My body shivers, and I swipe at my bare skin and my hair to shed any stowaways. Chains clank with every movement I make.

I look down. Manacles are still attached to my wrists and ankles, their broken chains dangling. Something pierces my biceps. There, in my flesh, is a small piece of metal. I pinch it and draw out the long remnant of the hypodermic needle. I flick it to the floor.

At the center of the mass of insects lie the broken remains of the stone altar. What's left of my torn and tattered shirt is draped across one corner. Glancing around the room, I can see a fragment of stone imbedded in the wall, with a broken chain hanging from its surface.

Near the cabinet, I spy my jacket and boots. Careful not to

step inside the circle, I grab my clothes then hurry to the door at the other side of the room. It's locked.

I bang on the door and pull on my coat. "Hey! Let me out of here!" My throat is sore, and I fear to consider why that might be.

"Dear, is that really you?"

"Cut the shit, Fiona, and let me out."

"That's her," she says to someone on the other side. Moments later, I hear a click, and the door opens.

Not waiting for the door to open all the way, I push through and into the hallway. I shield myself when I see both Fiona and Ammon standing down the hall, each posed in a defensive magic stance. Fiona's hands are extended, generating a shimmering energy. Ammon points a golden and bejeweled staff right at me.

"Don't magic me!" I shout, not sure if that's the right term. "It's me! It's Darcy!"

I peer past my outstretched hands. Fiona lowers her hands, and the energy dissipates. Hesitantly, Ammon points his staff at the ground.

Jack Skellington moves past them toward me, holding a tray with a single glass of water. Not waiting for permission, I grab the glass and take a drink. The water is amazingly refreshing, and I suspect it has some magical qualities. Within seconds, my throat is no longer raw.

Ammon hurries past me and shuts the door to the chamber. His shirt is missing a sleeve, and his pant leg has rips going down the side. Fiona's usually perfectly styled hair is a mess. Then there's the fact that both of them are splattered with blood. My blood. Or Dudley's blood.

"I trust that went well," I mutter.

"Percival," Ammon says. I'm not sure what that's supposed

to mean until Jack Skellington appears beside me with the two wooden boxes. He shoves them into my chest even though I'm still holding my boots.

"*Maftūh*," Ammon says. The manacles open on their own. The one on my right wrist falls and crashes down on my pinky toe.

"Ow!" I shout and grab my foot with a free hand.

Ammon turns to Fiona. "Get her out of here." He marches down the hall and disappears around a corner.

Percival turns to Fiona. "Follow me."

Fiona grabs me by the arm and begins to drag me down the hall behind Percival but immediately pulls her hand away. It's the first time the normally touchy-feely Fiona has ever recoiled from our contact. She looks at my eyes as if she's never noticed them before.

"It's me," I assure her, still rubbing my toe.

"We'd best be off right away."

"Hold on. I don't have my boots on."

"Put them on in the lift." She grabs me again and hauls me through the club, this time not letting go. The members are lined up and watch from a safe distance as we walk past. They are on guard, so I suspect whatever ruckus I made in that room penetrated the walls.

Percival waits at the elevator, holding the door open for us. I limp inside then realize I'm alone. When I turn, I catch a glimpse of Fiona hesitating. Whatever she saw in that chamber has given her second thoughts about climbing into an enclosed box with me. She steels herself and steps inside the elevator.

The doors close, and we're descending. I plop down on the floor with my boxes and pull my socks and boots on. I stay seated on the elevator floor, my legs sprawled out before me.

"Did he get what he wanted?" I ask.

Fiona doesn't respond. She begins fumbling in her purse as if I'm not there.

I push for a response. "What happened in there?"

She pulls out a plastic zipper bag with two peanut butter cookies. "Here," she says, extending it to me without looking.

Just like a trip to the Red Cross. I snatch the bag and tear into the cookies.

As the elevator settles, Fiona finally says, "You need to get that cursed thing out of you."

Chapter 28

————◆————

The coffee shop where we meet Paige is quite nice. Fortunately, they have full leather club chairs—perfect for collapsing into a ball after an afternoon of failed demonology.

Paige's eyes bounce up and down as she looks at me. "What happened to you? Where's your shirt?"

I pull the warm tweed jacket closed and munch on my peanut butter cookies while Paige harasses me about what happened upstairs. The cookies are pretty good, so I take a few moments to enjoy them despite Paige's verbal assault that drones on and on.

Fiona orders coffee at the counter. Just before she entered the café, she donned big dark sunglasses to hide her identity. Her incognito mode doesn't work, so she has to sign autographs and pose for two selfies with fans while she waits for her order.

Paige refuses to relent, so I'm compelled to tell her what happened upstairs. She goes ballistic.

"Calm down. It was my decision," I tell her.

"Calm down?" she says, even more furious now.

Fiona returns and hands me a cup of coffee. Paige directs her anger on her. "You selfish old hag! I knew we shouldn't have trusted yo-*fth*—"

Without saying a word, Fiona calmly zips her purse closed. Paige's lips tighten. She struggles to open her mouth but can't.

"Let's not make a scene," Fiona warns her, glancing around. "I cannot afford to have this tirade appear on social media. I still have a reputation to uphold. Please calm yourself."

Fiona daintily lifts her coffee and takes a sip. She turns to me. "Drink up, dear. I promise it'll set you right."

I have no doubt of that. Paige sits here, arms crossed, and listens silently as Fiona and I reveal why I did what I did and what is in the two boxes.

When my coffee is finished, I do feel much better. After two peanut butter cookies and a cup of joe, it's like my hit points are back to full. Fiona unzips her purse, and Paige's jaw drops open. She rubs her mouth to get the feeling back, glaring at Fiona.

"I'm sorry, but you were grousing like a fool, and it was neither the time nor place."

"Don't ever use your witchcraft on me again," Paige says.

Fiona reaches for her purse again. When I grab her hand, she flinches. I try to make eye contact with her, but she refuses to look me directly in my yellow eyes. I must have done a number on her.

"Knock it off, both of you," I say, trying to move past the awkward moment. "Paige, we did what we had to do, and I need you to get on board. Fiona, no more hexing Paige. Got it?"

I'm chastising them and putting my foot down. A new dynamic has settled on the three of us, and I'm the grownup. It's weird, and I don't like it.

"Fine," Paige says. "What's our next move?"

"Well," Fiona says, standing up, "I'm quite sorry, but I'll

be leaving you for the rest of the afternoon. I have meetings at my office."

"You're not coming with us?" I ask, concerned.

Her eyes still refuse to meet mine. "You can use the Rover," she says, tossing me the keys. "I'll be at the lot. Come to us when you're done."

"What if we need your help? I don't even know how to use these things," I protest, indicating the two boxes from Ammon.

Fiona pulls out a pad and pen and proceeds to jot something down. "It's quite easy. The command word for the pendulum is *Finna* to find someone. For instance, *Finna Paige.*"

The box lurches and shifts toward Paige. I have to hold it before it slides off my lap. Paige flinches, still gun-shy from Fiona's prior spell.

"*Stöðva* to stop," Fiona says.

The box settles down. She tears off the piece of paper and hands it to me. When I reach out to take it from her, she lightly tosses it in my direction to keep her distance from me. As if suddenly aware of how she's acting, Fiona composes herself and straightens her outfit.

"Good luck." She disappears out through the door.

"What was that all about?" Paige asks.

Whatever I—or Dudley—did scared the living shit out of Fiona, and she's a witch. The last thing I need is to scare Paige. She's the only person left standing by my side.

"I think I embarrassed her upstairs in front of her friends," I say.

~

Paige drives Fiona's Land Rover east on Hollywood Boulevard. I ride shotgun, the pendulum dangling from its chain in my hand. It sways with the momentum of the moving car. Sunlight refracts clearly off its surface, bouncing clear beams inside the car.

Looking at Fiona's note, I read the words out loud. "*Finna Elizabeth.*"

The crystal continues to swing but does not point anywhere.

"Did you break it?" Paige asks.

"I didn't break it."

"Then why didn't it work?"

I consider and try again. "*Finna Santa Muerte.*"

The pendulum begins to rock more. Without any provocation from me, it spins on its chain. This is not something it did in Ammon's office, so I'm concerned that maybe I did break it. Suddenly, it swings up and hovers at a perfect right angle, pointing east.

"Well, I guess we're going east," I say.

We head into Los Feliz, where the street takes us south. Still going east, we head up into the hills. We zigzag our way past the residential houses and hit a dead end when we come upon the Silver Lake Reservoir.

This isn't going to be easy.

We decide to take a gamble and head back and north toward the other side. After two hours of dead ends and circling around, we finally find ourselves in Montecito Heights. It's a residential neighborhood where the architecture ranges from modern and craftsman to the outdated Victorian. We go through some parts that are clearly upscale but, two blocks later, find ourselves in a poorer area. Paige and I make our way up the meandering roads until we reach a turnoff. The next road is unpaved and poorly kept, and the car's wheels vibrate. We are forced to park the Land Rover when we arrive at a chain-link gate that blocks our path.

Fifty yards beyond is a seemingly abandoned collection of houses that surround a cul-de-sac. The pendulum continues to point past the barrier. I gather the veil and ready myself.

"Do you know how to use that?" Paige asks, staring at the piece of delicate fabric in my hand.

I wonder how I can test to see if it works. I look at Paige.

"What?" she asks, then her eyes widen. "Oh, come on. I've already had one spell cast on me today!"

"Paige, please. You know I never ask you for anything."

Her eyes widen. "You ask me for shit all the time!"

"I need to know if this can help me!"

I must look pretty desperate. Paige looks into my face. She knows the situation we're walking into and that the veil could literally save my soul.

She rolls her eyes and shakes her head. "I can't believe the crap I let you put me through. How does it work?"

I try not to smile. "Ammon said that whoever wears this veil is compelled to tell the truth." I raise the delicate cloth toward the top of her head. "I guess we just put this on your—"

Before I can even finish sentence, the veil flies from my hand. It wraps itself around her head and pulls itself taut around her face. Immediately, her mouth opens, and she struggles to breathe. The veil tightens, stretching over her face like rubber.

Instinctively, I reach out to pull it away. Then I stop. "My red-and-white cashmere sweater…"

Paige's eyes widen under the gauze. She shakes her head vigorously as she tries to inhale.

"You said the dry cleaner lost it. Was that true?"

Paige closes her eyes, but it doesn't take long before she's finally able to inhale. When she breathes, the words pour out. "I never took it to the dry cleaner's. I donated it to a thrift store." The veil loosens then collapses around her neck. She yanks the fabric away and flings it at me.

"I loved that sweater!" I yell.

"It was the single most hideous thing you ever owned! Who wears Christmas colors in the middle of September?" She opens the car door, stumbles outside, and slams it behind her. I open my door and follow her to the driver's side. She stands there, hands on her hips, catching her breath. "Not cool."

"I'm sorry, but I had to know it worked." I give her a moment. "Was it really that ugly?"

"You looked like Waldo."

It's hard to be angry with Paige when she's always looking out for me—or putting herself at risk by letting me test unknown magical artifacts on her. "Thank you," I say.

She nods. "So, are we going to find this death saint now or what?"

I approach a concrete marker with a bronze plaque that stands beside the road. It reads:

Sterling Terrace has been designated as a Historic Neighborhood and includes twenty Victorian homes constructed between the years 1885 and 1888.
City of Los Angeles, Cultural Heritage Commission

We climb over the fence and find ourselves walking down the middle of the street of an abandoned neighborhood. The Victorian houses are forgotten and dilapidated. Overgrown grass, broken windows, and graffiti mar all the homes we pass. I notice pieces of paper on every door.

I detour from my path and approach one of the homes. The once-red tag has faded over time. "Unsafe," I read. "Do not enter or occupy."

Paige looks around. "Every house has this."

"They're all earthquake damaged."

"No one's lived here for years."

We keep walking, following the crystal's navigation. At the top, the street loops around a center island on which sits a decrepit and stained gazebo. The circular structure stands on four posts wrapped in garlands of dead flowers. In the center of the gazebo is an elevated stone structure painted over with spray paint. I circle around the island. As I move, the crystal continues to point right at the center.

"The gazebo?" Paige asks.

I nod. "*Stöðva*," I command. The pendulum droops back down. I wrap the silver chain around my neck so the crystal dangles at my chest, then I retrieve the veil and clutch the fabric. *Just in case.*

Thousands of dead petals litter the dead grass on the island. Most have turned brown, but some still bear their vibrant colors. Ashes, feathers, and remnants of char can be traced on the dirt and the flowers. Covering most of them is a thin string of wax that seems to have glued them in place. There's a pattern to the detritus. The various leaves, flowers, and feathers form concentric circles expanding from the gazebo.

I peel a feather off the ground and inspect the burnt ends. "We've seen this before."

"Santa Muerte," Paige says.

I nod. We step onto the island and approach the gazebo. More wax drippings coat the ground. There are even piles of it in some places.

The circular stone structure in the center was probably once a fire pit. Cement has been poured inside, creating a flat surface. Underneath layers of spray paint, I can make out now-familiar imagery carved into the filling—an angry Aztec god holding a heart in each hand.

"We saw that at the museum," Paige says.

"The Aztec sun stone."

Paige leans in close to inspect past the graffiti that obscures it. "Why just the face? Why not the outer rings?"

I point to the concentric circles that surround us. "Those are the outer rings. This entire island forms the rest of the symbol."

The fact that somebody would devote such much time and energy to crafting this shrine gives me an uneasy feeling. *Why did they do it?* is the sixty-four-thousand-dollar question. I scan the fire pit. It reminds me of Malbrook and the Witching Well where Vivien and I would spend our afternoons.

Paige looks down the edge of the stones. "Darce?" She points to thick drops of dried blood on the waxy floor. It's a lot of blood. "What do we think?"

"Not good."

Her head down, Paige moves away from the gazebo. "I think I found a trail."

A red line leads onto the street. We follow the trail until it becomes clear where we're going—the house at the top of the loop. It stands higher than the others, but this home is in better shape than anything else on the cul-de-sac. Its rounded corner tower offers a view of every house on the block. Though it's aged and worn and tilts slightly to one side, there isn't a spot of graffiti on its gray-and-red facade.

The trail of blood leads directly to the door. Another faded red tag is stapled to it with the warning *Unsafe*.

Paige reaches into her cardigan and pulls out a gun.

"I forgot you had that," I say. "You can't even see that tucked under your sweater."

"I know, right?" she says, pulling open her cardigan to reveal the tiny shoulder holster tucked beside her breast. "It's so skinny you can't even see it."

"You know how to use it?"

"I've used this before."

"Yeah, and you almost shot me," I say, remembering how she shot Santa Muerte last time. "Just keep the gun at your side until you're ready to aim. Finger off the trigger until you're ready to shoot."

And there it is, the echo of my father's voice coming out of my mouth. Every time we went shooting, that was what he would tell me, drilling it in my head. Here I am, trying to hunt down an evil spirit, and now I have family issues to contend with. I do my best to shake them off and focus.

"And don't shoot Santa Muerte. I need Elizabeth alive."

"Then why do I even have the gun?" she asks.

"Look, you can shoot anyone except you, me, and Elizabeth."

"Fine."

"Fine."

We walk up to the front porch. The boards creak under our weight, bending as both of us stand on the deck. The trail of blood disappears under the front door. I reach for the knob.

"What if someone's in there?" she asks.

"That's why we're here."

"Right. Shit. Okay." She gets the gun ready and presses her shoulder against the doorjamb. I turn the knob, but it's locked.

"Remember, leave Santa Muerte to me," I say, clutching the veil.

"Can I admit something?" Paige asks.

"Sure."

"I wish Fiona were here."

"Me too."

I aim my foot carefully and kick down the door. The wood splinters inward easily. I probably could have pushed down the door if I'd tried.

Paige follows me, gun drawn, as we step slowly into the house. It smells of mildew, tobacco, and… lemon. There is no furniture. Empty cans of food, beer, and soda are littered throughout the house, along with Sterno cans. Thick dark spots pepper the old carpet that stretches the length of the floor, giving it a leopard pattern.

"Maybe we should get a leopard-print rug," I tell Paige, nodding at the floor.

She scowls. "Do you want me to move out?"

Carefully, we make our way to the kitchen. Various pots and pans sit on the stove and countertops. Dried sprigs of herbs dangle from the walls and ceiling, tied into bundles with straw. The small table in the corner is covered in glass bottles filled with God knows what.

We return to the living room, staying close together. On the far side of the room, I notice a map pinned to the wall. I pull Paige with me as I walk toward it. It's a municipal map of Los Angeles, with various pushpins pressed into its surface. Immediately, I find a pin pressed into place in Pasadena, marking Carmen's house.

Paige points out another location—our apartment. Whoever was here was looking for Carmen and for us. Evidently, they found both. I wonder who all the other addresses belong to. I pull out my cell phone and take a photo of the map.

Looking around, I find nothing else here to inspect. Paige points upstairs. I head up the stairs, and Paige follows, gun pointed. On either side of each step is a cluster of unlit and half-melted candles. The wax runs down the entire staircase, like a waterfall frozen in time. As we climb, each step creaks under our weight. At the top of the stairs, we reach a small landing with a closed door on either side. The blood trails to our left.

I look at Paige and mouth, "Ready?"

She nods and lowers the gun. *Gun at your side until you're ready to aim. Finger off the trigger until you're ready to shoot.*

Using my fingers, I count down. *One... two...*

Ring!

Something rattles against me, and I jump to the side. My shoulder bumps into Paige, and she fires.

Bam! A bullet pierces the floor right by my boot.

I bounce away. "Jesus Christ!" My ears ring from the gunshot in such a small space.

"What the hell?" Paige screams.

Ring!

It's my cell phone. I pull it out and look at the display. Paige breathes a sigh of relief but keeps her gun pointed at the door.

Ring!

Nothing happens. No one seems to be around.

"I need to take this," I say.

"Now?" she asks like I'm crazy.

I click Answer and put it on speakerphone. "Carmen?"

Paige shoots me a surprised look.

Carmen's familiar voice speaks on the other end. "Are you okay?"

"I'm fine. Where are you?"

"I'm with Father Ramon. Darcy, it was Santa Muerte! The Holy Angel of Death! It came to my house. I saw it. It killed Leona."

It. I don't think she knows *it* is her daughter.

"You must believe me," she pleads.

"I do." I exchange a look with Paige. "I was there last night too. I saw it. Wait." I think about last night's timeline. "When were you there? When did Santa Muerte come?"

"I don't know. It was very late. I barely escaped."

She must have escaped shortly before Paige and I arrived. If

I hadn't been shot, if we hadn't stayed so long at the retirement home, maybe Leona would still be alive.

"She must have my Elizabeth," Carmen says. "Oh, *mija*! Do you think she's okay?"

"I'm still looking for her," I assure her. My eyes zero in on the blood trail that disappears under the closed door.

"What if she's..." Carmen trails off.

"Don't think that." I'm afraid to open the door... afraid of what might be inside. "Not for one second. I'm going to find her. Where are you?"

"Father Ramon has given me sanctuary at the Cathedral."

"Downtown?"

"It's the only place safe for me anymore. Can you come?"

"I'll be there as soon as I can," I say.

"Thank you."

I hang up.

"What do you think?" Paige asks, her eyes fixed on the door.

"There's only one way to find out." I reach out and turn the handle.

The moment the door opens, a putrid stench punches us like a fist. Paige gags then bolts downstairs to vomit. I cover my nose and mouth with my sleeve and examine the space. The windows are boarded, so I use the flashlight app on my phone to see. In the center of the room is a stained mattress on an iron bedframe. Empty handcuffs dangle from the four posts at each corner of the bed. Piled on the floor is a red sweater. I lift it and find the gold letters USC embroidered on the chest. I've seen this sweater before. It's the one Elizabeth wore in the photos in her room.

In the corner of the room is a plastic bucket. It's the source of the smell and tells me all I need to know about the horrible conditions this poor girl was kept in. She never stood a chance.

I hurry out, closing the door behind me and taking a deep breath of fresh air. I run downstairs to find Paige outside, leaning against the wall of the house. A garden hose is in her hand, but no water comes out.

"Are you okay?"

"What the hell was that?" she asks, still choking back her revulsion.

"They kept her in that room to weaken her. She was trapped, given only enough food and water to keep her from dying." I remember what she looked like at Carmen's house. Weakened. Pale. Eyes darkened. The poor girl is just a host. "When she couldn't fight anymore, they offered her body to Santa Muerte."

"Jesus." While Paige dry heaves, I hold her hair. "What about the blood?" she asks when she's able to talk.

My eyes follow the trail of blood. It wasn't going *to* the house—it was coming *from* the house and heading to the gazebo with its floral garlands—to the stone fire pit marked with Aztec symbols. The candle wax, flower petals, and feathers all make sense now. I've seen those before at the temple on Whittier.

"That's an altar," I say. "That was where they did it. That was where Elizabeth's body was offered as a host to Santa Muerte."

Chapter 29

When Carmen said she was at the Cathedral, I knew exactly what she meant. The Cathedral of Our Lady of the Angels is the home of the Archdiocese of Los Angeles. It's a massive complex of postmodern buildings, completely rejecting the decades—or centuries—of classical architecture one usually sees in churches. The Cathedral is a concrete geometric structure with hundred-foot walls the color of sunbaked adobe. Despite its blocklike construction, it possesses no right angles.

I call Carmen and ask her to meet across the street at the park on Temple Avenue—a safe distance from the Cathedral's hallowed grounds. She's reluctant and pleads with me to meet her at the clergy residence where Father Ramon has secured her a room. I don't want to mention the whole I'm-possessed-by-a-demon-and-can't-step-on-holy-ground thing, so I tell her I need to meet in an open place where we can't be surprised. When I hear Father Ramon's reassuring voice on her end, I know he'll find a way to convince her it's safe to step out.

Minutes later, Carmen hurries across the street. She's

wearing big sunglasses, a hat, and a scarf. In her effort to look inconspicuous, she could not attract more attention if she tried. She looks like Fiona. Beside her is Father Ramon. Today, he's dressed in the full Catholic cassock, a black tunic that drapes from his shoulders to the ground.

When Carmen reaches me, she greets me with a hug. I wave to Father Ramon. "I'm so happy to see you're safe," she whispers.

We find a park bench and sit down together. "What happened?" I ask.

Carmen takes a deep breath to steady herself and reaches for Ramon's hand. "It was evening, so the staff had gone home. Except Leona. I was in the kitchen, cooking dinner. Leona had been outside, tending to our rose garden. I was alone. When I turned around, I saw her. *Santa Muerte*.

"I didn't know what to do. I stood there, frozen. It stared at me with those eyes. Then Leona came back in. She was holding those flowers. Before she could scream, that thing raced across the room. It was all so fast. The next thing I saw, it was holding Leona's…"

She trails off. "I ran out of the house as fast as I could."

I recall the surveillance team outside her house that night. Evidently, they didn't see anyone leave. When I ask Carmen about that, she has an answer.

"I knew someday I would have to escape the confines of my own home. My staff and I had developed a plan for just such an occasion. And that escape route was not going through my front door but to the house next door, which I also own. There was a car there, waiting for me, with the keys inside. That's how I escaped."

It's not an answer I like, but it makes a lot of sense. Anyone who's a target with a lot of enemies would probably have planned an escape route a long time ago.

"You have no idea how horrifying it was. It was pure evil," she says, shivering.

"I do know."

She nods. "Then you have seen the face of evil."

Every morning in the mirror. "It's best that you're here with Father Ramon," I assure her. "It probably can't harm you on hallowed ground."

"You should stay here too," she offers.

"Why didn't the spirit attack you?" Paige interjects. It's a good question. When I struggled with the spirit, it was alarmingly fast and strong. It should have been able to catch Carmen.

"Perhaps because I showed her this," Carmen answers, reaching into the collar of her shirt.

She pulls out a gold medallion. It's circular, with the image of a monk holding a cross in his hand and Latin text along the margins. I give one glance and recoil. My reaction is instinctual and not at all subtle. My stomach rumbles in pain, and I gag momentarily while doubling over.

"Darcy, are you okay?" Paige asks, patting me on the back.

I hold my hand up to signal I'm okay. When I sit up, I have to wipe the tears in my eyes. The medallion is back in her shirt.

"Are you all right?" Carmen asks.

I nod. "Caught something in my throat." The look on Carmen's face tells me she's not buying this at all.

Father Ramon steers the conversation forward. "It's the Saint Benedict Medal. I gave it to Carmen last week as a protection for her in this time of need. A blessed, *very powerful* tool against evil."

I am all too familiar with its powers. The Saint Benedict Medal is a tool priests use during an exorcism to combat the powers of evil. It's what Father Ramon used the few times he attempted to exorcise me. *Works like a charm.*

"Where was Hugo?" I ask when I can speak clearly again.

"He wasn't there. I'm not sure."

"Have you seen or heard from him since?"

"Do you think he had something to do with this? You don't think he took Elizabeth?"

"He knew how to find her. He knew how to get into your house to attack you and kill Leona. And I believe he was involved in Santa Muerte."

"My God," she says. "I've known him for years. My husband trusted him. We all trusted him."

"And he probably used that trust against you."

"Promise me, Darcy," she pleads. "Please find my daughter. Please bring Elizabeth home to me."

Still trying to catch my breath, I promise to do just that.

Father Ramon takes me aside before they leave. "I'm sorry about that," he says, referring to the incident with the Saint Benedict Medal. "Are you sure you're all right?"

I nod. I didn't expect the medal, so it felt like a sucker punch. I need a minute to recover.

"Are you sure you're okay?" he asks again.

Everyone keeps asking me that, so I must look pretty bad. I assure him I'm fine. Paige and I watch him escort Carmen back onto the cathedral grounds before we get into the Land Rover and drive away.

Chapter 30

By the time we arrive on the studio lot, the sun has started to set in the west. Even by Los Angeles standards, it's a beautiful sunset. Hues of orange and red blend into each other, creating a blanket of warmth across the sky so that everything in the city is diffused by the same light. Some people say it's the smog that gives us these beautiful sunsets. I guess you can find something positive in the worst of circumstances.

I text Fiona, who directs us to park outside Stage 9. Once we're there, Paige moves to the back seat. When Fiona exits the stage door, she jumps straight into the driver's seat.

Fiona revs the engine and pulls away. "You're both still alive." She pulls into traffic and starts navigating her way through the busy streets. "I trust everything went well."

"We didn't find Santa Muerte," I report. "But I think we found where they conducted the ritual to summon her."

"The spirit wasn't there? That's odd."

"There was a shrine to Santa Muerte. Maybe that was it." I hold up the pendulum and examine it. "Or maybe I did break it."

Paige chimes in with, "Told you."

"Oh, and Carmen's still alive," I tell Fiona. "She's found sanctuary at the Catholic church downtown."

Fiona chuckles. "That won't protect her. The spirit of Santa Muerte is not a visitor from hell." She casts a sideways glance at me. "It'll protect her from you, though."

It seems like Fiona is still sore from my nearly killing her earlier.

"It's still evil," Paige argues. "I thought evil can't set foot on hallowed grounds."

I have to agree, based on personal experience.

Fiona shakes her head. "My dear, there's evil that goes to church every day."

As we drive along Sunset Boulevard, I ask Fiona to tell me more about Melchora.

"She joined the Mancery about a year ago. I don't know much about her background. Hers is not a name I had encountered before. Most new members make an effort to ingratiate themselves to the community, and Melchora was no exception. She offered to host some lectures on Mesoamerican magic and was an active participant in our exchange program."

I stiffen. "Is that the program where you pawned my demonic emissions?"

Fiona ignores my snide remark. "I learned a lot from her. My practice goes back a long way, as you know, but there was much I didn't know about magic from the Americas. It was informative."

"Did she talk about Santa Muerte at all?" Paige asks.

"No," Fiona says. "I don't see why she would. Witches are known for sharing with other witches. Magic is something we want to see develop and grow. But we keep our best spells to ourselves."

"Is there any other way to find her?" I ask.

Fiona shakes her head. We continue driving in silence until we near Fiona's house, and she finally speaks up. "Darcy, maybe it's best you don't stay with me tonight."

I have been expecting this. After the incident at the Mancery, I figured my days of staying at Fiona's home were numbered. And apparently, that number was one—I got one whole night there.

"Why?" Paige asks.

Pretending not to hear, Fiona continues. "I've booked a suite for you at the W. It's a two-room suite, so you and Paige should be quite comfortable there. My treat, of course. Until this whole thing blows over."

When Fiona pulls into her driveway, the sun has set in the west and the sky has completed its transformation into night. The city lights bounce off the clouds above, making this night a much brighter one than usual.

"I'll have Eva Jean send over a car to take you to the hotel," Fiona says as we walk from her Land Rover to her house.

"Thanks," I say.

Fiona's home is a welcome retreat after a long and taxing day. She heads straight to her sanctuary in the kitchen. As Paige and I head to the bedroom to pack, Fiona calls, "Why don't you come with me to the kitchen? I'll fix you some supper before you go."

Paige and I exchange a look. Our silent communication echoes the same question—*why the sudden change of tone?* One second, we can't stay. The next, she's offering us dinner.

Still, I'm never one to turn down a good meal, so I drag Paige with me into the kitchen. We sit at the counter as Fiona begins pulling out ingredients and placing them on the counter.

She delicately lays out a selection of herbs and spices.

She then moves to her range top and turns on all six flames for her burners. "I have always found cooking to be a great way to prepare for any situation." Fiona continues to lay out the ingredients for her dish.

It's been a long day, and with dinner on the horizon, I decide to take some Klonopin as an aperitif. As soon as I pull the bottle out, Fiona clamps her hand over mine and pushes it down. "A good meal is the recipe for whatever trials and tribulations we must confront."

I let go of my pills, and she releases my hand. She pulls open a canister of seeds and spills them across the counter in front of us. Her hands wave over the seeds. When I look down, I can see they've reorganized themselves into letters to spell out a simple phrase: *We are not alone.*

Looking at the seed letters, Paige grabs my arm. I meet Fiona's eyes.

"Everything I need to face today day can be found in the kitchen." Fiona pops open several silver canisters one by one.

Only now do I notice the other ingredients she's laid out. Salt, crystals, gold coins, copper wire... they're not ingredients. They're spell components.

"And I always have the perfect recipe for any guest that comes into my home."

Without hesitation, I dive on top of Paige and take her to the floor. It's not a moment too soon as a dozen of tiny darts fly across the air.

Ting-ting-ting-ting-ting! Fiona catches them all in the lid of a stainless-steel pan, shielding herself like an Amazon warrior. She lowers the lid to inspect the projectiles. They're not darts at all. They're actually small silver feathers.

The skeletal figure of Santa Muerte hovers above the

ground in Fiona's kitchen. Her blue-and-red robes flow like gossamer caught in a tide of invisible water. Her skull-like face scowls directly at me. There is no trace of Elizabeth in this body. It's as if she's completely consumed by this entity.

Standing beside Santa Muerte is a spindly old woman wrapped in a cloak of silvery gray feathers. When she moves, they catch the light as if made of metal. Her wiry white hair flows across her head like a mane. Soulless eyes stare at me through cloudy wide pupils. Her nose is sharp and hooked, resembling a beak.

Paige and I scramble to our feet.

"Hello, Melchora," Fiona says.

Slowly, Melchora's foggy eyes turn to Fiona. Her lips stretch into a sinister smile. "It's good to see you, old friend," she hisses. "I wish you had not become involved."

"Me, too, dear."

Bam! An explosion behind me makes me flinch. Melchora's body bounces back, forcing her to stagger for balance.

All eyes turn to Paige. She stands with two hands on her smoking gun, which is pointed right at Melchora. The witch hisses at Paige, not at all affected by the bullets.

"You shouldn't have done that," Fiona says. "Now you've made her angry."

With that, Fiona extends an outstretched hand toward the kitchen range. In an instant, the blue flames leap from the burners to her fist. She grabs the fire like a whip then flings the flames at Melchora.

With inhuman speed, Melchora sidesteps the fiery attack as it crashes onto the floor. She blows air into her fists then thrusts forward her open palms. A powerful wind blasts out of her hands and knocks Fiona back, scattering all the ingredients in her kitchen and extinguishing the flames behind her.

Without taking her eyes from Fiona, Melchora extends her

bony finger toward me. She says one word to the spirit beside her. "*Matar.*"

Santa Muerte's skeletal face contorts into a grotesque smile. "Stay behind me," I tell Paige.

She takes a step to stand beside me, ready to fight. Santa Muerte floats toward us, looking to strike. Her figure sways from side to side like a serpent as she approaches. Paige and I back away.

She strikes, her bony claw rushing toward my chest, and I grab her by the wrist, stopping her. Paige shoulder-checks Santa Muerte, catches her arm, and pulls it away from my heart. I hold Santa Muerte's arms tightly and feel skin sliding over bone. With Paige's strength, I'm able to keep the entity from plunging her fingers into my sternum.

Santa Muerte attacks again, this time trying to bite at me with her jagged teeth. Unable to release my grip on her still-extended arms, I twist away and try to keep our arms between us as a defense. *Clack, clack, clack!* The jaws chomp with such force that bits of teeth break off and fly into my face.

The alarm on my watch starts beeping. My heart rate is accelerating. Blood warms in my body. The power starts to surge, and I test my strength, pushing back the claw. It works. Dudley's power is starting to build.

Santa Muerte stops, and our eyes lock. This is the creature who holds the key to my salvation. If I could grab the veil, I could restrain her and get the name.

My eyes remain on Santa Muerte, but I can hear the chaos around me. Crashing metal and flashes of light hint at the epic battle between the two witches. With Paige gripping one arm, I try to hold the entity with one hand and reach with the other to grab the veil from my pocket. Santa Muerte pushes back, and I need all my strength to keep her at bay.

The ebb and flow of our struggle spins us around.

Somewhere in the room, I hear the flapping of wings. Gray feathers fly in my peripheral vision.

Santa Muerte releases me and floats backward. Her black eyes shift to Paige.

Shit.

She lunges, extending her bony claws toward Paige's chest. Now Paige is pushing, and I'm pulling Santa Muerte off her. We rotate our momentum into a circle, slamming ourselves into the kitchen counter.

I try to protect Paige by keeping myself between her and Santa Muerte. Out of the corner of my eye, I see lightning bolts scatter across the ceiling. Fiona's body sails through the air and lands with a thud against a nearby wall.

Momentarily distracted, Santa Muerte reaches around me and grabs Paige by the arm. My defense shifts, and the entity takes the opportunity to bite down onto my neck. She doesn't just take one bite but tears repeatedly into my skin like a wild animal. Flesh is ripped from my body, and I scream in agony. Warm blood flows easily from my wound, soaking into the collar of my shirt. Sweat drips from my brow as I struggle, and I suddenly become aware of how hot I am.

I know now why Fiona didn't want me taking any Klonopin. She was counting on Dudley's help. I clutch at the specter's hair and yank her back to pull her jaws away from me.

"Get the veil now!" I shout. Paige struggles to reach into my coat pocket.

My mind races to think of something calming, but all I can think about is the wild creature attacking me. I know that this really is Elizabeth, but all I can see is something as demonic as I am. All I see is Santa Muerte.

Paige's hand digs furiously into the pockets of my coat. "Pants pocket!" I yell. She switches gears, searching in every wrong pocket of my jeans. Finally, she gets the right pocket, but when I raise my thigh to kick against Santa Muerte, Paige's hand gets stuck.

Melchora slams against the ceiling, crushing a lamp. Sparks rain down. She remains pinned to the lighting fixture by some invisible force.

Then Paige screams. I look back and see that Santa Muerte's bony claws have torn at Paige's sleeve, leaving four bloody marks. She hurt my friend.

The secondary alarm sounds on my watch. My heart rate is at one hundred ninety beats per minute. Screw flight—I'm in fight mode. A monstrous roar bellows from within.

Santa Muerte's eyes turn to me. I can sense her fear.

I charge forward with all my strength—with Dudley's intensifying strength—and lift her above my head then slam her against a glass table. The table shatters as we crash to the floor.

"Darcy!" Fiona shouts. "Control it!" The sound is muffled.

My hands are wrapped around the throat of Santa Muerte as I lean over her. Melchora falls to the floor beside us. She reaches out to me to stop. Her face is filled with panic. She looks suddenly vulnerable, but it doesn't matter. It's too late.

Blood drips from the wound in my neck onto the spirit. Santa Muerte flickers, and for a moment, Elizabeth's eyes appear, begging me to stop. I can't. Dudley won't let me.

Fiona pulls Paige back, dragging her away. I can see she's shouting something, but I can't hear what it is. I can't hear anything. Everything is moving in slow motion.

Melchora approaches. From her robes, she pulls a feather. Its shaft shimmers like metal.

Shards of glass from the broken table rise around me. Melchora shields her face with her forearms. Everything goes black.

Chapter 31

H*ell.* My eyes remain closed, but I know that's where I am. Intense heat envelops me and scorches my skin. A flickering glow penetrates my closed lids and burns my eyes. I'm facedown on the hard ground. This must be brimstone.

I'm afraid to open my eyes and see my final destination. The temperature increases, and I cannot remain still any longer. My eyes open.

An inferno consumes my vision. Fire licks at my skin, my face, and my clothes. The flames are everywhere. *This is all I will ever see or ever feel*, I think. *This is my eternity.*

Then a stream of water splashes my head. The flames die down as the torrent continues to wash over me. As the fire dies, the light dims. It's dark, and my eyes can't focus. The water continues to blast me. I raise my hand to stop it. Eventually, the torrent ceases.

When I can finally focus, I see Paige standing before me, holding a hose. Her lips move as she shouts. I hear nothing at first, then a muffled noise. Sounds slowly return.

"Darcy, get up!"

I turn back to the fiery hell. It's not hell. It's Fiona's house.

Too tired to stand, I crawl away from the flames. I was close, too close. Smoke rises from my clothes as fabric sears my skin. The tweed coat, though damaged, has resisted the fire quite well. The pendulum dangles from a chain, still wrapped around my neck.

On my wrist is a melted glop of black rubber—remnants of my watchband. The device itself is gone. I try to wipe it away with my other hand and only succeed in spreading the smudge everywhere.

When I'm farther away from the house, Paige tries to lift me. Her hands recoil. I'm too hot to touch.

I rise to my feet and trudge away. The partially melted soles of my boots stick to the ground with every step. My skin is covered in soot, ash, and melted plastic. I turn around to find Fiona's house fully ablaze. Rafters collapse, and smoke and embers rise into the night sky.

Paige takes a tentative position a few feet beside me. She has a scared look in her eyes. "Darcy?" she says, looking ready to run.

She's never seen it happen before firsthand. We've known each other for three years and lived together for two. I've done everything in my power to make sure she's never seen the evil inside me. Tonight, she finally met Dudley.

"It's me," I say, taking a step toward her. She takes a step back, her hands shaking uncontrollably.

It breaks my heart that I've frightened her. My best friend in the world. My only true friend. *What if she never trusts me again? What if she will always be afraid of me?*

Fiona's Land Rover pulls up beside us and screeches to a halt. The driver's-side window rolls down. "I wasn't here," Fiona says.

"What?" I'm still trying to catch up on what just happened.

"Listen! I wasn't here. I let you stay while I was away on business to Vancouver. Say it!"

I shake the cobwebs from my head. "You were on a trip."

Fiona takes a last look at the fire. Her eyes well up. Then she looks at me. "You've destroyed me."

The SUV starts to pull away when I shout, "How do I stop her?"

Fiona, fortunately, hits the brakes.

I plead with her. "How do I stop Melchora?" Her eyes stay focused on the road out of here. I can tell she's tempted to drive away. "Please," I say.

"You can't," she answers. Then she turns to look at me. "Maybe *it* can."

"There must be some other way," I say. I'm not willing to leverage Dudley if I don't have to.

Fiona shakes her head. "Only magic can defeat her, Darcy Caine. If you're lucky, maybe the power you possess can destroy her… if it doesn't destroy you first."

She hits the gas, and the Land Rover peels away. It smashes through the gates—she is not even bothering to wait for them to open right away. The red taillights disappear on Mulholland.

I turn to Paige. She's looking at me, still afraid. "If you run, too, I'll understand." I don't know what she just witnessed, but judging by the destruction beside me, it was awful. I add, "Maybe it's better if you did."

She takes a few hesitant steps toward me then changes to a run. She throws her arms around me and holds me tightly. "Don't you get it, Darcy?" she says, her arms gripping me tighter and tighter. "You're all I have in this world. We're the only family we have. I would walk through fire for you. And if anything were to happen to you if…"

She struggles to get the thought out, but I know what she means. *If I were to die and go to hell.*

"If anything happened to you, I wouldn't let you go there alone. I would be right by your side. Forever."

My knees give, but she holds me up. My arms hold on to her as I collapse. The tears pour out. Sirens wail in the distance.

Paige and I decide not to wait for the fire department—there are too many questions we're not prepared to answer. With only one road in to Fiona's house, we have to hurry along a walking trail that leads down to the next property on the hill side. We sneak past the house that sits below Fiona's and finally arrive at another street.

"Should we call for a ride?" I ask.

Paige pulls out her cell phone. "I've got no reception out here. What about you?"

I reach into my jacket pocket and pull out my phone. The screen is shattered, and the phone case has melted around the device. It's a horrible thing to admit, but I'm devastated to think that my phone is ruined.

Then I realize that Paige lost her computer, and guilt settles on me. Her laptop is everything—her work, her life—Christ, even her investigation into her mother. She tries to tell me not to worry about it, that she had backups to the cloud, but I still worry that she might have lost something that couldn't be replaced.

We take inventory of what we have left. Paige still has her wallet, her cell phone, and the gun Fiona gave her tucked into the back of her jeans. I still have the pendulum around my neck, and Paige still has the veil in her pocket.

We continue our walk back to civilization along the dark, quiet road. Paige tells me what happened tonight. Once Dudley had taken over my body, Melchora attacked me. It distracted the demon and prevented my killing Santa Muerte—whose death might have resulted in Elizabeth's death as well. Then I—or Dudley—went on a rampage in the house. Melchora's magic was nearly useless on me. Everything she tried—fire, wind, electricity—I deflected, and the spells wound up hitting the walls, the furniture, and the curtains. Within moments, the house was ablaze.

With no hope of winning this fight, Melchora retreated out of the house. She used her feathered cape to literally fly out of a window, breaking through the glass, and disappeared into the night. Once she was out, Santa Muerte was magically pulled out of the window by the invisible force. Just like at the library. Just like at Carmen's.

As we continue down the dark road, two fire trucks with sirens blaring screech around a narrow corner. Paige and I squeeze ourselves against an embankment as they zip by, no doubt to fight the fire from below.

Paige continues her story. When the fire was too overwhelming, Fiona grabbed Paige and pulled her out of the house—while I was still inside. She tried to protest, but Fiona must have used some magic, because Paige claims Fiona carried her out like a rag doll.

Paige was frightened I would die in there. Then I emerged from the flames and collapsed on the front porch. That was when Paige sprayed me with a hose.

By the time we reach the bottom of the mountainside, the sun is rising in the east. From our position below, we can see the smoke still rising from Fiona's property at the top of the hill, where several news helicopters hover. The normally quiet and secluded community at the top of the hills is now the focus of a lot of attention.

My gears turn, and something suddenly occurs to me. "How did they find us?" Of all the places in Los Angeles, Melchora and Santa Muerte tracked us to Fiona's home. "No one knows we were staying at Fiona's. And they came looking specifically for me. How did Melchora find out?"

Paige considers this. "There were only two people who knew we were staying there. Fiona…"

"Right."

"And David."

"Right."

⟡

We decide to pay David a visit and confront him about the suspicious coincidence that he was the only person who knew I was staying with Fiona, yet somehow, Melchora found me. Since I'm not quite ready to confront him smelling of barbeque, and since it's probably still dangerous to go home, Paige and I take a rideshare to the Century City mall first. I'm in dire need of warm clothes, and we could both use caffeine and breakfast. Once again, we've pulled an all-nighter, and we still have battles to fight.

We find a café that serves hot breakfast and hot coffee and bide our time until the first store opens at ten o'clock. We sit in the restaurant, trying to act casual despite our tattered clothes and lack of shoes and the fact that we're covered in soot and dirt. As Paige enjoys her breakfast sandwich and the people watching that Los Angeles provides, I ask a question that's been on my mind. "What did I look like?"

Paige stops eating and turns to me. She trembles slightly, either from the terrible memory or from the fear of telling me. No one who has ever witnessed the full episode has told me what I look like. After the first exorcism, I was rather successful in keeping myself sequestered when it was happening. But now I've had three episodes in the past week—two in the past twenty-four hours. That's never happened before.

Judging by the recent aftermaths, the full demonic possession is worse now than it was when I killed Bennet. The priests never described to me what they saw, and my family banished me before I could ask. Not ever Father Ramon has seen the demon in all its unholy glory. But despite my best efforts and our success over the years, Paige has finally witnessed it.

"I want to know," I say, coaxing her.

She shakes her head. "I don't want to say."

This wasn't the answer I was expecting. "Why not?"

Paige considers her answer carefully. "I don't want you to be afraid of yourself. I don't want you to be afraid of being around me."

My heart sinks. This is worse than her actually describing it. "Is it that bad?"

"It's not what I was expecting. I mean, you're still you. It's still your body. Just... also..." She struggles for the right words. "Not you? Does that make sense?"

"Not even a little bit."

She visibly deflates.

"You really don't want to tell me?" I ask.

She shakes her head.

I consider pressuring her—demanding it from her. If I did, she would probably relent. I also understand why she doesn't want to tell me. Paige and I are a couple of orphans in this great big city, and we sometimes tread lightly around topics that might push the other away. Like she said, she doesn't want me to be afraid of being around her. She doesn't want me to run away. Again.

Once Bloomingdale opens, I get a pair of jeans, some boots, and a brand-new field jacket. Paige insists this new jacket be a step up in quality from what I normally get, and since she's paying with her credit card, I'm not allowed to decline. Since last night's fire proved that tweed is naturally fire-resistant, we opt for one made of wool. Admittedly, it fits like a glove and provides me with the perfect warmth. Paige buys herself a knit blazer with an inside pocket so she can stop carrying the Glock in her waistband.

We then walk into a salon for a quick wash and cut—something to trim off the split ends and fire-singed hair. The stylist is horrified, so we provide a generous tip for her troubles. When she has finished, I finally feel like my old self again. It's time to meet David.

Chapter 32

The Central Police Station is a giant monolith of redbrick in the middle of Downtown Los Angeles. A giant mural depicting the LAPD's commitment to the community marks the entrance to the station. We walk inside the lion's den and approach a young desk sergeant who mans the lobby.

"I'm here to see Detective David Resnick," I tell him.

"Is he expecting you?"

I glance up at the clock. It's eleven thirty in the morning. "No, but I'm sure he's looking for me. Just let him know Darcy Caine is here."

Per the desk sergeant's recommendation, Paige and I take a seat on the bench. There are about a dozen other people here, some filling out reports, some waiting their turn to be called inside. Some of them seem to just be killing time, although that's probably not really the case.

A minute after the desk sergeant places a call, David charges into the lobby. Without saying a word, he grabs me by the arm and pulls me in to follow. Then he immediately lets go. "What happened to your shoulder?"

"What?" I ask.

"You were shot," he says, noticing it's no longer in a sling.

I exchange a look with Paige. "It got better?"

He ignores my question, grabbing my hand again and leading me into the station. I take Paige's hand, and we follow him like a chain of monkeys.

"You don't look surprised to see me," I say.

"You're lucky I don't arrest you," he mutters.

"On what charge?"

He leads us through the station bullpen. Detectives sit in cubicles, typing out police reports on old PCs, one finger at a time. There are a handful of civilians in here, probably talking about various cases of theft, assault, and worse.

"We could start with lying to me about getting shot."

"I didn't lie."

"Gunshots don't just get better," he growls. "Then I get here at eight in the morning to see—on every single goddamn news station—that Fiona Flanagan's house burned to the ground last night." David marches us to the back of the station. "You're not answering my calls or my texts. You're on thin ice, Darcy."

He drags us to an open door and gestures inside. "Get in."

"No." I glare at him with my yellow eyes. "With all due respect, Detective," I whisper, "I'd feel safer out here with witnesses."

The surprised look on his face melts into frustration. His hand drops, and he takes a step back as he glances around the bullpen. Through gritted teeth, he mutters, "Please?"

I exchange a look with Paige, silently asking her, *What's the worst that could happen?* She nods, so I step inside the room.

Paige moves to follow, but David stops her with his arm.

"I'd like to speak to Darcy alone." Again, through gritted teeth, he adds, "Please?"

Now is my turn to nod to Paige. I don't mind, and besides, I could use someone standing guard. She acquiesces, and David follows me inside and closes the door.

It's an empty room with three chairs and a cheap table—an interrogation room. Unlike the ones on television, there's no one-way mirror for the peanut gallery, just a dome camera on the ceiling tucked away in the corner.

I hurry to stand beneath the camera, outside the view of the lens.

David gestures to an empty chair. "Wanna have a seat?"

My feet stay planted. "Someone tried to kill us last night."

"Who?"

"I'm not sure," I lie, not yet ready to tell him all the unbelievable details. "We were ambushed and escaped before we could see who it was."

"Wait. Hold on. You're telling me that you were attacked by some unseen assailant? And that this same person also caused the catastrophic fire at Fiona Flanagan's mansion, burning it to the ground along with two acres of nearby property?"

"That's right."

"That's your statement? You want me to report—"

"You are the only other person who knows where we were," I say.

His eyes narrow as he realizes what I'm suggesting. "What the hell is that supposed to mean? You've given me nothing. But I've got seven dead bodies at three murder scenes—all of which I can place you at. Then this shit last night. Now you show up after dodging my calls to say *you* don't trust *me*?"

I refuse to be put on the defensive. "It took twenty-four hours for someone to find where I was hiding."

"Do I need to remind you that I'm the one who's kept you out of jail for the past week?"

"Why is that?" I ask, taking two steps toward him, forcing him onto his heels. "Why have you been going through all this trouble to keep us as far away from a police station as possible?"

David's not having it. "Because I didn't want you in jail." He takes two steps forward, and I back up until I bump up against the wall. His body moves in until I'm pressed against the wall. I tense up at the sensation of being cornered. Maybe I could push him off or shift out of the way. But I don't. I don't want to.

He looks me up and down, sensing my vulnerability. Then he asks a simple question. "Do you really think I would let anything happen to you?"

I swallow, not sure how to answer. Deep down inside, I can't imagine that David would want to see me hurt. Then again, it's the people I trusted most who have hurt me the most.

"I don't know," I say.

David leans in close, his voice barely a whisper. "I was protecting you."

I'm acutely aware of how close his chest is to mine. I can feel the heat of his body. "Why?" I ask in little more than a whisper.

"Because you needed it."

I take a deep breath. "Even if I did, why?"

His demeanor softens as I stare into his eyes. He struggles with what to say next—I can see him running through various responses in his head. I think about what he could say and what I want him to say.

Just say you care.

He steps back, creating some distance. "It's my job."

I try to hide my disappointment, but it's not a good effort.

Detective David Resnick reads me like a guilty suspect. "I didn't tell anyone where you were. You have to believe I'm trying to keep you safe. That's all."

He didn't have to add that last part, but I nod, accepting his answer. "Someone knew how to find us," I say, trying to steer us back to business. "Only the four of us knew." I meet his eye again. "Right?"

David's eyes widen in realization, and he snaps his fingers. "Come with me." He opens the door to the bullpen. I compose myself before following, making sure my eyes are dry.

Paige intercepts me the minute I step out. "What's wrong?" I wonder whether it's that obvious or if she's that good a friend. I hope it's the latter.

"Nothing," I say, grabbing Paige and pulling her as I follow David. "But I think he has a hunch."

David approaches an empty cubicle then moves to a second and third cubicle. "Where is everyone today?" he calls to no one in particular. Another officer walks by, and David turns to him. "Simmons! Did anyone hear from Snyder yet?"

Simmons shakes his head. "Nothing yet, Detective."

David turns to me.

"You told your partner?" I ask.

"I had to. He was threatening to file a complaint with the captain that I was knowingly releasing a suspect in a murder case back onto the streets."

"Then where is he?" I ask, looking around. "You thought he would be here. Why isn't he?"

David looks around then pulls out his cell phone. He dials, and I can hear the phone ringing on the other end while he waits. A woman's automated voice picks up on the other end—voicemail.

"Damn it." He hangs up and starts marching out of the

bullpen. "Let's go," he calls back without looking at us.

Paige and I hurry to keep up. "Where are we going?" she asks.

"Ed's house," David says.

Chapter 33

----◆----

O nce again, I find myself in the back seat of David's Charger while Paige sits shotgun. The car rumbles along Sunset Boulevard—the crappy part in the east, not the nice part in the west.

"How long has Ed been your partner?" I ask, now curious about their history.

"A few months. Since right when I started Homicide."

"So you don't know him that well?"

"He's a veteran on the force. Been with LAPD for twenty years. He worked Gangs and Narcotics, Vice, and Robbery-Homicide. The man's a legend."

"That doesn't answer my question."

David shoots me a look through his rearview mirror. "I know him well enough."

He steers his car into the affluent suburbs of Franklin Hills. The streets are narrow and winding, so he drives slowly up the hillside to avoid hitting parked cars and retaining walls that prevent the entire mountain from sliding down.

We arrive at a large home near the top. From the outside, it looks like a typical Spanish-style Los Angeles home. A long path of terra-cotta tiles leads up the stucco-walled fortress. Red-clay tiles top every inch of the home, including the posts and overhangs.

"This is a nice house," Paige remarks. It's easily a multimillion-dollar home and pairs nicely with the brand-new Jaguar parked in the driveway.

"Really nice. You cops must make a lot more than I thought," I say.

"Take it easy," David scolds.

"Tell me again that he's clean."

David turns to me when we arrive at the doorstep. "Just... don't say anything."

I zip my mouth shut.

"Too soon," Paige mutters to me.

He rings the doorbell. We wait. Nothing.

He rings again then tries the door handle. It's unlocked, and the door swings right open.

Without hesitating, David pulls out his gun. "I want you two to stay right—" He looks at Paige. I turn and see that she's holding her gun, too. "What are you doing?"

"Backup?"

"Put that away."

Paige holsters the gun.

David looks at me. "Are you armed?"

"Nothing you need to worry about," I answer. Paige and I exchange a look. *Hopefully.*

He shakes his head. "Wait in the car. No, wait." He looks like he's mulling the options. "Shit."

David pulls out his cell and dials three numbers. "Hi, this

is Detective David Resnick with the LAPD. Yes. I'm at 254 Ronda Vista Drive, requesting a black-and-white for a possible B and E. I'm going inside. Please advise. Thanks." He hangs up and turns to us. "Stay close. And don't touch anything."

Just before he goes in, he hesitates. "If you do have to use that thing," he says, glancing at Paige's gun, "you know how to use it, right?"

Paige scowls. "I've used a gun before." That is technically true. She tried to shoot a death saint, almost shot my foot in an abandoned house, and tried to murder a witch.

David's not entirely sold. "Just keep your finger off the trigger until you're ready to shoot." He goes in first, gun drawn and pointed. I follow with Paige behind me. She keeps her hand on her gun but leaves it holstered. We move carefully throughout the house, clearing every room.

Judging by the decor and the view of downtown LA, there's no way this cop is clean. David carefully sweeps the room, gun aimed wherever his eyes are directed. As he looks around, I notice something on the stairs.

"David," I whisper, pointing.

His eyes zero in on what I'm seeing. On the cream-colored carpet that runs down the steps are red footprints—boot prints, to be more precise. They look like faded red stamps on the fabric, with the toes pointed out. The tracks are more pronounced on the top steps, growing paler toward the bottom.

I recognize these prints. These aren't from normal casual boots. They're flat with pointed toes. Cowboy boots. And only one person I know wears cowboy boots—Hugo.

We move upstairs slowly. At the landing, David sweeps the area and ensures that no one is waiting down a hall or in a closet. The prints saturate the carpet in a deep crimson hue.

They come directly from the bedroom. The door is ajar.

Through the opening, I can see red stains on the white bedspread.

We move forward in unison. David keeps the barrel of his gun pointed high, and he gently nudges the door with his foot. Inside the room is a horrific sight.

Two dead bodies are in there. The first is Snyder, still in his pajamas, lying supine on the couch. The second is a woman, heavyset and wearing a nightgown, lying on the floor. Both of them have huge holes in their chests. Pools of blood are everywhere, with one pair of footprints leading directly from the bodies.

"Christ," David mutters. He looks around the room, still aiming his gun. "They could still be here."

Paige and I have been through enough in the past few days to know that no one is here. We stand idly by until David finishes his sweep. Then we walk back outside, careful not to step on the prints.

David looks up and down the street. "Where's the damn car?"

It takes ten minutes for the black-and-white to arrive. David chastises the two uniformed officers the moment they step out of the vehicle. "What took so long? There is a dead police officer in this house!"

The two officers exchange a look. The female cop responds. "Haven't you heard what's going on?"

David shakes his head.

"This is the fourth dead detective reported this morning."

David's jaw drops.

The other detective adds, "Someone's going around killing cops."

⌇

As soon as David hears about the deaths, he orders Paige and me into his car. He gets on his phone and starts making numerous frantic phone calls. More police cars arrive. Crime-scene tape goes up, and within a half an hour, we have a police base camp set up. More detectives arrive in unmarked but still obvious police vehicles. The medical examiner soon follows in his paneled van.

Then the news crews show up. First there are a few individuals snapping pictures on smart phones to post online and share via apps as citizen journalists. Then come the local news vans and Los Angeles tabloids. Within an hour, it's a full-blown circus.

Paige and I are still sitting in the back seat of the Dodge when someone shouts, "Where's Resnick?"

I turn to see David's captain, Reginald Hollis. He's a tall African American man with a barrel chest and clean-shaven head. He bears a constant scowl, like a disappointed football coach. Hollis hurries out of the car and takes long strides past the other officers before disappearing into the house.

"He looks pissed," I say.

"Yeah, and it sounds like he's pissed at David."

I nod.

"You have to admit," Paige says, "David's taken a lot of heat for you the past few days."

"I know."

Hollis's voice booms from inside the house. A couple of uniformed officers scurry outside, taking shelter from the storm inside. I can only imagine what David must be dealing with. He can't possibly explain to his boss what's going on when I haven't given him the full picture. He has spent all this time trusting me at every turn, and I haven't told him the truth.

I open the car door.

"Where are you going?" Paige slides out and follows me.

"I'm tired of waiting in the wings," I say as I charge to the door. "This whole *wait in the car while the men do the work* thing is crap."

In order to get past the guarding police officer without benefit of badge or credentials, I do my best to imitate the confident stride Captain Hollis used. When the cop allows me to pass without a second glance, I'm surprised it worked. Then again, why bother stopping someone this deep into the crime scene?

There's a wide strip of plastic on the floor leading through the house, and I follow it into the living room. Several crime-scene technicians are busy collecting evidence from the scene—dusting for fingerprints, analyzing a computer, rifling through mail. At the far end is the den, where David and his captain are having a heated conversation. I trust that my arrival will help ease the tension, so I march right inside.

The moment David sees me, he moves to intercept. "Wait in the car!"

I brush right past him and extend my hand to his captain. "Darcy Caine, private investigator."

Hollis ignores me and addresses David over my head. "Who is this, and what is she doing here?"

"Darcy Caine," I repeat. "I'm the PI hired by Carmen Viramontes to find her daughter." David tries to pull me away, but I stand my ground. "I have reason to believe my case might have something to do with Detective Snyder's death—and perhaps the death of the other detectives."

Hollis points his long finger at me. "Young lady, if you have information pertaining to this investigation, you had better reveal it."

I point my finger back at him. "That's what I'm trying to do. Sir."

He turns to David. "Seriously, who is this?"

David changes tactics and now ushers Hollis out of the den. "I'll handle this, sir. I'm taking her to the station for a statement."

As soon as Hollis is out of earshot, he whirls on me. "What the hell, Darcy? Are you trying to get me fired?"

"I'm trying to help you."

He rubs his face with both his hands in frustration, stretching it into a funny expression. "Does she drive you this crazy?" he asks Paige.

"Every day."

"Hey!" I say to her. That wasn't nice. I turn back to David. "I'm serious. This has something to do with the disappearance of Elizabeth Viramontes."

David acquiesces. "You think Elizabeth has something to do with the seven dead detectives?"

"That's righ—seven?" I ask. The number has grown since I've been in the car.

David nods. "Seven."

I take a deep breath. "The bloody prints. Those belong to Hugo Escalante."

David looks into the living room, where the crime scene technicians are photographing the stairs. What he probably doesn't notice—but I certainly do—is another technician carrying down a plastic bag filled with a handful of gray feathers. Melchora was here, too.

"Carmen's thug?" He turns to me. "Why is Hugo Escalante going around killing detectives? What does any of this have to do with the kidnapping of Elizabeth Viramontes? What does Snyder have to do with this?"

I steel myself. I have a theory, but I need David to listen to me until I finish. "You said Ed worked in—"

"Detective Snyder," David interrupts.

I'm already losing him. I remind myself that he just lost his partner. "Sorry. Detective Snyder worked in the Gangs and Narcotics Division."

"That's right."

"Did all the other detectives killed today work in GND?"

"No," David says definitively. "Not all of them. And they weren't from the same divisions, either."

"Well, Detective Snyder was no longer with GND, but did the other detectives previously work in GND?"

David stands there, staring at me. I can see the wheels turning in his head. Finally, he says, "Don't move," and walks away. I follow him. He turns back to look at me.

Before he can say anything, Paige chimes in. "You know she's not going to listen to you."

"Let's go," he grumbles and keeps walking. I follow on his heels as he approaches a technician with a tablet computer. "Cortez, can I see that?" David grabs the computer from him. He taps into the device then turns to Cortez. "Who were the other detectives found today?"

"Let's see. Bill Bryce at Rampart. Miguel Nuñez at Rampart. Simon Shaw at Hollenbeck. Michelle Lin at Pacific…"

David waves him off. "Okay. Stop." He keeps typing into the tablet. Reads. Types again. Reads. Types again. Reads.

When he looks at me, I can tell my theory was accurate. All the detectives recently murdered have worked in Gangs and Narcotics at one time or another. David tosses the tablet back to the technician.

"Do you want the other names?" the tech asks.

Instead of answering, David grabs me by the elbow. I allow him to pull me this time. We head into an empty room.

Paige follows, and David closes the door once the three of us are inside. By the look of the desk, filing cabinets, and stacks of papers, this must have been Snyder's office. There's even a framed picture of the woman who was murdered with him—his wife.

David takes a seat in a chair and appraises me. "What's going on in that brain of yours?"

Paige leans against the desk with her arms crossed, and I suddenly feel like I'm about to make a presentation to my classmates. *Here goes.* "All the detectives were at one time or another involved with the LAPD investigation into the Galeana Cartel."

"How did you know?" David asks.

"I told you. This has something to do with Viramontes."

"You know there are some things I can't discuss."

"Can we cut the BS and work together on this? People are dying, David." He doesn't answer, but I can tell I'm finally getting through to him. "How did you know I was working on her case?" I continue. "Why all the activity around her?"

Paige turns, angling her body toward David. I take a step forward, and suddenly, he's on the hot seat as we converge and hover over him. He takes a deep breath before speaking. "A few months ago, Carmen Viramontes reached out to the LAPD. She wanted to make a deal. Testimony. Evidence. Names. In exchange for immunity and permanent residence in the US for her and her daughter."

Carmen was trying to go straight. That must have been cause for alarm if anyone in the cartel found out.

"I can't imagine there would be a lot of people happy about that," Paige says, echoing my thoughts.

"Not just that," David adds, "but her whole empire is incredibly complex. The electronics business—a money-laundering front. Her bank, same thing. There are networks upon networks invested in this operation. Farms—coca, marijuana, poppy. Smugglers. Distributors. Not to mention the competitors she was willing to implicate. A woman like that threatens to unravel an empire…"

"And everyone becomes an enemy," I finish.

If Hugo were with the spirit when they killed Ed—Detective Snyder—then he must be working with Melchora. Hugo must have found out what Carmen was trying to do.

"The LAPD was working with the DEA on this one," David says. "I'm not in Gangs and Narcotics anymore, but this task force was close to getting all the evidence they needed to shut down the empire and take down her accomplices and competitors."

"Until Elizabeth was kidnapped," Paige says.

"That makes sense," David adds. "A buddy who was on the Galeana case told me that Carmen Viramontes went radio silent two weeks ago. After all the work, all this time, she suddenly became a ghost. We weren't sure if she was alive or had left the country. But that would have been around the time Elizabeth disappeared. A few days later, some girl with black hair and yellow eyes shows up at her front door and gains access to one of the most heavily fortified drug compounds in Los Angeles."

Darcy Caine, to the rescue.

"How were you communicating with Carmen in the first place?" Paige asks. "You said no one has ever seen her."

"We were talking to the only person she trusted."

"Leona," I say.

David nods. Leona did a lot of the talking when I met with Carmen, not only to communicate for her but to protect her as well. She was probably the only person Carmen could trust.

"So let me get this straight," Paige says. "Carmen Viramontes sends Leona to talk to the LAPD and DEA to broker a deal for protection. Hugo finds out and kidnaps Elizabeth to stop her."

I give Paige a look, silently begging her not to reveal too

much. We finally have David on our side.

"Carmen stops the deal and hires Darcy to find her daughter." Paige points at me. "Hugo tries to stop you and ends up killing Lupe at the museum."

Yes and no. Santa Muerte and Melchora tried to stop me. Hugo wasn't there. But he knew what I looked like, which was why Santa Muerte tried to kill me.

"Then Hugo finds out Leona was working as the liaison," Paige continues, "brokering the deal on Carmen's behalf. So he murders Leona."

"And tries to kill Carmen, too," I say. Hugo, Melchora, Santa Muerte—they must all be working together.

Paige turns to David, her brow furrowed as she tries to understand everything. "The other detectives were no longer in narcotics. Why kill them? Why kill Detective Snyder?"

"Clean house," David says. "Get rid of everyone who knows anything. Why stop with the current investigators? Go back as far as you can."

"Were any of the victims on the current case?"

"At least two," David says.

My next question is difficult to ask. "David, did you ever work on the Viramontes case?"

He stiffens. "Two years back. Didn't go anywhere at that time, so we had to let it go. Not enough evidence for the DA."

It's pretty clear what this means. Hugo and Melchora must have a list that includes David's name. He's in as much danger as I am.

"Well, David, I think we're officially in this together."

David looks up. A defeated chuckle escapes his lips. He's a hunted man now.

"Shit," he says.

Chapter 34

David reports to Captain Hollis with our findings and our theory. Paige and I stand beside David's car and watch the exchange. The moment David explains the connection between the detectives and my investigation, everything shifts to DEFCON 2. Police officers scramble, the scene is sealed off, and the entire force retreats into the vehicles and off the site.

David jogs to his car and points for us to get inside. I'm so sick of riding in the back. I commandeer shotgun before Paige has a chance.

A caravan of police vehicles and unmarked cars hurries down the hill and through the streets of Los Angeles. I have a front-row seat as I watch motorcycle cops block traffic so our motorcade can quickly make its way downtown. Every detective in the city is now a target, including David and the other officers in other cars.

As we approach the skyscrapers downtown, SWAT vehicles merge into our group. On either side are fully armored vehicles. We're a convoy now.

We don't so much as hesitate at a stoplight or intersection. In a few minutes, we're back at the Central Police Station. Vehicles from other convoys merge into our queue as we take a tight turn and head down into the parking structure.

Cars screech to a stop inside, and we jump out of the vehicle. Police in full tactical gear guard our arrival as we hurry into the entrance. I hold Paige's hand, and we follow David through a series of halls. Other civilians are ushered out to the lobby as we continue to follow David to the detectives' bullpen.

"Sit here," David commands, gesturing toward Snyder's desk. His tone is authoritative, but when he looks at me, his eyes plead that just this once, in front of all his detective friends, I comply without sassing him.

Fine.

Paige and I sit across from Detective Snyder's former desk and watch as David directs a photographer to take photos of it. This is a crime scene now. Flashes of light fill the room.

Captain Hollis arrives, and he and David listen to an investigator report the findings of the murder.

"ME's initial report estimates time of death was between oh three hundred and oh four hundred this morning. Cause of death for both victims was most likely trauma to the front upper torso. Cause of injury is still unclear. ME reports the hearts of… the hearts of both victims were missing."

David shoots me a look. He's still trying to understand this particular mystery of who is tearing the hearts out of the victims. He's probably wondering if it's another cartel fear tactic. I can't give him an answer to that yet.

The medical examiner continues. "One pair of bloodied footprints—size-ten cowboy boots—were found leading away from the crime scene, down the stairs, and outside. There was no sign of forced entry…"

All this I already know. My eyes are focused on Snyder's desk and the flashes of light that glint off his belongings. Flatscreen monitor, keyboard, and mouse. Landline. Mesh pencil cup filled with pens and a pair of scissors. Stacks of manila folders overflowing with sloppily inserted pieces of paper. Opened Coke can. Stapler. White mug with coffee stains.

Opened Coke can.

Snyder was a lean guy. He didn't look like someone with a big soda habit, but every time I saw him—at my apartment, at Carmen's—he had a can of soda.

"There were signs of forced entry at Detective Shaw's home—"

"Did Detective Snyder drink soda?" I ask loudly.

All eyes turn to me. Hollis's gaze is clearly full of contempt. "What is she doing here?" he barks at David.

David shakes his head, but finally, he's willing to listen. "Hold on, Sir." Then he asks me, "What?"

"Was he a big soda drinker?"

"No."

I gesture toward the desk. David looks then nods. "Right. No, he chewed."

Chewed. He chewed tobacco—and spit tobacco into the can—or presumably, the floor. Or carpet.

I remember the stains on the carpet, like a leopard print, in the house in Sterling Terrace. I'm quiet as all this goes through my mind. David steps closer, not interrupting but knowing I have something to say. I scan my audience—chief of police, detectives, sergeants, beat cops. What I have to say is going to piss a lot of people off.

"Detective Snyder was an informant for a drug cartel."

All eyes turn to me again. No pair is opened as wide as David's. In the deafening silence, I hurry to keep talking before someone shoots me.

"He was meeting with members of a rival gang that's been working to take over the Galeana Cartel. That's how Hugo knew the names and addresses of all the detectives who were murdered last night." My eyes laser in on David's, needing at least him to believe me. "That's how they found out where Paige and I lived, and that's how they found us hiding at Fiona's."

I wait for David to respond. He stands there in shock. He'll have to wrap his head around the fact that his partner was working with a drug cartel. I wonder if I've lost him.

"That's a pretty serious accusation, young lady," Hollis says pointedly. "Do you have evidence to back that up?"

I stand up. "I can take you to their meeting place. You'll find all the evidence there."

$$\sim\!r$$

I tell Captain Hollis and David about the hideout in Sterling Terrace. I mention the map we found in the old Victorian house, which I now realize must have pinpointed the addresses of all the detectives. I show them the photo I took with my phone. At first glance, it's difficult to discern the details of the various streets. However, the vicinities do suggest a correlation with the addresses of the murdered detectives. I then mention the empty soda cans and stains on the carpet—stains, I also now realize, that were caused by tobacco spit.

Hollis is dismissive, but David pulls him away to talk in private. Paige and I continue to listen to the chatter around us. As of now, eight detectives were murdered last night. All remaining detectives, especially those with connections to the Galeana Cartel cases, have been pulled into their respective stations for safety.

My accusation of Detective Snyder has not been greeted with appreciation or even belief, but after last night, the police aren't taking any chances. Since this morning, even family members of detectives have gone into hiding. Their whereabouts have not been announced to the LAPD.

Paige and I continue to sit for an hour in the bullpen. Our only sustenance comes from a vending machine we find in the hall. As we sit in the break room, munching on candy bars and trail mix, Paige asks me when I'm going to tell David about Santa Muerte.

"I just accused his partner of working with the drug cartels. I think I'll need to give it a minute before I bring that up." He already thinks I'm crazy, so I don't need to stoke that fire.

"We have to warn them," she says. "You know what that thing can do. You can't shoot it. You can't run away from it. Santa Muerte is going to hunt them all down and rip their hearts out one by one. Including David's."

"I have to go with him. Protect him. Wherever he goes, I need to be there, ready to fight."

"Protect him? How? You heard Fiona—only magic can defeat Melchora. And you don't have..." Paige stops, and I can see realization dawning. "You can't control Dudley."

I can't explain something this fantastic to David, so using my supernatural advantage is our only option. "I have to try. It's the only thing I can do to protect David."

Paige considers this. "You know I'm coming with you, right?"

I know. "When the time comes, I'll tell you to run," I say. "Run, and make sure no one else is around."

David enters the break room. "We're thin right now, but I've secured a four-member SWAT team to accompany us to the site. They'll be here in an hour. Darcy," he says, turning to me, "I need to know where we're going."

"We're going with you," I say, standing. Paige stands with

me. "We've been there. We know the lay of the land."

"It's too dangerous," he says. But I can tell he has little fight left for me. I'm going to win this argument.

"David, Paige and I can warn you about any traps."

"Fine," he says. "You two and I will hang back until they secure the area."

When the SWAT team arrives, I'm given a municipal map of the city of Los Angeles. It's been abandoned so long that it's not even on the current map. It's strange for me to be surrounded by armored soldiers and uniformed officers while I hold court and direct them to Sterling Terrace. Paige and I are dwarfed by everyone, including the one female officer on the team. Once I'm done, David, the SWAT team, and the four uniformed officers come up with a plan.

We return to the parking garage and wait by David's blue Charger. Outside, a SWAT vehicle called a BearCat pulls up. It's a four-wheeled armored vehicle that looks military ready. Two more black-and-whites and a Field Investigative Unit truck also join us before we head out.

David arrives, carrying two ballistic vests with LAPD stamped across the heart. "You know how to put these on?"

"We've got it," I answer, taking the vests. Paige and I help each other zip up and strap in. When no one is looking, I help her holster her Glock into one of the vest pockets.

"Can I admit something?" I ask her.

"Of course."

"I'm glad you have the gun."

Our convoy arrives at the chain-link fencing blocking access to the abandoned community of Sterling Terrace. A tactical officer cuts the lock with bolt cutters. Colorful bits of debris are pressed against the fence—red, lavender, yellow, and orange. A wind passes through the fence, sending a scattering toward us. Paper-thin and no bigger than potato chips, they float toward us and pass by the car.

"What are those?" David asks.

"Flower petals," I answer, watching a handful drift past the window.

Once the gate is opened, the convoy drives down the road over a floral path that has been laid out for us. As we approach the cul-de-sac, there is something decidedly different about the neighborhood from the last time we were here.

Hundreds of Santa Muerte statues are arranged along the street. Porcelain figures of various shapes, sizes, and colors stand on every porch and clutter every yard. They even fill the island in the center of the neighborhood and surround the gazebo. Their skeletal faces seem to watch our slow-moving convoy as we proceed up the block.

"What the hell is this?" David mutters.

I exchange a look with Paige. "This wasn't here before. Something's not right."

"Which house?" he asks, ignoring my warning.

I direct David to the last house on the top. The vehicles circle around the loop and park. My attention is drawn, again, to the center island. The gazebo is now fully decorated as a shrine to Santa Muerte. Fresh flowers have been strung on the posts. Glass containers hold votive candles. The stone fire pit has been cleaned of all graffiti. Statues stand on the perimeter, guarding the altar. And thousands of flower petals cover every inch of the area. Huge piles swell with each passing breeze as if emerging from the ground itself.

"Stay here," David warns as he exits the vehicle. He doesn't go far but stands beside his car and directs the two officers from the second vehicle to remain stationed outside. All four uniformed officers arm themselves with shotguns and visually sweep the area for danger.

"What do we think about all these statues?" Paige asks, looking around.

"Nothing good," I respond. My stomach groans in the anticipation that we're walking into a trap. Something in my body is telling me we're in trouble. "I think she's here."

"Melchora or Santa Muerte? Shit—doesn't matter. We should warn David," Paige says as she watches four SWAT team members approach the front door. They signal to each other.

I open the door and swing my legs out of the car. David turns to face me the moment I do. "I told you to stay inside."

"David, none of this was here before," I say, standing. "They knew we were coming."

"Wait," he says, holding a hand to stop me.

The SWAT officer on point opens the door and sweeps his weapon as he enters. The other officers quickly follow to clear the inside of the house. They disappear inside. David waits patiently, a hand on his radio.

I speak up again. "I'm worried this is a trap."

His radio crackles to life. "We're all clear."

David looks around, assessing the situation. "Shit. Too late to back out now." He waves to uniformed officers to follow, as well as the field investigative technicians. He turns to Paige. "Do you still have your gun?"

She nods, patting the pocket of her vest. David waits. "Oh!" she chirps and pulls it out.

He follows the team, and Paige and I follow him.

"Finger off the trigger," I remind her.

The place is as it was before. Dirty. Dilapidated. Deserted. The tobacco spots remain on the dingy carpet—remnants of Detective Ed Snyder's significant time spent here.

Two things immediately throw me off. One, I can smell something cooking in the kitchen. And two, there's no SWAT team here.

One of the investigative technicians steps into the room and approaches the map on the wall. "Is this the map?"

Brilliant detective work.

David's eyes and gun sweep the area. He searches for the rest of the team then sidles next to me. "Answer him casually," he whispers to me as quietly as possible.

"Yep. That's the one." I pull Paige close. The three of us take a defensive position—back-to-back-to-back.

Oblivious, the technician continues to examine the map. He points. "That's Detective Snyder's place. Detective Brice. Lin. All here."

I peer into the kitchen. I can see a big pot on the burner. Something is boiling, and steam rises from inside.

Two gunshots echo from outside the house. David rushes to the door and carefully cracks it open. In the distance, I can see Hugo and a handful of other men marching down the road, armed with assault guns. Two officers lie dead on the ground.

One guy aims, and a bullet splinters the doorframe. David ducks and slams the door shut. The rest of us hit the floor.

"Shit." He points at the female officer. "Watch the back." He looks at the other officer. "Call for backup."

The second officer grabs his mic. "This is One-Adam-Fifty-Six. We've got two officers down at Sterling Terrace in Montecito Heights. Numerous assailants converging on remaining officers. Requesting immediate backup and helicopter unit!"

The female officer shouts, "I see at least two more coming up the back!"

The radio crackles to life. "Copy that, One-Adam-Fifty-Six.

All units, we have a code three at Sterling Terrace…"

David turns to me. "Other entrances?"

I point through the kitchen.

David gestures for the second officer to guard. He crawls toward the kitchen door. I look at the boiling pot. The steam rising from the top thickens then redirects itself through the air. It snakes its way toward the door. The vapor slowly begins to materialize into little ashen clouds. As I watch, the clouds turn into tiny feathers.

Feathers. Shit.

"No!" I slam the door shut. *Thwack! Thwack! Thwack!* The feathers puncture the door from the other side, their needlelike shafts barely penetrating the wood. The officer shoots me a look, and I shout, "Someone's in there!"

He quickly aims his gun at the door.

I turn to Paige. "Melchora."

She visibly tenses, looking around. If Melchora's here, there's also a good chance Santa Muerte is here.

Another technician shouts, "We're surrounded!"

I hear gunshots. Bullets fly into the house around us. Bits of wood spray across the room like confetti. Glass shards rain down on anyone unlucky enough to be near a window. We all dive and cover our heads. The moment the barrage ends, I rise and sprint for the stairs.

"Darcy!" David shouts.

More bullets fly through the first level as I race up the stairs and land face-first on the upstairs carpet. A bulky vest jabs my stomach. Under me is the dead body of a SWAT office, his open eyes frozen in horror. I look up and find the bodies of the three other SWAT officers on the carpet. Standing at the end of the hall is Melchora. She's cloaked in her silvery gray feather cape. Her dark eyes stare at me.

Still lying on my stomach, I wait for the sound of bullets to end downstairs. When they do, I make a T with my hands and call, "Time out."

Paige's voice echoes from downstairs. "Darcy?"

"I'm alive!" I shout as I stand and brush myself off. "Paige?"

"Yeah?"

"Run!"

I can hear her swearing quietly and conferring with David.

Gunfire erupts again from downstairs. This time, it sounds like we're returning fire. Then there is more return gunfire from outside. Meanwhile, I stand here facing a witch, and I wish I were back downstairs.

Melchora removes a handful of feathers from her cape. "You are difficult to kill, demon. I think, this time, I will not fail." She cocks her arm, ready to launch the projectile.

I slap myself hard. Melchora hesitates. She's momentarily confused.

I do it again. My open palm swings as hard as it can against my cheek. *Come on, you little shit. You want to be free, Dudley, so come out and play.*

Again and again, I slap myself, trying to get my adrenaline pumping. Trying to get my pulse up. Trying to release the rage and anger inside me. Melchora watches, confused and delighted.

Right hand. Left hand. I think about all the things that piss me off. Bennet's death. My family banishing me. Lupe. Strike after strike leaves my face feeling hot and sore. My hearts beats harder, faster.

"Enough!" She flings the feathers at me. Their needle-sharp shafts aim directly for my heart.

"No!" I shout.

Just like at Fiona's home, a gust of wind blasts from my body. It funnels down the hall and disrupts the trajectory of the feathers, casting them aside. Their steely points impale themselves on the walls and floors around me. The air flows from my body and knocks Melchora on her back.

Wind still blowing in her face, she scrambles to look at me. She screams. The sound of her screams and the blowing wind begin to muffle. I know this moment—the prelude to Dudley's arrival. I must keep him close and also at bay—that fine line between control and chaos. I close my eyes.

My memory shifts into overdrive, and I recall the words Fiona said when she tested me. *Bhí an saol ina chalm.*

I say them over in my mind. *Bhí an saol ina chalm.*

The noise returns and is no longer muted. I open my eyes. The wind continues to howl. *"Bhí an saol ina chalm!"* I shout.

I'm still in control. I'm doing this. I march toward Melchora. The air intensifies as I get closer. It all concentrates on her.

She scrambles to her feet and plants them firmly on the floor to resist my tempest. With a sneer in my direction, she vaults herself into the air and wraps her feathered cloak around her body. Midair, her body warps into a spiral. The hem of her cape expands, except it's no longer a cape—it's wings. In mere seconds, she transforms into an owl. Using the gust of air, she catches the wind and explodes out of the window behind her. Glass rains down as she disappears through the frame.

I sprint for the window. The storm dissipates as I no longer focus on it. Through the broken glass, there is no sign of Melchora, only the house next door.

My body is warm, but my heart is calm. I'm still in control, and I'm still me—but I'm not sure for how long.

"Darcy!" shouts a voice behind me.

David stands there, gun in hand. Paige is behind him, leaning against the wall, where a dozen feathers are impaled. She inspects the feathers.

There's no time to debate. Using all my strength, I take three running steps and launch myself through the open window. Without even an ounce of grace, I land on my shoulder. My body crashes on the porch roof of the house next door.

I hear shouting in Spanish and turn to see Hugo aiming an assault rifle at me. Bullets whiz in my direction, peppering the shingles around me. Next to me is a second-story window, and I dive through it, broken glass scraping and cutting my skin. I brush off the bits embedded in me. Blood seeps from the wounds.

An explosion rocks the walls around me. Through the window, I can see a fireball rising into the air, following by thick black smoke. It's a war zone out there.

I'm in an empty bedroom. There's an open door to an empty bathroom and a closed door that presumably leads out of the room. I twist the handle, but it doesn't budge. Something's blocking it from the other side.

My body is cooling, so I know I'm losing Dudley. I slap myself a few more times, but it's not working. I'm running out of thoughts that will piss me off, as I'm focused on not getting shot. It's going to take some next-level agitation to bring him out.

I grab a piece of the broken window, take a deep breath, and slice it along my palm. Blood flows easily from the cut, and I clench my fist repeatedly. Each time I squeeze, the pain intensifies.

My temperature rises. My pulse quickens. It's flight-or-fight time. I use my strength to break through the door... which is a really stupid thing to do.

My momentum carries me through the door and across a narrow hall. A weak wooden handrail is the only thing that could stop me from plummeting down to the first floor. It doesn't. So I do.

My body lands with a thud on the ground floor. Dust and debris erupt around me, momentarily clouding my vision. The dust settles, and I am horrified.

There are crosses everywhere. Wood. Iron. Brass. Silver. With Jesus. Without. Crucifixes of every shape, size, and color surround me like a forest of toxic trees.

Nausea hits me like a truck. Unable to control myself, I gag and cough. The energy of the symbols radiates through me and instantly weakens me. I try to stand but can't.

This was the real trap. When I hear the cackling behind me, I know Melchora has defeated me. Using all my strength, I crawl. When I try to lift my head, it hurts.

Melchora stands before me. Beside her is the flowing form of Santa Muerte. At this level, I can see the hem of her dress hovering inches off the ground. No feet underneath. No shoes. Just air. They stand amid the cloud of dust I created, with the light of the setting sun streaming through the picture window behind them.

I thrust my hand into my pocket and clench the veil. I wrap it around my fist and lift my eyes to meet Santa Muerte. She's two feet away. She has the answer to my final riddle. If I could just reach her…

"It was a foolish thing to do," the old witch hisses, "trying to come after me without Fiona to protect you." Her hand sweeps around to the crosses. "The source of our power is your weakness. What makes us stronger kills you."

I summon the last of my strength and try to pounce on Melchora. Just as I rise, Santa Muerte pushes an iron cross on top of me. It slams against my back and flattens me against the floor. It feels as though it weighs a thousand pounds and burns like molten metal.

I'm weak. The influence of the cross on top of me radiates

into my being. Whatever strength is inside me is suffocated.

In the distance, I can hear a few sputtering gunshots. From where I am lying, they sound like firecrackers. Melchora looks up, listening to the sporadic sounds. "It's over. Your friend is dead. The police are almost all dead. You, soon, will be dead."

Paige. David.

Melchora crouches down before me and plucks a feather from her cloak. This close, I can see it refract in the light that spills in through the windows. Its point is razor-sharp.

I make my last plea for help. "Elizabeth," I mutter.

Melchora laughs. "Elizabeth?" she says, turning toward Santa Muerte. I crane my head up. The skeletal face looks at me with a blank expression from behind its draped hood.

"She is gone. There is no Elizabeth anymore. Only the Holy Death."

I turn to Melchora. As she smiles, her dried, cracked lips reveal crooked yellow teeth. The cloudy eyes stare through me.

"I know what demon lies inside you." She holds up the feather. "You've been wanting to know its name? You'll soon find out. In hell." She raises the feather above me, its sharpened shaft pointed down at my head.

There's a crash behind her—glass shattering. *Thump! Thump! Thump!* Feet pound on the hardwood floor. Melchora turns.

Paige charges through the living room at full speed. She launches herself and dives for Melchora with two fists extended. Paige howls at the top of her lungs.

Melchora holds out her hands, but it's too late. In Paige's fists are clusters of gray feathers—Melchora's own magical feathers.

She plunges them deep into the witch's eyes. Paige's momentum carries them both to the ground, and Melchora slams down beside me in a heap.

Paige stabs repeatedly as Melchora cries out in agony. "No! No! No!" Blood splashes and sprays everywhere. Despite the witch's attempt to bat her away, Paige refuses to relent. Her fists hammer away.

A startled gasp turns my attention to Santa Muerte. The specter falls to its knees, the robes pooling around her. Whatever magical power Melchora was wielding over the spirit is diminished as Paige attacks. I see a brief flicker of Elizabeth behind the skull-faced facade. Her simple girlish features look momentarily shocked as she regains control of her body. She's still there. Still alive. Then fear washes over as her face is swallowed by the image of the skull.

The specter returns, but a sense of panic remains on her face. A force jerks her backward. Santa Muerte tries to grab hold of a cross but fails. She goes flying backward.

But not before I grab the hem of her robe with my free hand. As she flies back, I'm pulled out from beneath the cross. We go flying out through the front door, smashing the wood to bits.

Outside, Santa Muerte is dragged across the front lawn. My hand holds on for dear life as we both slide across the dirt and dried grass. We bulldoze through the armies of Santa Muerte statues, knocking them aside like bowling pins.

Her body breaks through the front gate and across the street. I'm dragged across the asphalt as we're pulled toward the fire pit under the gazebo. Santa Muerte clutches at empty air, trying to stop the progress. She flashes between the skeletal ghost and Elizabeth, with equal expressions of terror.

We reach the center island, and I use my other hand to grab onto the curb. We jerk to a stop, but Elizabeth sways toward the gazebo. My hand, wound with the veil like a fighter's wrist wrap, barely clutches the concrete edge with four fingers. Stronger now that I'm away from the crosses, I use all my strength to hold on. I look down, and Elizabeth's face stares back at me.

"Help me!" she cries.

The spirit returns. Time and strength are running out on me. This is my last chance.

"What's my name?" I yell.

The spirit sneers.

I have one chance left—one chance to use the veil. I let go. We fly toward the shrine. I loosen my grip on the cloth to untangle it, but it gets caught in the wind. The veil pulls out of my grasp and out of reach.

Elizabeth shoots into the gazebo then spills onto the fire pit. Instead of landing on its surface, she slips over the edge and disappears. I jam my feet against the base to stop myself from following her. My torso and arms dangle over the edge, and I'm shocked by what I see.

Elizabeth dangles inside the fire pit. The cement that once filled the structure is gone, leaving a bottomless void of inky black. Wind whirls inside, threatening to pull Elizabeth and me into its depths. I use one hand to hold onto her arm and my free hand to stop both of us from falling in. Elizabeth's panicked face disappears, and now Santa Muerte looks up at me. She grins then starts to pull me in.

Shit.

"What's my name?" I yell out again.

The spirit flashes and disappears, and Elizabeth's frightened face reappears. "Don't let me go!" she screams.

My strength is weakening. I need Dudley. I strain against the force and pull Elizabeth up.

Pockets of rock and debris explode out of the wall inside the well. Hundreds of blackened arms emerge from the inner wall and flail about, blindly searching for Elizabeth. Those that find her start to pull her down.

"No!" I cry out.

Flames appear at the bottom of the void. The heat is so intense it burns my face. Elizabeth looks down and screams.

Another flash. Elizabeth turns up to me, her face transformed back into Santa Muerte. She opens her mouth. Jagged teeth snap at my hand.

The disembodied limbs that once reached for her now start grabbing at me. I recoil and let go… another flash. Elizabeth returns in time to watch her fingers slip through mine. She disappears into the black maelstrom, falling toward the fire.

As I stand straight up, the concrete reforms, sealing off the portal. The black void disappears beneath me. "No!" I shout, slamming my hands on the flat surface. It's solid, as if it were always there.

Elizabeth is gone. Another life has slipped through my fingers.

I collapse in defeat and lean back against the altar. In my peripheral vision, I see flames and black smoke rising from the SWAT vehicle. The veil flutters in the wind and falls next to me in the gazebo. My hand rests on it.

A shadow washes over me. Hugo looks down on me, a gun pointed at my face. An expression of absolute hatred covers his face. He offers me one word before he pulls the trigger. "*Puta.*"

Bam!

I flinch, knowing this is the end.

But it's not. His chest blossoms into splattering red as a bullet explodes out of his shirt. Blood sprays from the exit wound and onto my face as Hugo collapses into a heap on the floor beside me.

I look up and see David running toward me, two hands

holding his still-smoking handgun. He keeps it trained on Hugo until he reaches me. Then he pulls me up.

Instinctively, I lean into his chest and press my face against his ballistic vest. My legs can barely keep me up, but with one arm wrapped around my waist, he keeps me from falling.

"Are you okay?" he asks.

I don't answer. I look around the cul-de-sac. Bodies lie everywhere, dead. Both vehicles are burning.

Paige emerges from one of the houses. Her right arm is extended, and from it dangles a dull gray object. It's not until she's near that I can see what it is—a large owl, its wings spread out wide. Blood seeps from its eyes, which have been gouged out.

This is all that's left of Melchora. When Paige is sure I've seen the remains, she casts the bird aside and helps David to keep me standing. From down the street, a convoy of police vehicles approaches. Their red and blue lights and flash across the faces of the houses, cutting into warm hues from the sunset.

I'm not focused on them. I look at the shambles of what remains of the shrine. I stare at the sealed-off altar. With Melchora's death, Santa Muerte has been pulled back into whatever netherworld she came—and with her, Elizabeth. And with Elizabeth, my name.

Chapter 35

Only four of us survived tonight. Paramedics load the injured body of the technician into the back of the ambulance. The cargo doors shut, and the vehicle rolls away into the night.

My eyes sweep across the neighborhood of Sterling Terrace. Giant spotlights sit atop cranes and illuminate every inch of the area. What feels like a hundred cops and detectives mill about, examining the aftermath.

Paige and I sit on the hood of a squad car, wrapped in police blankets. It must be three in the morning, and it's an uncommonly chilly night in Los Angeles. With each breath, clouds of vapor escape my lips.

David comes walking up with a heavy white plastic bag and a cardboard tray with two drinks. "Hungry?"

The only response he gets from Paige and me is our tearing into the bag and pulling out two burgers. I bite into the lukewarm sandwich, grateful for anything to eat at this point.

"You're welcome," he says as he joins us on the hood of the car.

He watches in silence as the scene wraps up. Plainclothes detectives are returning to their cars and pulling away. A forensics team transitions from evidence gathering to cleanup.

Finally, David asks, "Do you know whatever happened to Elizabeth?"

I stop eating and tell him the truth. "I don't know."

He nods. Paige casts me a sideways glance.

"So who has her?" David asks.

No one does. The witch who had the power to keep Santa Muerte in this plane of existence is dead. Elizabeth is gone.

"Maybe she'll turn up." David sighs. "Whoever has her, there's no point anymore. Maybe they'll let her go."

"Maybe," I lie.

David slides off the hood. He turns to look at me. We've been through a lot in the past twenty-four hours. I can tell he wants to say something reassuring—or something wise and profound. Or maybe he wants to proclaim his love for me.

Instead, he walks off without a word. *Typical.* I should be accustomed to this kind of disappointment by now. I'm not.

The sun still hasn't risen when David drives Paige and me to the Cathedral. I wait with David across the street, leaning against his parked blue Charger, while Paige goes onto the grounds to get Carmen. As we stand there in silence, I notice a couple of black-and-white cruisers parked down the street. Then I see an unmarked sedan few yards from us and a few panel vans at each corner.

"What happens to Carmen now?" I ask, nodding toward vehicles.

David turns and looks. "It's complicated."

I know that. She's an undocumented immigrant and the head of a major drug cartel. Or was. I'm sure her hold over the organization has disappeared by now. Whatever leverage she had for making a deal with the DEA is all but gone. Any chance of going straight is dead.

"Are you going to arrest her?"

"She's not a good woman, Darcy. She's a drug dealer. Don't think she hasn't done terrible things just 'cause she's a mom."

I'll be the first to admit I put blinders on because she was a mom—because there was a missing daughter out there. There are some things in this world I don't wish upon anyone. Losing a child is one of them. I think about my mom and how Bennet's death affected her. Then she pushed me away and lost a second child.

"Are you going to arrest her?" I ask again.

He shakes his head. "Not today. They'll keep an eye on her until the various attorneys can decide who has jurisdiction and who gets to proceed."

Paige finally emerges from the grounds. Along with Father Ramon, they escort Carmen down the stairs from the church grounds, heading toward David and me. There is no hiding the bad news, and I'm sure whatever neutral tone Paige tried to strike when she woke Carmen and Father Ramon did little to calm the woman's nerves. Across the street from where I stand with just David—no Elizabeth—Carmen collapses on the steps to the Cathedral and wails in anguish. Father Ramon and Paige do their best to hold her up, but she's deadweight.

She continues to cry and scream as David and I sprint toward her and Father Ramon. Halfway across the street, I slide to a stop, remembering where I am. David slows down when he realizes I'm not by his side. He looks back at me, bewildered.

I stand in the middle of the deserted street, unwilling to

move any closer. I can't console Carmen in her moment of agony or even try to help—not as long as she stays on the side of the boundary that separates the faithful from the unholy.

David turns away from me and rushes to Carmen's side. She leans into his chest and sobs uncontrollably. Two weeks ago I told her I would find her daughter. I failed. And now I can't even comfort her.

Chapter 36

It's been a week since the incident at Sterling Terrace. Since then, any hope of finding Elizabeth has dried up. Hugo's dead. Melchora's dead. Yury Yury might as well be dead for as quiet as he is. Carmen remains confined to the Cathedral with LAPD on surveillance—they even put an ankle monitor on her to make sure she wouldn't slip away.

With no leads and no more clues, the case of Elizabeth Viramontes is officially closed. Whenever I'm done with a case, I think things will get back to normal. They never do. My life isn't normal.

⌒

"Can we talk?"

I look up from my laptop to find Paige standing before me. For most of the day, she's been locked in her room, leaving me to program my new smartwatch on my own. That's not too difficult, though I was only able to set one heart-rate alert instead of the two she had done.

Now Paige has finally emerged from her rabbit hole, looking very serious. There was no reason for her to retreat, so I can only imagine what she was doing in there all day and what finally brought her out this evening. I close my laptop and push it aside.

"Do you know what I'm going to ask?" she says.

I cringe inside. I've been waiting for Paige to ask a favor of me ever since the case ended. I guess tonight is the night. "Yes. When do you want to go?"

"Now?"

"Let me change."

Paige and I sit in my Mini Cooper in the driveway of our apartment building. It's a warm spring night—well, warm for everyone else. Tolerable for me.

I cast a glance at Paige. She nods.

Okay, then.

"*Finna…*" I hesitate, not sure what to say next. "Paige's mom?"

The pendulum around my neck begins to sway. Then it rises and points west. I hand the crystal to Paige. It continues to point us west. I press my foot down on the gas, and my Mini Cooper pulls onto the street.

My car meanders up the winding roads of the Pacific Palisades, high above Sunset Boulevard. The Palisades are an affluent suburb deep in the Santa Monica Mountains, perched above the coastline. This is where many celebrities live, insulated from the noise and crowds of Los Angeles.

It's dark, with no streetlights anywhere. Large mansions sit behind tall hedges and iron gates. Some loom large and encroach on the edge of the street. I glance sideways at Paige, who looks at the surrounding neighborhood. I can only imagine what's going on her in mind as she compares these rich surroundings with the areas where she was raised.

The pendulum continues to dangle from her hand, pointing us deeper and deeper into the neighborhood, higher and higher into the mountains. Eventually, we come to a line of cars funneling onto one particularly popular street. We sit in a queue for twenty minutes, watching cars drive back down the street then park in our vicinity. Valet drivers hop out of the parked cars and hustle back up the street.

Instead of waiting for our turn, I park the Mini in the first spot I can find. Once again, I have to move my car a bit when I realize I can't open the British-side door because of the high curb. Paige and I stand together and look at the crystal. It points due north, to the house at the top of the hill, where the partygoers are headed.

"*Stöðva*," I say.

The pendulum falls and dangles from Paige's fist. I take the crystal from her and stuff it in my pocket while Paige begins the march up the hill. It's difficult to keep up with her determined pace as we stalk past car after waiting car.

We finally arrive at the entrance of a large Tudor mansion. Marble statues of lions guard the entrance on either side. Dozens of guests in suits and cocktails dresses stroll up a long cobblestone walkway lit by Victoria streetlamps and illuminated fountains. Everything just glows.

We pass through a double-door entryway into the house itself. Everything is grand and opulent. Eighteenth-century paintings hang in the foyer, bordered by ornate gold frames. I half wonder whether I'm walking into someone's home or a museum.

Servers in red vests hold silver trays of hors d'oeuvres for the arriving guests—caviar on French blini, lobster toast with avocado, bruschetta on warm sourdough, spinach puffs, and minced-chicken lettuce cups.

Paige marches through the living room, scanning the crowd for some hint of her target. We navigate our way through the many people in fine clothes who chat and sip champagne while talking about the film industry, real estate prices, and the stock market. These are important people discussing important things. Paige and I are ignored as we move through the house, cloaked by our insignificance.

As we finally reach the end of the living room, Paige suddenly stops. My momentum carries me forward, and I bump into her back. I follow her gaze and see a familiar face in sitting in the corner—Judge William Whitaker.

The moment he sees us, he stands up. The immediate shock that registers in his face is quickly followed by sincere sadness. He takes a step toward us.

Worried that he means to stop us, I push Paige forward. "Keep going."

We emerge into what seems to be a backyard but more closely resembles a private park. In the darkness of the evening, it's impossible to tell how far the grass extends into the hills. Lights on strings crisscross above our heads, so everyone sitting at the various patio tables sits in perfect lighting.

I've been to many beautiful and expensive homes in Los Angeles, but this one is the most impressive. Everything is topnotch, from the architecture to the decor to the service. I feel like I'm in an old Hollywood movie, and I'm half expecting to see Clark Gable and Jean Harlow regaling guests with sordid stories of their recent weekend up at Hearst Castle.

I can't even imagine what is going through Paige's mind right now. For fourteen years, she grew up in conditions that would break a lesser woman—poverty, abuse, and things she won't talk about even to me. And here she stands, in a palace of good fortune and luxury.

Why is her mother here? Who is this woman?

I notice a foam-core poster near the large swimming pool. Paige sees it, too, and we're drawn slowly toward it. It's a teenage girl's high school portrait. Her hair is a chestnut shade with light streaks peeking through the waves that cascade to her shoulders. She's beautiful and bears a subtle similarity to Paige with her athletic build, high cheekbones, and striking eyes—Paige's eyes.

Written in silver letters above and below the photo are the following words:

Congratulations Emma!

Good luck at Harvard!

I glance at Paige. She stares blankly at the photo, and I'm not sure if she can register the resemblance like I can. Her expression is impossible to read. *Pain? Anger? Resentment?*

We hear a roar of laughter to the side, and our attention turns to a crowd near the cabanas—yes, this place has cabanas. Over the heads of a circling crowd, I spy a couple holding court. The man is tall, with a salt-and-pepper beard that matches his salt-and-pepper hair. But it's the woman beside him who catches my attention. Or more accurately, it's her long blond hair.

Paige approaches slowly, and I follow. Out of the corner of my eye, I see Judge Whitaker watching from a distance. I can tell from his expression that nothing good will come of this.

My eyes zero in on the woman's hair, the only thing I can see above the throng of guests that surround her. The incandescent light bounces off her golden locks and acts as a shining beacon. Paige moves deliberately toward it, shoulder-checking anyone in her way. She doesn't notice their sneering looks as they move aside.

The last of crowd finally parts, revealing the woman. She's beautiful, with perfectly chiseled features and smooth tan skin. I can tell by her posture and the way her blue evening gown clings to her body that she keeps herself fit and healthy. Her teeth shine as she smiles at her husband, admiring the way he can own a room. This is the woman from the faded Polaroid in Paige's pocket.

She looks like Paige—they are practically clones. I feel as though I'm looking at Paige in twenty years. The similarity is unsettling.

The woman laughs again, then her eyes fall upon the crowd. Her eyes fall on me. Then they fall on Paige. As her husband continues to talk, her smile begins to fade. Her eyes are locked on Paige, unable to look away.

Paige stares back. Her expression is blank, but I can tell by the way her cheeks flush that emotions are boiling within. The world around us moves in slow motion as each of the two women stare at the other as though trying to grasp the weight and truth of this moment.

The woman's eyes well with tears as realization finally hits home. She drops her champagne glass, and it pops on the ground in an explosion of shards. Her husband and the crowd go suddenly quiet.

The husband rests his hand on her shoulder to see if she's all right. She's not. The man with salt-and-pepper hair turns to Paige and looks her over. He doesn't register the similarity between his wife and my friend. *How could he miss it?*

He turns to the woman. "Priscilla? Is everything all right?" *Priscilla.*

She ignores him as if she can't hear anything. After an eternity, she finally speaks. "Paige?" she asks, her voice quivering with emotion.

Paige stands frozen. For as long as I've known her, she has been gearing up for this moment. She has rehearsed it over and over in her mind—what she would say, what she would do. So I stand there, anticipating the release that's about to erupt from Paige.

Nothing comes out. Not a sound. Not an action. Nothing.

A woman's disembodied voice calls out from the crowd. "Mom? Is everything all right?"

I turn, half expecting to see young Emma. But instead, a woman with wavy jet-black hair breaks through the crowd. She's elegant and striking. Her cocktail dress is flattering but not revealing. She's tall, like her father, with dark eyes, like her father.

But here's the thing—she's roughly the age as Paige and me. And nothing in her features bears any resemblance to Priscilla.

"Mom," the woman repeats, "are you okay?"

Paige casts a sideways glance at this woman who called Priscilla "Mom." She looks her up and down as though trying to comprehend the math and the DNA to explain all this.

I appraise the trio, doing my own mental gymnastics to understand the relationship. Judging by the dominant genes in this young woman's features, she's clearly the man's daughter. She bears no resemblance to Priscilla, the woman she just called "Mom." Priscilla must be her stepmom.

Before I can continue my analysis, young Emma emerges. She wraps her arms around Priscilla in concern. "Mommy, are you okay?" she says in an infantile tone.

Then Emma's eyes fall on Paige. Her confused look melts into one of recognition. The father's expression remains polite, but I can see a sneer develop as he realizes who this person standing before him is.

Paige and I stare at this family—this perfect picturesque

quartet that once was happy and content, staring back at two interlopers who have ruined their evening. Priscilla takes a step forward. Paige flinches and recoils back a step. Her arm rises slightly as if to defend herself against a strike.

This is it. This is Paige's moment to confront the woman who abandoned her—who dumped her in a foster system that nearly broke her. It wasn't because of drugs or poverty or any of the myriad reasons Paige concocted in her imagination. It was so this woman could come live here. Paige's journey of suffering—every strike, every insult, every unwanted touch—was for the benefit of this woman's comfort.

As I wait for Paige to say these things—to kick into gear and fight the way she has her whole life—I become aware of the silence, not just from the crowd around us but from Paige as well.

I turn to look at my friend. She's paralyzed. After all this time spent searching and preparing for this encounter in her mind—this one moment that she's built her entire life around—she's frozen. I look closer at her. She's practically catatonic.

I've known her to withdraw into depression before but never this quickly or deeply. She's not just hurt—she's broken.

"Paige?" Priscilla calls again.

I whip my head around and stare daggers at this woman. She takes a step back when she sees my eyes. Her whole family does.

My hands curl into shaking fists, and my blood boils. *How dare she address my friend after what she's done?* I very much consider unleashing hell on her and everyone here. I could, too. It's two hours past my regular dosage, and the demon inside me rages to be released. I don't think I would regret it one bit if I did.

The alert goes off on my new smartwatch. The beeping jolts

Paige from her daze. She looks down at my watch, then up at me, then at my targets. She reaches out, and her fingers insert themselves into my fists, relaxing my grip. Our fingers interlock. When I turn to look at her, she shakes her head.

I close my eyes and take deep, steady breaths. My shoulders relax, then my arms, my hands, then my entire body. By sheer will, I force my heart rate to slow down. After more deep breaths, I am in complete control.

I open my eyes and turn to Paige. I need to get her out of here, away from this place and these people. "Paige," I whisper, "let's go home."

She doesn't resist as I lead her out, shoving men and women out of our way. They stumble back, and I even knock a couple of men off their feet. When I try to glare one last time at Judge William Whitaker, he's disappeared.

We exit the backyard and leave the guests behind. We don't look back as we storm through the house. With my arm wrapped around her waist, I escort Paige off the property. We're halfway to my car when Paige stumbles. Her knees buckle, and she nearly falls forward before I catch her.

"Come on," I say, "we're almost there."

She struggles to breathe, gulping for air like she's drowning. She's not drowning—she's sobbing. As her legs give way under her own weight, I guide her to the steps of a nearby house. We collapse beneath the light of an illuminated archway of someone's front lawn.

I hold Paige against my shoulder as she wails. Tears pour out as she comes to terms with what just happened. A life of misconceived notions, hopes, and dreams has been dashed away in a single moment. Her body convulses as if trying to control the overwhelming emotional pain.

"She didn't want me," she sputters between sobs. "She

didn't want me."

I hold her closer, not knowing what to say to make things better.

"Why didn't she want me?" she whimpers. "Why didn't she love me?"

Tears stream down my face as I think about that four-year-old girl who was abandoned—who tried to understand why her mom suddenly disappeared from her life. She had no home, no family, no one to love her. She must have been so lost. So confused. My hold tightens around Paige, and I wish I could have been there for her twenty-one years ago. I wish I could have held that little girl as tightly then as I'm holding her now. It's all crashing down on her in this one moment—the mother who left, the foster parents who abused her, the system that forgot about her, the men who used her.

"What's wrong with me? Why can't anyone love me?"

"I love you," I say, trying as best as I can to comfort my best friend. I envelop her in my arms, shielding her from the world around us. "I'm so sorry. But I promise you, I'll always be here for you. You and me until the end."

Paige continues to cry, releasing the anguish from a lifetime of pain.

⌇

It takes me fifteen minutes to stop crying. It takes Paige another fifteen after that. Even then, her misery doesn't subside—I think she has simply run out of tears.

We're in no rush, so we continue to sit on the steps of a stranger's house, tucked away from the sidewalk in an alcove formed by tall hedges. Her head remains on my shoulder, my arms wrapped around her tightly. My mascara streams down onto her hair, and hers drips down onto my jacket.

Footsteps click on the side, slowly getting louder. We don't bother to hide and compose ourselves. *Fuck people.*

A silhouette appears before us on the sidewalk. In one hand, he holds two small bottles of water, and in the other is a lowball glass filled with an amber liquid. He takes a step forward and extends the water bottles to us.

For a moment, we stay still. We've been wrapped together like this for so long that we're slow to move. Then simultaneously, we both reach out for the water.

"Thanks, Judge," I say.

Judge Whitaker steps forward. His kind, handsome face emerges into the light before us. "I'm sorry."

Paige and I open the water and drink. The water is clean and crisp and soothes our dry throats.

I point at the judge's glass. "Bourbon?"

"Scotch."

I beckon for the glass. "Close enough."

He hands me the glass, and I offer it to Paige first. She takes a sip then hands it back to me. The liquid is rich and smoky when it meets my lips.

"I wanted to make sure you two were okay," he says, looking up and down the street. "I didn't want to intrude."

"You're friends with them?" Paige asks.

Again, he looks up the street. "I should go."

"The secret's out, Judge," I say, handing Paige the glass of scotch. "Whatever you don't tell us tonight, we'll figure out tomorrow."

He nods reluctantly. "I've known him for thirty-plus years. I've known her for twenty."

"Twenty-one," I add.

"That sounds about right," he admits. "They're not good people. You have to believe me."

"Who is *he*?" I ask, curious about the husband.

"Thomas Thorne," he says with slight disdain. "He's a partner in a law firm in Century City. Real piece of work."

"The kids?" I ask.

Whitaker grimaces. "Older one is Taylor Thorne, his daughter from a previous marriage. Works for him."

A previous marriage. That confirms that Taylor was in the picture when Thomas and Priscilla met. Thomas kept his daughter, while Priscilla abandoned hers. This also makes Paige's mom wife number two—at least.

"And Emma?" asks Paige.

Paige knows the answer. I think she asks so she can hear the words out loud, as an act of masochism. He's not going to tell her anything she doesn't already know.

The judge hesitates then says, "Emma is your half sister."

Paige digests this. She takes another sip of the scotch then looks up at him. "Why?" she asks with pleading eyes as if hoping for an answer that will make this acceptable, if not forgivable.

Whitaker crouches down before her. "They are not good people, Paige. None of them. Not him, not the girls, not your mother. She abandoned you for her own selfish desires. I meant what I said before—you're better off without her in your life."

Paige doesn't protest but doesn't agree with the judge either. I take the scotch back and knock back the last sip. "If they're so terrible," I ask, handing the empty glass to Whitaker, "what were you doing at the party?"

Whitaker shrugs. "Even judges have to practice politics with the devil."

"That's a poor choice of words," I say.

"I'm sorry, Paige." He reaches into his coat pocket, pulls out a business card, and hands it to her. "If you ever need anything, please call me."

Paige looks over his card as he walks away. "Judge

Whitaker," she calls. He stops and looks at her. "Can you answer one last question for me?"

He cocks his head, waiting.

"I don't even know if you remember, but I was wondering, what's my name? My real name?"

He nods. "Paige. Alexandra. Chandler."

Paige inhales deeply, her breath stuttering as she receives that one last piece of the puzzle. With that, Judge William Whitaker hikes up the sidewalk, back to the house of Thomas Thorne and family.

Chapter 37

The drive is quiet. There's not much left to say after this evening, which is fine. I'm still trying to process it all myself. I try to imagine the series of events that transpired twenty-one years ago that led Priscilla to abandon her four-year-old daughter and begin a new life as Mrs. Thomas Thorne.

Who was she before? Who was Priscilla…? I can't imagine what was so objectionable about bringing Paige into the family, if Thorne already had a daughter.

As I'm pondering this on the quiet drive back, Paige suddenly screams. It's a primordial release of anger, frustration, and pain. It startles me, and I nearly lose control of the car and come close to hitting someone's mailbox.

"I'm sorry," Paige says. "I just needed to let that out."

"That's ok—"

"But I'm okay. Really. You know why? Because I did it. I finally found her, and now I can move with my life."

I keep driving, not sure where Paige is going with this.

"So what if she's not some homeless vagrant? So what if

she's not a doped-up prostitute living in the projects? So what if she's not running from the mob or hiding from feds or if she didn't accidentally kill someone in a hit-and-run accident?"

"You thought she might have killed—"

"The point," Paige says, shutting me up, "is that I found her, and she's okay. She's healthy and safe, just like I hoped for. She tried to hide from me—fine—but I found her. So I win. Right?"

Before I can answer, Paige keeps going. I'm not sure what stage of grief this is. Maybe the gloating or ridiculing stage. We're way past acceptance.

"Right," she continues. "*I* found *her*. That's what I should have said. *I* found *you*, you, you contemptible bitch. That's what the judge called her, right? A bitch?" She looks at me, waiting for an answer.

"Yes. He did." *I'm just going to agree with everything right now.*

"Yep. Bitch," she blurts. "A rich bitch. Up in the Palisades with her rich husband and two kids. No, one kid! Because apparently, he already had a daughter! So I was, like, a car you trade in for a new model. Get rid of the blond four-year-old— I'd like to try the brunette this year! What's her name? Taylor? And can you believe what she called her? 'Mom'? Give me a break. Mom? Mom! That's such BS! You want to know why? That woman in there—that bottle-blond trophy wife playing hostess with all these snobby assholes—is not her goddamn mother!"

I slam on the brakes, and my Mini Cooper screeches to a halt.

ᴊᴄ

Paige's words rattle around in my head. "Not her goddamn mother."

The floodgates open, and memories wash over me. I think back to the first time I was at Carmen's house. When I was upstairs I looked over all the family portraits, something struck me as odd even then.

Images of Elizabeth growing up and professional photographs of Carmen, including some that suggest she used to be a model or an actress... There are no candid shots. These are posed portraits, assembled to show a family. Curiously, they don't show the entire family together. Everyone is there, just in different pictures.

Even Paige has a picture of her and her mother. Why are there no pictures of Carmen and Elizabeth together? Then I remember when I first walked into Carmen's kitchen and found her cooking. Not the housekeeper. *Carmen.* And Leona was the one in control.

"¡Váyanse!" Leona commands. The two other servants stop what they're doing and quickly leave.

Leona never left me alone with Carmen—ever. They exchanged a lot of strange looks every time Carmen had something to tell me. Leona wasn't having it when I tried to grill Carmen about Elizabeth and Hugo.

"She's done answering your questions today," Leona says.

Was Leona protecting her or keeping her quiet? I sensed something was off, even then.

There's a lot Carmen's not telling me, and she won't tell me, especially with Leona protecting her. Maybe Leona is more than a maid.

If Leona was more than a maid, what was she? Who was she? Maybe she wasn't just Carmen's confidante. Maybe she was more. Then David's words come back to me.

"She's dangerous, Darcy" he says. "A ruthless, manipulative, evil, and incredibly smart woman who won't let anything stand in her way… No one in law enforcement has even set eyes on her—she stays in that compound twenty-four seven."

No, that can't be. Leona was the housemaid killed by Santa Muerte, and Carmen was the mother trying to save her child. Right? Then the family photos come back to me, again.

These are posed portraits, assembled to show a family. Curiously, they don't show the entire family together.

What proof do I have that Carmen was actually Elizabeth's mother? Who, then, is Carmen? Who is the woman hiding from Santa Muerte at the Cathedral of Our Lady of the Angels? I remember what Fiona said when I reported back to her about Carmen.

"Oh, and Carmen's still alive," I tell Fiona. "She's found sanctuary at the Catholic church downtown."
Fiona chuckles. "That won't protect her. The spirit of Santa Muerte is not a visitor from hell." She casts a sideways glance at me. "It'll protect her from you, though."

If Carmen wasn't protecting herself from Santa Muerte,

could she have been protecting herself from me? That's only possible if she knew I had a demon inside me—and only Santa Muerte and Melchora knew that.

Was Carmen working with them? Melchora was in command of Santa Muerte, right? Again, I hear Fiona's words echoing in my ear.

"Frankly, I'm surprised Melchora is able to wield such magic," Fiona says. "I didn't think she was that powerful a witch."

"Some spells are so powerful that two or more witches are needed to harness the energy."

"Two or more witches," Fiona said. That can't be. How can that be? Then there was that other thing Fiona said:

"My mother. She was a very powerful witch herself, and she taught me everything she knew."

Then I remember Carmen's words.

"My mother," Carmen says proudly. "She taught me everything I know."

Oh shit...

✧

"Darcy!"

Paige's screaming in my ear jolts me from my thoughts. A car zooms by on the left, honking its horn in frustration.

"What's wrong?" Paige asks, concerned.

"Elizabeth's mom," I answer slowly.

"Carmen?"

"No," I say. "Leona."

Paige looks at me quizzically. Then she registers what I'm suggesting. "No. That can't be."

"Carmen was a facade. An actress pretending to be the head of the cartel. She was a smokescreen in case the feds were going to bust Leona or a rival cartel was going to assassinate her. But Leona... she was the real leader. She was the real wife of Marcos Viramontes, who inherited his empire. The real mother of Elizabeth. The real Vibora Negra. No one knew what the real woman looked like. David said it himself—no one's ever seen her. But he was wrong. Everyone had seen her. Everyone had spoken to her. It was Leona talking directly to the police to make a deal *for herself* the whole time!"

Paige speaks hesitantly. "Then... then who took Elizabeth?"

"It was Carmen's plan. She found out Leona was going to make a deal with the DEA and had Elizabeth kidnapped to put a stop to it—Carmen, Hugo, and Melchora working together." My mind shifts into overdrive as I put the pieces together. "Not only did taking Elizabeth stop Leona's plan, but it also provided a body for Santa Muerte to possess. That was Melchora's doing. A two-for-one deal. It wasn't enough to stop Leona—they also needed to kill the investigators involved in the deal and stop any rivals from taking over during the power vacuum."

"Like Yury." Paige is catching up.

"Exactly. Yury knew Elizabeth was gone, and he intended to move into her business the moment Leona went down. The business was vulnerable. Carmen had to make sure that didn't happen and used Elizabeth—Santa Muerte—to make it happen."

"My God. Then Elizabeth killed her own mother."

I nod, remembering the ghost of Leona and the look on her

face. She must have known, in the end, who was about to kill her. I then recall Carmen's crocodile tears when we went to tell her Elizabeth was gone. I remember Paige, David, and I trying to console her.

I turn to Paige. "It's not over. She's not done."

"What do you mean?"

"She was trying to kill everyone involved in the case. That means…"

"David," Paige finishes.

I pull out my cell phone and dial David. Not waiting for him to pick up, I put the car into gear and start heading east.

"You've reached David Resnick with the Los Angeles Police Department. Please leave a message after the beep." *Beep.*

"David!" I yell into the phone. "That woman at the church, Carmen, is not Elizabeth's mom. Call me back. And be careful!" I hang up and toss my phone to Paige. "Keep calling."

"Where are you going?" she asks, dialing again.

"To the police department."

I floor my little Mini and head east. The Central Police Station is clear across town, twenty miles. That's a relatively short distance, but it could take me an hour to get there from the Palisades. As I race through the dark and winding Sunset Boulevard, part of me hopes a cop will spot me and pull me over. At least then I could get a hold of David.

No such luck. We merge onto the 405 and navigate through the late-night commuters clogging the freeway.

Paige has no luck calling David on his cell, so she finally breaks down and calls the dispatch at the department. She pleads with them to get a hold of him, and after ten minutes of negotiating, they finally tell her they can't reach him either.

"Where do you think he is?" she asks.

I don't answer, but I have a theory. I make it to downtown

in record time and take the Temple Street exit. This drops me off right next to the Cathedral.

My heart sinks when it turns out that my theory is correct. A blue Charger is parked across the street. David's car.

My tires screech as I pull up behind it and shut off the engine. There's no sign of David through his rear window. Muffled gunshots echo from the Cathedral across the street. Without hesitating, Paige swings open the passenger door and sprints across the street toward the church.

"Wait!" I yell, but the sound of my voice doesn't travel as fast as Paige does.

I whip open my door—only to have it crunch against the curb. *Shit.* Paige is already up the steps and disappearing into the courtyard. I drag my body over the passenger seat and tumble into the street. A passing sedan nearly clips me as I struggle to regain my balance.

A few yards down, I see the panel van parked by the curb—police surveillance. As fast as I can, I sprint to the driver's-side window and start banging on it. "Open! It's Darcy! Detective Resnick is in trouble!"

There's no answer. That's not good. I circle around to the sliding door and yank it open. I poke my head inside, and more of my worst fears are realized. Two dead detectives lie inside, their hearts ripped out.

Santa Muerte is back.

I look down the street at the marked and unmarked police cars stationed around the Cathedral. I have no doubt the other officers have suffered the same fate. I crawl into the van, check the waist of the closest detective, and unholster his sidearm. Then I grab an extra magazine and stuff it into my back pocket.

I race across the empty street toward the Cathedral then slide to a stop. My toes meet the boundary of the church grounds, where an actual seam is carved into the surrounding sidewalk. At my feet, I find a metal placard: Right to Pass by Permission and Subject to Control of Owner.

I can already feel the nausea growing. The holy force field around the property repels me like the wrong poles of a magnet. I look through the open gate into the empty plaza. Paige didn't pack her gun tonight. She's in there, completely defenseless. And David—poor David—probably got lured into a trap. And Father Ramon… *Please, God, let him be okay.*

More gunshots ring out. There isn't a single pedestrian in earshot, and a handful of cars zip by with their windows up, none the wiser. There are thirteen million people in the Greater Los Angeles Area, and it's my luck that none of them are nearby tonight.

I pull out my cell phone and dial 911.

"Nine-one-one. What's your emergency?" answers a woman's voice.

"Yes, I'd like to report gunshots at the Cathedral of Our Lady of Angels."

"You're hearing loud bangs?"

"No, gunshots! As in, someone is shooting a gun in the church! Please send the police here as soon as possible!"

"And what is your name?"

Two more gunshots ring out.

All I can think about is that all my favorite people in the world are hurt, or worse, and I'm standing out here, dealing with customer service. Despite knowing the agony that awaits me on the other side of this perimeter, I can't wait here any longer.

I drop the phone, hoping they'll put a trace on it. Steeling myself, I step over the seam that marks the boundary of the church grounds and pass under the archway that supports the carillon bells.

I vibrate as I trespass farther into hallowed ground. The air pressure tightens around my entire body, weighing down on me. Each step is like marching through water. Not willing to admit defeat, I drop to my hands and knees and crawl up the stairs to the plaza. My right hand keeps a firm grasp on the pistol.

Pressure turns to heat. A burning sensation radiates from within my body. It's a sear—a fire that wants to tear its way out of me and escape this place. A fire named Dudley. I can feel him festering inside me. He's in pain, probably more pain than I'm in. I worry that the moment I let him have control, he'll flee this place and take my body with him. I cannot let him. I won't.

With my eyes shut in agony, I finally reach the top of the steps. I'm well onto church grounds. My head throbs with a weapons-grade migraine. I vomit on the granite ground. I take deep breaths, trying to control myself—trying to control Dudley.

The burning intensifies. The gun becomes too hot to hold, and I let it clatter to the ground. Still on my knees, I tear off my jacket, hoping that might alleviate the fiery pain and let the heat escape. It doesn't. The fire moves from inside my chest to my skin. I look at my arms, expecting to see blisters forming.

Instead, I see something else. My arteries pulse with a radiant orange blood that courses from my heart. Tiny rivers of vibrant magma flow beneath my skin and through my arms. My hands glow like red-hot irons where the blood vessels concentrate. On the tips of my fingers, black talons have replaced my nails.

As I twist and stretch my arms to inspect my transformation, my arm begins to hyperextend. My elbow pops and cracks as my forearm bends unnaturally and my hand inches toward my triceps. Inside the taut sleeve of my skin, my hand rotates at the wrist until I'm grabbing the underside of my own arm. There's no discomfort, but the shock of seeing this contortion causes me to convulse in revulsion. My arm snaps back to its original articulation.

I look down at my chest. The area beneath my breast emits a bright orange light. With each heartbeat, more radiant blood pulses through my body. With each heartbeat, more power flows. This is it. This is Dudley.

I've never been conscious long enough to see this transformation. Somehow, despite the pain and fatigue, I am still me. I think about how Fiona said all I needed was to believe I could control it.

I remember how Father Ramon said, "The question is, how do you control yourself?"

I have to find a way. I close my eyes and focus on what has brought me this far. Paige. Ramon. David. They are not just my friends—they are my family. They are my life. I cannot let them down. If Dudley wins, they're lost.

I scream, channeling all my rage and frustration and letting it out. My roar echoes off the high-rises that surround me, reverberating across the entirety of Downtown Los Angeles.

I consider my hands again. *Yes, Dudley is out.* The agony that overwhelmed me moments ago is now manageable. The demon has come to fruition… but I am in control.

I look up. Before me is a fountain, raised above the ground like a floating disc. Water spills over all sides. And on the edge, someone lies in black priest robes. The water that flows around his motionless body is dyed red with blood.

Father Ramon?

I steel myself and rise to my feet. My body aches all over— my hands, my legs, my chest, my back. But no amount of pain or nausea can stop me from sprinting to him.

When I reach the body, I realize it's not Father Ramon. It's another priest, an innocent victim. In his chest is a deep black hole. His heart lies in the fountain beside him, staining the water red as it spills over the side.

My attention is drawn to the Cathedral. High on the wall, panels of translucent alabaster extend from the facade like a giant geometric bay window. The glass panes surround an architectural cross made of the same sand-colored concrete as the rest of the structure. Warm light projects into the night sky like a beacon. Another source of light spills out from the cracks of the closed double doors that mark the entrance to the Cathedral.

I summon all my strength and return to retrieve the pistol I left on the ground. The heat from my hand warped the plastic grip. When I try the trigger, it's jammed. With so many polymer parts inside, there's no telling what I melted while holding it.

Dudley is the only weapon I need right now, so I toss the useless gun aside and march toward the church. With each step, the pain intensifies. I reach the double doors. Strange symbols are carved on the bronze surface—cryptic cyphers I don't have time to identify. My hands press against the doors and push them open to reveal the entryway of the church.

I make my way inside. Three pairs of glass double doors stand before me. All are shattered, and glass shards lie scattered on the ground. My boots crunch over the bits of glass as I cross the threshold. The pain worsens. I worry that at any given moment, I will collapse to the ground and explode into a ball of flames.

I push myself forward, deep into the church corridor. On either side of it hang enormous paintings in gilded frames. One is of the Virgin Mary looking over the California Missions. Another depicts Jesus's ascension.

A loud bang reverberates behind me. I whirl around to find that the double bronze doors have slammed shut by themselves, trapping me inside. I have an idea who did this.

"Welcome, Darcy," a soothing voice purrs.

I recognize that voice. *Carmen.* She's nowhere to be seen, but I find Santa Muerte hovering at the end of the hall. She stares at me with her dark hollow eyes.

"Have you come to pray at the altar?" rings Carmen's disembodied voice. "Have you come to join your friends?"

Santa Muerte drifts away and disappears down an adjacent corridor. This is bait, and I know it, but it's bait I have to take. I walk down the long corridor.

On the right, I find what I initially assume is an alcove but then realize is the first entrance into the nave of the structure. My view of it is blocked by a stone wall that guides visitors inside.

Instead of following Santa Muerte, I proceed to the hall, thinking perhaps I can intercept her. I step cautiously in and up. The interior of the church is massive. A ceiling of slatted wood rises a hundred feet into the air. The same sand-colored blocks that form the outside make up the walls inside the cathedral. Huge tapestries depicting dozens of Catholic saints are draped on all sides. The only light in here is from the hundreds of lit candles in various corners and the glowing alabaster windows that form the architecture cross high on the back wall.

The altar sits in the center of the sanctuary—a huge slab of bloodred marble set on a black-and-gold pillar. Behind the altar stands the crucifix, planted firmly on the floor.

The figure of the Christ moves, and I stop. It's not Christ. Father Ramon is on the crucifix.

The pain is no match for my worry now. I sprint down the ramp to make my way deeper inside. On the stone floor is the bronze Jesus that once hung on the cross. Blood drips from where Father Ramon's arms and bare feet are nailed to the wood. Instead of nails, the length of his arms and legs are embedded with metallic feathers, like those from Melchora's robes, except instead of silver, these feathers are gold.

"Ramon?" I ask, worried.

I instinctively place my hand on his bloody foot. There's a burning shock the moment I make contact, and my glowing hand recoils.

His body spasms. His head rolls toward me, and his eyes flutter open. "Darcy?"

I force myself not to touch him. If only I could help get him down. If only I could comfort him. Save him.

He smiles. "It's okay. I'll see you again soon."

I shake my head. "No." *God, please, not him.*

A sharp blast of wind passes by my ear. Something rushes past me and plunges itself into his heart. Another gold feather.

I spin around to find Carmen at the far end of the cathedral some two hundred feet away. Like Melchora, she's draped in a cape formed from hundreds of feathers—golden feathers that shimmer in the light. She stands there, and even at this distance, I can see her smiling. My attention returns to Ramon. His head droops, and his eyes close one last time.

"No!" I shout, and now the tears come.

"Welcome, demon," Carmen says behind me. "I see you've found your true form."

When I turn to face her, she looks me over with a smile, her eyes admiring me. "I heard so much about you. I didn't think it could be true, but here you are, the picture of evil in the house of God."

I carefully move toward her, knowing that a trap lies here somewhere. As I walk, I scan the area for Santa Muerte. She's nowhere to be found.

"I thought it would be appropriate," Carmen says, pointing behind me, "that he die like the martyr he worships—a helpless, careless god. The same god that allowed you to be possessed by a weaker demon. The same god that doesn't care what happens to you. The same god that will let you die here, in his house, tonight."

"The same god that let your mother die?" I ask, wiping tears from my eyes.

Her smile disappears. She pulls a gold feather from her robe. As much as I want to stop everything and grieve for Ramon, this man who did so much for me, I can't. I must be ready to fight. This is the game she wants to play—taunting me so my emotions run wild and good judgment disappears and I lose control.

I keep walking past the pews. A wave of pain overwhelms me, and I'm forced to rest my hand on the back of a bench. The glow from my arteries intensifies when I make contact, and the wood smolders under my touch.

Carmen registers this. "Demons are weakened in this house—on this ground. But not me. Not Nuestra Señora de la Santa Muerte. This place—your god—grants us power as it takes it from you."

I ignore her and push myself back up. "Melchora was your mother, wasn't she?" I continue walking toward her. "Melchora taught you everything you know. Including how to be a witch and how to connive your way into power."

She seethes. "How dare you speak her name!"

Now *she's* losing control, so I keep talking. "Fiona Flanagan didn't believe Melchora was capable of possessing Elizabeth with the spirit of Santa Muerte—there had to be someone else who could wield such magic. Someone powerful enough but also someone in the middle of this. It was you. Hugo kidnapped Elizabeth—at your direction. Melchora secured the components—that you needed. Melchora kept Elizabeth hostage, preparing her for the possession ritual—using your instructions." Carmen swells with pride as I pepper her with accusations. "*You* conjured Santa Muerte. *You* gave her a body to possess. *You* directed her to kill everyone who threatened the cartel. The cartel you wanted to control."

"That I had to control," she corrects. "Leona was going to destroy us all. And do you know what her excuse was? Her daughter. She didn't want Elizabeth to inherit the business. Instead of giving it to those who deserved it, she was going to betray us!"

I'm close now and stop. A mere twenty feet separates us.

"Poetic, then," she continues, "that the child she was trying to save was the child who killed her."

The image of Leona dying resonates in my memory. I think about that look of shock. She probably knew it was her daughter in those final moments. I wonder if Elizabeth knew.

Did Santa Muerte release its hold long enough for Elizabeth's eyes see her mother's heart in her hands? Was Santa Muerte as sadistic as Dudley was when I killed Bennet?

"As poetic as when your mother was killed by her own magic?" I say, looking at her cape.

This time, she doesn't hesitate to attack. She sweeps her cape across her body. Dozens of feathers slip from the cape and fly at me—too many for me to dodge. I twist my body and raise my arm to block my face.

Stinging spikes pelt my forearms, torso, and legs. The force of the strike knocks me back, and I tumble across the hard floor for twenty feet before coming to a stop. I gingerly look at the damage on my arms and body. A dozen golden feathers are imbedded in me.

Slowly, I rise to my feet. It's not Dudley's strength but my own that's keeping me standing. Grimacing, I swipe the feathers off me. Metallic bloodstained darts clatter to the stone floor.

Carmen smiles at me and shakes her head. "I'm so glad you could join us. Tonight I can finish my plan. Goodbye, Darcy."

The hairs on the back of my neck stand at attention—something is behind me. I whirl around and come face-to-face with Santa Muerte. I grab her bony wrist before she's able to plunge it into my chest. Her skeletal face is inches from mine. My other hand grips her neck to stop her from biting.

We struggle. I can sense her claw searching for my heart, which continues to glow within my chest, giving her an easy target. Her strength pushes forward, and her sharp nails scratch away at my shirt and into my skin. Warm blood drips down my chest. Her strength is overwhelming.

I'm weakening and close my eyes.

In the darkness, I can hear Santa Muerte whisper, "*Muere.*"

In my mind, I can hear the echo of Fiona's words. *You can control it.*

I think about Father Ramon dying in front of me. I wonder where David is and if he's safe. I wonder if Paige is alive.

I won't believe they're dead. They're alive. They have to be. And the only way to keep them alive is to stop Carmen and Santa Muerte.

I am in control. I focus on her claw in my hand. My grip glows brighter then hotter. Santa Muerte's skin begins to smoke from our contact. She's confused.

The pain becomes too much for her. She jerks her arm away from me and holds her skeletal hand up. It's on fire.

The spirit releases an unearthly wail that echoes through the cathedral. She floats away from me and maintains her distance. I look at my hands—they smolder and burn, but I am not in pain. Not anymore.

I turn back to Carmen, ready to end her. I expect her to be

surprised by the shift in momentum, but instead, she smiles. She steps aside, revealing a basin behind her—a large cross-shaped baptistery. I realize too late what that means.

With a sweep of her arm, she summons a column of water from the basin. It flies toward me, and a deluge of holy water blasts me. I'm knocked off my feet and land with a thud on the hard limestone. The water stings like a cold burn, and the pain returns. It douses the fire inside me, and the radiating blood in my veins dims.

I struggle to my feet, not ready to give up. Steam rises from my body and clothes. I run then leap toward her. My feet barely touch the ground as I tackle her and wrap my hands around her body.

She's strong, like me. She whips me around and uses my inertia to push me past her. I keep hold of her as we go flying.

We collapse in the baptistery with a splash. I'm burning as I find myself submerged in an entire pool of holy water. I struggle to resurface, but Carmen pushes me down.

From her neck hangs the Saint Benedict Medal. Its holy energy forces me to the bottom of the basin, preventing me from rising. I swallow water, drowning.

With one hand, I grab the medal, and it sears my palm. Despite the pain, I rip the medallion from her neck and fling it out of the water. I'm almost out of air.

The basin boils as the temperature rises around our bodies. Carmen tries to escape, but I keep hold of her and pull her under with me. Her screams bubble under the surface as the heat from the water scalds her.

Her robe flaps like metal wings, yanking her out of the water and me with her. We sail into the air, arcing across the cathedral. A trail of smoke and steam follows in our wake. Then we crash to the floor and slide across the stone tile, and her metallic cape shatters into pieces.

I look up and see that Carmen is barely conscious. Her skin is blistered, like mine. Unlike me, she's not used to the pain. I need to stop her but am not sure how.

Then I remember Paige. I crawl across the floor with supernatural speed. My distorted joints propel me in a grotesque gait toward my target. I grasp a feather from the floor and pounce on Carmen then bring it down with all my strength. The shaft pierces her flesh and pins her right wrist to the stone tile. She awakens, and screams. I snatch another feather and stab it through her left wrist. She screams again and struggles to rise. Her body writhes and contorts, but like Melchora when Paige attacked her, she's defenseless against her own magic. She tries to pull her arms free, but the wide metallic vanes keep her wrists pinned to the floor.

My attention turns to Santa Muerte. The specter stares at me a moment then floats backward. She withdraws into the shadows, disappearing around a corner to somewhere unknown. I stand and follow her.

"Leave her alone!" Carmen shouts.

For a moment, I think she's speaking about Elizabeth. Then I can see the worry in her eyes. The spirit of Santa Muerte must be the last ounce of power she has left in this world.

There's still one more secret to uncover, and I will get it from Santa Muerte one way or another. I summon every ounce of strength I have. Again, a fire builds inside me. This time, it doesn't burn me—it warms me. I'm comforted by its familiar heat. My heart glows again, and the blood coursing through my arteries intensifies in brightness.

I pursue Santa Muerte around the corner and down the ambulatory. There are more alcoves—passages that reveal hidden corners and dark rooms. I pause and listen.

From behind me, I hear a scuffling. I whirl around and discover a staircase I missed before. Dimly lit signs indicate it's the path to a mausoleum.

I slowly descend the stairs into the shadowy bowels of the cathedral. A sloping tiled path lies at the bottom, leading directly to a glowing stained-glass portrait of a saint.

Standing before the glass is Santa Muerte. She waits. As I approach, a set of double doors opens to her left. She floats out of the hall and through the doors. A moment later, I hear the shattering of glass falling to the floor.

This is another trap, but I can't stop now. I move forward with trepidation. To my right is a mosaic-glass portrait of the Virgin Mary. I catch my reflection in the glass and stop.

Despite the fractured imagery, I can finally see my full demonic form. The now-familiar glowing amber heart beats beneath my white shirt, sending the radiant blood along my bare arms and concentrating in my hands. But it is my face that horrifies me. It's still my likeness, despite the blistered skin damaged by the holy water. My black hair lies flat on either side of my head. My eyes are the same shade of yellow, but now they burn brightly. In this dark hall, they are all the more menacing.

My jaw is fuller, and when I open my mouth, my fears are realized. Two rows of razor-sharp fangs gnash against each other like those of a vicious animal. I take it all in—the glowing yellow eyes, the malformed joints, the fangs, the molten blood, the burning heart. I am truly demonic.

My fist flies at the stained glass, and it shatters into a thousand pieces. Multicolored shards of the Virgin Mary rain down around me then clatter onto the limestone tiles. I scream. From deep inside, Dudley's demonic voice bellows through the halls of the dead.

This monster that has killed so many—too many—is more

real to me now than it's ever been. I'm shaken by what I become when the evil takes over, especially now that I've seen it for the first time.

In my despair, my control is waning. Then the fire begins to burn again—not by my doing but by his. Now is not the time to worry about the monstrosity I have become but about the friends I still have to save.

I march down the main hall then turn into the mausoleum. It's a maze of large marble crypts stacked four blocks high. The corridors appear to go on forever, disappearing in the shadows after a few yards. A few sconces are lit, leaving the far reaches of the mausoleum shrouded in darkness.

The doors slam shut behind me. I catch a glimpse of blue robes disappearing around a corner. When I catch up and look around, she's gone. Before me is another endless row of crypts, intermittently lit. The remains of the shattered glass lie on the floor. As I continue down this new path, the only sound I hear is the footfalls of my boots. I try to walk with lighter steps, but in the silence around me, each footfall is like a thundering stomp.

A blast of cool air hits me on the back of the neck. I look back to find nothing but an empty hall of marble vaults. More glass breaks behind me. When I spin around, I see a corridor disappearing into a black nothingness and the remains of a broken sconce on the floor. She's leading me deeper into the catacombs and entombing me in shadows.

My eyes shift to another corridor, and I glimpse the robes rounding another corner. I can no longer see to the end of the passage. Each hallway now ends in a deep inky shadow.

After a few more turns, I'm lost. I'm at a dead end, where a handful of crypts and cremation niches form the walls. For a moment, I think I'm losing my mind. The center crypt before me reads *Darcy Caine*. Below it are two dates—the date of my birth, and today's date.

Glass crunches behind me. I spin around, ready to strike. A woman screams, and I find Paige crumbling before me. She scrambles backward and cowers against a marble wall. Her eyes widen in fear. I can see her recalling what I did the last time she saw me like this.

I take a step back and drop to a knee. "Paige, it's me. It's still me."

It takes a moment for her to register my voice coming out of this body. She furrows her brow, not sure what to believe. "It can't be." She's ready to run, reluctant to fall for the trap.

So I sing.

"Cheer, cheer for old Notre Dame,
"Wake up the echoes, cheering her name."

Her eyes widen in recognition. She rises and inspects me, trying to see through the facade and find the real me inside. "How?"

"I'll tell you later. Do you know where David is?"

She shakes her head. "When I got into the cathedral, I heard the gunshots coming from down here. I ran here then got locked inside."

"Do you know where David is?"

"No. What about Ramon?"

She doesn't know. If she ran through the nave, she might have missed seeing him on the cross.

"Darcy?" she prods.

I shake my head. Her hand covers her mouth and muffles her gasp. "I'm so sorry," she whispers.

"I need to find Santa Muerte," I say, changing the subject.

Paige rises to her feet. "What about Carmen?"

"She shouldn't be bothering us anymore."

"You killed her?"

It's a legitimate question, given my current state. "No. She's just… stuck."

Paige furrows her brow.

More glass shatters a few rows away. Down an adjacent hall, a light is extinguished. I move toward it.

Paige gingerly grabs hold of my arm. "She's luring you."

For a brief moment, I find it comforting to know that Paige and I are in sync.

"Yeah, well," I say, "I don't have much a choice, so stay behind me."

We move down the corridor, passing several intersections, but I can't see down to the end of any row. I suspect we're in the middle, but it's impossible to tell. We proceed cautiously past the alcoves as each one is now completely dark. Anything could be hiding in them.

More glass shatters behind us. When we turn, it's clear we're running out of lights. The shadows are getting closer. We continue walking.

We come to the only hallway still lit, a single stretch that ends with a backlit mosaic projecting a kaleidoscope of colors. Before it rises a pale stone altar. A figure steps into view. I would know his silhouette anywhere.

"David!" I shout. My only concern is for him, so I sprint down the corridor to rush to his side before any harm can befall him.

Everything happens in a split second.

"Darcy, no!" shouts Paige behind me.

David's silhouette turns to face me. I recognize the item in his hand and the muzzle flash when it fires. Paige grabs my legs, tripping me. I fall face-first as a bullet ricochets off the marble and past my head.

"Darcy?" David calls from the shadows.

I'm okay, but Paige's deadweight on my legs sends me into a panic. I roll over and check on her. "Paige!" I shout, lifting her head from the floor.

Her eyes flutter open as she struggles to regain her equilibrium. A giant red bump swells on her forehead, from where it struck the floor. She lets out a groan.

Approaching footsteps clack on the stone tile. Paige's eyes widen, and she scrambles to her feet. David nears, and the moment he sees me as this monstrosity, he aims his gun again. I cringe into a ball, waiting for the shot, as Paige slides between us, her arms spread to protect me.

"It's Darcy!" she shouts.

David freezes, but his gun stays pointed. I make no sudden move. I don't even breathe. I wasn't thinking when I ran to him. I can only imagine the horror he sees—a demonic creature emerging from the dark while he's trapped in the catacombs of a church.

"It's okay. Trust me." Nothing happens. "It's Darcy," Paige repeats.

Slowly, I raise my face and crane my neck around Paige's defensive position. David's gun is still pointed at me. As I come into view, his face is an expression of revulsion and fear. His finger stays on the trigger.

I shrink and look down. I wish I had never seen that look. Now burned into my mind is his expression as he debates whether or not to kill me. Part me wishes he would pull the trigger just so this terrible moment would end.

He doesn't. "Darcy?"

I look up. David stands there, his gun down at his side, finger off the trigger. Paige moves aside, allowing David to see me.

With nothing left to hide, I stand. My arms crisscross over my body to hide my glowing heart as my pulse anxiously quickens. But there's no hiding the bright orange arteries running through my arms. I keep my face down so he doesn't have to take it all in at once.

Santa Muerte's plan is clear now—to lure me into the mausoleum and lead me to David. She was gambling on the fact that a cop would shoot first and ask questions later when confronted with a creature like me.

David takes a step closer. "Is that really you?"

I look up, making sure my mouth stays closed and my fangs stay hidden. I nod.

He looks me over, trying to figure out if this is real or some trick of makeup and costume design. "How?"

More glass breaks behind us. We're now in a pocket of light, with each hallway around us disappearing into shadows. I scan our surroundings, looking for Santa Muerte.

"And what the hell is it doing that?" David asks.

When I turn to face him, I see a skull emerging from the shadows behind him. I grab him by the shirt and pull him past me as Santa Muerte's hand reaches for him. David goes sliding, and I intercept her outstretched hand with my own. Flames erupt the moment we make contact.

She unleashes an unholy scream, and I whip her around to throw her down the hall. Keeping hold, she pulls me with her. We shoot down the corridor like a bullet down a barrel. The inertia is so strong it feels like we're flying.

We smash into the far wall, our bodies slamming against stone. Santa Muerte tries to use the sudden brake as an opportunity to plunge her claws into my chest, but I'm too fast. My hands wrap around her wrist, instantly burning her.

She gives another cry but doesn't stop. The force is so great that it pushes me off my feet, and we go flying down another dark corridor. My hands remain wrapped around her wrists as she propels us down the hall. Flames erupt around us. We're a ball of orange light shooting down a shadowy passage.

My back crashes into an altar, and I can feel my spine bend unnaturally from the impact. A rapid sequence of crackling sounds follows. Santa Muerte flies over and past me. The flames are extinguished, and I crumple to the floor, trying to catch my breath from the sudden stop.

For a moment, I'm worried I fractured my back. But there is no pain, and I am able to pull my knees under me. Blood seeps from the damaged and burnt skin on my hands. Each drop is like lava, forming tiny flaming candles on the floor.

Santa Muerte leaps over the altar and lunges at me, mouth open to bite. She pins me backward against the floor, and I wrap my hands around her neck to stop her gnashing teeth.

When her claws dig into my chest, I realize my mistake. My sternum cracks as her fingers break through, and the air seeps from my lungs. She hovers above me, forcing the weight of her body into me.

Her bony claw scratches at my heart, struggling to get a hold. I try my best to push her away. Her nails sink deeper. The light from my hands dims. I dim. Everything dims. I howl in pain, my voice echoing through the mausoleum. If I don't fight back at this moment, I'll be dead.

Footsteps echo down the hall, followed by a voicing shouting, "Let her go!" From my peripheral vision, I can see David above us with Paige next to him. His gun is pointed at the spirit.

Santa Muerte lifts her horrific face to him, and it's probably the first time he's seen it, because he shouts, "Jesus!"

"Don't shoot her!" Paige warns him—not that bullets will do anything, as she and I know.

Santa Muerte ignores them and focuses on me. Her skeletal face smiles wickedly. "They're next," she spits.

No, they're not.

My heart beats faster and harder. I fight against her crushing claws. My hands brighten in intensity as the blood flows again. My fingers wrap around her arm, my talons digging into her flesh. Slowly, I pull her fingers out of my chest. I summon Dudley's strength—all of it—and push her back.

Wind blows like a cyclone around us, the result of our combined powers. Through the vortex, I can hear David's confused voice as he continues to swear. I can see Paige trying to pull him away.

Santa Muerte's fingers slip from inside me. She cannot overpower Dudley. She cannot overpower us.

I rise to my feet, forcing her onto the altar. We are in the eye of my storm, and there's nowhere for her to go. She struggles to escape, but the fight is over. I loom above her, in control of my body and hers.

I remove one hand and dig into my pocket. My fist rises above her face, holding the veil from Ammon. I let it fall.

By its own accord, the veil unravels and spreads itself wide. Santa Muerte freezes, staring at the veil. For a moment, the fabric floats above her face. Then it drops suddenly. It wraps itself around her head and across her face then slowly constricts. Through its translucent fabric, I can see Santa Muerte struggling.

For a moment, the spirit disappears. In its place is Elizabeth. When she sees my demonic face, she recoils. "No!" she shouts through the ever-tightening fabric. "Please!"

"What's my name?" I scream.

The body writhes beneath me, trying to escape. The wind

continues to whirl around us, whipping her loose clothes like flags in a hurricane. Santa Muerte's visage returns, and she roars in my face.

"What's my name?"

Elizabeth returns. "Help me!"

"Tell me my name!"

She's confused. Her eyes search for an answer. "I don't know!" she cries.

This isn't supposed to happen. The veil is supposed to make her tell the truth. Except... she doesn't know. Santa Muerte does.

The spirit returns, this time noticeably weaker. *Yes!*

"The name!" I command. "Say it!"

Santa Muerte begins to speak, as commanded. "Your... name... is..." Then she's gone, and Elizabeth's face returns.

No!

Elizabeth is also weaker and struggling to breathe. The veil is too tight now. Her life force is waning, and I have only moments left.

"Give! Me! The! Name!" I shout. Santa Muerte knows the answer, and she can't hide forever. I need this key. I need this thing out of me. I need this hell to be over. "Come back! I command it!" *Please.*

Elizabeth gasps for breath.

Paige breaks through the cyclone that surrounds us and hurries by my side. "Darcy! You have to stop!" she cries above the wind. "You're killing her!" David is behind her, trying to make sense of what is happening before him.

Paige is panicking, but I am in control. I am in control. "The name!" I plead.

Elizabeth's eyes flutter.

"Stop!" Paige shouts, her voice barely piercing the howling

air as it intensifies.

Santa Muerte returns and snarls at me in defiance.

"The name!" I demand.

Elizabeth returns, unconscious.

"Darcy, stop!" Paige repeats. Her voice is barely a whisper in a tornado. "Think about Ben..." Her voice trails off, overcome by the cacophony around us. I look up to tell her to back off.

Instead, I see Father Ramon. His bloodstained robes whip in the wind. Ramon shouts above the wind, but I can't hear him. He holds onto his stomach, grimacing. His lips move, and I know what he's saying: *Please. Stop.*

I'm momentarily relieved to see him alive. I look back at Elizabeth, who is possessed by a force she doesn't understand. That poor girl unknowingly killed someone she loves.

I see myself in her. "I'm sorry," I say, pulling away the veil. It delicately slips off her face, releasing its hold the instant I tug on it. The key to my salvation now dangles from my hand like an ordinary piece of fabric.

The wind dies down, and Elizabeth lies still. Her face fluctuates between her own and Santa Muerte's. Back and forth it goes, neither force strong enough to maintain control.

Father Ramon approaches Elizabeth's still body and lays one hand on her face while another makes the sign of the cross. My eyes stay fixed on him, watching him prepare for the exorcism that will save Elizabeth and banish Santa Muerte.

A tinge of jealousy courses through me. I can't help it. I want this to be over.

As he lays his hands on Elizabeth, Paige circles around the altar to stand by him. Instead of stepping next to Father Ramon, she passes right through him. Or rather, right through his ghost.

For a moment, his image ripples like a reflection on the

surface of water, then it regains its form. His mouth moves to utter a silent prayer in a voice I will never hear again. My heart breaks a second time when I accept that Father Ramon is dead.

I stumble backward and to the ground. My body is drained, and I wilt to the hard stone floor. The tears return. My hands are no longer glowing, but my skin still reddens from the pain of being in the church. I don't care. I sit there, waiting for the pain I deserve.

I watch as Father Ramon's ghost continues to pray. Then he stops, confused. Nothing is happening to Elizabeth. He looks at me, lost. His mouth asks a silent question. *Name?*

He needs the spirit's true name. That's the only way to exorcise the entity. Santa Muerte is not her true name—it's just the title she's been given.

But I know her true name. I've heard it before. *I remember it.* I speak each syllable slowly, just like he taught me. "Meek-tay-kah-see-wah-tl."

Mictecacihuatl. Lady of Death. Ruler of the Underworld.

Silently, Father Ramon speaks the name and finishes his prayer. A wisp of light rises from Elizabeth's body. It forms into the image of Santa Muerte and hovers. The light transforms, and the robes fall from her body to reveal a seminude woman. Her skin is covered in black and white paint, and she wears only a feathery skirt and a gold-plated bib necklace that covers her breasts. On her head is an enormous crown of feathers.

Mictecacihuatl stares back at me through dead black eyes. Her lips curl into a snarl, and she lunges. Father Ramon inaudibly cries out, and before Mictecacihuatl reaches me, her body vaporizes and disappears into a wisp of smoke.

Father Ramon smiles at me. Then, slowly, he fades away into nothing. I try to yell for him, but I make no sound. My voice is hoarse, unable to even moan.

I vomit what's left in my stomach, choking on my own bile. The pain is inside me now. The church has regained its dominion over me and is rejecting me like a bad organ. The warm glow from my arteries diminishes. My joints contract, popping back into their sockets. Blisters form on my skin.

Paige's voice cries above me, "We need to get you out of here!"

Elizabeth coughs. Her body convulses on the altar as she rolls to her side. Her eyes meet mine.

Paige hoists up my dead weight. "Help me!"

Another set of hands grabs me—David's. He lifts my limp body into his arms. I look up at him.

The fear and revulsion he had before are gone. Now he's concerned and confused, probably wondering what happened to me and why I can't stay in here.

"Hurry!" Paige pushes him down the corridor as my head dangles past his arms. She lifts the weakened Elizabeth off the table then follows us as David leads the way out.

Chapter 38

A bright light shines in one eye then the other. Once the light is extinguished, I'm blinded until my pupils readjust to the night.

"I think you're going to live," Dr. Savell says.

Once again, I find myself sitting on the hood of David's blue Charger. It's still parked across the street from the Cathedral, where a small army of LAPD, city officials, paramedics, and clergymen are cleaning up the mess. I'm wrapped in several space blankets, including one draped over my head like a hood. Paige sits behind me, cradling me in her arms so I can rest against her body. She's my human recliner.

Dr. Savell puts the penlight back into his case, which sits next to me. "Thanks, Doc," I say. "And thanks for coming."

As soon as we made it out of the Cathedral, Dr. Savell was Paige's first call. She knew the paramedics wouldn't be able to do anything for me, and she did her best to keep them at bay while he rushed to be here. Luckily, David backed her up.

Once he arrived, Dr. Savell took responsibility for me and

did what he could. Four injections later, I'm feeling better, but I'm still in bad condition. My arms and legs are wrapped in gauze, which covers the puncture wounds of the tiny feathers thrown by Carmen and the blisters from my overextended visit to hallowed ground. A gaping wound from Santa Muerte's claw scars my chest between my breasts—also covered by gauze. Every breath is a struggle from the internal damage.

But I can feel myself healing, albeit slowly. I'm no longer bleeding, and all the wounds have closed. What once looked like third-degree burns on my face now seem like second-degree burns. I stay under my tinfoil covers, trying to remain inconspicuous while Dr. Savell ensures me that I am indeed going to live.

Paige and I watch as a commotion forms at ground zero around the cathedral. The organized chaos opens a lane as a gurney is carried down the steps. From this distance, I can see that it's Carmen in that gurney. They must have finally extricated her from my impalement. She's strapped into the cart, and her wrists are bandaged and cuffed.

She's awake and soon sees me across the street. She smiles her wicked smile, and I can tell she's already plotting her escape and revenge. I worry that I should have killed her when I had the chance. Now that she's free of the magical feathers I used to pin her down, I can't imagine there's a jail cell in the state that can contain her.

The gurney is hoisted into the back of an ambulance. A tall paramedic appears at the cargo doors and closes one. Then he turns to look directly at me. It's Jack Skellington.

Or... what's his name? Percival.

Percival nods at me in a manner that ominously communicates that he's going to take care of things. Then he shuts the other cargo door. The ambulance rolls away.

We continue to watch as another gurney is carried down the steps. Lying on this one is a young girl with long dark hair. An oxygen mask covers her face, but I can see that she's awake and alert. Elizabeth is wheeled to another ambulance, which speeds away once she's inside.

Finally, two last gurneys come down the steps with less urgency. These hold closed body bags. I think about Father Ramon. I think about every kind thing he ever did for me. I think about the man who was my sole source of hope in this godforsaken world. He was the only man left I could find who was willing and prepared to conduct the exorcism—the man who was helping me find this demon's name. I selfishly wonder who's going to help me now.

As if to remind me, Paige's arms gently but firmly squeeze me from behind. Paige is going to be here. No matter how horrific I become, no matter how bad I get, she's not going to abandon me. My hand finds hers and squeezes it in appreciation.

She perches her chin on my shoulder and whispers, "I'm going to miss him."

"Me too," I say, watching the medical examiners place his gurney into a nondescript panel van.

Then I see him. His ghost stands at the entrance to the courtyard. Police walk casually through him as if he doesn't exist. But he does.

Father Ramon waves at me. I'm not sure how long he will be around, but it doesn't look like he's going anywhere for a while. Maybe that's why he waves—to let me know he'll be there even if he can't talk to me. Maybe he's hoping it will comfort me. It does, and I smile. Then I notice Dr. Savell staring at Father Ramon. I can even see the hint of a smile.

"What are you looking at?" I ask.

Dr. Savell turns to me. He doesn't hide the smile. "It's a

beautiful church, isn't it? Oh, I know you've been through a lot tonight. And I'm sorry for your loss." He turns back to the grounds, but I can tell he's still looking at Father Ramon and not the actual cathedral. "Still, she's a magnificent building."

I'm not quite convinced. *Could there be more to Dr. Savell than he's told me?*

He closes his medical bag and addresses Paige. "Call me in the morning, and let me know how she's doing. If she needs anything else, I'm happy to come by."

Over his shoulder, I can see David approaching. Paige must see him, too, because she slides out from behind me and offers to walk the doctor back to his car.

David doesn't say anything. Without hesitating, he lifts the cowl of my space blanket hood and inspects my face, lifting my chin and moving my head from side to side. He checks my bandages arms then even looks down my cleavage to ensure that the wound is properly dressed.

I'll be honest—it feels nice to be touched by him, even though it's like I'm being poked and prodded like a show dog. He has seen my demonic self, but he shows no trepidation. His contact is calm and assured. Even Paige recoiled from me after I turned. Not David. He's not afraid of me.

When he's satisfied, he releases a deep sigh of relief. "You look better. You look... amazing."

I don't. I look terrible. But I know what he means—I'm healing miraculously fast. I close my eyes and pretend he means something else. When I open my eyes, he's staring at me and smiling. I smile back.

David shifts his weight as if he's getting ready to tell me something difficult. I know it's coming, and I'm ready when he says, "Darcy, what happened in there? What... are you?"

After all this time of evading his questions, I'm finally ready to explain everything to him. "It's a long story."

He takes a step closer. "I've got time."

I take a deep breath. "So, ten years ago—"

"David!" a woman's voice interrupts.

David turns, and I follow his gaze to the source. From out of the crowd of police officers emerges a beautiful Asian woman. She's tall and slim, with the posture of a runway model. Even wearing jeans and a T-shirt, she outclasses everyone around her.

"David!" she calls again, searching.

"Grace?" David answers.

Grace turns, and the moment she sees David, she sprints to him. She throws herself in his arms and grabs him. "I came here as soon as I could," she says, nuzzling her head into his chest. "Are you okay?"

He holds her closely, comforting her. "I'm fine. How did you know I was here?"

"One of the other ADAs called me and told me you were here." She releases him. "Why didn't you tell me you were working on a case tonight?" Then she kisses him.

My insides collapse. None of the wounds I endured tonight match the pain this image causes me.

After an agonizing amount of time, she finally lets go. "I was so worried." Then she turns to me.

"Right," David says as if to answer. He takes her hand and guides her toward me. I shrink inside my nest of foil blankets, hoping the darkness will hide me. "Grace, I want you to meet Darcy. She saved my life tonight. Darcy, this is Grace. My fiancée."

When he mentions this, I can sense Dudley wanting to emerge. My heart beats faster. My blood boils. It must be Dudley. *Right?*

"You saved his life?" Grace asks, shocked.

"Well, I…"

I don't have time to finish. She wraps me in a bear hug. "Thank you."

It's agonizing—not only because my whole body is still tender but because she is my new mortal enemy.

"Actually," David says, peeling her off, "she's a bit sore right now after tonight."

"Oh! I'm sorry," Grace says. "Do you need to go to the hospital? I can get an EMT here right away." She peers into my cowl. "Oh!" she says, recoiling from the damage.

"She's fine," David says.

"She doesn't look—"

"Like her usual self," he interrupts. "But she's fine. She's already been seen by a doctor." He looks at me. "She's a tough girl."

Not right now, I'm not.

"Are you sure?" she asks me.

I wave her off. "I'm fine. Nothing a good facial won't fix."

She digs into her pocket and pulls out a business card. "If there is anything I can do for you, please let me know."

I look down at her card. Grace Zhang, Assistant District Attorney, City of Los Angeles.

"Thanks," I mutter.

"Thank you," she says, "for saving David."

I don't say anything—no *You're welcome* or *My pleasure* or snarky comment. I don't know what to say. The uncomfortable silence lingers.

She looks between David and me then says, "I'm sorry. I'll let you get back to it."

Then she hugs him again. I can sense her relief in knowing he's safe. I can sense her reluctance to let go. They kiss.

Out of the corner of my eye, I notice Paige watching this

exchange from a distance. The expression on her face is one of disheartened sadness. She looks how I feel.

The kiss finally ends, and Grace walks away. David turns to me. Part of me wants to ask about his fiancée. *Why didn't he tell me about her? Why didn't he tell her about me? Am I that insignificant? Or is it something else—something worth hiding?*

He coughs, using it as a transition. "You were going to tell me what happened in there?"

I shake my head. "Not tonight, David."

He nods, seeming to understand. "Right. Okay. Are you going to be all right getting home?"

"Yes."

He nods again. There's not much else he can do. "Well, I think I've got everything covered here. I've got your statement. I've told the captain everything… well, almost everything. Most this I can't even begin to explain." He chuckles knowingly. I say nothing. "So… I don't need you… to stick around if you don't want to."

Ouch. "Okay," I say.

"Okay." He starts to walk away then turns back. He takes a couple of steps toward me, words trying to come out.

Please, say something. Apologize for not mentioning Grace. Tell me you feel something between us. Tell me you're torn. Tell me that's why you never mentioned me to her or her to me. Tell me you're afraid, and I'll tell you I'm afraid. Tell me literally anything.

He shakes his head, turns, and walks away. *Why are men such idiots?*

I watch as the first person he returns to is Grace. She latches onto his arm, and they head back to the church grounds.

Paige comes walking up slowly. "Are you okay?"

"Can we go home, now?" I ask.

She nods. "I'll drive."

I gingerly get into the passenger seat of my Mini. Paige gets in and turns the ignition. The car rolls away, and the police open a path for us. I look through the window, watching David and Grace disappear into the crowd. I see Father Ramon waving as if this would comfort me. It doesn't.

Chapter 39

A week later, the incident at Our Lady of the Angels is still in the news. I'm in bed, watching yet another newscast of what purportedly happened there. They don't have all the details, but they do have the gist of it.

Detective David Resnick—once again a hero in the city—solved the case of the murders of a dozen police officers. *Wrong.* There's no mention of me, but that's probably for the best. I don't need the attention right now. But you know, it'd be nice for business.

Carmen Viramontes, a suspected drug lord, was working with another suspect to murder multiple police officers. The coconspirator, Hugo Escalante, was murdered earlier in a shootout. Viramontes was hiding at the Cathedral of Our Lady of Angels under surveillance by the LAPD. *Mostly true.*

When Detective Resnick confronted Ms. Viramontes about her involvement in the murders, they engaged in an altercation, and she attacked Detective Resnick with violent force. Detective

Resnick took appropriate actions to protect himself, and Ms. Viramontes sustained injuries in the conflict and was taken to an area hospital, where she later died. *Mostly wrong.*

However, the part that gets me is that Carmen Viramontes is dead. The last time I saw her, she was very much alive. I wonder what happened to her after those ambulance doors closed. I wonder what Percival was able to do.

There is no information about Elizabeth on the news. For better or worse, the LAPD has left me alone since that night. No follow-up interviews or interrogations. No calls. No updates either. Elizabeth's current situation is a complete mystery to me.

The only contact attempted by the LAPD has been from David—three text messages, two phone calls, and one voicemail asking if I'm okay. I've chosen to ignore them, deciding distance is the thing I need right now. I do wonder what is going to happen to Elizabeth. I wonder if she's okay and if Santa Muerte is gone from her life forever. I hope so.

A knock on the door pulls my attention from my laptop. Paige is not home, which means I'm going to have to get up and scare some unfortunate courier. After a week, my face still hasn't fully healed. Granted, it's better, but my complexion is still reddened, and the blisters have been replaced by a shedding of dead skin like the world's worst sunburn.

I get up, covering my head with the hood from my sweatshirt. When I open the door, I find Ammon standing in the hallway. He wears the same suit I saw him in before and holds a red gift box with gold ribbon.

"Hello, Darcy," he says coolly.

"Ammon?" I'm a bit shocked to see him, and though I try to match his casual tone, my uptalk reveals my surprise.

"I hope I'm not intruding."

"Just watching the news." I nod at the box. "Is that for me?"

"If you might consider inviting me in."

"What are you, a vampire?"

"No," he says matter-of-factly. It's as if I asked if he were hungry or wanted a diet soda.

"Uh, sure. Come on in."

Ammon steps inside and looks around my apartment. "You have a lovely home. It's very…" He searches for the right word. "Youthful."

I look around, trying to figure out if that's a compliment or a criticism. "Thanks." I usher him to our couch and offer him something to drink, which he politely declines. "I guess you're not afraid to be in the same room as me anymore?"

He smiles. "Our last encounter was less than ideal. I hope we can both move past our mutual first impressions."

I point at the box. "Is the gift for me?"

"From Fiona. She said she wanted to apologize for the way she left things with you after…"

"After I burned down her home and everything she owned?"

He smiles then tugs on the golden ribbon and lifts the lid. The four sides of the box collapse outward, revealing a small chocolate cake inside. Beside it is a single gold fork. The metal of the handle winds itself into a Celtic knot at the end.

"A cake?"

"It's a dacquoise," he corrects me.

"That sounds like Fiona."

"Yes," he admits, looking at the dessert. "When she found out what you had done and what you had gone through, she decided to make you something special. It has certain properties." He looks at me, his eyes dancing across my face. I hope the hood keeps me well enough in the dark to hide the worst of my complexion. Probably not. "Certain healing properties."

As I reach for the fork, Ammon interrupts. "Perhaps I might persuade you to retrieve the items you have on loan before you enjoy your cake?"

Of course, he's here for his magical objects. I retrieve the two boxes containing the pendulum and the veil from my bedroom and hand them to Ammon. Then I dig into the cake. It's only a couple of bites. Well, a couple of Darcy-sized bites.

He sits there, watching me chew. I raise my eyebrows. It's pretty good.

"I'm sorry you didn't learn the demon's name," he says, pointing at his own eyes as an indication that he can see that mine are the same yellow color as always.

"I think it'll be okay."

He appraises me. "You seem different. It's still inside you, but... something has changed."

Part of me is surprised he noticed. Then again, Ammon is a... whatever he is. I nod. "Ever since my last episode, I've had more control. Not just over my body but over its powers as well."

Ammon looks intrigued. "How so?"

I reach into the gift box and remove one of the paper dessert doilies. Pinching it between two fingers, I raise it up for him to see. I concentrate on my right arm, trying to recall the sensation I felt at the cathedral.

My arteries start to glow. Once again, vibrant orange blood flows through my arm. My whole hand radiates with a burning heat. The paper doily flashes into a flame then disappears in a wisp of smoke.

When I relax, my hand dims, and the molten blood fades until it returns to normal. This is a trick I've been working on for the past week. I can summon just enough of Dudley's strength but still keep him at bay. Some powers don't require any effort. I'm stronger than I was before—stronger even than

Paige. She doesn't like that.

Ammon watches, seeming amused. "You have it under control. I guess we don't have to worry about… what's his name, Dudley?"

"I was watching the news," I say, changing the subject, "and saw reports about Carmen Viramontes. You know, she was the witch who cursed the girl I was looking for. It wasn't Melchora."

"Yes," he says, "I am aware."

"The reports are that she's dead."

"Yes." Again, he is stoic.

"Did you kill her?"

Ammon doesn't even hesitate. "Do you really want to know?" His manner is too calm and casual. It's a warning against asking questions to which I don't actually want the answers.

"I want to know if you're someone I can trust."

"You, of all people, shouldn't trust anyone."

Yeah, that's a warning. "I need to know who I'm dealing with. What I'm dealing with."

"She's not dead."

I release a gasp. This was not the answer I was expecting— it's worse. Carmen Viramontes is still loose. "She's dangerous. A murderer! She could come back and—"

"You won't want to worry about her. Carmen Viramontes is alive but not free. Obviously, we could not allow her to remain in police custody. That would be too dangerous. But neither could we pass sentence on someone who was merely practicing magic, dark though it may be."

My eyes narrow. "Who's 'we'? The Mancery?"

He chuckles, the first unchecked response he's offered so far. "Dear, no. Nothing as sectarian as that. Just a few of us like-minded individuals."

"Fiona?"

He nods.

"Where is Carmen now?" I ask.

"She… contained."

He carefully takes hold of his boxes and stands. This marks the end of this conversation. "I'm sorry these did not help you find the answers for which you were searching," he says, gesturing to the boxes. "Perhaps there is a reason. Some grand plan."

I can't help but wonder if he's already planning how to use this extended affliction to his benefit. *He already has my blood. What's next?*

With his free hand, he pulls the hood off my head. I stiffen as he looks over my face as if he's appraising me. He raises his hand to my cheek, and I close my eyes, anticipating his gentle touch. It never happens. When I close my eyes, I can see him pull away. Only then do I remember the last time we touched and how the brief contact burned my hand.

He smiles. "It has worked wonders. You're back to your beautiful self."

I blush.

"We should thank Fiona when next we see her." Ammon opens the door to leave.

We are both surprised to find David pacing in front of my door, his fingers digging into his hair. He turns to us, just as surprised. "Oh, hey."

Ammon says, "Good day, Darcy. I hope to see you soon." He steps past David and nods to him. "Detective." Then he strolls down the hall without looking back.

David watches Ammon walk away. "Who is that guy? And how did he know I was a detective?"

"He's a friend." I emphasize the word *friend*. "And he probably saw you on the news."

David nods, apparently buying the explanation. We wait an

awkward moment. Then I finally decide to let David in.

As he walks past me. he takes notice of my face. "Wow. You look... much better. Except"—he points at his teeth—"you've got some..."

I panic and look in a mirror near the door. As Ammon said, I'm noticeably better. I'm back to my old self. I bare my teeth. *Yep. Chocolate all over the place. Thanks, Ammon, for telling me.*

I rub my teeth and dig as much out as I can. "So, what brings you by?"

David takes a seat on the couch. "You've been ignoring my calls."

"Oh. That."

"Yeah. That."

I take a seat on the couch—on the far end and look David over, trying to read his body language to determine what he's thinking. All I see is his doing the same thing to me. Neither one of us is willing to reveal our emotions. Instead, we sit there, completely still, completely relaxed.

Knowing this could go on forever, I move on to business. "Why don't you tell me what's happening with Elizabeth."

He shakes his head. "You need to tell me what happened back at the church."

"I will. But since I'm about to bare my soul, I think the least you can do is tell me what's going to happen to Elizabeth."

He sighs. "It's out of my control, Darcy." Already, I know this isn't going to be good. "One, she's undocumented. Two, she's the daughter of a drug kingpin."

"Queenpin."

"I don't think that's a word."

"Feminism will fix that."

"Is feminism really worried about equality in the criminal world?"

"David," I say, killing the banter. "What's going to happen to Elizabeth?"

He sighs. "She's getting deported."

"It's not her fault…"

"It's not my call. Honestly, maybe it's better for her if she goes back to Mexico. If she stays, there's a pretty good chance the feds would seek to prosecute her for even being the daughter of drug trafficker."

"She's just a kid. There's got to be something we can do."

"I asked," he said. "Grace says the DA is dead set on having her deported."

The moment he says "Grace," I feel the sting. He looks away, and I can tell I didn't hide the pain very well.

"What happened in there?" he asks after a long awkward silence. He looks back up at me. "I've been trying to understand it all week. I've had so many questions." His speech quickens. "And my report—you have no idea the verbal acrobatics I had to go through to explain my version of the incident. I have three different supervisors on my ass about my report, plus the chief of police, *and* I have to submit testimony to the police board at the end of the month. And I can't even begin to describe what I've had to do to keep the entire force away from you. I'm doing all this, and I still have no idea what happened!" He takes a breath, calming himself down. "So I'm asking, what was that thing you were fighting in the mausoleum? What… are you?"

I take a moment. Prepare myself. Then I start. And I tell him… everything. What happened to me in Malbrook. My brother. My search for the demon's name. Father Ramon. The case to find Elizabeth. Santa Muerte.

The words spill out like an avalanche, describing the hell that is my life and the evil that dwells inside me. I tell him everything he needs to run away from me and never look back.

He doesn't run. He sits there, taking it all in, listening to every insane word.

So I keep going, trying to drive him away. I tell him it was my fault Lupe was murdered in the library. I tell him about what I did in the meth house in Harvard Park. I take the blame for Fiona's house fire.

When I'm finally done, David has enough ammunition to throw me in jail and forget I ever existed. Instead, he sits there and digests my whole sordid story. I sit at my end of the couch, waiting for him to storm away or pull out the handcuffs. He continues to do nothing. *Infuriatingly typical.*

Finally, he slides across the couch and gingerly takes my hand in his. His skin is warm to the touch but still sends shivers up my spine. "I never told you this, but I used to sell drugs when I was a kid."

I'm taken aback—this wasn't the response I was expecting. But he's talking, finally, so I listen.

"My parents were both dealers. When I turned twelve, they put me on the streets to start selling. When my little brother turned twelve, he joined me. Adam. My parents would split a g-pack of heroin between us to sell on the streets. Adam was fourteen when he was murdered. The found his body on Hudson, by the power station on the shore. He was stabbed a dozen times. His life was worth five hundred dollars."

David pauses, struggling with the memory. "Next day, my parents give me the whole g-pack to sell. 'Go raise money for his funeral,' my mother said. Jewish guilt." He chuckles, more out of discomfort than because he finds his story humorous. "That was it. I was done. Done with them. Done with drugs. Done with New York. I moved here with no money. I was homeless for the first few months, working odd jobs. Couch surfing. Then I joined the academy. You know the rest from there."

David has never told me any of this. He's sharing—trading. My dark secrets for his.

"Do you remember when we first met? You were surveilling a drug dealer I was building a case against, back when I was in narcotics. You helped me bust him. That wasn't just any case for me. That was personal. I never thanked you for that. It meant a lot."

I squeeze his hand. *You're welcome.*

He squeezes it back then squares himself to face me on the couch. "I know what it's like to lose the people you love. I know what it's like when the people you trust abandon you. I want you to know that nothing you told me is scaring me off."

I wipe away the stupid tears before he can see them.

"I'm here," he continues. "You need help with research, I can do that. If you need support, I'll help. Whatever battles you have to fight, I'll be by your side. I'm not going anywhere."

I can't help myself and lean into his chest. His arms wrap around me and squeeze. For a moment, I let all the cluttered thoughts escape my mind and allow myself to exist in this one perfect moment.

If I could stop time, this could be my happily ever after. Time doesn't stop. Eventually, sadly, I have to pull myself away.

"What do we do now?" he asks. "How can I help you?"

"I need to find its name. That's the key."

He nods. "And your friend Father Ramon was helping you to find the name of this demon?"

"Yes."

"Then you need to have the exorcism performed, right?"

I hesitate. I consider what to say next, wondering if I should tell him a truth I've never admitted to anyone else. It's something I hid from Father Ramon—something I never even told Paige.

He looks at me, waiting. I decide to confess. "No."

He wrinkles his brow. "I thought—"

"That's not enough," I add. "An exorcism removes the demon from my body. It sends this thing back to hell. But I don't want to send this thing back to where it came from. It murdered my brother. It doesn't deserve to just go home. That's not enough."

He furrows his brow. "What else can you do?"

I take a deep breath and tell him my secret. "I'm going to kill it."

About the Author

————◆————

G.S. Fortis was born and raised in Southern California and now makes his home in the city of Los Angeles. For many years he worked as both a development executive and as a screenwriter in the entertainment industry. He eventually decided the story of a demonically-possessed private detective on a quest for her own salvation might make an interesting book.

When not writing, he enjoys exploring the nooks and crannies of LA. One of his favorite hobbies is taking photos, particularly of the weird and wonderful architecture of the city.

A NAME IN THE DARK is his first novel.